ROBERT SILVERBERG
and KAREN HABER

Fantasy
The Best of 2001

KU-547-620

ROBERT SILVERBERG's many novels include *The Alien Years*; the most recent volume in the Majipoor Cycle, *The King of Dreams*; the bestselling Lord Valentine trilogy; and the classics *Dying Inside* and *A Time of Changes*. He has been nominated for the Nebula and Hugo awards more times than any other writer; he is a five-time winner of the Nebula and a five-time winner of the Hugo.

KAREN HABER is the bestselling co-author (with Link Yaco) of *The Science of the X-Men*, a scientific examination of the popular superhuman characters published by Marvel Comics. She also created the bestselling *The Mutant Season* series of novels, of which she co-authored the first volume with her husband, Robert Silverberg. She is a respected journalist and an accomplished fiction writer. Her short fiction has appeared in *The Magazine of Fantasy and Science Fiction*, *Full Spectrum 2*, and *Isaac Asimov's Science Fiction Magazine*, and *Science Fiction Age*.

OTHER ibooks TITLES
BY ROBERT SILVERBERG

FANTASY
THE BEST OF 2001

ROBERT SILVERBERG
and KAREN HABER

Editors

ibooks
new york
www.ibooksinc.com

Contents

FANTASY
THE BEST OF 2001
AN INTRODUCTION

by Robert Silverberg
and Karen Haber

Fantasy is the oldest branch of imaginative literature—as old as the human imagination itself. It is not at all hard to believe that the same artistic impulse that produced the extraordinary cave paintings of Altamira, Lascaux, and Chauvet, fifteen and twenty and even thirty thousand years ago, also produced astounding tales of gods and demons, of talismans and spells, of dragons and werewolves, of wondrous lands beyond the horizon—tales that fur-clad shamans recited to fascinated audiences around the campfires of Ice Age Europe. So, too, in torrid Africa, in the China of prehistory, in ancient India, in the Americas; everywhere in the world, in fact, on and on back through time for thousands or even hundreds of thousands of years. Surely there have been storytellers as long as there have been beings in this world that could be spoken of as "human"—and those storytellers have in particular devoted their skills and energies and talents, throughout our long evolutionary path, to the creation of extraordinary marvels and wonders.

The tales the Cro-Magnon storytellers told their spellbound audiences on those frosty nights in ancient France are lost forever. But surely there were strong components of the fantastic in them. The evidence of the oldest stories that *have* survived argue in favor of that. If fantasy can be defined as literature that depicts the world beyond that of mundane reality, and mankind's struggle to assert dominance over that world, then the most ancient story that has come down to us—the Sumerian tale of the hero Gilgamesh, which dates from about 2500 B.C.—is fantasy, for its theme is Gilgamesh's quest for eternal life.

Homer's *Odyssey*, with its shapeshifters and sorceresses, its Cyclopses and many-headed monsters, is fantasy. The savage creature Grendel of *Beowulf,* the Midgard Serpent and the dragon Fafnir of the Norse Eddas, the immortality-craving Dr. Faustus of medieval German literature, the myriad enchanters of *The Thousand and One Nights,* and many more strange and wonderful beings all testify to the endless fertility of humankind's fantasizing imagination.

In modern times fantasy has moved from being a component of the human mythmaking process to a significant form of popular entertainment. The wry tales of Lord Dunsany, the grand epics of E.R. Eddison and H. Rider Haggard, the archaizing sagas of J.R.R. Tolkien, the sophisticated novels of James Branch Cabell and the furious adventure stories of Robert E. Howard demonstrate the reach and range of fantasy in the past century and a quarter. And in today's publishing world it has established itself in a vastly successful commercial form that manifests itself as immense multi-volume series that carefully follow expected narrative formulas.

The present anthology is intended to show that reach and range as it is demonstrated nowadays in the shorter forms of fiction. You will find very little that is formulaic here, although we have not ignored any of fantasy's great traditions. There are stories set in the familiar quasi-medieval worlds to which modern readers are accustomed, and others rooted in the authentic myth-constructs of high antiquity, and several that depend for their power on the juxtaposition of fantastic situations and terribly contemporary aspects of modern life on Earth. There are philosophical and theological speculations. There is even one science-fiction story—although one that carries scientific thinking to a fantastic extreme—by way of showing that science-fiction, rather than being a genre apart, is simply one of the many branches of fantasy literature.

These eleven stories—which we think are the best short fantasies published in 2001—are reassuring proof of fantasy's eternal power even in this technological age.

—Robert Silverberg
Karen Haber

THE BONES OF THE EARTH

URSULA K. LE GUIN

IT WAS RAINING AGAIN, and the wizard of Re Albi was sorely tempted to make a weather spell, just a little, small spell, to send the rain on round the mountain. His bones ached. They ached for the sun to come out and shine through his flesh and dry them out. Of course he could say a pain spell, but all that would do was hide the ache for a while. There was no cure for what ailed him. Old bones need the sun. The wizard stood still in the doorway of his house, between the dark room and the rain-streaked open air, preventing himself from making a spell, and angry at himself for preventing himself and for having to be prevented.

He never swore—men of power do not swear, it is not safe—but he cleared his throat with a coughing growl, like a bear. A moment later a thunderclap rolled off the hidden upper slopes of Gont Mountain, echoing round from north to south, dying away in the cloud-filled forests.

A good sign, thunder, Dulse thought. It would stop raining soon. He pulled up his hood and went out into the rain to feed the chickens.

He checked the henhouse, finding three eggs. Red Bucca was setting. Her eggs were about due to hatch. The mites were bothering her, and she looked scruffy and jaded. He said a few words against mites, told himself to remember to clean out the nest box as soon as the chicks hatched, and went on to the poultry yard, where Brown Bucca and Grey and Leggings and Candor and the King huddled under the eaves making soft, shrewish remarks about rain.

"It'll stop by midday," the wizard told the chickens. He fed them and squelched back to the house with three warm eggs. When he was a child he had liked to walk in mud. He remembered enjoying the cool of it rising between his toes. He still liked to go barefoot, but no longer enjoyed mud; it was sticky stuff, and he disliked stooping to clean his feet before going into the house. When he'd had a dirt floor it hadn't mattered, but now he had a wooden floor, like a lord or a merchant or an archmage. To keep the cold and damp out of his bones. Not his own notion. Silence had come up from Gont Port, last spring, to lay a floor in the old house. They had had one of their arguments about it. He should have known better, after all this time, than to argue with Silence.

"I've walked on dirt for seventy-five years," Dulse had said. "A few more won't kill me!"

To which Silence of course made no reply, letting him hear what he had said and feel its foolishness thoroughly.

"Dirt's easier to keep clean," he said, knowing the struggle already lost. It was true that all you had to do with a good hard-packed clay floor was sweep it and now and then sprinkle it to keep the dust down. But it sounded silly all the same.

"Who's to lay this floor?" he said, now merely querulous.

Silence nodded, meaning himself.

The boy was in fact a workman of the first order, carpenter, cabinetmaker, stonelayer, roofer; he had proved that when he lived up here as Dulse's student, and his life with the rich folk of Gont Port had not softened his hands. He brought the boards from Sixth's mill in Re Albi, driving Gammer's ox team; he laid the floor and polished it the next day, while the old wizard was up at Bog Lake gathering simples. When Dulse came home there it was, shining like a dark lake itself. "Have to wash my feet every time I come in," he grumbled. He walked in gingerly. The wood was so smooth it seemed soft to the bare sole. "Satin," he said. "You didn't do all that in one day without a spell or two. A village hut with a palace floor. Well, it'll be a sight, come winter, to see the fire shine in that! Or do I have to get me a carpet now? A fleecefell, on a golden warp?"

Silence smiled. He was pleased with himself.

He had turned up on Dulse's doorstep a few years ago. Well, no, twenty years ago it must be, or twenty-five. A while ago now. He had been truly a boy then, long-legged, rough-haired, soft-faced. A set mouth, clear eyes. "What do you want?" the wizard had asked, knowing what he wanted, what they all wanted, and keeping his eyes from those clear eyes. He was a good teacher, the best on Gont, he knew that. But he was tired of teaching, didn't want another prentice underfoot. And he sensed danger.

"To learn," the boy whispered.

"Go to Roke," the wizard said. The boy wore shoes and a good leather vest. He could afford or earn ship's passage to the school.

"I've been there."

At that Dulse looked him over again. No cloak, no staff.

"Failed? Sent away? Ran away?"

The boy shook his head at each question. He shut his eyes; his mouth was already shut. He stood there, intensely gathered, suffering: drew breath: looked straight into the wizard's eyes.

"My mastery is here, on Gont," he said, still speaking hardly above a whisper. "My master is Heleth."

At that the wizard whose true name was Heleth stood as still as he did, looking back at him, till the boy's gaze dropped.

In silence Dulse sought the boy's name, and saw two things: a fir cone, and the rune of the Closed Mouth. Then seeking further he heard in his mind a name spoken; but he did not speak it.

"I'm tired of teaching and talking," he said. "I need silence. Is that enough for you?"

The boy nodded once.

"Then to me you are Silence," the wizard said. "You can sleep in the nook under the west window. There's an old pallet in the woodhouse. Air it. Don't bring mice in with it." And he stalked off towards the Overfell, angry with the boy for coming and with himself for giving in; but it was not anger that made his heart pound. Striding along—he could stride, then—with the sea wind pushing at him always from the left and the early sunlight on the sea out past the vast shadow of the mountain, he thought of the Mages of Roke, the masters of the art magic, the professors of mystery and power. "He was too much for 'em, was he? And he'll be too much for me," he thought, and smiled. He was a peaceful man, but he did not mind a bit of danger.

He stopped then and felt the dirt under his feet. He was barefoot, as usual. When he was a student on Roke, he had worn shoes. But he had come back home to Gont, to Re Albi, with his wizard's staff, and kicked his shoes off. He stood still and felt the dust and rock of the clifftop path under his feet, and the cliffs under that, and the roots of the island in the dark under that. In the dark under the waters all islands touched and were one. So his teacher Ard had said, and so his teachers on Roke had said. But this was his island, his rock, his dirt. His wizardry grew out of it. "My mastery is here," the boy had said, but it went deeper than mastery. That, perhaps, was something Dulse could teach him: what went deeper than mastery. What he had learned here, on Gont, before he ever went to Roke.

And the boy must have a staff. Why had Nemmerle let him leave Roke without one, empty-handed as a prentice or a witch? Power like that shouldn't go wandering about unchanneled and unsignaled.

My teacher had no staff, Dulse thought, and at the same moment thought, The boy wants his staff from me. Gontish oak, from the hands of a Gontish wizard. Well, if he earns it I'll make him one. If he can keep his mouth closed. And I'll leave him my lore-books. If he can clean out a henhouse, and understand the Glosses of Danemer, and keep his mouth closed.

The new student cleaned out the henhouse and hoed the bean patch, learned the meaning of the Glosses of Danemer and the Arcana of the Enlades, and kept his mouth closed. He listened. He heard what Dulse said: sometimes he heard what Dulse thought. He did what Dulse wanted and what Dulse did not know he wanted. His gift was far beyond Dulse's guidance, yet he had been right to come to Re Albi, and they both knew it.

Dulse thought sometimes in those years about sons

and fathers. He had quarreled with his own father, a sorcerer-prospector, over his choice of Ard as his teacher. His father had shouted that a student of Ard's was no son of his, had nursed his rage, died unforgiving.

Dulse had seen young men weep for joy at the birth of a first son. He had seen poor men pay witches a year's earnings for the promise of a healthy boy, and a rich man touch his gold-bedizened baby's face and whisper, adoring, "My immortality!" He had seen men beat their sons, bully and humiliate them, spite and thwart them, hating the death they saw in them. He had seen the answering hatred in the sons' eyes, the threat, the pitiless contempt. And seeing it, Dulse knew why he had never sought reconciliation with his father.

He had seen a father and son work together from daybreak to sundown, the old man guiding a blind ox, the middle-aged man driving the iron-bladed plough, never a word spoken. As they started home the old man laid his hand a moment on the son's shoulder.

He had always remembered that. He remembered it now, when he looked across the hearth, winter evenings, at the dark face bent above a lore-book or a shirt that needed mending. The eyes cast down, the mouth closed, the spirit listening.

"Once in his lifetime, if he's lucky, a wizard finds somebody he can talk to." Nemmerle had said that to Dulse a night or two before Dulse left Roke, a year or two before Nemmerle was chosen Archmage. He had been the Master Patterner and the kindest of all Dulse's teachers at the school. "I think, if you stayed, Heleth, we could talk."

Dulse had been unable to answer at all for a while. Then, stammering, guilty at his ingratitude and incredulous at his obstinacy—"Master, I would stay, but my work is on Gont. I wish it was here, with you—"

"It's a rare gift, to know where you need to be, before you've been to all the places you don't need to be. Well, send me a student now and then. Roke needs Gontish wizardry. I think we're leaving things out, here, things worth knowing . . ."

Dulse had sent students on to the school, three or four of them, nice lads with a gift for this or that; but the one Nemmerle waited for had come and gone of his own will, and what they had thought of him on Roke Dulse did not know. And Silence, of course, did not say. It was evident that he had learned there in two or three years what some boys learned in six or seven and many never learned at all. To him it had been mere groundwork.

"Why didn't you come to me first?" Dulse had demanded. "And then go to Roke, to put a polish on it?"

"I didn't want to waste your time."

"Did Nemmerle know you were coming to work with me?"

Silence shook his head.

"If you'd deigned to tell him your intentions, he might have sent a message to me."

Silence looked stricken. "Was he your friend?"

Dulse paused. "He was my master. Would have been my friend, perhaps, if I'd stayed on Roke. Have wizards friends? No more than they have wives, or sons, I suppose . . . Once he said to me that in our trade it's a lucky man who finds someone to talk to . . . Keep that in mind. If you're lucky, one day you'll have to open your mouth."

Silence bowed his rough, thoughtful head.

"If it hasn't rusted shut," Dulse added.

"If you ask me to, I'll talk," the young man said, so earnest, so willing to deny his whole nature at Dulse's request that the wizard had to laugh.

"I asked you not to," he said. "And it's not my need I spoke of. I talk enough for two. Never mind. You'll know what to say when the time comes. That's the art, eh? What to say, and when to say it. And the rest is silence."

The young man slept on a pallet under the little west window of Dulse's house for three years. He learned wizardry, fed the chickens, milked the cow. He suggested, once, that Dulse keep goats. He had not said anything for a week or so, a cold, wet week of autumn. He said, "You might keep some goats."

Dulse had the big lore-book open on the table. He had been trying to reweave one of the Acastan Spells, much broken and made powerless by the Emanations of Fundaur centuries ago. He had just begun to get a sense of the missing word that might fill one of the gaps, he almost had it, and—"You might keep some goats," Silence said.

Dulse considered himself a wordy, impatient man with a short temper. The necessity of not swearing had been a burden to him in his youth, and for thirty years the imbecility of prentices, clients, cows, and chickens had tried him sorely. Prentices and clients were afraid of his tongue, though cows and chickens paid no attention to his outbursts. He had never been angry at Silence before. There was a very long pause.

"What for?"

Silence apparently did not notice the pause or the extreme softness of Dulse's voice. "Milk, cheese, roast kid, company," he said.

"Have you ever kept goats?" Dulse asked, in the same soft, polite voice.

Silence shook his head.

He was in fact a town boy, born in Gont Port. He had said nothing about himself, but Dulse had asked around a bit. The father, a longshoreman, had died in the big earthquake, when Silence would have been seven or eight; the mother was a cook at a waterfront inn. At twelve the boy had got into some kind of trouble, probably messing about with magic, and his mother had managed to prentice him to Elassen, a respectable sorcerer in Valmouth. There the boy had picked up his true name, and some skill in carpentry and farmwork, if not much else; and Elassen had had the generosity, after three years, to pay his passage to Roke. That was all Dulse knew about him.

"I dislike goat cheese," Dulse said.

Silence nodded, acceptant as always.

From time to time in the years since then, Dulse remembered how he hadn't lost his temper when Silence asked about keeping goats; and each time the memory gave him a quiet satisfaction, like that of finishing the last bite of a perfectly ripe pear.

After spending the next several days trying to recapture the missing word, he had set Silence to studying the Acastan Spells. Together they finally worked it out, a long toil. "Like ploughing with a blind ox," Dulse said.

Not long after that he gave Silence the staff he had made for him of Gontish oak.

And the Lord of Gont Port had tried once again to get Dulse to come down to do what needed doing in Gont Port, and Dulse had sent Silence down instead, and there he had stayed.

And Dulse was standing on his own doorstep, three eggs in his hand and the rain running cold down his back.

How long had he been standing here? Why was he standing here? He had been thinking about mud, about the floor, about Silence. Had he been out walking on the path above the Overfell? No, that was years ago, years ago, in the sunlight. It was raining. He had fed the chickens, and come back to the house with three eggs, they were still warm in his hand, silky brown lukewarm eggs, and the sound of thunder was still in his mind, the vibration of thunder was in his bones, in his feet. Thunder?

No. There had been a thunderclap, a while ago. This was not thunder. He had had this queer feeling and had not recognised it, back—when? long ago, back before all the days and years he had been thinking of. When, when had it been?—before the earthquake. Just before the earthquake. Just before a half mile of the coast at Essary slumped into the sea, and people died crushed in the ruins of their villages, and a great wave swamped the wharfs at Gont Port.

He stepped down from the doorstep onto the dirt so that he could feel the ground with the nerves of his soles, but the mud slimed and fouled any messages the dirt had for him. He set the eggs down on the doorstep, sat down beside them, cleaned his feet with rainwater from the pot by the step, wiped them dry with the rag that hung on the handle of the pot, rinsed and wrung out the rag and hung it on the handle of the pot, picked up the eggs, stood up slowly, and went into his house.

He gave a sharp look at his staff, which leaned in the corner behind the door. He put the eggs in the larder, ate an apple quickly because he was hungry, and took up his staff. It was yew, bound at the foot with copper, worn to satin at the grip. Nemmerle had given it to him.

"Stand!" he said to it in its language, and let go of it. It stood as if he had driven it into a socket.

"To the root," he said impatiently, in the Language of the Making. "To the root!"

He watched the staff that stood on the shining floor. In a little while he saw it quiver very slightly, a shiver, a tremble.

"Ah, ah, ah," said the old wizard.

"What should I do?" he said aloud after a while.

The staff swayed, was still, shivered again.

"Enough of that, my dear," Dulse said, laying his hand on it. "Come now. No wonder I kept thinking about Silence. I should send for him . . . send to him . . . No. What did Ard say? Find the center, find the center. That's the question to ask. That's what to do . . ." As he muttered on to himself, routing out his heavy cloak, setting water to boil on the small fire he had lighted earlier, he wondered if he had always talked to himself, if he had talked all the time when Silence lived with him. No. It had become a habit after Silence left, he thought, with the bit of his mind that went on thinking the ordinary thoughts of life, while the rest of it made preparations for terror and destruction.

He hard-boiled the three new eggs and one already in the larder and put them into a pouch along with four apples and a bladder of resinated wine, in case he had to stay out all night. He shrugged arthritically into his heavy cloak, took up his staff, told the fire to go out, and left.

He no longer kept a cow. He stood looking into the poultry yard, considering. The fox had been visiting the orchard lately. But the chickens would have to forage if he stayed away. They must take their chances, like everyone else. He opened their gate a little. Though the rain was no more than a misty drizzle now, they stayed hunched up under the henhouse eaves, disconsolate. The King had not crowed once this morning.

"Have you anything to tell me?" Dulse asked them.

Brown Bucca, his favorite, shook herself and said her name a few times. The others said nothing.

"Well, take care. I saw the fox on the full-moon night," Dulse said, and went on his way.

As he walked he thought; he thought hard; he recalled. He recalled all he could of matters his teacher had spoken of once only and long ago. Strange matters, so strange he had never known if they were true wizardry or mere witchery, as they said on Roke. Matters he certainly had never heard about on Roke, nor had he ever spoken about them there, maybe fearing the Masters would despise him for taking such things seriously, maybe knowing they would not understand them, because they were Gontish matters, truths of Gont. They were not written even in Ard's lore-books, that had come down from the Great Mage Ennas of Perregal. They were all word of mouth. They were home truths.

"If you need to read the Mountain," his teacher had told him, "go to the Dark Pond at the top of Semere's cow pasture. You can see the ways from there. You need to find the center. See where to go in."

"Go in?" the boy Dulse had whispered.

"What could you do from outside?"

Dulse was silent for a long time, and then said, "How?"

"Thus." And Ard's long arms stretched out and upward in the invocation of what Dulse would know later was a great spell of Transforming. And spoke the words of the spell awry, as teachers of wizardry must do lest the spell operate. Dulse knew the trick of hearing them aright and remembering them. When Ard was done, Dulse had repeated the words in his mind in silence, half-sketching the strange, awkward gestures that were part of them. All at once his hand stopped.

"But you can't undo this!" he said aloud.

Ard nodded. "It is irrevocable."

Dulse knew no transformation that was irrevocable, no spell that could not be unsaid, except the Word of Unbinding, which is spoken only once.

"But why—?"

"At need," Ard said.

Dulse knew better than to ask for explanation. The need to speak such a spell could not come often; the chance of his ever having to use it was very slight. He let the terrible spell sink down in his mind and be hidden and layered over with a thousand useful or beautiful or enlightening mageries and charms, all the lore and rules of Roke, all the wisdom of the books Ard had bequeathed him. Crude, monstrous, useless, it lay in the dark of his mind for sixty years, like the cornerstone of an earlier, forgotten house down in the cellar of a mansion full of lights and treasures and children.

The rain had ceased, though mist still hid the peak and shreds of cloud drifted through the high forests. Though not a tireless walker like Silence, who would have spent his life wandering in the forests of Gont Mountain if he could, Dulse had been born in Re Albi and knew the roads and ways around it as part of himself. He took the shortcut at Rissi's well and came out before midday on Semere's high pasture, a level step on the mountainside. A mile below it, all in sunlight now, the farm buildings stood in the lee of a hill across which a flock of sheep moved like a cloud-shadow. Gont Port and its bay were hidden under the steep, knotted hills that stood inland above the city.

Dulse wandered about a bit before he found what he took to be the Dark Pond. It was small, half mud and reeds, with one vague, boggy path to the water, and no tracks on that but goat hoofs. The water was dark, though it lay out under the bright sky and far above the peat soils. Dulse followed the goat tracks, growling when his foot slipped in the mud and he wrenched his ankle to keep from falling. At the brink of the water he stood still. He stooped to rub his ankle. He listened.

It was absolutely silent.

No wind. No birdcall. No distant lowing or bleating or call of voice. As if all the island had gone still. Not a fly buzzed.

He looked at the dark water. It reflected nothing.

Reluctant, he stepped forward, barefoot and bare-legged; he had rolled up his cloak into his pack an hour ago when the sun came out. Reeds brushed his legs. The mud was soft and sucking under his feet, full of tangling reed-roots. He made no noise as he moved slowly out into the pool, and the circles of ripples from his move-ment were slight and small. It was shallow for a long way. Then his cautious foot felt no bottom, and he paused.

The water shivered. He felt it first on his thighs, a lapping like the tickling touch of fur; then he saw it, the trembling of the surface all over the pond. Not the round ripples he made, which had already died away, but a ruffling, a roughening, a shudder, again, and again.

"Where?" he whispered, and then said the word aloud in the language all things understand that have no other language.

There was the silence. Then a fish leapt from the black, shaking water, a white-grey fish the length of his hand, and as it leapt it cried out in a small, clear voice, in that same language, "Yaved!"

The old wizard stood there. He recollected all he knew of the names of Gont, brought all its slopes and cliffs and ravines into his mind, and in a minute he saw where Yaved was. It was the place where the ridges parted, just inland from Gont Port, deep in the knot of hills above the city. It was the place of the fault. An earthquake centered there could shake the city down, bring avalanche and tidal wave, close the cliffs of the bay together like hands clapping. Dulse shivered, shuddered all over like the water of the pool.

He turned and made for the shore, hasty, careless where he set his feet and not caring if he broke the silence by splashing and breathing hard. He slogged back up the path through the reeds till he reached dry ground and coarse grass, and heard the buzz of midges and crickets. He sat down then on the ground, hard, for his legs were shaking.

"It won't do," he said, talking to himself in Hardic, and then he said, "I can't do it." Then he said, "I can't do it by myself."

He was so distraught that when he made up his mind to call Silence he could not think of the opening of the spell, which he had known for sixty years; then when he thought he had it, he began to speak a Summoning instead, and the spell had begun to work before he realised what he was doing and stopped and undid it word by word.

He pulled up some grass and rubbed at the slimy mud on his feet and legs. It was not dry yet, and only smeared about on his skin. "I hate mud," he whispered. Then he snapped his jaws and stopped trying to clean his legs.

"Dirt, dirt," he said, gently patting the ground he sat on. Then, very slow, very careful, he began to speak the spell of calling. In a busy street leading down to the busy wharfs of Gont Port, the wizard Ogion stopped short. The ship's captain beside him walked on several steps and turned to see Ogion talking to the air.

"But I will come, master!" he said. And then after a pause, "How soon?" And after a longer pause, he told the air something in a language the ship's captain did not understand, and made a gesture that darkened the air about him for an instant.

"Captain," he said, "I'm sorry, I must wait to spell your sails. An earthquake is near. I must warn the city. Do you tell them down there, every ship that can sail make for the open sea. Clear out past the Armed Cliffs! Good luck to you." And he turned and ran back up the street, a tall, strong man with rough greying hair, running now like a stag.

Gont Port lies at the inner end of a long narrow bay between steep shores. Its entrance from the sea is between two great headlands, the Gates of the Port, the Armed Cliffs, not a hundred feet apart. The people of Gont Port are safe from sea-pirates. But their safety is their danger: the long bay follows a fault in the earth, and jaws that have opened may shut.

When he had done what he could to warn the city, and seen all the gate guards and port guards doing what they could to keep the few roads out from becoming choked and murderous with panicky people, Ogion shut himself into a room in the signal tower of the Port, locked the door, for everybody wanted him at once, and sent a sending to the Dark Pond in Semere's cow pasture up on the Mountain.

His old master was sitting in the grass near the pond, eating an apple. Bits of eggshell flecked the ground near his legs, which were caked with drying mud. When he looked up and saw Ogion's sending he smiled a wide, sweet smile. But he looked old. He had never looked so old. Ogion had not seen him for over a year, having been busy; he was always busy in Gont Port, doing the business of the lords and people, never a chance to walk in the forests on the mountainside or to come sit with Heleth in the little house at Re Albi and listen and be still. Heleth was an old man, near eighty now; and he was frightened. He smiled with joy to see Ogion, but he was frightened.

"I think what we have to do," he said without preamble, "is try to hold the fault from slipping much. You at the Gates and me at the inner end, in the Mountain. Working together, you know. We might be able to. I can feel it building up, can you?"

Ogion shook his head. He let his sending sit down in the grass near Heleth, though it did not bend the stems of the grass where it stepped or sat. "I've done nothing but set the city in a panic and send the ships out of the bay," he said. "What is it you feel? How do you feel it?"

They were technical questions, mage to mage. Heleth hesitated before answering.

"I learned about this from Ard," he said, and paused again.

He had never told Ogion anything about his first teacher, a sorcerer of no fame even in Gont, and perhaps of ill fame. Ogion knew only that Ard had never gone to Roke, had been trained on Perregal, and that some mystery or shame darkened the name. Though he was talkative, for a wizard, Heleth was silent as a stone about some things. And so Ogion, who respected silence, had never asked him about his teacher.

"It's not Roke magic," the old man said. His voice was dry, a little forced. "Nothing against the balance, though. Nothing sticky."

That had always been his word for evil doings, spells for gain, curses, black magic: "sticky stuff."

After a while, searching for words, he went on: "Dirt. Rocks. It's a dirty magic. Old. Very old. As old as Gont Island."

"The Old Powers?" Ogion murmured.

Heleth said, "I'm not sure."

"Will it control the earth itself?"

"More a matter of getting in with it, I think. Inside." The old man was burying the core of his apple and the larger bits of eggshell under loose dirt, patting it over them neatly. "Of course I know the words, but I'll have to learn what to do as I go. That's the trouble with the big spells, isn't it? You learn what you're doing while you do it. No chance to practice." He looked up. "Ah— there! You feel that?"

Ogion shook his head.

"Straining," Heleth said, his hand still absently, gently patting the dirt as one might pat a scared cow. "Quite soon now, I think. Can you hold the Gates open, my dear?"

"Tell me what you'll be doing—"

But Heleth was shaking his head: "No," he said. "No time. Not your kind of thing." He was more and more distracted by whatever it was he sensed in the earth or air, and through him Ogion too felt that gathering, intolerable tension.

They sat unspeaking. The crisis passed. Heleth relaxed a little and even smiled. "Very old stuff," he said, "what I'll be doing. I wish now I'd thought about it more. Passed it on to you. But it seemed a bit crude. Heavy-handed ... She didn't say where she'd learned it. Here, of course ... There are different kinds of knowledge, after all."

"She?"

"Ard. My teacher." Heleth looked up, his face unreadable, its expression possibly sly. "You didn't know that? No, I suppose I never mentioned it. I wonder what difference it made to her wizardry, her being a woman. Or to mine, my being a man ... What matters, it seems to me, is whose house we live in. And who we let enter the house. This kind of thing—There! There again—"

His sudden tension and immobility, the strained face and inward look, were like those of a woman in labor when her womb contracts. That was Ogion's thought, even as he asked, "What did you mean, 'in the Mountain'?"

The spasm passed; Heleth answered, "Inside it. There at Yaved." He pointed to the knotted hills below them. "I'll go in, try to keep things from sliding around, eh? I'll find out how when I'm doing it, no doubt. I think you should be getting back to yourself. Things are tightening up." He stopped again, looking as if he were in intense pain, hunched and clenched. He struggled to stand up. Unthinking, Ogion held out his hand to help him.

"No use," said the old wizard, grinning, "you're only wind and sunlight. Now I'm going to be dirt and stone. You'd best go on. Farewell, Aihal. Keep the—keep the mouth open, for once, eh?"

Ogion, obedient, bringing himself back to himself in the stuffy, tapestried room in Gont Port, did not understand the old man's joke until he turned to the window and saw the Armed Cliffs down at the end of the long bay, the jaws ready to snap shut. "I will," he said, and set to it.

"What I have to do, you see," the old wizard said, still talking to Silence because it was a comfort to talk to him even if he was no longer there, "is get into the mountain, right inside. But not the way a sorcerer-prospector does, not just slipping about between things and looking and tasting. Deeper. All the way in. Not the veins, but the bones. So," and standing there alone in the high pasture, in the noon light, Heleth opened his arms wide in the gesture of invocation that opens all the greater spells; and he spoke.

Nothing happened as he said the words Ard had taught him, his old witch-teacher with her bitter mouth and her long, lean arms, the words spoken awry then, spoken truly now.

Nothing happened, and he had time to regret the sunlight and the sea wind, and to doubt the spell, and to doubt himself, before the earth rose up around him, dry, warm, and dark.

In there he knew he should hurry, that the bones of the earth ached to move, and that he must become them to guide them, but he could not hurry. There was on him the bewilderment of any transformation. He had in his day been fox, and bull, and dragonfly, and knew what it was to change being. But this was different, this slow enlargement. I am vastening, he thought.

He reached out towards Yaved, towards the ache, the suffering. As he came closer to it he felt a great strength flow into him from the west, as if Silence had taken him by the hand after all. Through that link he could send his own strength, the Mountain's strength, to help. I didn't tell him I wasn't coming back, he thought, his last words in Hardic, his last grief, for he was in the bones of the mountain now. He knew the arteries of fire, and the beat of the great heart. He knew what to do. It was in no tongue of man that he said, "Be quiet, be easy. There now, there. Hold fast. So, there. We can be easy."

And he was easy, he was still, he held fast, rock in rock and earth in earth in the fiery dark of the mountain.

It was their mage Ogion whom the people saw stand alone on the roof of the signal tower on the wharf, when the streets ran up and down in waves, the cobbles bursting out of them, and walls of clay brick puffed into dust, and the Armed Cliffs leaned together, groaning. It was Ogion they saw, his hands held out before him, straining, parting: and the cliffs parted with them, and stood straight, unmoved. The city shuddered and stood still. It was Ogion who stopped the earthquake. They saw it, they said it.

"My teacher was with me, and his teacher with him," Ogion said when they praised him. "I could hold the Gate open because he held the Mountain still." They praised his modesty and did not listen to him. Listening is a rare gift, and men will have their heroes.

When the city was in order again, and the ships had all come back, and the walls were being rebuilt, Ogion escaped from praise and went up into the hills above Gont Port. He found the queer little valley called Trimmer's Dell, the true name of which in the Language of the Making was Yaved, as Ogion's true name was Aihal. He walked about there all one day, as if seeking something. In the evening he lay down on the ground and talked to it. "You should have told me. I could have said goodbye," he said. He wept then, and his tears fell on the dry dirt among the grass stems and made little spots of mud, little sticky spots.

He slept there on the ground, with no pallet or blanket between him and the dirt. At sunrise he got up and walked by the high road over to Re Albi. He did not go into the village, but past it to the house that stood alone north of the other houses at the beginning of the Overfell. The door stood open.

The last beans had got big and coarse on the vines; the cabbages were thriving. Three hens came clucking and pecking around the dusty dooryard, a red, a brown, a white; a grey hen was setting her clutch in the henhouse. There were no chicks, and no sign of the cock, the King, Heleth had called him. *The king is dead*, Ogion thought. *Maybe a chick is hatching even now to take his place.* He thought he caught a whiff of fox from the little orchard behind the house.

He swept out the dust and leaves that had blown in the open doorway across the floor of polished wood. He set Heleth's mattress and blanket in the sun to air. "I'll stay here a while," he thought. "It's a good house." After a while he thought, "I might keep some goats."

LEGERDEMAIN

(In memory of Robert Cormier)

JACK O'CONNELL

Dear F:

I am, primarily, a reader. No, let's be factual—
I am *only* a reader. In all other things, I have
been, let's confess, an abject failure. As husband, father,
son, brother, friend, lover, I have been a consistent disappointment. In the last letter you called me a "writer"
and I reared back upon reading the word.

I am a correspondent. No more and no less. And I
come from a time when this was known to be a different
avocation from "writing." While both writer and correspondent wish to make contact, the purpose of that contact differs with each role. With each state of being.

But today, on this one and only occasion, I do have
a story to tell. Whether or not you believe the story is
not my concern. I ask only that you follow it to the
conclusion and try to remain open-minded and atten-

tive. At such a late date, is this too much to ask?

We must start the story with a disclaimer. We must offer up my motivations for what will be, very likely, my final letter. Yes, the worst has been confirmed. The third and most vigorous course of chemotherapy has failed. In some perverse and utterly characteristic way, it is a relief. No more plastic bags of useless fluids leaking into my veins day and night. No more thumbing through dense (and badly written) journals for the latest news about acute myelocytic leukemia. I checked myself out of St. John the Divine last night over the outrage of a physician young enough to be my grandson. It was as if my choice to die far from the sterility of the hospital were an affront to his newly minted degree. The young have not read enough, my friend.

But look at whom I aim my windy summations. For years now you have read all of my discursive epistles and I need for you to know, now more than ever, how much this has meant to me. No one could guess the nature of our connection. And soon there will be only one primary source available to the historians. The blood on this page fell from my nose. Not an encouraging sign, but I won't tear up the sheet and start again. Time is simply too precious.

So now that you know the context, I will pass on to you all that I have to bequeath. The last tale and the best. Librarians and book clerks are not known for the enormity of the estates they leave behind. But, if they can identify the appropriate heirs, there is usually a legacy to be passed down, an antique or two of some value. Take this story with my thanks and my blessing. Perhaps one day you will tell it in my memory.

In my youth, there was a time when I was obsessed with playing cards. At the de Sale School I was, by far, the best card player. This is no great boast, however. I came of age too late, at a time when boys had, by and large, abandoned the love of a long card game. The art of the deal and the play and the bluff was no longer inculcated in the young. After the first few times I cleaned out the rare poker enthusiasts on campus, no one wanted to go to the green felt with me. I was left to a dozen variations of solitaire and, more importantly, manipulation.

I believe at some point I have written of my boyhood enthrallment with sleight-of-hand magic. My interest began with a young fan's appreciation for the Masters—Arthur Lloyd, Herbert Brooks, the great Archie Tear. In due course I began to emulate my idols and found that I had a). the long, tapered fingers that are made for such a skill and b). the infinite patience and the love of repetition and the satisfaction of my own company that allows for the kind of endless practice that the skill requires in order to be elevated into art. I trained compulsively, to the detriment of my studies and my friendships, but before long I could handle a Greek Shuffle or a Mongolian Crimp with the nonchalance of a professional. I could palm and riffle, spring and jog in my sleep. I had two Svengali decks, one of which had been made in London by Elmsley himself (or so the salesman told me). I amazed my dormitory mates with a slew of vintage tricks, all of which were new to these rubes. They sat in the hallway late into the night, sipping their tonics and trying not to blink, their backs rigid against the ancient horsehair plaster as I led them like lemmings through the O'Henry and the Gemini, through Liar Liar and the King's Robbery.

I won't go into the details of my downfall at the school. Suffice it to say that I fell prey to the magician's oldest temptation. The audience's adulation and frustration were not enough for me. Soon, I went for their wallets. They were all young enough to love wagering on illusion. And I was young enough to think I could strip them of daddy's allowance without repercussion. That I spent the money on an Oriental stripper deck with its own enamel case only further annoyed the dean of discipline and it was upon receipt of his letter that my sister, my legal guardian, summoned me home to the Capital.

So, that morning, boarding the train out of Quinsigamond, I thought I would calm myself with hours of one-handed shuffling, making Jacks vanish from sight, as I pondered ways to explain and excuse my expulsion.

I was riding the old Portland-Columbia line—this was just a few years before it went bust. My train, the Seaboard Star, once the showcase of a more tasteful era, was showing evidence of extreme fatigue. The stained glass in the solarium was cracked and the brass moldings in the dining car were tarnished beyond any hope of a future gleam. These signs of obsolescence combined with the disgrace of my dismissal and my fear of my sister's anger to produce in me a premier case of the blues. So, as I found my seat in the last economy coach (car 29—I've never forgotten), I set at once to my favorite cure-all. I put my duffel between my legs and began to rummage for a deck. And I came up empty.

Shocked, I pulled open the mouth of the bag until the seams were ready to burst and searched again. My hand grabbed blindly; fondling sweatshirts and dirty socks, but I soon knew the truth. There were no cards to be found. In my haste to disappear from the campus, I had forgotten to pack even a single deck. I can't convey how unsettling this discovery was. I always kept a deck within reach. The cards had become a kind of talisman for me, a calming instrument, unconsciously handled in the way others finger prayer beads or pill bottles.

It's true, I could have marched down to the club car and purchased a new pack. But the dean had ordered me to reimburse my marks with interest and I was suddenly experiencing some severe economic difficulties. I had only enough money for either a skimpy lunch or one of the train's horribly flimsy souvenir decks—the ones that sport a line drawing of a locomotive. The trip was a ten-hour ride. Though I knew that my stomach would carry the day, still, my decision, though logical, was an insult to what I saw as my calling. And so, though I knew it was futile, I allowed myself some angry rummaging before I resigned myself to my fate.

That was when Klingman approached me. Let me take a moment to describe the man's face as that first glimpse remains with me, just as clear, to this day. I know that I overestimated his age, a common mistake for a schoolboy. At that time, age had only two demographic categories: Youth, someone such as myself, an aspiring magician with all the time needed to learn the conjuring arts. And lack-of-youth, which meant irrelevant and musty and unintelligible.

Klingman was, I would now guess, no more than fifty years old. His skin, however, was already giving in to the cruelties of gravity if not sunlight (he was not an outdoorsman and, today, I might speculate that he was anemic). He was short and round, a pear-shaped lump of dough. He had bushy gray eyebrows, purple caverns below the eyes. There was a long-faded scar on the bottom of his chin. Sea-green eyes and a badly cut monk's crown of hair. There were liver spots speckling his dome. He needed a shave and a conscientious barber would have trimmed the nose hair without waiting to be asked. He wore wire-rimmed glasses of the old variety, round lenses with either a rust-colored or industrial silver frame.

His clothes were an indignity, I thought at that time, when I was as stylish as I was arrogant. But Klingman was surely unaware of this humiliation. I can see the worn, dark suit that smelled like camphor and was many fashion-seasons out of date. A yellowed handkerchief was pushed up one sleeve. I know he wore his faded white shirt open at the neck and there was a ribbed undershirt beneath.

He said to me, "Did you lose something?" in a tone too concerned and friendly. Too informal, as if he were an uncle I'd known since birth.

I looked at him without responding, one hand still thrust in my duffel, though I already knew there was no hope of retrieving any cards.

Klingman stood in the aisle staring at me as I stared back. A woman turned sideways and shimmied past him. She was carrying a sleeping baby. I remember the infant was dressed in white lace.

"Because," he said, "I could lend you one of mine." And with that he positioned himself and lowered his bulk into the seat next to mine. Trust me when I tell you he was not a naturally coordinated man.

My mood went from disappointed to suspicious with the speed only an adolescent can summon. Klingman pulled into his lap an oversized valise made, I swear to you, of some sort of imitation red leather. It was cracked and torn and he opened it delicately.

"Nothing worse," he said, "than being caught on a long train ride without your book."

"I was looking," I said, delivering the words with what I hoped was the right combination of contempt and apathy, "for a deck of cards."

"You are a card player?" he asked and I waited a beat for emphasis before blowing a heavy gust of air out my nose and giving my head the tiniest shake. This greasy bumpkin was the last thing I needed. I was about to speed toward my sister's fury for three days of debate about my attitude and my future.

"My father was a card player," he said. "Do you know the game My Aunt, Your Aunt?"

This brought me up short. I did, in fact, know the game fairly well. But, understand, it had already fallen through the cracks of popular entertainment. It was a complicated affair, requiring both a good memory and an actor's instincts. Some real money could be made during a night with the Aunts. But I'd never before met anyone who was an informed player.

I sat in my seat and gave him a smile. I said, "You wouldn't have a deck of cards in there?" indicating his bag.

At this he laughed.

"Cards?" he said in a put-on voice and made a little show of opening the valise and bringing his head down to its mouth. "No, no cards in here," as if I were a child in need of amusement. At that moment I thought him less the hick and more likely an Old Mavis, as we called them at de Sale.

He rooted in the valise and I thought for a second he was mocking me, imitating my search through the duffel. After a moment, he pulled free two books, both paperbacks. He held one in each hand and hefted them a bit as if trying to guess the weight of each. As he did this, he pushed out his bottom lip, which gave him a moronic, unevolved look. The books appeared old and second-hand. The spines were both broken and peeled in so many places that you could no longer read the titles.

"A difficult decision," he muttered, it seemed, to himself. "Always, a tricky choice."

He let his head fall back against the fibrous white paper that protected the headrest and closed his eyes, then his left arm jerked sideways and presented me with one of the books.

Today, it interests me that I tried to decline the gift. I shook my head but his eyes were still closed, so I was forced to say, "No thanks."

"It's a long trip," he said with an annoying, sing-song delivery. It didn't occur to me to ask how he supposed he knew where I was headed. It wasn't an express train. There were a dozen or more stops before we would arrive at the Capital.

"I'm not much of a reader," I said.

"That," as his eyes opened, "is a shame. But not a tragedy. Do you know why?"

I didn't want to have a conversation but I didn't

know how to make this clear without being rude. And so I set out immediately to be rude. I pushed my seat back in a reclining position, turned away from the man and made as if to nap.

Of course he continued talking.

"Because this is something you can change. This is a condition you can alter at once. Without too much difficulty."

I felt the book tap my arm, rolled forward and looked at him.

"Hey, mister," I said, "give me a break."

But as I said the words, I surprised myself and took the book from him. I turned it over in my hands and studied the cover. To say that it was striking would give the wrong impression, call up, I think, notions of color and flash. This was not at all the case, more the opposite I would say, but the design did intrigue me and made me want to discover what was inside.

The title of the novel was *Refugee*, the word written in large, black type. Many years later, it occurred to me to attempt to replicate the presentation of the title on the page. I spent weeks with a felt pen and a sketchpad, but, as you know, I am no artist and when I took my rendering to a designer acquaintance, she offered several possibilities as to the typography. I looked up all of her speculations and the one that seemed to come closest to my memory of the title on the page was known as "Urban Remington." It approximates an old typewriter style and upon seeing this I recalled that part of the design was an uneven distribution of the ink, some letters darker than others, but all in the utilitarian blockiness of a manual typewriter dating from mid-century.

I had an instantaneous attraction to the illustration below the title. I can no longer recall whether it was a photograph or an artist's rendering, but if the latter, it was done in an extreme style of photo-realism. It was precise and detailed. Perhaps I did not know at first glance if it were photo or painting. It had something of a sepia quality to it, though it was surely in color, mostly muted browns and blues.

What shall I describe for you first? It would be simple to say the cover featured a young man on a highway. But while technically accurate, I fear this would instill precisely the wrong impression. The "young man" is more an adolescent forced into an early maturity. Yet, how can I say that I knew this on first glance since the figure was depicted in the distance and his back was to the reader's eye? The "highway" was actually an older, two-lane road, nothing like the interstate monsters of our own age. There was no traffic. There were no reflective-green road signs. No gas stations. No halogen lamps rising into the clouds. The landscape was pastoral—the road was framed by forests of bare trees, stark with the autumn season. The young traveler carried a sailor's tote. He was attired as a working man, in blue jeans, a coat of leather or canvas, boots. He approached a covered bridge, partly shrouded in mist, set in the distance, in the upper right-side of the cover, just below the last "e" of the title.

Now, the first oddity that should have been evident was the absence of an author's name anywhere on the cover. But I failed to realize this until I finished reading the novel.

After studying the cover, I attempted to hand the book back to its owner, who was busy trying to cram his valise under his seat. When he finally sat back and saw the extended book, he waved it away, saying, "Trust me, you'll like it."

"I told you," I countered, "I'm not a reader. I don't want it."

He smiled and let his head give a series of fast, patriarchal nods.

"Yes," he said, "I heard you. You do not read. You do not like books. I hear it quite often."

But still he would not take the book from me. Instead he pulled in a phlegmy breath and said, "You keep the book. No need to read it if you don't want. But just in case you change your mind."

"I'm not going to change my mind," I said, more loudly than I intended.

"You give it to me at the end of the trip."

"I don't—" I began, but he held a finger up to his mouth and made a shushing sound as if trying to quiet an infant.

I was caught so completely off-guard that I canceled the end of my protest and he said, "You know, if I remember correctly, there's a wonderful card playing chapter someplace near the middle."

I stared at the man and decided to walk away. I got out of my seat and saved it with my duffel, tucked the book into my back pocket and walked toward the club car, fuming. By this time, the train was ready to pull out of the local station and I'll confess that the knowledge that I was leaving de Sale for the last time inflamed my regret and my sense of shame. I had experienced as many happy as sad days on the hill and since my parents' accident, it was the closet thing I had to a home. The thought of living with my sister was as unappealing to me as it was to her husband. So, as I wormed my way into the overheated club car, the weight of the unknown future came to me in the form of a subtle panic.

When a seat opened near the window, I raced for it against someone's dog-faced grandmother and claimed it without any remorse. The bitter righteousness of the orphan and all. The table was littered with the remains of the previous occupant's breakfast, a small lake of spilled coffee and powdered sugar. I mopped and brushed with a napkin and looked out the window at the decrepit, ash-covered landscape of mills and row houses that had come to represent New England to me.

We picked up speed slowly and the train occasionally lurched, but for the most part there was a steady, nap-inducing sway to the motion that produced in me a kind of low-grade trance, a state perpetually on the border of sleep, but never crossing fully into that territory. When the waiter finally arrived, he had to grunt to signal his presence. I ordered a cherry soda and he immediately launched into a bored, well rehearsed explanation that the tables were reserved for "full-meal dining only." I asked for a corn muffin to go with the soda and the man gave me a dismissive look and moved off toward the galley.

Everyone else in the car seemed in high spirits, dressed up for travel and looking forward to reuniting with a distant clan. The sound of all this anticipated happiness made me more fearful than angry and I suddenly wished I had taken one of the interstate bus lines with their bad ventilation and horrific toilets.

I leaned back into the booth and felt Klingman's book press against my coccyx. And then came, depending on your point of view, the moment of my redemption or my damnation.

I'm sorry to be so melodramatic, my confrere. But I know, beyond any possibility of doubt or confusion, that this moment, this simple action, the basic kinetics of my arm reaching behind my back and extracting the book, that *this* was the moment when my life jumped tracks and veered wildly in a new direction.

I went beneath that picture of the wandering young man and started to read his story. Within a paragraph, the train began to vanish and the world of the refugee began to assert itself into my consciousness with such power and clarity that I was helpless in its presence.

At some point, I assume, I paid for and ate my muffin. But I did so without thought or taste. At some point, the club car must have emptied of its breakfast customers and filled with a lunch crowd, disposed of the sandwich eaters and swelled with the supper shift. For reasons I still do not understand all these years later, no one bothered me. No one disturbed the universe of my reading. Not even my surly breakfast waiter.

You want, at this point, some sense of the novel. I'm hesitant to even attempt such a gift. In the end, it's a cheat, isn't it? At best, I'd be offering the shadow of the experience. Which is to say, I'd be offering you nothing. Less than nothing. You could, of course, try to track down the novel and read it yourself. Let me save you the effort. You'll never find it. I know this as surely as I know my own name. And even if you could locate a copy, your experience of the book could never be my experience. Have you never heard the saying, *the reader creates his own book*?

But for the sake of my story, let me write that the novel was a *Bildungsroman*. A coming of age tale. The protagonist was a boy my own age and, if you can believe it, also an orphan. The title referred to his sense of unbelonging and chronic displacement. The boy wandered the country, chapter to chapter, region to region.

At one point, he even rode the rails, as I was doing. The hero worked odd jobs along the road. He met fascinating characters and had all manner of adventures.

Am I making the novel sound like a lark, a series of lighthearted episodes? It was anything but. A dark tale, there was a sense of the ominous and the morose on every page. More than any plot-driven danger that befell the boy, there was at the heart of the narrative an aura of foreboding evoked by the prose itself. And in the end, the hero remained the refugee of the title, still unsettled, still unembraced. After all those pages, the boy continued to live as a wanderer and stranger in the land of his birth.

I finished the book two stops before we pulled into the Capital. The sun had gone down. My backside was in a state of advanced paralysis. I hadn't eaten since breakfast and my bladder was on the verge of rupture.

I want to write this as precisely as I am capable because it will inform your sense of my entire story: when I finished that book, I felt as if I had been remade. I felt as if I had been changed into another person somehow. As if my consciousness had not been simply opened up, but redesigned and redirected, refocused, trained to think, to imagine, in an entirely new manner.

I closed the book and tried to stand and stumbled on my sleeping legs. I used the table tops as crutches and made my way to the rest room where I urinated for some record-breaking span of time. I splashed my face and neck with water. And then, instinctively, I ran to find Klingman.

My duffel was on my seat where I had left it, but Klingman was not in the adjoining chair. I looked up and down the aisles. No Klingman. I thought of searching the Seaboard Star, car by car, from coach to first class. But before I could begin, the train began to move again. And as it pulled out of the station, I saw the old man outside, seated on a wooden bench on the boarding platform. He was staring at me, smiling. He brought one hand away from the book he was reading and gave me a single, slow motion wave. I moved into my seat and brought my face to the window and watched him recede and grow smaller. I stood there, one knee resting on my seat, my arm above my head braced against the window, until Klingman disappeared from my sight. And in the instant that he vanished, I was overcome with a sense of what I now swear was pure grief.

I have come to know grief all too well and too often in my life. As anyone my age has. Grief is what age insists on teaching us. And the sensation of utter loss I experienced in that train car, watching a stranger fade into the distance, was akin to the dispossession and the cold sorrow I had felt when my parents were killed on an icy highway in Manitoba.

I think I might have dissolved into tears had I not felt the hand on my shoulder. I jumped and turned to find my breakfast waiter smiling at me. He removed his hand but I couldn't bring myself to ask what he wanted. He leaned forward and whispered, "Klingman says, 'You're welcome.' "

I cringe again as I write this because on the page it may read a presumptuous statement. But I have never doubted that the message contained anything but genuine warmth and good wishes.

The waiter moved on and left my car. I sank into my seat and held the book in my lap as if it were a fragile pet. For the rest of my trip I looked from the book cover to the countryside passing my window. My mind was empty and exhausted and my entire body was chilled. I knew, sensed, that something had happened to me but I could not begin to understand what it was.

When we arrived at the Capital, I pushed the book into my duffel and buttoned my coat. I was the last to exit the train. My sister and her husband were waiting for me. For some reason, they were both dressed formally, as if on their way to an opera. They had the same tired, dour look on their faces. I knew they wanted some immediate groveling—enough so that I'd embarrass myself without making a scene. And honestly, I would have complied but I was tired enough to collapse.

I followed them to the parking garage and climbed into the back of their sedan for the drive to the country house where we were to spend the holiday. Under the guise of weary concern, my sister lectured me the entire way, grounding all of her many opinions regarding my character in the disappointment and disgrace that our mercifully dead parents would be feeling if they could see how badly I'd turned out. My brother-in-law played Greek chorus, warning of the ravages the future would hold should I fail to "turn things around."

Somehow, I managed to stay awake and take all of the berating in a silence that I hoped passed for contrition. When we arrived at the house, I passed, politely, on the dinner that Sis had kept warm in the oven. I apologized one last time for my mistakes, promised we would talk in the morning and climbed upstairs to one of the guestrooms.

I closed and locked my door, threw the duffel on the loveseat and opened it, intending to climb into bed with the book. Not to read it, mind you—my eyes and my brain were beyond reading at this point. No, I simply wanted to hold it close to me, the way a child might hold a stuffed bear. But the book was not in my bag. I emptied all the contents, all of my possessions, and sorted through each item. Then I resorted over and over again until it was clear there was no book to be found. You can imagine how frantic I was.

I made myself settle down enough to think logically and decided that the book must have fallen out in the car on the ride home. My brother-in-law was an erratic driver at best and my sister's non-stop scolding had only degraded what little skill he possessed. We had taken some sharp corners getting onto and off of the expressway. My duffel had been sitting in the rear passenger footwell and had, most likely, toppled during one of those turns. The book, which had been sitting atop the rest of my gear, likely fell out of the bag and was now resting beneath the driver's seat.

I managed to wait until I heard my hosts retire for the night, then I made my way downstairs and out through the laundry room into the attached garage. The sedan was unlocked and I performed an elaborate, let us say obsessive search, but there was no sign of the book.

I returned to the guestroom and went through the bag again and again and came up empty each time. I lay down on the bed, fully clothed, and tried to think of the other possibilities. I'd either dropped the novel on the train, in the station, or in the parking garage. Tomorrow, I decided, I would find a way to return to the station and comb the area. Perhaps locate a lost and found office. If nothing turned up, I could inquire with the train line—I still had my ticket stub with all the pertinent information. The worst case scenario, I imagined, would involve purchasing a fresh copy of the novel at a bookstore. Though I didn't have an author's name, I had the title and that, I thought, should be sufficient. This was a distasteful option, however. I very much wanted the copy that Klingman had given me. I wanted, needed, that specific book. That *object*.

But with a plan of action decided, I attempted to sleep. Of course, it was futile. By 3 A.M., I was consumed with a level of anxiety I had never known. Even my expulsion hearing paled in comparison to the worry and nervous tension. I experienced that night. I paced the floor. I tried to exhaust myself with sit-ups and push-ups. I raided the medicine cabinet and swallowed a handful of aspirins. And I went downstairs and rifled my sister's library drawers until I found an incomplete Pinochle deck. (That they called this book-free room a "library" has always amused me.) I took the deck upstairs and spent an hour running through my various routines, making cards disappear and reappear and trade places. And for the first time since I'd initiated myself in the brotherhood of monty, the cards failed to bring me any solace.

Can you imagine, old friend, how desperate I felt in this moment? It was the kind of realization that reroutes the intestines and bites into the heart. What I did next should inform you of my state of mind that night. As my anxiety began to trammel my reason, I started to repack my duffel. When I was done, I slipped downstairs, found the key to my sister's convertible in her pocketbook and borrowed her car. My brother-in-law, up until the day he died, was incensed with my use of the word "borrowed." But as I backed out of their driveway, I had every intention of returning before morning.

I tried to retrace the route to the Capital and got lost several times. Finally, I secured directions at a highway gas station. It was only after I'd parked in the train station garage that I realized I had no money for the exit fee.

I searched the garage and the areas of the station that I'd passed through. There was no trace of the book. The lost and found office was closed but I pestered a ticket clerk until she opened the door and let me inspect every bin. I inquired about a search of the train I'd arrived on, the Seaboard Star, and was informed that it had just been thoroughly cleaned before its imminent departure and that no books had been discovered.

An analyst I knew briefly once theorized that my actions that night were the result of the accumulated traumas I'd been experiencing since the death of my mother and father. That my parents' demise and my banishment to de Sale and my expulsion from the school all coalesced and exploded inside of me. And that the force of that explosion propelled me back onto the train.

The truth is that as I sat on a bench in the cold of the National Station, I felt all my panic and doubt slip away from me and I became as focused as a young Houdini. And at the heart of this utter calmness I found the certainty, the absolute conviction, that if I did not recover the Klingman copy of *Refugee*, I would die. This confession, I would guess, leads you to believe that I was not in my right mind when I decided to re-board the Seaboard Star and ride north once again, in search of the book and, perhaps, in search of Klingman.

But you must trust me, F, when I write that I was as

sane as I have ever been. Sane enough to approach every conscious soul in the station and proffer my father's vintage Hamilton "Mason"-model wristwatch for the price of a train ticket. This was self-inflicted robbery, but it took me until the last boarding call before I found an elderly porter who knew the value of what I offered. He paid me what I'd asked and threw in the cost of breakfast and lunch.

For hours, I walked back and forth through all the cars of the northbound Seaboard Star, looking under every seat, checking every rest room, inquiring of every uniformed hand. But there was no trace of my lost paperback.

And so I tried, with a surprising degree of success, to re-create the book in my head. I closed my eyes and slouched down in my chair, huddled into myself and let the rocking of the car lull me into a kind of lucid dreaming, a recollection of the story that was, if not a perfect re-creation, even more interesting for its discrepancies. Where my imagination insisted on rewriting the author, it managed, to my delight, to retain the overall mood and tone and, if you can stand it, theme of the book.

I'd had only enough cash to get to Manchaug, a one-horse valley town in the farmlands a few hours west of Quinsigamond. My exact plans as I got off the train have faded over time, but I believe I hoped to find a ride into the city and to look up all the Klingmans in the phone directory. Before I left the depot, however, something made me stop at the ticket counter and inquire if there were any bookstores nearby.

Remember that this was when people still retained a degree of literacy *and* civility. The clerk explained that Pittsfield was my best bet for selection, but there was a local antiquarian shop about ten miles down Route 4.

"Of course," the clerk added as I turned away, "they'll both be closed for the holiday."

I turned back to him and he smiled and said, "I doubt anyone will be open on Thanksgiving."

The word hit me like a rubber bullet for two reasons. Yes, I felt some guilt over my flight from my sister and the worry I must be have caused her. But, as cavalier and selfish as it will sound, more than any guilt was the fear that I faced a delay in locating *Refugee* or Klingman.

I left the station and walked out onto the road, trying to think. If I turned right, I'd be headed in the direction of Quinsigamond and de Sale and the possibility of food and shelter from a pitying headmaster. The possibility, as well, of finding Klingman. He had, after all, like me, boarded the train at Gomper's Station.

But as you have already guessed, my friend, I turned left. And for the first, but certainly not the last time in my life, I began to hitchhike. You have to understand, I was obsessed. However lofty it might sound in retrospect, I can only tell you that at the time it felt as if I were on a kind of quest. And, as in the case of most quests, neither fatigue nor reason could dissuade me.

There was little traffic and I decided that it would be best to walk as I hitched. Route 4 was a lazy two-laner that had recently been made obsolete by the interstate. And by the time I had my thumb out, most travelers had already arrived at their destinations and were sampling the cider and cheese. I'm sure I looked suspicious to the few cars and trucks that did roll by, what with my slept-in clothes and uncombed hair and vintage seaman's duffel large enough to hold a small body.

But I didn't much mind. The day was brisk, but I was wearing my father's old Navy pea coat. And I had time to think, once again, about the book. This time, however, I let myself extrapolate freely, taking the refugee into sideline adventures that his author had never considered.

About two hours later, I rounded a bend in the road, looked out on a classic New England covered bridge and fell to my knees in near faint. The sensation of collapse vanished almost as quickly as it had come. But I sat on my duffel breathing through the aftershock of it. My legs and arms had gone numb and, simultaneously, a chill had coursed through my body like a current.

When I collected myself, I attributed the spell to hunger and sleeplessness and the general upsetting of the past week. I picked myself up and continued across the bridge and on the other side I saw a red-shingle cabin with a sign on the roof that announced

SCHEHEREZADE'S
RARE AND USED BOOKS

There was a porch fronting the house and on the porch sat wheelbarrows filled with books.

I confess that I ran across the road without looking, dropped my duffel in a pile of leaves and leapt up the three stairs to the porch. I began pawing through the offerings. It was a real mishmash—hardcovers and paperbacks, fiction and non-fiction and textbooks, atlases and magazines and even postcards. I went through it all like a man panning for gold. But I think I knew, as I looked, that I would not find *Refugee*.

When I'd exhausted the offerings and confirmed my suspicion, I sat down on the stairs to decide my next move. And soon after that I heard a bell ring. I turned around to see a man standing behind me. He would have been my first choice to play a farmer in the local production of *Oklahoma*. He was gaunt and tall and serious looking, craggy-faced and with a head of thin steely hair that he combed straight back over his bulging dome of a skull.

"Can I help you?" he said in a tone that implied I'd better have a good reason for sitting on his steps and I'd better deliver it fast.

"I was looking for a book," was all I could think to say.

He squinted and said, "We're closed. It's Thanksgiving."

"I understand," I said and stood up. "Sorry to bother you."

I got as far as the shoulder of the road when he yelled, "What book were you looking for?"

I turned back and yelled the title. He was the kind of man who wore his thinking on his face. I watched his eyes glaze a little in concentration as he scratched at his chest through his flannel shirt.

"I don't know it," he yelled. "Who's the author?"

I took a step back toward him and said, "I have no idea."

This seemed to surprise him and, after looking back into the shop, he said, "Come on in here for a minute."

His name was Albert Southard. And he lived like a monk in a back room of the store. In the years since we met, I've often wondered what became of him. And I've wondered what became of that unlikely store in the middle of nowhere. Inside, it proved bigger than it had looked from the road. It is, in my memory, a haven of cozy warmth, a honeycomb of small shelf-lined rooms, each one fitted with an easy chair or a sofa, all of them draped with quilts and comforters and pillows. Of course, there were books everywhere, spilling off the shelves, forming pyramids in the middle of the corridors. I could see that a sense of order was not the shop's chief virtue.

Mr. Southard offered me a seat in front of his desk. On top of the desk, in the center of his blotter, steamed a TV dinner of turkey and mashed potatoes. Southard took his glasses from his shirt pocket and asked me to tell him about this book that I seemed to need so desperately. I gave the same details that I've given to you. (Over time, that description of the book became a kind of prayer, repeated so often that I could say it in my sleep.) At the end of my recitation, Southard shook his head. He began to walk to his piles of reference volumes, asking, over his shoulder, where I found my original copy of the novel. I started my story and when I mentioned Klingman's name, Albert Southard stopped in his tracks.

He returned to the desk and said, "Now that you mention it, I think I do know the book." It was a rare volume, he said. The print run had been minimal. It could be a costly investment. What was the maximum I'd be willing to pay?

The possibility that I couldn't afford the book had not occurred to me. Mr. Southard must have seen the crestfallen look on my face because before I could respond, he added, "But we're getting ahead of ourselves. First we'll see if we can locate this *Refugee*."

He told me to make myself at home, to feel free to browse the store while he made some calls.

I looked down at the aluminum tray organizing his Thanksgiving feast and said, "I don't want to interrupt your meal."

He seemed confused for a second, then he said, "Have you eaten?"

I admitted I had not. He said he had another Swanson's in the freezer. Would I like to join him? I hadn't had a bite since finishing a cheese sandwich somewhere in Smyrna. I thanked him for the hospitality and he went off to pop a tray into his toaster oven.

I did as he advised, let myself ramble through the maze of the store, running my finger along rows of spines, silently reciting titles and author's names as if they were train stops along an extended journey.

Sometime later Mr. Southard found me in the rear of the place, sitting on the floor with a tower of books at my knee.

"Dinner's served," he said and I looked up to see him holding my TV dinner in a oven-mitted hand.

We ate on opposite sides of the desk. I devoured every scrap. Washed it all down with warm ginger ale.

"I've got some leads," he said to me as we ate.

He spoke, quite knowledgeably, and, at times, quite humorously, about various used bookstores all over the country and their often eccentric proprietors. And by the time we got to our cherry cobbler desserts, he surprised me by asking, "By any chance are you looking for a place to stay?"

I had imagined I would be sleeping in a train station, waiting until I got so cold and hungry that I had no choice but to call my sister.

"It's no shame to need a place to stay," Southard said. "Come here."

I got up and followed him back to the front of the shop. He put my duffel on the largest couch and said, "It's not four star, but it's warm and the sofa is comfortable."

Before I could reply, before I could argue or thank him, he slipped into his overcoat and said, "I have to visit my sister and her family. I'll be back in the morning. We'll have some breakfast and talk some more about this book of yours." Then he was out the door and I was locked inside.

You're thinking what I thought: What kind of a man leaves a complete stranger alone in his home overnight? Let me tell you something. Southard was part of a tribe that is larger than you might expect.

Can you begin to imagine the flood of doubt and fear and, yes, excitement and hope I experienced that night? Alone in an unknown town, without a dime to my name, I felt as if I were living someone else's life, as if a mistake had been made and my mundane existence had been swapped for one of adventure and freedom and danger and absolute chance.

Is it any surprise that I could not sleep that evening? I made some coffee. I ate the pear and the jar of nuts that I found on the desk. And I carried several armfuls of books, more books than I could read in a lifetime, to the couch and spent a delightful if hallucinatory night sampling all manner of story.

Over hot oatmeal and bananas the next morning, Mr.

Southard offered me a job. I knew, even at that tender age, that this was nothing but charity. That he had no need for an employee. But I was not in any position to be proud. I took the job and stayed for three months, saving up my money and learning the basics of the book trade. And more than this. I began that morning a dialogue that would continue the rest of my days. I entered into an exchange about books and writers and stories and what they can mean to a life.

Every other week or so, Southard would make a vague comment about a lead he had on *Refugee*. But nothing ever came of them.

When I finally left Scheherezade's with the intention of moving, in general, westward, Albert Southard gave me the name of a bookstore in Milwaukee that had purportedly sold a copy of *Refugee* last year. He also mentioned that the proprietor might have work for me.

And so I became a traveler, a traveling reader, staying briefly in some places, much longer in others. And devouring books as I went. My general purpose remained the search for my elusive paperback and the man who had given it to me. But as time passed, it became a passive quest. It was not that I gave up looking so much as I came to understand, to feel, that it would take years to conclude my search.

I worked in libraries and bookshops mostly, referred from one owner or manager to another. But I can also claim employment as night watchman, parking lot attendant and house sitter. All jobs that allowed me to read for long, uninterrupted hours.

I attempted to settle down once, in the exact middle of my life. It was an emotional time and I let a rare bout of loneliness influence me. I tried, very hard, please believe me, to make a family. But I was not suited to the role of patriarch and I hurt too many people for too many years. It was not that I did not love my wife and the twins. Never that. I loved them to my full capacity and to this day I ache with regret at the way I failed them. But I was driven, compelled—just as I'd been compelled to jump on the Seaboard Star and flee the Capital all those years ago—to live a different life than the one they required and deserved.

Is it any wonder that so many religious traditions insist their priests remain celibate? It is a setting apart, is it not? It is a way to claim them as acolytes of another way, another tradition, separate from the satisfactions of the domestic world.

I'm trying to say that on the day Klingman gave me that book, he claimed me for another way of life, initiated me into something wondrous and ruined me for the joys of the grounded.

I'm saying that I followed the only road open to me. I continued my wandering, a kind of tin pan asceticism. I came to see most of my native land and much of the rest of the world. I traveled as often as possible by train because I found that, though I never attained the depth of intensity I'd known with *Refugee*, the rails always provided a heightened reading experience.

It was early in the travels that I began to understand the phenomenon I titled, at some point, "the seizure," the numbing faint and chill that would overcome me from time to time, just as it had on Route 4 when I first glimpsed that covered bridge on my way to Sheherezade's.

The second occurrence happened in Peru, Kansas, where I was working in a small shop called The Bookworm. I had not been long in the Prairie State but I'd already assisted a customer in securing a rare first edition of a C. Gus French novel. The collector, a pharmaceutical salesman who passed through our region every other month, was so thrilled that he invited me to join him for a night on the town. His cheer was so genuine that I accepted, not knowing that a night on the town meant sitting in on a longstanding game of draw poker in a Road King motel room. The other players were friendly but wary of the youngster. I soon replaced their wariness with surprise and then, annoyance, when, by 10 P.M., I was smirking behind most of the chips on the table.

My experience at de Sale had taught me nothing, however, and I let my early good fortune make me cocky. Also, there was liquor present and while I only nursed a beer or two, I was new to the charms of alcohol and perhaps my play grew more sloppy than usual.

Whatever the reason, my good fortune faded rapidly and by the end of the game I was busted. It was as I got up from the table and walked into the bathroom that the seizure hit me. I managed to close the door behind me and steady myself against the sink. There was a cold sensation throughout my body, particularly along my joints. This was followed by a near faint, which, in turn, was followed by the most vivid and powerful feeling of déjà vu I had ever known.

Only it became apparent to me in seconds that it wasn't déjà vu at all. It was an episode from the novel, from *Refugee*. On the Seaboard Star, I had read an almost-exact description of everything that took place in that motel room. Everything that had happened to the novel's protagonist—the arrival in Kansas, the invitation to a private card game, the flush of early success and the subsequent loss of all the winnings—had been replayed in my life. I *was* the protagonist.

It happened again two years later in East Texas where I was robbed at gunpoint while exiting a movie theater.

It happened in Denio, Nevada, where I was arrested for vagrancy and through a series of miscommunications and bad luck, ended up serving thirty days of county jail time.

And in Castile, New York, where I met a belly dancer named Glynnis and ended up in a hot air balloon celebrating her birthday.

And in Lowell, Massachusetts, where I met my wife-to-be for the first time as she served up a sausage omelet at the Paradise Diner.

In some strange way, for reasons that to this day I do not understand, my life was foretold in a forgotten, spine-cracked paperback novel titled *Refugee*.

I last experienced a seizure on the day that we met, my friend, on that train to the Capital. (I've never told you, but I was heading to see my sister who was living in a nursing home not far from the National Station. One last visit to apologize and say good-bye.)

I want to apologize to you as well. I know I appeared overbearing during our initial meeting, but when you reach my age you will see that sometimes one must dispense with manners when time is in short supply. And I hope my little gift made up for my rudeness.

No need to track me down to say, "thank you." Giving the right book to the right person is a joy I've long treasured. Beyond this, it is my duty.

Which is why it's no surprise that this is where I find myself in the end. On a train. Rattling and swaying, out of the world and into another story. But perhaps it will surprise you to learn that when I boarded this particular train and made my way to the last car (still traveling in the economy coach, of course), and located my seat, I found a large and shabby passenger in the adjoining chair.

Klingman was reading *Refugee*. He'd left another,

more slender volume on my seat. He lifted it, with one hand, without breaking off from his reading. And I took it from him as I squeezed into my place without a word. It has been over an hour now and still we have not spoken. I've stolen a few glimpses and he looks the same as he did when I first met him. When my nose began to bleed at the start of this letter, he pulled his yellow handkerchief from his sleeve and offered it to me. It smelled like old paper.

There is so much that I want to ask him but I don't want to interrupt his joy, the beauty and wholeness of his moments enveloped in the story of my life. My guess is that he is anxious for me to put down this pen and pick up my last book.

I'll trust the porter to mail this for me.

In case you're wondering, the volume currently in my lap appears to be more short story than novel. There is no author's name on the cover. And this time there is no title. Only a picture, a faded cover illustration of an old man sitting in a train car reading a book whose cover features an old man sitting in a train car reading a book.

I have no idea where this engine is headed or if I'll have time to finish the tale. I have no interest in knowing. The countryside passing me now looks like no land I've seen before. But then, my eyes are not what they once were. What is? Even my hands, once so strong and agile, capable of tricks that could make you distrust yourself, are, today, gnarled and stiff. By the time I finish turning the last page, they'll be good for nothing.

You, on the other hand, have much to do. Places to go, as they say, and people to see. I'm sentimental enough to ask that you think of me from time to time. Hopefully, in a favorable light. I ask that you try to understand why I did what I did. Why I chose you out of the world and initiated you. Why I made you into a reader.

I ask, if possible, that you forgive me, my friend. Please know that I wish you all the best, despite any evidence to the contrary.

And now, if you'll excuse me, I have some reading to catch up on.

Sincerely,

DIVING THE *COOLIDGE*

BRIAN A. HOPKINS

THE WATER OF ESPIRITU Santo harbor was a thick, chalky cobalt against which our diving lights struggled in vain. At a depth of sixty feet, motes of tiny marine life hung like stars in the ethereal glare, vanishing toward the bottom where the U.S.S. *President Coolidge* reposed in the gloom. Except for the bubbles from our regulators, it was deathly quiet. The silence of a grave. The silence of a museum. The silence of half a century and more.

The ship lay on her port side, empty lifeboat davits reaching toward the surface. She was coated with a thick shag of marine growth: sponges and coral and great purple sea fans. Her bow lay just below us, near the top of the reef, while her stern lay downslope, held against the sandy harbor floor by two hundred feet of sea water. The holes where U.S. mines had gutted her starboard hull were still visible.

Edward ran the headlights of his sled along the *Coolidge's* promenade, while I shot photos. We'd been diving together for six years, Edward locating the wrecks with that eerie combination of sixth sense and sonar sensitivity that I'd come to expect (and even take for granted), me shooting my photos. I remember when he spotted that B-17 lying off Rabaul. We hadn't even been looking for anything that day, but the depth finder had been running, plotting a rough outline of the sea floor in blocky LCD pixels. Without a word, Edward had slowed the engine and brought the boat around. He pointed at what, to me, appeared to be nothing more than another stretch of coral reef.

"That's an airplane," he said. "A *big* airplane."

"I think you're full of shit."

"A hundred dollars says I'm right."

So we dove, and we found the B-17 embedded in the reef 150 feet beneath the surface. The photos I took made the cover of *Newsweek*. The B-17 had gone down in 1943, caught in severe weather after skip-bombing a Japanese cruiser. I paid Edward his hundred and bet him double or nothing he couldn't locate anything else on the crude depth finder. In rapid succession, he found several more wrecks. First, a Japanese Zero, teeming with tiny silversides and encrusted with sponges and coralline algae, completely unrecognizable from more than twenty feet away—but as soon as it appeared on the depth finder, Edward had pointed to what he said was the prop and identified not just that it was a plane, but the exact type of plane. Ten minutes later, I was sitting in the cockpit of the Zero, accompanied by an iridescent blue parrotfish, and staring at the butts of the twin 7.7 millimeter machine guns, wondering what it had been like to fly her, to hear the roar of those guns whipping past. How had she come to rest here, I wondered, cupped in the maritime museum of the sea? Had she been outmaneuvered by an F-4U Corsair or a P-38 Lightning? Had she been forced to ditch when she ran out of fuel? With better equipment, we'd find many more Zeros in the days to come—nearly three hundred of the Japanese fighter planes were shot down over Rabaul—but that first one was special.

National Geographic saw the photos and commissioned a story. I was suddenly an expert on World War II wreckage at the bottom of the South Pacific. The assignment for a coffee table book came next. Edward and I were suddenly inseparable. We shot long forgotten Japanese warships like the *Hakki Maru* in Simpson Harbor, placed there by B-25s on January 17, 1944. And one of those same B-25s, not a hundred feet away, had bullets still racked and ready to fire from her twin .50 caliber guns. I photographed tractors and jeeps and tanks lost from the holds and decks of battleships and cargo vessels. Scuttled submarines. Torpedoed patrol boats. The flotsam and jetsam of the last great war. Throughout the Solomon Islands, across New Guinea and Vanuatu, we searched and we found them, one by one, each with its own story to tell.

Edward would find them. And I would photograph them.

I don't know how he did it. Sometimes, he didn't even look at the equipment. Sometimes we weren't even *near* the equipment. I remember the Kawanishi flying boat he foun d just off shore. We were sitting on the beach at Rabaul, watching Papua New Guinean children playing in the surf. Edward's wheelchair was firmly entrenched in the loose sand. I was dreading the struggle involved in getting him back to the Bougainville Resort, when Edward suddenly sat up and stared out at the turquoise water.

"What is it?" I asked.

"There's something out there," he said. His face had that haunted look I had come to know. "A plane."

I got to my feet and looked. The waves curled white and foamy, broke around the brown legs of the children, and scattered tiny bivalves on the beach. "I don't see anything."

He called over some of the children and tried to talk to them, but of course they didn't speak English. Somehow he got through to them that he thought there was something on the ocean bottom, there just outside the breakers. They rolled their eyes. Of course there's something out there, their expressions said. One of the older boys held out his arms and soared around the beach making airplane noises, his rags flapping in the breeze, while the other children laughed and jabbered in Malaysian. Edward bribed them to ferry us out beyond the surf in their outriggers—dangerous, as we didn't have our dive gear with us. The children were careful with him, though. Besides, they lived their lives in those canoes, tooling about the islands the way an American child would ride around town on a bicycle. We stood more chance of being swallowed by a whale than one of the children tipping a canoe and letting Edward drown.

Not more than eight feet beneath the surface, we found the Kawanishi. The children had played in it all their lives.

As I said, I don't know how he found them. He would laugh about it when I insisted there was something paranormal about the whole experience. He would point to the sonar and the depth finders and all the fancy equipment that the National Geographic Society had bought us. He would deny that there was anything strange going on.

And then we dove the *Coolidge*.

In January of 1942, Japan captured Rabaul on New Britain Island and established a garrison of 100,000 troops, five airstrips, and a naval base. From this vantage point, Japan attempted to invade Port Morseby, an allied base in New Guinea. They were turned back in the Battle of the Coral Sea. In July, Japanese troops took Guadalcanal in the Solomons. U.S. Marines attacked a month later and for twenty-six weeks a channel called the Ironbottom Sound accumulated the detritus of war. American reinforcements were sent in from Espiritu Santo in the New Hebrides (now Vanuatu). It wasn't until March 1943, in the Battle of the Bismarck Sea, that Allied forces skip-bombed the Japanese Navy at Rabaul to ribbons. In November, U.S. aircraft from the carriers *Saratoga* and *Princeton* entered Rabaul's Simpson Harbor and bombed the Japanese fortress to impotency. But from 1942 on, Espiritu Santo, protected by a series of underwater mines, was the staging area for our operations against Rabaul.

It was one of those mines—*one of our own mines*—that sank the *President Coolidge*.

Sometimes life works that way. The mine you step on is the mine you laid years ago, the trap you set for someone else, not realizing the ultimate target was yourself. Long forgotten, but still waiting.

Sometimes you are your own worst enemy. And the most grievous of injuries are those which are self-inflicted: the guilt you carry with you, the lies you tell yourself.

Edward sipped his rum and tried to look comfortable, but I knew him too well. He fidgeted with the wheel brakes on his chair and made a great show of adjusting his bicycle gloves. Public places make him nervous, especially places like this remote bar which had never heard of accommodations for the handicapped. It had been a struggle just to get the wheelchair maneuvered through all the tables and, once there, our table was too low, meaning that Edward's chair had to sit out in the aisle, a good arm's length and a stretch from his drink. He'd told me before that it seemed everyone stared at him in places like this. That he could feel a million eyes on him, wondering how he'd ended up in the chair, wondering just how wasted were the remnants of his legs, hidden beneath the tweed throw. Edward was most comfortable in the sea, where the Farallon DPV gave him greater range and speed than any diver I knew. Even before he'd been able to afford the Diver Propulsion Vehicle, though, his powerful arms had made him an accomplished diver. Here . . . in the resort's surfside bar . . . he was truly a fish out of water.

"You want to go on up to your room?" I asked. "I can take care of this."

He shook his head. "No, I'll stay. I want to make sure Gunter knows he has to have room for the Farallon."

"After six years you don't trust me?"

"Oh, I trust you, Mickey. It's your memory I don't put much faith in. Sometimes," he snickered playfully, "I think you might have skipped a decompression or two."

I pointed at him with my shot glass. "Don't make me have to come over there and let the air out of your tires."

"You'd have to catch me first. We both know I can outrun you on land, too."

It wasn't true, but I laughed as if it was. I thought it ironic that Edward would joke about speed, when it was speed that had made him a paraplegic to begin with. According to him, he'd been outrunning a speeding ticket, his Camaro Z28 clocking over a hundred when an old woman had pulled out in front of him. He'd chosen a roadside ditch over her Chrysler LeBaron, and the rest was history. He joked that the Highway Patrol had still written him the speeding ticket.

"How'd you find this Gunter guy anyway?"

I shrugged. "Phone book. We need him. No one dives the *Coolidge* without a guide." Vanuatu laws were very specific about this.

"Well, you could have found one who knew how to tell time."

I let it go. He was just irritable because the bar made him uncomfortable. "You want another drink?"

"Tell me that's not our man," he said, pointing.

Gunter was fortyish. Long hair. Khaki shorts. Flip flops. Hawaiian shirt, mostly hidden by the fact that his right arm hung in a white sling. He spotted us, waved, and made his way through the tables. "Mick Beai?"

"It's pronounced *bay-eye*," I told him, taking the offered hand. "You're our guide?"

He nodded vigorously. "Yes. Guide. That's me. Gunter." His accent was the thick guttural of Northern Germany. Hamburg maybe. His w's were v's. The end of each word was clipped off. His vowels came from somewhere deep within his gut. How he'd come to be in the South Pacific was probably quite an involved story.

I introduced him to Edward.

"Forgive me for asking," Edward said, "but how the hell do you plan to dive with your arm in that sling?"

Gunter cocked an eyebrow. "*You* would ask Gunter such a thing?" Then he laughed, a great hearty bear laugh, and slapped Edward's wasted thigh (an offense for which I surely thought Edward would actually rise from his chair and kill the German). "I'm kidding, friend. Gunter will not dive." He pulled out a chair. "Sit? Yes?" He dropped into the chair, which groaned under his weight.

"The law," Gunter said "says you need guide. Need Gunter. Law does not say that Gunter must dive with you." He grinned, knowing we knew he was full of shit, but that we wouldn't say anything. "Gunter take you out to mooring at bow of *Coolidge*. You dive. Gunter wait up top. You bring nothing up with you. Law say that everything must stay in wreck. First dive, you maybe go as far as the Lady, but no further into ship, no further down toward stern. Depth maybe 45 meters. You use safety lines inside, cause Gunter does not like to dive for corpses, and the *Coolidge* . . . she is very possessive. Very often there are silt-outs. Next day you swim to stern. Over 70 meters."

"Decompression?"

"Forty minutes."

It was a bit much by my quick mental estimate, but I understood his caution. The nearest chamber was in Australia. "Gunter show you deco stops. Lovely coral garden. Lots of fish. Maybe moray eel." He tried to sound sinister, but his voice was already a nightmare. "Maybe shark or two!" He laughed. "You take pictures. You swim around and look at fish. Decompression time go very slow for you."

"Fast."

"Oh. Yeah. Time go fast." He laughed again. "You have great dive, Mick. Tell all friends Gunter is the best guide 'cause he not breathe over your shoulder the whole time." He patted his injured arm. "Dislocated shoulder."

"Do you have maps of the interior?" Edward asked. We had our own, but local guides usually have maps that they've annotated. The interior of a ship that's been on the bottom as long as the *Coolidge* would hardly match her original blueprints.

"Gunter show you maps. First day, though, no further than the Lady. Everyone wants to see the Lady. Toilets, too," he guffawed. "Everybody wants to see the toilets!"

"The two divers who died in '96," I asked, "what happened?"

Gunter shrugged. "No guide. No safety lines. Caught in silt-out . . . and drowned."

* * *

The *President Coolidge* began her career as a luxury liner in 1931. Built by Newport News Shipbuilding, her interiors were paneled in rare woods, draped in silk, lit by skylights of cathedral glass. She displaced nearly twenty-two thousand tons and was more than six hundred and fifty feet long. Her two steam turbine engines were capable of sustaining twenty knots. In 1942, just after the Japanese entered the war, she was converted to an Army troop transport and put into service in the South Pacific. Her finery was ripped out. Her promenade deck was crowded with three rows of extra toilets to accommodate the large number of troops onboard. Guns were mounted on her decks.

On her seventh voyage for the military, while entering Segond Channel on approach to Espiritu Santo, staging base for hard-pressed Allied troops on Guadalcanal, the *Coolidge* missed a warning signal from shore and hit two U.S. mines. She was carrying more than five thousand men, most of them from the 43rd Infantry Division. The ship's Master, Captain Henry Nelson, ran her aground on a coral reef to give the men time to abandon ship. Just over an hour later, the *Coolidge*, which had listed almost completely over on her port side, slipped off the reef and sank. By this time, nearly all the men on board had been evacuated. Dead were a fireman, Robert Reid, killed by the second explosion, and an Army Officer, Captain Elwood Euart, whose death remains something of a mystery. He and another Army Officer, Warren Covill, were instrumental in saving hundreds of lives by rigging a line to guide men across the treacherously tilted deck. When everyone was clear, they went to make their own escape, but Euart turned back and went below. The ship slipped from the reef. Covill was sucked under and barely escaped alive. Euart was never recovered. It's believed that, in the confusion, Euart thought there were still men below decks. He was posthumously awarded the Distinguished Service Cross.

Today, the *Coolidge* is the largest, intact, accessible shipwreck. And she's certainly one of the best known. People have come from around the world to see the last bit of refinery left to her: the Lady. The Lady waits in the main smoking lounge, over the marble fireplace, an Elizabethan figure with a unicorn. The rare woods of the fireplace have been eaten by teredo worms, and the unicorn has lost his horn, but the marble and the Lady remain. In her fine white gown with its gold ruffles and brocade, she watches, a somber sentinel to the waste at the bottom of the sea.

Shipwreck divers can't help but believe in ghosts. You don't spend your life diving ocean graveyards such as the South Pacific without acquiring an affinity for the drowned. It's always there, the possibility of death; just an equipment failure or stupid mistake away. Nor can you photograph such wreckage without imagining the last minutes of those who've gone before you: the frantic haste to abandon ship, the crushing weight of all that water sweeping over the deck, the agony of waiting for that last breath and then seeing that final air bubble squeezed from your lungs, meandering, fading with your darkening vision, toward an impossibility distant surface.

World-renowned underwater photographer David Doubilet has said, "the minute a ship crosses that final barrier between air and surface, as it settles into the sea, it loses the heat and the pain and the blood and the smell, and it becomes a sculpture."

The *Coolidge* lay beneath us like a surreal work of art in the murky depths: Descending the mooring line, with Gunter waiting above in his boat, I was aware of the demarcation of light and dark. The scintillating surface above. The gray-green hue of the sea between. And the black mass of the wreck below us, her stern vanishing in the gloom. Edward hit the lights on the Farallon and they played over the *Coolidge*'s bow. I snapped a photo, capturing the chain locker, a three-inch gun battery, and the dark opening of her forward cargo hold. Her masts were still in place on the foredeck, their tips buried in the sand. The crow's nest was still in place. A massive anchor leaned against the nearly vertical deck, replete with fairy shrimp and feather duster worms, its chains tangled with the masts and metal cables and several long silent hoists. Everything was coated with heavy marine growth, a veil of wet, brown-green dust that swirled murkily in the eddies behind Edward's sled.

We proceeded to the cargo hold where Edward let his lights penetrate the gloom. The hold was crammed with the mechanisms of war: six-wheeled Studebaker trucks, Jeeps, huge artillery guns, aircraft drop tanks, rifles, Thompson submachine guns, helmets, barrels, mysterious and mostly decomposed crates, and even a typewriter. Everything was jumbled together against the port bulkhead, seething with marine life.

I snapped my pictures, trying to capture the ghosts and the voices. Such a picture should do more than tell a story. Such a picture should haunt, should echo with those final moments.

We entered through the gaping windows of the bridge and worked our way aft along the promenade. The deck here was littered with discarded equipment: rifles, gas masks, metal ladders, helmets, .303 cartridges, plates, cups, cooking utensils ... a single inexplicable tuba, now the home for an octopus. The famous toilets— tightly spaced with absolutely no concern for privacy— gleamed white, their porcelain surface immune to the assault of the reef.

From the promenade, we entered the main dining hall. Here, the quarters became too tight for Edward's sled. Also, there was the very real danger that the Farallon's fan might stir up too much of the silt in the wreck. Though the walls of the promenade had collapsed, leaving an easy escape through the remaining steel girders, technically this was still a penetration dive with all due caution. Divers had become confused and died in similar conditions. Silt can be blinding. With no easy orientation, a man can become confused, can forget all the basics, and wind up joining the vast number of dead in the sea.

Edward removed one of the spotlights and proceeded by arm strength alone, propelling himself from different surfaces like an astronaut in zero gravity, his dead legs trailing behind him. When he couldn't reach a surface, he pulled himself through the water with his arms, his upper body strength more than a match for the dead weight below his waist. While he swam, the spotlight hung from a strap around his neck, its light playing madly across the canted interior of the *Coolidge*, sweeping across the skeletal ribs that separated us from the open sea. I would tap my tank to get his attention and indicate a shot I wanted. He'd hover then, the light casting its own ghosts. With hand signals we'd worked out years ago, I'd move him around until I had just the effect I was looking for. The underwater Nikon would whir and click in my hand, the noise of its tiny motor magnified tenfold by the pressure of all that water. Another ghostly image recorded. Another piece of history laid bare.

Beyond the promenade, moving steadily deeper as we ventured astern, we entered the main dining hall, the tables and chairs long gone to rot, now just a deep bed of silt to port. Beyond that massive room, we entered the smoking lounge and found the Lady. She stood guard over a dangerous looking rampart of bed frames. The beds had been brought in to house the troops. Looking at the twisted mass of rusted metal, like some mad fence around a concentration camp, I couldn't even begin to guess how many thousands of men must have been crammed into this one room. Like the toilets, there couldn't have been any privacy.

With Edward holding his light, I photographed the Lady. Her colors were remarkably bright for her age: red dress with gold brocade and ruffled collar; yellow hair pulled back from a high Elizabethan forehead; green vines and pink flowers behind her. The unicorn was still as white as porcelain of the toilets on the promenade. He was reared up on his hind legs, his tail raised and his mane, though hidden behind the long, trailing sleeve of the Lady's gown, appeared swept by a strong breeze. The Lady's expression was one of beatific benevolence, her arms raised as if she were welcoming all those who came to visit, as if she was grandly gesturing to the splendor all around her. Only the splendor of the *Coolidge* was long gone. Nothing but ghosts remained.

I didn't realize Edward was gone until the light rolled free of where he'd wedged it. I was turning to frown at him for not holding it still, when I caught movement from the corner of my eye. In the threshold of an aft exit, I saw something white slip around the corner and vanish. Edward's neoprene suit was black, like my own, so it couldn't have been him. I'd chalked it up to some sort of fish turning the corner, my peripheral vision making it larger and brighter than it probably was. The light continued its roll, playing across the exit, revealing a dense cloud of silt rising from the floor, tossed up by whatever I'd seen.

Edward was gone.

With the camera housing, I tapped my tank three times in rapid succession, then did it again—our distress code. The silt cloud by the doorway expanded, all but obliterating the opening. Setting aside my mounting fear, I turned and swam for the abandoned spotlight, moving carefully so as not to create any additional turbulence in the room. When I'd retrieved the light, I immediately focused it on the doorway. The light reflected back from the cloud of silt, blinding me.

I tapped my tank again.

Nothing.

Damn you, Edward, if—

But there he was, pulling himself back through the open doorway; pushing off the frame and gliding through the expanding silt. I let the light blind him, wanting to see his face. Just before he squinted his eyes and turned his face away from the light, I saw fear, an expression I'd never known Edward to wear, not in all our diving experiences.

When he was close enough, I caught him by the vest

and dragged him toward the bow, ignoring the great clouds of silt that billowed up from my flippers. We outran the silt into the dining hall and then onto the bridge where I shoved Edward rather too harshly toward his sled. He didn't look back at me as he powered the thing up and shot for open water. I can well imagine his rage at being handled that way.

We made the decompression stops. Edward fiddled with his sled, showing me his back. It took forever to reach the surface.

Gunter checked his watch when we broke the surfaced.

I stripped off my mask and spit out my regulator, grabbing for Edward. "What the hell were you doing down there?" I screamed at him.

"You didn't see it?" He was hanging onto the Farallon and it was still running. He was using it to keep himself afloat. I'd never seen him do that before. He looked exhausted. He was shaking.

"See what?" I asked, some of my anger subsiding.

"The ghost."

"I lied to you."

"About what?" I asked, signaling our waitress for another round. It had taken two to get Edward talking.

"Everything," he said without meeting my eyes. "The accident that put me in this chair. About my father."

I tried to recall what he'd told me over the years

about his father. Very little. I knew the man was dead, but couldn't recall how he'd died. In the rare conversations in which either of our parents had been a topic, I'd gotten the sense that Edward's father had been one of the absentee types, that Edward had seen very little of the man. He'd never given me any indication that this had been a problem for him, though.

"I never owned a Camaro. Never owned *any* automobile, for that matter."

The waitress brought out drinks. As she turned away, I pushed Edward's closer to him, using it as an opportunity to lean out and squeeze his forearm. "Hey, man, forget it. We all tell little white lies from time to time. Remember that time I told you about feeling up my older brother's girlfriend? Hell, that was really my brother and his best friend's girl. He used to tell that story all the time. I just kind of adopted it as my own when I was younger and it's stuck with me all these years. Hell, I've been telling that lie for so long that it really seems as if it did happen that way."

"In time we all come to believe our own lies," Edward said with a slight nod. He still hadn't looked at me.

"No lie," I said, still trying to lighten the mood. It didn't work. "Look, Edward, why don't you just tell me what you saw on the *Coolidge* and—"

"When I was young," he said, looking up at last, "my father and I were inseparable. I told you I grew up on the Outer Banks? That was the truth. But I lied when I said my father was a carpenter. He was a fisherman."

A chill ran up my spine. "Look, Edward, I think I know where you're going with this. If you're just trying to pull off some elaborate hoax . . ."

"Shut up and listen, Mickey. For once, just shut the fuck up."

I pushed back a bit from the table. "Sure. But if you're going to tell me your father's boat went down at sea one day, all hands lost, and now you've seen his ghost swimming around in the *Coolidge*, I'm going to be forced to remind you how far we are from the Outer Banks. If the old man was such a great swimmer, then he never should have drowned in the first place." I regretted it as soon as it was out, regretted it even more when I saw the hurt and anger in Edward's eyes, but I'd always been quick to put my foot in my mouth.

Edward reached for the wheels of his chair.

"Wait," I stammered, catching the arm of his chair. "Damn, but I'm sorry, Edward. You know what a stupid fuck I can be sometimes. Please forgive me. Let's start over, okay? You said you never owned a Camaro. Why don't you start by telling me how you wound up in the chair? Let's get that out of the way first. Then we can talk about your father. Okay?"

He said nothing. The thick cords of muscle in his forearms were set to propel the chair backward. I knew I wouldn't be able to hold onto it if he did.

"You have to agree to go back to the *Coolidge* with me tomorrow."

"Sure, Edward. I'll go back with you." It was, after all, what we'd come for.

"And this time, we do a deep penetration. Past Gunter's maps. Down into the stern, all the way into the bilge hold if necessary."

I nodded. "If you promise me that we'll follow proper safety procedures. Rig guidelines. Run a safety line between us. Carry some extra lights."

"Agreed."

I leaned back in my chair. "Tell me then. Start from the beginning."

The *Coolidge*'s third cargo hold had been used for medical storage. More serious than the loss of the vessel itself or the equipment of the 43rd had been the loss of the medical supplies stored there. The *Coolidge* had been carrying Atabrine to fight malaria on Guadalcanal. Most of the supplies have been salvaged, but they say if you dig around in the silt against the port bulkhead, you can still find a few intact phials of Atabrine and morphine among the eye droppers and syringes, tubing and surgical clamps and so on. Edward and I passed through the hold without probing her mysteries, tethered by thirty feet of nylon line. I only shot a few halfhearted photos without fussing over the lighting or the angls.

We were both carrying flashlights this time. I had a spare clipped to my vest, along with two spools of iridescent monofilament line, one of which was already reeling out through a hatch that led to the promenade.

Edward took a corridor astern, heading deeper. I followed, checking to make sure the guideline didn't become entangled behind me, kicking easy so as not to disturb the silt. In the tight passageway, it would be all too easy for a diver to create a blinding cloud with his flippers.

The passageway brought us to the ship's swimming pool, mosaic tiles still in place. Beyond it waited the soda fountain and beauty shop. Stranger even than the swimming pool turned vertical was the barber's chair standing out from what seemed to be the wall. The soda fountain was littered with old Coca-Cola bottles. Edward continued past all of this, barely allowing me time for a single photo. When I delayed too long, the line between us snapped taut, and I was forced to continue or be dragged.

"Though I loved him dearly, my father was an alcoholic," Edward had told me last night. "The only time he didn't drink was when he was working on the boat, which made those times with him at sea the best times in my life. Oh, it was a lot of hard work, especially for a kid, but I didn't mind.

"I was ten when he stopped off that night in the bar after a day on the boat, leaving me to wait outside. The night he wrecked the car because he was drunk. The night he put me in this wheelchair for the rest of my life." There was no bitterness in his voice, just a deep regret and a comfortable resignation. Edward had come to terms with all this years ago, had hidden whatever anger and resentment he still felt behind the lies that had come to be more real to him. But the lies spoke of guilt, and I wondered if somehow Edward didn't blame himself.

We were beyond the annotations on Gunter's maps now. Edward moved deeper into the bowels of the ship, ever astern and toward the keel on our left. The line on the first reel of monofilament was almost gone: nearly 250 feet of line strung out behind us through the twisting warrens of the vessel.

"Guilt ate the man alive," Edward continued, as if he'd read my thoughts. "He never took me out on the boat with him again. 'It's no place for a cripple,' he'd say, not meaning to be cruel, just stating fact in the unvarnished manner that he'd always used. Yes, it would have been difficult, but not impossible. The real reason he didn't want me on the boat is because it would have reminded him of all those times before the accident. It would have driven home the fact that his son would never be whole again and the fact that it was his fault.

"He drank more than ever. He even started drinking while working the boat."

He was getting careless, stirring up more and more of the fine silt that littered the *Coolidge*. I tugged on the tether to signal for him to slow down. He ignored me. I checked my air supply, checked the time, checked our depth. We were a hundred and seventy some odd feet beneath the surface. At this depth, I had maybe twenty minutes of air left. It was time to turn back, head up to our first decompression stop where our remaining air would last longer.

"You guessed the rest. There was a storm. He'd been drinking. He never came home." The pain I'd expected to see in Edward's eyes wasn't there. Instead he shrugged and said, "He's been haunting me ever since. It's Dad who whispers in my ear, tells me where things are at the bottom of the sea. Oh, don't look at me like I'm crazy, Mickey! I don't mean that literally, but even you've said there's something unnatural in my ability to find these things. I get these intuitions that manifest themselves as a voice in my head. It's the voice of my father."

I'd tried to laugh it off, told him I wished his father would tell him where the *Santa Maria* was laid to rest. Having broken apart on a reef off the coast of Hispaniola and never found, Columbus' flagship is something of a Holy Grail to underwater archeologists.

"He's not really interested in shipwrecks," Edward replied. "My father wants me to find *him*."

I tugged the line again. The silt and the gloom and the narrow corridor prevented me from seeing Edward, but his weight was still there at the end of the line. I needed to stop, tie off the guideline, and start the second spool. More importantly, we needed to turn back. I braced a flipper against the bulkhead and hauled back on the tether, attempting to stall Edward. As I did, I saw the end of the monofilament slip from the empty spool and slither back toward the bow, vanishing in the dark and the swirling silt.

"So," I asked, my blood gone cold, "you saw your father in the *Coolidge*?"

"No. I saw a cat."

"A cat? What do you mean, a cat? What would a cat be doing underwater? And I thought you said you saw a ghost?"

"I did. I saw the ghost of a cat. A white Siamese."

"Edward, this is getting ridiculous..."

I pulled on the tether, but it wouldn't give. I tapped the distress code on my tank with my flashlight. I kicked furiously, attempting to draw Edward back down the corridor toward me. My actions stirred up great billowing clouds of silt.

"Used to be, all I ever heard in my head was my father's voice, but over the years I've started hearing others. Now I've begun to see them."

"But really, Edward—*a cat?*"

"I know it sounds crazy, but it's just the first step. My eyes have been opened now. Somewhere on the *Coolidge* there are other ghosts—I've heard them. I have to find them. If you see one ghost, it indoctrinates you. Before long, you'll be seeing more."

The tether went slack. The pounding in my heart eased somewhat. Since I wouldn't let him advance, Ed-

ward must have turned back. I reeled in the line, waiting
for it to pull taut again against his weight. It never did.
Thirty feet of line coiled in the muck swirling about my
feet . . . and then came the end of the line . . . with nothing attached.

Edward?

I plunged aft, heedless of the silt thickening about
me. My light was useless. I couldn't see the bulkheads,
the ceiling, the deck. My panic contributed to my diso-
rientation and in seconds I was unsure which way was
up. I no longer knew if I was heading fore or aft, if I'd
turned to port or starboard at the last intersection of
passageways. I tapped my tank. I banged the walls. I
removed my regulator and screamed Edward's name.

We were going to die down here.

I couldn't see my hand held out before my face.

I searched for the monofilament guideline, praying
for its bright strand to flash back from the beam of my
light. Nothing. I hung suspended in a directionless void,
my oxygen bubbling away with every—

My air bubbles! The *Coolidge* lay on a steep incline.
The bow was at the top of the reef. The bow was up. My
air bubbles were rising . . . up!

I followed the bubbles to the nearest surface, which
logic said had to run parallel to the starboard hull. Teas-
ing the bubbles to run along the surface rather than
adhere to the marine growth, I followed them to the next
intersection, where I faltered. Left had to be the direction

of the upper deck, but there were also salvage holes that had been cut to allow access to the engine room and the lower decks. Was one of those holes closer to open water than working my way back up to the promenade? I didn't have time to debate it. I didn't have the air to hesitate. I turned left and pressed on, propelling myself at top speed, ignoring the additional silt that I disturbed behind me.

Forgive me, Edward.

Another intersection. I proceed straight through. The beauty shop should be ahead with its barber chair. Beyond that—

The corridor came to an end against a series of unrecognizable doors. All closed. All rusted shut. I turned and made my way back to the corridor, took the left turn. The beauty shop should be—

Another intersection. I turned left again.

I checked my depth. Somehow I was moving deeper, which meant I was heading aft. No . . . wait. It could also mean I was heading to port. The port side of the ship was down. I retraced my path, came to the intersection and couldn't remember which way I had come from.

I was lost.

Bubbles flow up. Up is toward the bow. But up is also to starboard, isn't it?

I was running out of air. My panic just made it worse. At this rate, I wouldn't have enough air to decompress.

Something brushed my face mask. A long, thick

strand of brown. I caught it, ran my light over it. It was the end of a rope. What the hell—" It tugged in my hand, nearly escaping. I wrapped it in my fist and hung on.

Hand over hand, I climbed the length of the rope, even as it drew me through the ship. The clouds of silt swirled and eddied about me. I couldn't see anything but the rope where it vanished into the thick soup ahead of me. Then the dark faded to gray, and the gray to the green of the deep ocean. I could see it ahead, just the other side of the thinning silt and the splines of the girders surrounding the promenade. The rope played out, slipping through my hands. I floundered for a second in the silt-out, but then my hands found something . . . no, that's not right.

My hands found *someone*.

Edward! I'd found Edward! He'd pulled me to safety with the rope.

But where had the rope come from?

And why, when I should feel the neoprene of Edward's diveskin, was I feeling cloth that tore in my hands, cloth long rotted by the sea?

I clutched at my savior, but he was slipping away. Clothing parted in my fingers. My hand came up against something solid in the midst of the shredding cloth, and I wrapped it in my fingers, squeezing it tight.

Then the silt cloud dropped behind me. The *Coolidge* stretched up toward daylight, toward the mooring line at the bow. I checked my gauges. To rise now would mean death. But I didn't have enough air to make all the decompression stops. I wouldn't even make the first one, unless—

Edward's sled was where we'd left it on the promenade. I switched it on, gave it full throttle, and allowed it to carry me the length of the bow toward the coral garden and the first deco stop. There I paused, checked my air gauge, checked my watch. There wasn't enough time. There wasn't enough air.

I was a dead man.

A moment later, he came out of the sunlight, trailing a pony bottle, his arm still in that silly sling. Gunter.

While I decompressed, Gunter went down and brought out Edward. Hanging there, waiting for my friend's body, hoping for a miracle but knowing the sea rarely permits miracles, I examined the object in my hand. It was a name tag.

Euart.

He and Covill had used a rope to pull members of the 43rd Infantry to safety. The ship had listed so badly to port that it was impossible to cross the steep deck and reach the lifeboats. Without their heroic actions, many men would have gone down with the ship. Covill escaped, but Euart had gone back after something.

It would take me six months of research and phone calls, but I eventually located Warren Covill. He was old, but still alive. He remembered those days on the *Coolidge* like they were yesterday. He confirmed what I had already guessed. I know why Euart went back.

Army mess officer Captain Elwood Euart had kept a cat in his kitchen to keep the ship free of mice. A Siamese cat.

Edward, when Gunter brought him up, looked at peace. I wondered if he'd found his father. I wonder if they're both out there somewhere, haunting the South Pacific—or perhaps the Outer Banks.

In the folklore of many seafaring countries, those who drown depart their bodies and commend their souls to the sea, where they live forever, drifting with the tides, carried by the currents, the upsurges, and the swells. Is Edward there somewhere, relieved of the crippling weight of land and a physical body? Do he and his father enjoy the sea together as they did when he was young, before the accident and the guilt and the lies that Edward made of his life?

I can't be sure.

But I do know this.

What Edward said was true. There are ghosts in the depths of the seas. And once you've learned to see one, you eventually see them all.

I don't do freelance underwater photography anymore. I've taken a permanent job for a yachting magazine where I spend my time on the surface, shooting sailboat races and charter boat ads with lovely ladies in bikinis. Even there, though, I see the occasional ghost, perched on the rail of a passing merchant vessel, waiting on a pier, awash and alone in the surf. They're easily avoided. But the ghosts below the surface are all too real for me.

And far too insistent that I join them.

for Dietmar Trommeshauser, 1955–1998

THE MOULD OF FORM

ROSEMARY EDGHILL

Art thou aught else but place, degree and form
Creating awe and fear in other men?
—William Shakespeare, *Henry V*

I GROW AS TIRED as any man of hearing it said that one cannot know what those years were like unless one lived them, for such words make mock of that learning which is the mark of civilization and the adornment of an English gentleman, but even I must admit that in this case it is true, for only those who lived through those years of madness, hope, and possibility can understand how we thought in those days, as if all the world had been washed, new and there had been no Adam's Fall to mar us. It has been said that since the Restoration, there is no sin save bad form, and I think perhaps that is true as well. When the appearance of virtue is all that one retains then appearance matters.

I was born James Cruikshank—I have another name now, of a more suitable aspect—in London-town in 16—, when the Old King was a prisoner of his subjects and all men were architects of possibility. Our rulers were men no better than ourselves, and in that we saw the refashioning of the world. That they were as greedy and venal as the nobility we had cast down was something no one saw, for in those days, men lived on dreams.

The Protector had molded England's destiny since before I was born. My father had opposed him, King Charles' man first and last, and labored to the destruction of his entire fortune in hope of a deliverance that could only be years in some distant future, for the King was executed at St. James Palace in '49, and his heir was but a child. The Sealed Knot unraveled, like all such things of moonshine and phantasie, and my father died in poverty, fled to France to escape the condign punishment of the victors. Meanwhile my mother and I lived upon the charity of a distant cousin, in a cramped unloving house within the Great Smoke itself, and so upon the streets of London-town I supped full at the banquet of futures and possibilities, though circumstance had barred me from my place at the table.

Yet even in exile and death my father still had his friends, and it was through the sponsorship of one of them that I was given a chance to rise again in the world, for, by what influence I know not; this distant friend secured me a place at Eton.

In those days, Eton had become a resort of gentlemen, and the children of the New Men mingled here with the oldest blood of England. Friendships made here would lead to preferment later, for good form had made its first triumph over blood when the Old King died, and in the world men had made, the appearance of virtue was more important than its expression.

The school fees were large, as befit an institution founded by Great Harry, that profligate and luxurious monarch, and my mother was reduced to desperate stratagems to raise them. Her cousins, who grudged us both food and roof, wanted me put to a trade. The London of that day held more work than hands, and I might have found a ready place as a clerk, for I had already my letters and some Latin, but this my mother would not permit, seeing in it the long slow slide into obscurity and extinction. Our name, our blood, was all the world to her now that my father was dead, and in me she saw the opportunity to make his dead bones live again. And so she would see me established at Eton, and then Oxford, upon a path to *gentilesse* and advancement. Within her plans, I wove plans of my own: to become a partisan and supporter of that great Commonwealth that ushered my father so neatly out of position and life, to join with my peers in that freemasonry of ability that held all English in its giddy thrall.

In the end, I threw away all her hopes and my own for no more than childish pride.

The compass of my brief years had introduced me to hardship, to poverty and fear, but never had I imagined the existence that awaited me at school. It was as if I were cast into hell, there in the Long Chamber at the close of day. The strong preyed upon the weak subjecting them to unimaginable tortures while the masters of the school pretended to see nothing. Though I represented my condition as strongly as I could in my few letters home, my mother likewise refused to hear. Schooling was the hallmark of a gentleman, and schooling I must have, though it cost me my soul.

It is from those hellish days, I think, that my whole hatred of boys stems. For though I was fallen among that company of the bestial and cruel, there were those I hated more: the careless golden souls who walked through chamber and hall as if untouched by their surroundings. Prefects and tutors vied for their regard, and cruelties and punishments alike fell lightly upon their oblivious shoulders. Their futures were assured—futures of rank and privilege among men of learning and dignity. In light of such future satisfaction, the present was a dim and trivial shadow.

There was one of them, a boy named Peter, whom I hated with a particular rancor, for from the moment I met him, four years into Purgatorial exile, he treated me as his equal, showing me all consideration despite the difference in our estate. With careless ease, he drew me into his charmed circle, the world of barely remembered surety and privilege that I had known in dimmest infancy, and treated me as if I belonged there.

It was my downfall.

It did not seem so at first. Peter was just my age, but while I had a Puritan's face, with a long jaw and heavy coat of black beard which I had begun to shave in my twelfth year, Peter was all golden boyhood, the downy peach fuzz of his skin barely beginning to ripen into coarse manhood. His family had bent supplely with the prevailing political winds, but while many suspected them of Royalist sympathies, they were seen to be ardent supporters of the Commonwealth, and so had weathered the storms of the 'forties and 'fifties with their lands and consequence intact.

The difference between his family's fortunes and my own did not escape me, and I hated Peter all the more for it. But once he was seen to take an interest in me, the worst of my torments stopped, so simple self-preservation entailed smiling prudence, to follow Peter and his golden lads wherever Fortune led me.

You will find it odd, perhaps, that under his influence I became even more zealously Puritan than I had been before, for Peter was the living opposite of that vengeful, joyless philosophy. But my envious hatred, all the more ardent for its secrecy, was vexed to madness by his careless innocence, though at the time, it seemed to me only that I thought more clearly than ever before. The Old King and his favorites, those golden children of decadence and privilege, all had been swept away by the cruel modern winds of change that brought with them fierce possibility and clear-eyed rationalism. Just as there would be no more of ghosts and mummery at the Lord's Table, so our lives would not be guided by the dead hand of ancient kings, nor our destinies by blood and birthright. I saw explicitly what I had only dimly sensed before: that this new world, bright and hard and ruthless as steel, held a place for me that the old one never had.

But to claim it, I still must climb the ladder out of this hell, a ladder made out of favors and friendships, and of smiling, always smiling, when my heart turned to a crucible of vitriol within my bosom.

I have said that my family was impoverished, my mother little better than a pauper. Despite this she managed to send me small gifts of money from time to time; small money and pawnable trinkets. With these I maintained a foothold upon the society of Peter's set, though I was hard-pressed to repay even so simple a courtesy as a round of drinks at the corner alehouse. As for the young gentleman's other vices—whoring, gambling, hunting—they were as far beyond my reach as the mountains of the moon.

Peter affected to see none of this. At this remove, it is hard for me to say whether that indifference came from malice or a genuine greatness of heart, but I will tell you this: the damage they invoke is all one, and so

I despised him all the more for flaunting what I did not and could not have as if I might ever attain it. To withstand such blandishments forever would tax the fortitude of a sinless angel, and I was not made of such celestial stuff.

As I said, my mother did what she could for me financially, but in my fifth year at Eton, she died at last. Of grief, of melancholy—or of starvation and pneumonia at the delectable fountainhead of her cousin's charity, there is no man living who can say. But in her dying, a small legacy came to me, and in that moment of unexpected largesse I was at last able to seem what I truly wished to be—an independent gentleman of rank, a full member of that gilded company surrounding my insensible patron. With funds beyond the bare necessity at last at my disposal, I entered fully into the pleasures of the idle scholar. Gaming was forbidden by the rules of the school, but then, so were most of our diversions. The need for secrecy, for misdirection and confusion, gave our pleasures an added spice.

At first, it truly seemed that God had favored my commission. I wagered and won, increasing my wealth. I had a strong head for drink, and a cool head for cards. The combination was felicitous, and I won handily. What I should have seen as a warning, I saw instead as an opportunity, and in seizing it, doomed myself entirely.

Perhaps the sun of Peter's countenance began to

shine less brightly on me then. I began to have to work for that regard which I had heretofore unthinkingly accepted as a beggar's alms, to compete for my place where once I was assured it as of right. But to return once more to the outer darkness of an unsponsored life was unthinkable: those incubi who had withheld their blows when I entered this charmed circle of fellowship awaited me avidly should I be thrust from it, and I feared them with the sincerity with which I feared death and the pains of hell. Triumph and fear and a new coat of green velvet trimmed with modest gold lace made me reckless; I plotted my victories without regard for my standing among these charitable peers, badgering them into wagers that were heartless in their rapaciousness.

And when at last my luck began to fail, I saw what armor my temporary wealth had granted me, making tender a skin which had once been armored against the harshest blows of Fate. Having once been raised to the heights, I could not bear to acknowledge my poverty and return to my former place.

And so I began to cheat at cards.

This was a far graver offense than the trespasses against the law of the land which I had heretofore blithely committed. This was a transgression against Good Form itself, that hallowed and unspoken code by which a gentleman of England lived. Even poverty might be carried off with a certain elan, debt and lawlessness managed with insouciant grace, so long as one feigned obliviousness to one's humble estate—so long as one demanded with each unspoken word to be accorded the rights and privileges of a gentleman.

But I was no gentleman, if only in my heart, and so I cheated at cards.

At first I hoped only to halt the slow exsanguination of my assets, to blunt the worst of my luck. But in the months since I had come into my mother's legacy, some intangible line of credit had run dry, and what I had once received as a gift, I now must pay for. But I was without coin of any sort—not the Commonwealth's gold angels, not wit and style, and not the forbearance of Peter's friends. I had outstayed my welcome, and I was made to feel it. But still I could not bear to return to what I once was. I became more predatory in my games-manship, more reckless in my cardsharping.

And at last I was discovered.

It was a night like any other. We gamed, defiant of curfew, in a corner of the public rooms of a High Street tavern. I had added luck to the mechanic's skill, and I was emboldened to feel pleased with my success, until Peter's hand fell lightly upon my wrist and I stared into his merciless eyes. In that moment, I felt—not shame, but a vast groveling betrayal of self, the yearning to accept any punishment, any disparagement, if only this moment could never have come. Gladly would I embrace my tormentors, renounce my place, vanish into the vast unwashed obscurity of the proletariat, meekly accept all

I had raged against, all I had hoped for, if I could unmake the journey that had led to this moment. It was weakness, cowardice, and I, who had been a coward a thousand times over in my life, despised myself most of all for the despairing love I felt in the instant of its forfeiture.

"Bad form, Cruikshank," Peter said coolly, regarding the cards that spilled from my sleeve.

If demons had slain me in that moment, if the earth had opened beneath my feet and I had toppled into the fiery Pit, I would have been no more dead to him than I became in that moment. He withdrew his hand, the secreted cards dropped from my sleeve to the table, and my life was over. In moments I sat alone at an empty table, nearly swooning, and all around the tavern I could hear the venomous whispers growing: *Cheat . . . cheater . . . bad form . . . bad form. . . .*

When I came to my senses once more, I found myself walking through the fields outside of town, long after the locking of the school gates. I wondered if, by any faint merciful forbearance, I would be able to brazen out the scandal, knowing in my heart that it was impossible. When I returned to my lodgings in the morning, there were bailiffs outside my door to prevent my entry, my possessions forfeit to those I had preyed upon. Though technically I was still enrolled, Eton, like every public school, has a morals clause in its charter. I had forfeited my right to be called a man of good Christian character, and my remaining tenure within these hallowed precincts could be compassed in hours.

I left my lodging and began to walk vaguely in the direction of my cousins' house. Why, I do not know; there was no possibility that they would take me in once more, and in truth, I had become so much a Puritan in my sojourn at school that the thought of accepting their charity was repugnant to me for more than ordinary reasons. Still, I walked, drinking nothing on my way but Adam's ale, and as I did my spirits began to revive. In the new world that men had made of the conceit of kings, surely there would be a place for me. I would go to the City. I had yet a few coins in my pockets, and by the deployment of those wicked skills that Peter had so disparaged I could gain myself a stake to go on with. I might yet win through, now beholden to no man's favor.

But as I walked, a distant roaring came to my ears, as of a thousand voices raised in cheering, and I began to see curious sights along the road. The closer I came to London, the more people I encountered, and every man seemed privy to some great secret that had eluded me, for most of them were roaring drunk. Though after watching a few of them ride by me insensibly, I did attempt to attract the attention of the travelers so as to gain their news, I had no luck until at last I encountered a solitary man wheeling a barrow, upon which were piled what seemed to be all his worldly possessions.

"What news, man?" I asked him.

"News! Why the best news there ever was! Have you not heard?"

"Heard what?" I asked, bewildered. I had been seduced into oblivion by my vices, for so long that I no longer followed the daily doings of the Young Protector, Cromwell's son.

"The King has come again! The King has come again!"

It was not to Christ that this pagan reveler referred, but to Charles: the son of the Old King had returned from his French exile to lord it anew over his father's subjects. And every man who had seen the Old King out with such delight now cheered with equal delight for the return of the son, or so it seemed that morning. The doughty old yeoman I had hailed was journeying to London to see the king, having sold up his holding to do it. He urged me to drink a toast to the king's health, and I knew that to be less than eager would earn me a sound thrashing. And so I drank the health of that chiefest member of the band of gilded youth that was my nemesis in strong English ale, and went numbly on my way, as he did upon his. I did not need to see this new royal court to know that it had in it no place for me.

So I walked once more without destination, this time against the throng, heading to what circumstance I knew not. As the road filled with more and more Englishmen converging antlike upon London, the journey began to take on (for them) a carnival air, and (for me) the dress of nightmare. I did not lack for food—bread and even meat were pressed by the pilgrims upon their fellows—and surely I did not lack for drink, for the king's heath was drunk in wine, in gin, in ale, and in brandy with every passing mile. The same spirit of hectic jubilation seemed to possess my fellows as had possessed me in certain nights at the tables, a sense of soaring above the surface of the Earth, unfettered by its limits. But on this day I was as cast down as they were exalted, for the people's joy at the king's return seemed to me to be the final betrayal of the certainties of my brief existence. My head reeling with emotion and strong drink, I staggered at dusk from the road into the new-plowed fields to find what shelter I could in the night. It was spring, but I did not fear the night dews nor the other misfortunes that could befall one who slept far from bedstead and rooftree. Neither moon-madness nor the malice of the faeries had power over one whose heart had been burned away to ash.

So I thought then, and so I do still think, for I have never yet taken harm of the faeries, and indeed I account many of them to be my great friends. It is only mortal boys who yet have the power to wound me, and I hold all that race my implacable enemy. So I lay down that night with a bleak and carefree heart and slept, cushioned on a bounteous tide of drink. And as I slept, all the world changed.

I awoke in the depths of night, with the full moon just stepping down from midheaven, and got slowly to my feet, wondering what had summoned me from my only refuge. All around me was stillness and the sleeping English countryside, but there was no darkness while Diana, that witches' goddess, bleached the sky to paleness with her silver mirror. I felt alert and clearheaded, as lively as though someone had called my name, and in fact something had. In the distance a steeple clock rolled the hour, and went on tolling, madly, through two dozen strokes, then three. For a moment fury filled me, for I thought it must be tolling for the king, and waited hopefully for the angry verger to flog the sexton from his untimely celebration. But the bell tolled on, until I was certain that all within its sound must be deaf, or dead, or slumbering too deeply for it to waken them.

And then I saw that from which I would have run shrieking only days before, whether as staunch Puritan or hopeful scholar. But both scholar and divine have a stake in the world as it is, and to fling aside the laws of God and Nature for uncertain gain would seem to be very madness. But both God and Man had rejected me—for the king's return must surely be such a sign of Divine partisanship as to form a dire omen—and so I stood as still as if I had been elf-shot, watching the ship come on with a distant sense of wonder.

For ship it was, sailing grandly above the tilled springtime fields as serenely as any vessel ever sailedupon the sea. She was a full-rigged galleon, her hull bleached to moonlight silver and her lanterns burning with the red fire of hell itself. Only the faint creak of rigging and sails could be heard over the monotonous tolling of that distant bell, and I saw no sailors upon her deck or aloft. Whatever force sailed this ship, it sailed her as silently and as mysteriously as a cloud upon the wind. Her sails were black, a darker shadow against the sky, and I remember thinking at the time that this was the most profligate wonder of all, to spend such costly adornment upon that part of the ship which so often was carried to the bottom of the ocean by a storm. Though if a storm came here to trouble this vessel, and strip her of her gauds, would not the parts be cast merely to the ground, and lie there simple of recovery?

I have said that the White Ship was in every way like a ship of water, and so she was, save in one. When the ship reached me, she stopped as neatly as a carriage might stop at the coachman's command, and hovered above me in the sky. I had stood my ground all the time she had glided toward me in that unearthly silence, thinking, in so much as I thought at all, that the White Ship would pass me by and sail undisturbed upon her secret errand, leaving no proof of her presence behind.

But then she stopped, hanging perfectly motionless in the air above me, rocking as gently as a ship at anchor in calm harbor. I had thought her entirely a craft of moonlight and shadows, but now that she was upon me I could see her mermaid figurehead thickly crusted in silver leaf, and the letters that burned like fire along her carven bow. "Revenge" was what they spelled, and in that entranced, dazzled moment I realized I longed for her above all things: revenge, sweet revenge, to slake the guilt-filled burnings of my wounded heart. The land was closed to me—I would go to sea, turn pirate, drench the world in blood and sorrow until I had washed away all record of weakness and folly and the laughing faces of golden boys.

"Ahoy to the land below!" a voice called from above me. I looked up, and beheld, leaning over the edge of the railing, the most extraordinary personage I had ever seen, a tall man in a long gray velvet coat and smalls of silver satin that were no more bright than the silvery peruke upon his head. Around him stood his crew—small dark men the size of children, wearing nothing that I could see save paint and gold collars. I knew then that I had fallen among the Midnight Folk who sail upon the Sea of Dreams, and that the tolling of that bell which I had marked was but the striking of the hour of midnight, impossibly extended. When it had struck its full measure of twelve times twelve the ship would be gone, to sail other seas than this.

"Ahoy the ship!" I called in return. "Take you passengers?"

From my place upon the ground I saw the captain smile. "Nay, sirrah! We are no fat merchantman to cosset the frail bellies of landlubbers. We are honest working-men, pirates all!" He smiled at me, with teeth as long and white as a wolf's, and in that moment any sane man would have turned away, would have run until he reached the nearest church and there thanked God on bended knee for his deliverance.

I did not.

"Then take me for a pirate!" I cried, in that moment making my decision. A scrap of schoolboy Latin came back to me. *Alea iacta est:* the die is cast. "Take me with you, and if it please you, I'll have no more of the land!"

The captain turned to shout an order, and to my horror and despair, the *Revenge* began to move slowly away. But at the same time, a ladder was flung down to me, dangling down far below the keel, though yet a yard above my head. I ran after the White Ship, leaping up recklessly and grabbing for the sanctuary she offered. The rough hemp burned my hands where I clutched it, and it seemed to me that the ship was moving faster now, for I could feel a cold wind on my face. *It is not too late to jump*, I told myself, but I had no real desire to fling myself back into the world of men that had so betrayed me and itself. And so I climbed, into an unknown world that was yet friendlier to me than the one I was leaving.

The rope ladder swung and twisted, a pendulum with me its hapless weight, suspended between earth and air. At last I gained the relative stability of the ship's hull, and my ascent became swifter. I did not look down, but with some distant part of my mind I registered that the infernal tolling of the church bell had ceased. The only sound now was the creaking of the ropes, the wind whipping past my face.

At last I gained the rail, where there were hands waiting to pull me up, and after a seeming eternity, I had solidity beneath my feet once more. At last I could confront my rescuer face-to-face.

The captain was a tall man, as unearthly fair as starlight. I could see now what I had not seen before, that his eyes glowed with the lambent beastfire of one who has no soul. Such is the mark that God Himself has placed upon the brute creation, that it might be distinguished from the sons of Adam, and if I had not known before the nature of those into whose hands I had commended myself, I must in all justice know it now.

"Welcome to *Revenge*," the faerie captain said, and held out his hand to me. "Captain Goodfellow bids you greeting."

I took his hand right willingly, and a shock of cold at that touch thrilled through me to my very bones. It was, paradoxically, a warming thing to one numbed beyond sensation by the myriad blows of Fate, and in that spirit I welcomed it. I, who had set my foot upon so many paths to fortune, had found the last road I was to tread.

"Come, come," he said. "You will be weary from your

journey, and there is much for us to discuss."

He turned, leading the way to the master's cabin, and it was as if in looking away from me he at last freed my attention to inspect my surroundings. The crew were busy at their tasks as I had not seen them before—trimming the black sails, retrieving the ladder that had borne me aloft, performing the thousand tasks that must be enacted in every moment of a ship's life. Above me the stars were unwinking, the moon a bright coin burning as refulgently as the sun in this eternal midnight. Beyond the ship's rail, all that could be seen was cloud, blotting out the land below as we sailed to a destination outside my philosophies.

The painted men of the crew watched me with avid glowing eyes, but I felt no fear of them. Mortal man had dealt me all the sharpest blows of my life, and I did not fear those who were otherwise. At last, having gazed my fill upon this eldritch vessel, I followed my new master below.

I had never before been aboard a ship of any sort, so I knew not what to expect. But the captain's cabin was oddly familiar, bearing a more than passing kinship to the closets of the wealthy and powerful men whom I had visited in my life. There was a fine Turkey carpet laid upon the deck, and linen-fold paneling upon the walls, and the room itself was brave with candles. Their honest yellow light did much to reassure me, though had they been the blue and sulferous lamps of hell I would not have been deterred from the course I had set myself to follow, for all beneath my eye was in the first style of excess, and excess was like cool water to my fevered spirit. There was a wealth of bright silver plate upon the sideboard, and with his own hands Captain Goodfellow poured me a rich measure of a fine oporto, thick and red as blood. I drank it off at a gulp and felt its warmth race through my veins, steadying my nerves. Without a word from me, he poured another, and I drank that as well, at last feeling the cold of his handclasp fade from my bones.

"Well, now, Master Scholar. What think you of our company?" he asked.

"It matters not what I think, if you will have me," I blurted out with clumsy truthfulness. "For there is no place left on Earth for me."

"Bravely spoken," he answered. "And in truth, we welcome few as we have welcomed you. But as I have said, *Revenge* takes no passengers. Are you willing to become fully one of us, to enter into all our sport and amusement? For we sail the Sea of Dreams, and voyage to lands that few of the mortalkind have known. Before you I spread a table of riches and hardship, privation and glory."

He gestured, and I saw a table laid out in the center of the cabin. I had not seen it when I entered, and I would have been willing to swear, should any such oath have been asked of me, that it had not been there a moment before. It was dressed all in white damask, in the fashion of the table at the Lord's Supper, and upon its surface there were two tall silver candlesticks with tall white tapers aflame, an inkwell, and a book laying open before them.

"All who sail with us must sign articles," Captain Goodfellow said. "Loyalty to your fellows, confusion to your enemies, obedience to me, and no regret for what you have left behind."

"I can promise all these things," I said, and he clapped me jovially upon the shoulder.

I stepped up to the table then and gazed down upon my fortune. The Great Book was before me, its pages thick with signatures, but all the names indighted there were blurred, and I could not read them. When I touched the page, it was as cold beneath my fingers as black iron on Christmas Day, and there was a space at the bottom ready for my name.

Captain Goodfellow held the silver pen out to me. "Put down your name, Master Scholar, and you shall be one of us."

I clasped the pen between my fingers and dipped it into the captain's silver inkwell. I wrote my first name— James—in bold flowing letters, but then I hesitated. Not for weakness' sake, but for a notion that had come into my head. This was my birth into a new life, and I vowed that in it I would be the foolish and villainous Cruikshank no loner. Among this gallant company I would take a new name.

Something stronger.

Something sharper.

And so I signed. "James Hook" in a bold sweeping style, and sealed my destiny among the Midnight Folk.

The form is all that matters.

ETERNITY AND AFTERWARD

LUCIUS SHEPARD

PUNCTUALITY HAD COME TO be something of a curse for Viktor Chemayev. Though toward most of his affairs he displayed the typical nonchalance of a young man with a taste for the good life and the money to indulge it, he maintained an entirely different attitude toward his business appointments. Often he would begin to prepare himself hours in advance, inspecting his mirror image for flaws, running a hand over his shaved scalp, trying on a variety of smiles, none of which fit well on his narrow Baltic face, and critiquing the hang of his suit (his tailor had not yet mastered the secret of cutting cloth for someone with broad shoulders and a thin chest). Once satisfied with his appearance he would pace the length and breadth of his apartment, worrying over details, tactical nuances, planning every word, every expression, every gesture. Finally, having no better use for the time remaining, he would drive to the meeting place and there continue to pace and worry and plan. On occasion this compulsiveness caused him problems. He would drink too much while waiting in a bar, or catch cold from standing in the open air, or simply grow bored and lose his mental sharpness. But no matter how hard he tried to change his ways he remained a slave to the practice. And so it was that one night toward the end of October he found himself sitting in the parking lot of Eternity, watching solitary snowflakes spin down from a starless sky, fretting over his appointment with Yuri Lebedev, the owner of the club and its chief architect, from whom he intended to purchase the freedom of the woman he loved.

For once it seemed that Chemayev's anxiety was not misplaced. The prospect of meeting Lebedev, less a man than a creature of legend whom few claimed to have ever seen, was daunting of itself; and though Chemayev was a frequent visitor to Eternity and thus acquainted with many of its eccentricities, it occurred to him now that Lebedev and his establishment were one and the same, an inscrutable value shining forth from the dingy chaos of Moscow, a radiant character whose meaning no one had been able to determine and whose menace, albeit palpable, was impossible to define. The appointment had been characterized as a mere formality, but Chemayev suspected that Lebedev's notion of formality was quite different from his own, and while he waited he went over in his mind the several communications he had received from Eternity's agents, wondering if he might have overlooked some devious turn of phrase designed to mislead him.

The club was located half an hour to the north and west of the city center amidst a block of *krushovas*, crumbling apartment projects that sprouted from the frozen, rubble-strewn waste like huge gray headstones memorializing the Kruschev era—the graveyard of the Soviet state, home to generations of cabbage-eating drunks and party drones. Buildings so cheaply constructed that if you pressed your hand to their cement walls, your palm would come away coated with sand. No sign, neon or otherwise, announced the club's presence. None was needed. Eternity's patrons were members of the various *mafiyas* and they required no lure apart from that of its fabulous reputation and exclusivity. All that was visible of the place was a low windowless structure resembling a bunker—the rest of the complex lay deep underground; but the lot that surrounded it was packed with Mercedes and Ferraris and Rolls Royces. As Chemayev gazed blankly, unseeingly, through the windshield of his ten-year-old Lada, shabby as a mule among thoroughbreds, his attention was caught by a group of men and women hurrying toward the entrance. The men walked with a brisk gait, talking and laughing, and the women followed silently in their wake, their furs and jewelry in sharp contrast to the men's conservative attire, holding their collars shut against the wind or putting a hand to their head to keep an extravagant coiffure in place, tottering in their high heels, their breath venting in little white puffs.

"Viktor!" Someone tapped on the driver side window. Chemayev cleared away condensation from the glass and saw the flushed, bloated features of his boss, Lev Polutin, peering in at him. Several feet away stood a pale man in a leather trenchcoat, with dark hair falling to his shoulders and a seamed, sorrowful face. "What are you doing out in the cold?" Polutin asked as Chemayev rolled down the window. "Come inside and drink with us!" His 100-proof breath produced a moist warmth on Chemayev's cheeks.

"I'll be along soon," Chemayev said, annoyed by this interruption to his routine.

Polutin straightened and blew on his hands. A big-bellied ursine man of early middle age, his muscles already running to fat, hair combed back in a wave of grease and black gleam from his brow. All his features were crammed toward the center of his round face, and his gestures had the tailored expansiveness common to politicians and actors out in public, to all those who delight in being watched. He introduced his companion as Niall March, a business associate from Ireland. March gave Chemayev an absent nod. "Let's get on in," he said to Polutin. "I'm fucking freezing." But Polutin did not appear to have heard. He beamed at Chemayev, as might a father approving of his child's cleverness, and said, "I promised Niall I'd show him the new Russia. And here you are, Viktor. Here you are." He glanced toward March. "This one..."—he pointed at Chemayev—"always thinking, always making a plan." He affected a comical expression of concern. "If I weren't such a carefree fellow, I'd suspect him of plotting against me."

Asshole, Chemayev thought as he watched the two men cross the lot. Polutin liked to give himself intellectual airs, to think of himself as criminal royalty, and to his credit he had learned how to take advantage of society's convulsions; but that required no particular intelligence, only the instincts and principles of a vulture. As for the new Russia, what a load of shit! Chemayev turned his eyes to the nearest of the *krushovas* no more than fifteen yards away, the building's crumbling face picked out by wan flickering lights, evidence that power was out on some of the floors and candles were in use. The fluorescent brightness of the entranceway was sentried by a prostitute with bleached hair and a vinyl jacket who paced back and forth with metronomic regularity, pausing at the end of each pass to peer out across the wasteland, as though expecting her relief. There, he thought, that was where the new Russia had been spawned. Open graves infested by the old, the desperate, the addicted, perverts of every stamp. They made the stars behind them look false, they reduced everything they shadowed. If the new Russia existed, it was merely as a byproduct of a past so grim that any possible future would be condemned to embody it.

The prospect of spending an evening with his boss, especially this one, when so much was at stake, weighed on Chemayev. He was not in the mood for Polutin's condescension, his unctuous solicitude. But he could think of no way to avoid it. He stepped from the car and took a deep breath of the biting, gasoline-flavored Moscow air. A few hours more, and his troubles would be over. All the wormy, enfeebling pressures of the past year would be evicted from his spirit, and for the first time he'd be able to choose a path in life rather than accept the one upon which he had been set by necessity. Strengthened by this notion, he started across the lot. Each of his footsteps made a crisp sound, as if he were crushing a brittle insect underfoot, and left an impression of his sole in a paper-thin crust of ice.

Chemayev checked his pistols at the entrance to Eternity, handing them over to one of Lebedev's young unsmiling soldiers, and descended in an elevator toward the theater that lay at the center of the complex. The empty holsters felt like dead, stubby wings strapped to his sides, increasing his sense of powerlessness—by contrast, the money belt about his waist felt inordinately heavy, as if full of golden bars, not gold certificates. The room into which the elevator discharged him was vast, roughly egg-shaped, larger at the base than at the apex, with snow white carpeting and walls of midnight blue. At the bottom of the egg was a circular stage, currently empty; tiers of white leather booths were arranged around it, occupied by prosperous-looking men and beautiful women whose conversations blended into a soft rustling that floated upon a bed of gentle, undulant music. Each booth encompassed a linen-covered table, and each table was centered by a block of ice hollowed so as to accommodate bottles of chilled vodka. The top of the egg, some thirty feet above the uppermost tier, was obscured by pale swirling mist, and through the mist you could see hanging lights—silvery, delicate, exotically configured shapes that put Chemayev in mind of photographs he'd seen of microscopic creatures found in polar seas. To many the room embodied a classic Russian elegance, but Chemayev, whose mother—long deceased—had been an architect and had provided him with an education in the arts, thought the place vulgar, a childish fantasy conceived by someone whose idea of elegance had been derived from old Hollywood movies.

Polutin's booth, as befitted his station, was near the stage. The big man was leaning close to March, speaking energetically into his ear. Chemayev joined them and accepted a glass of vodka. "I was about to tell Niall about the auction," Polutin said to him, then returned his attention to March. "You see, each night at a certain time . . . a different hour every night, depending on our host's whim. Each night a beautiful woman will rise from beneath the stage. Naked as the day she came into the world. She carries a silver tray upon which there lies a single red rose. She will walk among the tables, and offer the rose to everyone in attendance."

"Yeah?" March cocked an eye toward Polutin. "Then what?"

"Then the bidding begins."

"What are they bidding for?" March's responses were marked by a peculiar absence of inflection, and he appeared disinterested in Polutin's lecture; yet Chemayev had the sense that he was observing everything with unnatural attentiveness. His cheeks were scored by two vertical lines as deep as knife cuts that extended from beneath the corners of his eyes to the corners of his lips. His mouth was thin, wide, almost chimpanzee-like in its mobility and expressiveness—this at odds with his eyes, which were small and pale and inactive. It was as if at the moment of creation he had been immersed in a finishing bath, one intended to add an invigorating luster, that had only partially covered his face, leaving the eyes and all that lay behind them lacking some vital essential.

"Why . . . for the rose, of course." Polutin seemed put off by March's lack of enthusiasm. "Sometimes the bidding is slow, but I've seen huge sums paid over. I believe the record is a hundred thousand pounds."

"A hundred grand for a fucking flower?" March said. "Sounds like bollocks to me."

"It's an act of conspicuous consumption," Chemayev

said; he tossed back his vodka, poured another from a bottle of Ketel One. "Those who bid are trying to demonstrate how little money means to them."

"There's an element of truth in what Viktor says," Polutin said archly, "but his understanding is incomplete. You are not only bidding for status . . . for a *fucking flower*." He spooned caviar onto a silver dish and spread some on a cracker. "Think of a rose. Redder than fire. Redder than a beast's eye. You're bidding for that color, that priceless symptom of illusion." He popped the cracker into his mouth and chewed noisily; once he had swallowed he said to March, "You see, Viktor does not bid. He's a frugal man, and a frugal man cannot possibly understand the poetry of the auction." He worried at a piece of cracker stuck in his teeth. "Viktor never gambles. He picks up a check only when it might prove an embarrassment to do otherwise. His apartment is a proletarian tragedy, and you've seen that piece of crap he drives. He's not wealthy, but he is far from poor. He should want for nothing. Yet he hordes money like an old woman." Polutin smiled at Chemayev with exaggerated fondness. "All his friends wonder why this is."

Chemayev ignored this attempt to rankle him and poured another vodka. He noted with pleasure that the pouches beneath Polutin's eyes were more swollen than usual, looking as if they were about to give birth to fat worms. A few more years of heavy alcohol intake, and he'd be ripe for a cardiac event. He lifted his glass to Polutin and returned his smile.

"To be successful in business one must have a firm grasp of human nature," said Polutin, preparing another cracker. "So naturally I have studied my friends and associates. From my observations of Viktor I've concluded that he is capable of magic." He glanced back and forth between Chemayev and March, as if expecting a strong reaction.

March gave an amused snort. "I suppose that means he's got himself a little wand."

Polutin laughed and clapped March on the shoulder. "Let me explain," he said. "During the early days of *glasnost*, Yuri Lebedev was the strongest man in all the *mafiyas*. He made a vast fortune, but he also made enemies. The dogs were nipping at his heels, and he recognized it was only a matter of time before they brought him down. It was at this point he began to build Eternity."

He gobbled the second cracker, washed it down with vodka; after swallowing with some difficulty he went on: "The place is immense. All around us the earth is honeycombed with chambers. Apartments, a casino, a gymnasium, gardens. Even a surgery. Eternity is both labyrinth and fortress, a country with its own regulations and doctrines. There are no policemen here, not even corrupt ones. But commit a crime within these walls, a crime that injures Yuri, and you will be dealt with according to his laws. Yuri is absolutely secure. He need never leave until the day he dies. Yet that alone does not convey the full extent of his genius. In the surgery he had doctors create a number of doubles for him. The doctors, of course, were never heard from again, and it became impossible to track Yuri. In fact it's not at all certain that he is still here. Some will tell you he is dead. Others say he lives in Chile, in Tahiti. In a *dacha* on the Black Sea. He's been reported in Turkestan, Montreal, Chiang Mai. He is seen everywhere. But no one knows where he is. No one will ever know."

"That's quite clever, that is," March said.

Polutin spread his hands as if to reveal a marvel. "Right in front of our eyes Yuri built a device that would cause him to disappear, and then he stepped inside it. Like a pharaoh vanishing inside his tomb. We were so fascinated in watching the trick develop, we never suspected it was a real trick." He licked a fleck of caviar from his forefinger. "Had Yuri vanished in any way other than the one he chose, his enemies would have kept searching for him, no matter how slim their chances of success. But he created Eternity both as the vehicle of his magical act and as a legacy, a gift to enemies and friends alike. He surrendered his power with such panache.... It was a gesture no one could resist. People forgave him. Now he is revered. I've heard him described as 'the sanest man in Moscow.' Which in these times may well serve a definition of God."

Apprehension spidered Chemayev's neck. Whatever parallel Polutin was trying to draw between himself and Yuri, it would probably prove to be a parable designed to manipulate him. The whole thing was tiresome, predictable.... Out of the corner of his eye he spotted a tall girl with dark brown hair. He started to call to her, mistaking her for Larissa, but then realized she didn't have Larissa's long legs, her quiet bearing.

"There is tremendous irony in the situation," Polutin continued. "Whether dead or alive, in the act of vanishing Yuri regained his power. Those close to him—or to his surrogates—are like monks. They keep watch day and night. Everything said and done here is monitored. And he is protected not only by paranoia. Being invisible, his actions concealed, he's too valuable to kill. He's become the confidante of politicians. Generals avail themselves of his services. As do various *mafiya* bosses." He inclined his head, as if suggesting that he might be among this privileged number. "There are those who maintain that Yuri's influence with these great men is due to the fact that his magical powers are not limited to primitive sleights-of-hand such as the illusion that enabled his disappearance. They claim he has become an adept of secret disciplines, that he works miracles on behalf of the rich and the mighty." Polutin's attitude grew conspiratorial. "A friend of mine involved in building the club told me that he came into the theater once—this very room—and found it filled with computer terminals. Scrolling across the screens were strings of what he assumed were letters in an unknown alphabet. He later discovered they were Kabalistic symbols. Some weeks later he entered the theater again. There was no sign of the terminals . . . or of anything else, for that matter. The room was choked with silvery fog. My friend decided to keep clear of the place thereafter. But not long before Eternity opened its doors, curiosity got the best of him and he visited the theater a third time. On this occasion he found the room completely dark and heard hushed voices chanting the same unintelligible phrase over and over." Polutin allowed himself a dramatic pause. "None of this seems to reflect the usual methods of construction."

"What's this got to do with your boy Viktor?" March asked. "He's planning a night club, too, is he?"

"Not that I know of." Polutin's eyes went lazily to Chemayev, like a man reassuring himself that his prize possession was still in its rightful place. "However, I see in Viktor many of the qualities Yuri possessed. He's bright, ambitious. He can be ruthless when necessary. He understands the uses of compassion, but if he wasn't capable of violence and betrayal, he would never have risen to his present position."

"I only did as I was told," Chemayev said fiercely. "You gave me no choice." Furious, he prepared to defend himself further, but Polutin did not acknowledge him, turning instead to March.

"It's in his talent for self-deception that Viktor most resembles Yuri," he said. "In effect, he has made parts of himself disappear. But while Yuri became an adept, a

true professional, Viktor is still a rank amateur...
though perhaps I underestimate him. He may have some
more spectacular disappearance in mind."

Chemayev's feeling of apprehension spiked, but he
refused to give Polutin the satisfaction of thinking that
his words had had any effect; he scanned the upper tiers
of booths, pretending to search for a familiar face.

"If I were to ask Viktor to describe himself," Polutin
went on, "he would repeat much of what I've told you.
But he would never describe himself as cautious. Yet I
swear to you, Viktor is the most cautious man of my
acquaintance. He won't admit it, not to you or me. Nor
to himself. But let me give you an example of how his
mind works. Viktor has a lover. Larissa is her name. She
works here at Eternity. As a prostitute."

"Don't tell him my business!" Chemayev could feel
the pulse in his neck.

Polutin regarded him calmly. "This is common
knowledge, is it not?"

"It's scarcely common knowledge in Ireland."

"Yes," said Polutin. "But then we are not in Ireland.
We are in Moscow. Where, if memory serves me, underlings do not dare treat their superiors with such impertinence."

Chemayev did not trust himself to speak.

"Larissa is a beautiful woman. Such a lovely face"—
Polutin bunched the fingers of his left hand and kissed
their tips, the gesture of an ecstatic connoisseur—"your

heart breaks to see it! Like many who work here, she does so in order to pay off a debt incurred by someone in her family. She's not a typical whore. She's intelligent, refined. And very expensive."

"How much are we talking about?" March asked. "I've a few extra pounds in me pocket."

Chemayev shot him a wicked glance, and March winked at him. "Just having you on, mate. Women aren't my thing."

"What exactly is your thing?" Chemayev asked. "Some sort of sea creature? Perhaps you prefer the invertebrates?"

"Nah." March went deadpan. "It's got nothing to do with sex."

"The point is this," Polutin said. "Viktor's choice of a lover speaks to his cautious nature. A young man of his status, ambitious and talented, but as yet not entirely on a firm footing . . . such a man is vulnerable in many ways. If he were to take a wife it would add to his vulnerability. The woman might be threatened or kidnapped. In our business you must be secure indeed if you intend to engage in anything resembling a normal relationship. So Viktor has chosen a prostitute under the protection of Yuri Lebedev. No one will try to harm her for fear of reprisals. Eternity protects its own."

Chemayev started up from the booth, but Polutin beckoned him to stay. "A minute longer, Viktor. Please."

"Why are you doing this?" Chemayev asked. "Is there a purpose, or is it merely an exercise?"

"I'm trying to instruct you," said Polutin. "I'm trying to show you who you are. I think you have forgotten some important truths."

Chemayev drew a steadying breath, let it out with a dry, papery sound. "I know very well who I am, but I'm confused about much else."

"It won't hurt you to listen." Polutin ran a finger along the inside of his collar to loosen it and addressed March. "Why does Viktor hide his cautious nature from himself? Perhaps he doesn't like what he sees in the mirror. I've known men who've cultivated a sensitive self-image in order to obscure the brutish aspects of their character. Perhaps the explanation is as simple as that. But I think there's more to it. I suspect it may be for him a form of practice. As I've said, Viktor and Yuri have much in common . . . most pertinently, a talent for self-deception. I believe it was the calculated development of this ability that led Yuri to understand the concept of deception in its entirety. Its subtleties, its potentials." Polutin shifted his bulk, his belly bumping against the edge of the table, causing vodka to slosh in all the glasses. "At any rate, I think I understand how Viktor manages to hide from himself. He has permitted himself to fall in love with his prostitute—or to think he has fallen in love. This affords him the illusion of incaution. How incautious it must seem to the casual eye for a man to fall in love with a woman he cannot possibly have. Who lives in another man's house. Whom he can see only for an hour or two in the mornings, and the odd vacation. Who is bound by contract to spend the years of her great beauty fucking strangers. Is this a tactical maneuver? A phase of Viktor's development. A necessary step along the path toward some larger, more magical duplicity. Or could it be a simple mistake? A mistake he is now tempted to compound, thus making himself more vulnerable than ever." He spread his hands, expressing a stagy degree of helplessness. "But these are questions only Viktor can answer."

"I bet I'm going to like working for you," March said. "You're a right interesting fellow."

"Nobody likes working for me. If you doubt this, ask Viktor." Polutin locked his hands behind his head, thrusting out his belly so that it overlapped the edge of the table; he looked with unwavering disapproval at Chemayev. "Now you may go. When you've regained your self-control, come back and drink some more. I'm told the entertainment this evening will be wonderful."

The countertop of the bar in the lounge adjoining the theater was overlaid with a mosaic depicting a party attended by guests from every decade of the Twentieth Century, all with cunningly rendered faces done in caricature, most unknown to Chemayev, but a few clearly recognizable. There was Lavrenty Pavlovich Beria, the bloody-handed director of the KVD under Stalin, his doughy, peasant features lent a genteel air by rimless pince-nez. He was standing with a man wearing a Party armband and a woman in a green dress—Beria was glancing up as if he sensed someone overhead was watching him. Elsewhere, a uniformed Josef Stalin held conversation with his old pal Kruschev. Lenin and Gorbachev and Dobrynin stood at the center of small groups. Even old Yeltsin was there, mopping his sweaty brow with a handkerchief. Looking at it, Chemayev, sick with worry, felt he was being viewed with suspicion not only by his boss, but by these historical personages as well. It wasn't possible, he thought, that Polutin could know what he was planning; yet everything he'd said indicated that he did know something. Why else all his talk of disappearances, of Larissa and vulnerability? And who was the Irishman with him? A paid assassin. That much was for sure. No other occupation produced that kind of soulless lizard. Chemayev's heart labored, as if it were pumping something heavier than blood. All his plans, so painstakingly crafted, were falling apart at the moment of success. He touched his money belt, the airline tickets in his suit pocket, half-expecting them to be missing. Finding them in place acted to soothe him. It's all right, he told himself. Whatever Polutin knew, and perhaps it was nothing, perhaps all his bullshit had been designed to impress his new pet snake . . . whatever he thought he knew, things had progressed too far for him to pose a real threat.

He ordered a vodka from the bartender, a slender man with dyed white hair and a pleasant country face, wearing a white sweater and slacks. The room was almost empty of customers, just two couples chattering at a distant table. It was decorated in the style of an upscale watering hole—deep comfortable chairs, padded stools, paneled walls—but the ambiance was more exotic than one might expect. White leather upholstery, thick white carpeting. The paneling was fashioned of what appeared to be ivory planks, though they were patterned with a decidedly univory-like grain reminiscent of the markings on moths' wings; the bar itself was constructed of a similar material, albeit of a creamier hue, like wood petrified to marble. The edging of the glass tabletops and the frame of the mirror against which the bottled spirits were arrayed—indeed, every filigree and decorative conceit—were of silver, and there were glints of silver, too, visible among the crystal mysteries of the chandeliers. In great limestone fireplaces at opposite ends of the room burned pearly logs that yielded chemical blue flames, and the light from the chandeliers was also blue, casting glimmers and reflections from every surface, drenching the whiteness of the place in an arctic glamour.

Mounted above the bar was a television set, its volume turned so low that the voices proceeding from it were scarcely more than murmurs; on the screen Aleksander Solzhenitsyn was holding forth on his weekly talk show, preaching the need for moral reform to a worshipful guest. Amused to find the image of the Nobel Laureate in a place whose moral foundation he would vehemently decry, Chemayev moved closer to the set and ordered another vodka. The old bastard had written great novels, he thought. But his sermons needed an editor. Some liked them, of course. The relics who lived in the *krushovas* sucked up his spiritual blah blah blah. Hearing this crap flow from such a wise mouth ennobled their stubborn endurance in the face of food shortages, violent crime, and unemployment. It validated their mulelike tolerance, it gave lyric tongue to their drunken, docile complaining. Solzhenitsyn was their papa, their pope, the guru of their hopelessness. He knew their suffering, he praised their dazed stolidity as a virtue, he restored their threadbare souls. His words comforted them because they were imbued with the same numbing authority, the same dull stench of official truth, as the windbag belches of the old party lions with dead eyes and poisoned livers whom they had been conditioned to obey. You had to respect Solzhenitsyn. He had once been a Voice. Now he was merely an echo. And a distorted one at that. His years in exile might not have cut him off from the essence of the Russian spirit, but they had decayed his understanding of Russian stupidity. People listened, sure. But they heard just enough to make them reach for a bottle and toast him. The brand of snake oil he was trying to sell was suited only for cutting cheap vodka.

"Old Man Russia." Chemayev waved disparagingly at the screen as the bartender served him, setting the glass down to cover Beria's upturned face. The bartender laughed and said, "Maybe . . . but he's sure as shit not Old Man Moscow." He reached for a remote and flipped through the channels, settling on a music video. A black man with a sullen, arrogant face was singing to tinny music, creating voluptuous shapes in the air with his hands—Chemayev had the idea that he was preparing to make love to a female version of himself. "MTV," said the bartender with satisfaction and sidled off along the counter.

Chemayev checked his watch. Still nearly three-quarters of an hour to go. He fingered his glass, thinking he'd already had too much. But he felt fine. Anger had burned off the alcohol he'd consumed at Polutin's table. He drank the vodka in a single gulp. Then, in the mirror, he saw Larissa approaching.

As often happened the sight of her shut him down for an instant. She seemed like an exotic form of weather, a column of energy gliding across the room, drawing the light to her. Wearing a blue silk dress that revealed her legs to the mid-thigh. Her dark hair was pinned high and in spite of heavy makeup and eyebrows plucked into severe arches, the naturalness of her beauty shone through. Her face was broad at the cheekbones, tapering to the chin, its shape resembling that of an inverted spearhead, and her generous features—the hazel eyes a bit large for proportion—could one moment look soft, maternal, the next girlish and seductive. In repose, her lips touched by a smile, eyes half-lidded, she reminded him of the painted figurehead on his Uncle Arkady's boat, which had carried cargo along the Dvina when he was a child. Unlike most figureheads this one had not been carved with eyes wide-open so as to appear intent upon the course ahead, but displayed a look of dreamy, sleek contentment. When he asked why it was different from the rest his uncle told him he hadn't wanted a lookout on his prow, but a woman whose gaze would bless the waters. Chemayev learned that the man who carved the figurehead had been a drunk embittered by lost love, and as a consequence—or so Chemayev assumed—he had created an image that embodied the kind of mystical serenity with which men who are forced to endure much for love tend to imbue their women, a quality that serves to mythologize their actions and make them immune to masculine judgments.

"What are you doing here?" he asked as she came into his arms.

"They told me I don't have to work tonight. You know . . . because you're paying." She sat on the adjoining stool, her expression troubled; he asked what was wrong. "Nothing," she said. "It's just I can't quite believe it. It's all so difficult to believe, you know." She leaned forward and kissed him on the mouth—lightly so as not to smear her lipstick.

"Don't worry," he said. "Everything's taken care of."

"I know. I'm just nervous." Her smile flickered on and off. "I wonder what it'll be like ... America."

He cupped the swell of her cheek, and she leaned into his hand. "It'll be strange," he said. "But we'll be in the mountains to begin with. Just the two of us. We'll be able to make sense of it all before we decide where we want to end up."

"How will we do that?"

"We'll learn all about the place from magazines ... newspapers. TV."

She laughed. "I can't picture us doing much reading if we're alone in a cabin."

"We'll leave the TV on. Pick things up subliminally." He grinned, nudged his glass with a finger. "Want a drink?"

"No, I have to go back in a minute. I haven't finished packing. And there's something I have to sign."

That worried him. "What is it?"

"A release. It says I haven't contracted any diseases or been physically abused." She laughed again, a single note clear and bright as a piano tone. "As if anyone would sue Eternity." She took his face in her hands and studied him. Then she kissed his brow. "I love you so much," she said, her lips still pressed to his skin. He was too dizzy to speak.

She settled back, holding his right hand in her lap. "Do you know what I want most. I want to talk. I want to talk with you for hours and hours."

Chemayev loved to hear her talk—she wove events and objects and ideas together into textures of such palpable solidity that he could lie back against them, grasped by their resilient contours, and needed only to say "Yes" and "Really" and "Uh huh" every so often, providing a minor structural component that enabled her to extend and deepen her impromptu creations. The prospect that he might have to contribute more than this was daunting. "What will we talk about?" he asked.

"About you, for one thing. I hardly know anything about your family, your childhood."

"We talk," he said. "Just this morning. . . ."

"Yes, sure. But only when you're driving me to school, and you're so busy dodging traffic you can't say much. And when we're at your apartment there's never time. Not that I'm complaining." She gave his hand a squeeze. "We'll make love for hours, then we'll talk. I want you to reveal all your secrets before I start to bore you."

He saw her then as she looked each morning in the car, face scrubbed clean of makeup, the sweetly sad pragmatist of their five hundred days on her way to the university, almost ordinary in her jeans and cloth jacket, ready to spend hours listening to tired astronomers, hungover geographers, talentless poets, trying to find in their listless words some residue of truth, some glint of promise, a fact still empowered by its original energy, something that would bring her a glimpse of possibility beyond that which she knew. For the first time he wondered how America and freedom would change her. Not much, he decided. Not in any essential way. She would open like a flower to the sun, she would bloom, but she would not change. The naiveté of this notion did not bother him. He believed in her. Sometimes it seemed he believed in her even more than he loved her.

"What are you thinking?" she asked, and smiled slyly as if she knew the answer.

"Evil things," he told her.

"Is that so?" She drew him close and slid his hand beneath her skirt. Then she edged forward on the stool, encouraging him. He touched her sex with a fingertip and she let out a gasp. Her head drooped, rested on his shoulder. He thrust aside the material of her panties. All her warmth was open to him. But then she pushed his hand away and whispered, "No, no! I can't!" She remained leaning against him, her body tense and trembling. "I'm not ashamed, you understand," she said, the words muffled by his shoulder. "I can't bear the idea of doing anything *here*." She let out a soft, cluttered sound—another laugh, he thought. "But there's no shame in me. I'll prove it to you tonight. On the plane."

He stroked her hair. "You'll be asleep ten minutes after take-off. You always sleep when we travel. Like a little baby."

"Not tonight." She broke from the embrace. Her face was grave, as if she were stating a vow. "I'm not going to sleep at all. Not until I absolutely have to."

"If you say so. But I bet I'm right." He checked his watch again.

"How long?" she asked.

"Less than half an hour. But I don't know how long I'll be with . . . with whoever it is I'm meeting."

"One of the doubles. There must be a dozen of them. I can't be sure, but I think I can tell most of them apart. They vary slightly in height. In weight. A couple have moles."

"What do you call them?"

"Yuri." She shrugged. "What else? Some of the girls invent funny names for them. But I guess I don't find them funny."

He looked down at the counter. "You know, we've never spoken about what it's like for you here. I know some of it, of course. But your life, the way you spend your days. . . ."

"I didn't think you wanted to talk about it."

"I guess I didn't. It just seems strange . . . but it's not important."

"We can talk about it if you want." She wrapped a loose curl around her forefinger. "It isn't so bad, really. When I'm not at school I like to sit in the theater mornings and read. There's nobody about, and it's quiet. Peaceful. Like an empty church. Every two weeks the doctor comes to examine us. She's very nice. She brings us chocolates. Otherwise, we're left pretty much to our own devices. Most of the girls are so young, it's almost possible to believe I'm at boarding school. But then. . . ." Her mouth twisted into an unhappy shape. "There's not much else to tell."

Something gave way in Chemayev. The pressures of the preceding months, the subterfuge, the planning, and now this pitiful recitation with its obvious omissions— his inner defenses collapsed under the weight of these separate travails, conjoined in a flood of stale emotion. Old suffocated panics, soured desires, yellowed griefs, lumps of mummified terror . . . the terror he had felt sitting alone at night, certain that he would lose her, his head close to bursting with despair. His eyes teared. He linked his hands behind her neck and drew her to him so that their foreheads touched. "I'm sorry," he said. "I'm sorry it took so long."

"It wasn't long! It's so much money! And you got it all in less than a year!"

"Every day I see enough money to choke the world. I could have fixed the books, I could have done something."

"Yes . . . and then what? Polutin would have had you killed. God, Viktor! You amazed me! Don't you understand? You were completely unexpected. I never thought anyone would care enough about me to do what you've done." She kissed his eyes, applied delicate kisses all over his face. "When you told me what you were up to, I felt like a princess imprisoned in a high tower. And you were the prince trying to save me. You know me. I'm not one to believe in fairy tales. But I liked this one—it was a nice fantasy, and I needed a fantasy. I was certain you were lying to me . . . or to yourself. I prepared for the inevitable. But you turned out to be a real prince." She rubbed his stubbly head. "A prince with a terrible haircut."

He tried to smile, but emotion was still strong in him and his facial muscles wouldn't work properly.

"Don't punish yourself. Can't you see how happy I am? It's almost over now. Please, Viktor! I want you to be happy, too."

He gathered himself, swallowed back the tight feeling in his throat. "I'm all right," he said. "I'm sorry. I just . . . I can't. . . ."

"I know," she said. "It's been hard for both of us. I know." She lifted his wrist so she could see his watch. "I have to go. I don't want to, but I have to. Are you sure you're all right?

"I'll be fine," he said. "Go ahead . . . go."

"Should I wait for you here?"

"Yes," he said. "Yes, wait here, and we'll ride up together. As soon as I'm through with Yuri I'll call my security people. They'll meet us at the entrance."

She kissed him again, her tongue flirting with his, a lush contact that left him muddled. "I'll see you soon," she said, trailing her hand across his cheek; then she walked off toward a recessed door next to the fireplace at the far end of the room—the same door that led to Yuri Lebedev's office and, ultimately, to the inscrutable heart of Eternity.

Without Larissa beside him Chemayev felt adrift, cut off from energy and purpose. His thoughts seemed to be circling, slowly eddying, as the surface of a stream might eddy after the sudden twisting submergence of a silvery fish. They seemed less thoughts than shadows of the moment just ended. On the television screen above the bar a child was sitting in a swing hung from the limb of an oak tree, spied on by an evil androgynous creature with a painted white face and wearing a lime green body stocking, who lurked in the shadows at the edge of a forest. All this underscored by an anxious, throbbing music. Chemayev watched the video without critical or aesthetic bias, satisfied by color and movement alone, and he was given a start when the bartender came over and offered him a drink in a glass with the silver initial L on its side.

"What's this?" Chemayev asked, and the bartender said, "Yuri's private booze. Everybody gets one. Everybody who meets with him." He set down the glass, and Chemayev viewed it with suspicion. The liquid appeared to be vodka.

"You don't have to drink," the bartender said. "But it's Yuri's custom."

Chemayev wondered if he was being tested. The courageous thing to do, the courteous thing, would be to drink. But abstinence might prove the wiser course.

"I can pour you another if you'd like. I can open a new bottle." The bartender produced an unopened bottle; it, too, was embossed with a silver L.

"Why don't you do that?" Chemayev told him. "I could use a drink, but . . . uh. . . ."

"As you like." The bartender stripped the seal from the bottle and poured. He did not appear in the least disturbed and Chemayev supposed that he had been through this process before.

The vodka was excellent and Chemayev was relieved when, after several minutes, he remained conscious and his stomach gave no sign that he had ingested poison.

"Another?" the bartender asked.

"Sure." Chemayev pushed the glass forward.

"Two's the limit, I'm afraid. It's precious stuff." The bartender lifted the glass that Chemayev had refused, offered a silent toast and drank. "Fuck, that's good!" He dabbed at his mouth with a cocktail napkin. "Almost everyone who tries it comes back and offers to buy a couple of bottles. But it's not for sale. You have to meet with Yuri to earn your two shots."

"Or work as a bartender in Eternity, eh?" Chemayev suggested.

"Privileges of the job. I'm always delighted to serve a suspicious soul."

"I imagine you get quite a few."

"People have every right to be suspicious. This is a weird place. Don't get me wrong—it's great working here. But it takes getting used to."

"I can imagine."

"Oh, I wouldn't bet on it. You have no idea what goes on here after hours. But once you've met Yuri"—the bartender slung a towel over his shoulder—"you'll probably be able to educate me. Everyone says it's quite an experience."

Chemayev downed the second vodka. Yet another video was showing on the TV, and something was interfering with the transmission. First there was an intense flickering, then a succession of scenes skittered across the screen, as if the video were playing on an old-fashioned projector and the film was breaking free of the spool. He glanced at the bartender. The man was standing at the opposite end of the counter with his head thrown back, apparently howling with laughter; yet though his mouth was open and the ligature of his neck cabled, he wasn't making a sound. His white hair glowed like phosphorus. Unnerved, Chemayev turned again to the TV. On screen, to the accompaniment of a gloomy folk song, two women in white jumpsuits were embracing on a couch, deep in a passionate kiss. As he watched, the taller of the two, a blond with sharp cheekbones, unzipped her lover's jumpsuit to the waist, exposing the slopes of her breasts. . . . It was at this point that Chemayev experienced a confusing dislocation. Frames began flipping past too rapidly to discern, the strobing light causing him to grow drowsy yet dumbly attentive; then a veneer of opaque darkness slid in front of the screen, oval in shape, like a yawning mouth. There was a moment when he had a claustrophobic sense of being enclosed, and the next instant he found himself standing in the blackness beyond the mouth. He had the impression that this black place had reached out and enveloped him, and for that reason, though he remained drowsy and distanced from events, he felt a considerable measure of foreboding.

From Chemayev's vantage it was impossible to estimate the size of the room in which he stood—the walls and ceiling were lost in darkness—but he could tell it was immense. Illumination was provided by long glowing silvery bars that looked to be hovering at an uncertain distance overhead, their radiance too feeble to provide any real perspective. Small trees and bushes with black trunks and branches grew in disorderly ranks on every side; their leaves were papery, white, bespotted with curious, sharply drawn, black designs—like little leaf-shaped magical texts. This must be, he thought, the garden Polutin had mentioned, though it seemed more thicket than garden. The leaves crisped against his jacket as he pushed past; twigs clawed at his trouser legs. After a couple of minutes he stumbled into a tiny clearing choked with pale weeds. Beetles scuttered in amongst them. Fat little scarabs, their chitin black and gleamless,

they were horrid in their simplicity, like official notifi-
cations of death. The air was cool, thick with the skunky
scent of the vegetation. He heard no sound other than
those he himself made. Yet he did not believe he was
alone. He went cautiously, stopping every so often to
peer between branches and to listen.

After several minutes more he came to a ruinous path
of gray cobblestones, many uprooted from their bed of
white clay, milky blades of grass thrusting up among
them. The path was little more than a foot wide, over-
hung by low branches that forced him to duck; it wound
away among trees taller than those he had first encountered. He followed it and after less than a minute he
reached what he assumed to be the center of the garden.
Ringed by trees so tall they towered nearly to the bars of
light was a circular plaza some forty feet in width, constructed of the same gray stones, here laid out in a
concentric pattern. In its midst stood the remains of a
fountain, its unguessable original form reduced to a head-
high mound of rubble, a thin stream of silvery water
arcing from a section of shattered lead pipe, splashing,
sluicing away into the carved fragments tumbled at its
base. Sitting cross-legged beside it, his back to Chemayev, was a shirtless man with dark shoulder-length
hair, his pale skin figured by intricate black tattoos, their
designs reminiscent of those on the leaves.

"March?" Chemayev took a step toward the man.
"What are you doing here?"

"What am I doing here?" March said in a contemplative tone. "Why, I'm feeling right at home. That's what I'm doing. How about yourself?"

"I have a meeting," Chemayev said. "With Yuri Lebedev."

March maintained his yogi-like pose. "Oh, yeah? He was banging about a minute ago. Try giving him a shout. He might still be around."

"Are you serious?" Chemayev took another step forward. "Lebedev was here?"

March came smoothly, effortlessly to his feet—like a cobra rising from a basket. He cupped his hands to his mouth and shouted, "Hey, Yuri! Got a man wants to see ya!" He cocked his head, listening for a response. "Nope," he said at length. "No Yuri."

Chemayev shrugged off his jacket and draped it over a shoulder. March's disrespect for him was unmistakable, but he was uncertain of the Irishman's intent. He couldn't decide whether it would be safer to confront him or to walk away and chance that March would follow him into the thickets. "Do you know where the door to Yuri's office is?"

"I could probably find it if I was in the mood. Why don't you just poke around? Maybe you'll get lucky."

Confrontation, thought Chemayev, would be the safer choice—he did not want this man sneaking up on him.

"What is this all about?" He gave a pained gesture

with his jacket, flapping it at March. "This thing you're doing. This . . . Clint Eastwood villain thing. What is it? Have you been sent to kill me? Does Polutin think I'm untrustworthy?"

"My oh my," said March. "Could it be I've made an error in judgment? Here I thought you were just another sack of fish eggs and potato juice, and now you've gone all brave on me." He extended his arms toward Chemayev, rotated them in opposite directions. The tattoos crawled like beetles across his skin, causing his muscles to appear even more sinewy than they were. In the half-light the seamed lines on his face were inked with shadow, like ritual scarifications. "Okay," he said. "Okay. Why don't we have us a chat, you and I? A settling of the waters. We'll pretend we're a coupla old whores tipsy on lager and lime." He dropped again into a cross-legged posture and with a flourish held up his right hand—palm on edge—by his head. Then he drew the hand across his face, pretending to push aside his dour expression, replacing it with a boyish smile. "There now," he said. "What shall we talk about?"

Chemayev lowered into a squat. "You can answer my questions for a start."

"Now that's a problem, that is. I fucking hate being direct. Takes all the charm out of a conversation." March rolled his neck, popping the vertebrae. "Wouldn't you prefer to hear about my childhood?"

"No need," said Chemayev. "I used to work in a kennel."

"You're missing out on a grand tale," said March. "I was all the talk of Kilmorgan when I was a lad." He gathered his hair behind his neck. "I foresee this is not destined to be a enjoyable conversation. So I'll tell you what I know. Your Mister Polutin feels you're on the verge of making a serious mistake, and he's engaged me to show you the error of your ways."

"What sort of mistake?"

"Ah! Now that, you see, I do not know." March grinned. "I'm merely the poor instrument of his justice."

Chemayev slipped off his shoulder harness, folded it on top of his coat; he did the same with his money belt. "So Polutin has sent you to punish me? To beat me?"

"He's left the degree of punishment up to yours truly," March said. "You have to understand, I like to think of myself as a teacher. But if the pupil isn't capable of being taught... and you'd be surprised how often that's the case. Then extreme measures are called for. When that happens there's likely to be what you might call a morbid result." He squinted, as if trying to make out Chemayev through a fog. "Are you afraid of me?"

"Petrified," said Chemayev.

March chuckled. "You've every right to be confident. You've got about a yard of height and reach on me. And what...? Maybe a stone and a half, two stone in weight? By the looks of things I'm vastly overmatched."

"How much is Polutin paying you?"

"Let's not go down that path, Viktor. It's unworthy of you. And disrespectful to me as well."

"You misunderstand." Chemayev tossed his shirt on top of the money belt. "I simply wish to learn how much I'll profit from breaking your neck."

March hopped to his feet. "You're a hell of a man in your own back yard, I'm certain. But you're in a harsher world now, Viktor old son." He gave his head a shake, working out a tightness in his neck. "Yes, indeed. A world terrible, pitiless, and strange. With no room a'tall for mistakes and your humble servant, Niall March, for a fucking welcome wagon."

Chemayev took great satisfaction in resorting to the physical. In a fight all of the vagueness of life became comprehensible. Frustration made itself into a fist; nameless fears manifested in the flexing of a muscle. The pure principles of victory and defeat flushed away the muddle of half-truths and evasions that generally clotted his moral apparatus. He felt cleansed of doubt, possessed of keen conviction. And so when he smiled at March, dropping into a wrestler's crouch, it was not only a show of confidence but an expression of actual pleasure. They began to circle one another, testing their footing, feinting. In the first thirty seconds March launched a flurry of kicks that Chemayev absorbed on his arms, but the force of each blow drove him backward. It had been plain from the outset that March was quick, but Chemayev hadn't realized the efficiency with which he could employ his speed. The man skipped and jittered over the uneven terrain, one moment graceful, dancing, then shuffling forward in the manner of a boxer, then a moment later sinking into an apelike crouch and lashing out with a kick from ground level. Chemayev had intended to wait for the perfect moment to attack, but now he understood that if he waited, March was likely to land a kick cleanly; he would have to risk creating an opening. And when March next came into range he dove at the man's back leg, bringing him down hard onto the stones.

The two men grabbed and countered, each trying to roll the other and gain the upper position, their breath coming in grunts. March's quickness and flexibility made him difficult to control. After a struggle Chemayev managed to turn him onto his back and started to come astride his chest; but March's legs scissored his waist, forcing him into a kneeling position, and they were joined almost like lovers, one wobbling above, the other on his back, seemingly vulnerable. Chemayev found he was able to strike downward at March's face, but his leverage was poor, the blows weak, and March blocked most of them with his arms, evaded others by twitching his head to the side. Soon Chemayev grew winded. He braced himself on his left hand, intending to throw a powerful right that would penetrate the Irishman's guard; but with a supple, twisting movement, March barred Chemayev's braced arm with his forearm, holding it in place, and levered it backward, dislocating the elbow.

Chemayev screamed and flung himself away, clutching his arm above the elbow, afraid to touch the injury itself. The pain brought tears to his eyes, and for a moment he thought he might faint. Even after the initial burning shock had dissipated, the throbbing of the joint was nearly unbearable. He staggered to his feet, shielding the injury, so disoriented that when he tried to find March, he turned toward the trees.

"Over here, Viktor!" March was standing by the fountain, taking his ease. Chemayev made to back away, got his feet tangled, and inadvertently lurched toward him—the jolt of each step triggered a fresh twinge in his arm. His brain was sodden, empty of plan or emotion, as if he were drunk to the point of passing out.

"What d'ye think, sweetheart?" said March. "Am I man enough for you, or are you pining yet for young Tommy down at the pub?" He took a stroll away from the fountain, an angle that led him closer to Chemayev but not directly toward him. He spun in a complete circle, whirling near, and kicked Chemayev in the head.

A white star detonated inside Chemayev's skull and he fell, landing on his injured elbow. The pain caused him to lose consciousness and when he came to, when his eyes were able to focus, he found March squatting troll-like beside him, a little death incarnate with curses in the black language scrawled across his skin and long dark hair hiding his face like a cowl.

"Jesus, boyo," he said with mock compassion. "That

was a bad'un. Couple more like that, we'll be hoisting a pint in your honor and telling lies about the great deeds you done in your days of nature."

Chemayev began to feel his elbow again—that and a second pain in the side of his face. He tasted blood in his mouth and wondered if his cheekbone was broken. He closed his eyes.

"Have you nothing to say? Well, I'll leave you to mend for a minute or two. Then we'll have our chat."

Chemayev heard March's footsteps retreating. A thought was forming in the bottom of his brain, growing strong enough to sustain itself against grogginess and pain. It pushed upward, surfacing like a bubble from a tar pit, and he realized it was only a mental belch of fear and hatred. He opened his eyes and was fascinated by the perspective—a view across the lumpy rounded tops of the cobblestones. He imagined them to be bald gray midgets buried to their eyebrows in the earth. He pushed feebly at the stones with his good arm and after inordinate labor succeeded in getting to his hands and knees. Dizzy, he remained in that position a while, his head hung down. Blood dripping from his mouth spotted the stones beneath him. When he tried to stand his legs refused to straighten; he sat back clumsily, supporting himself with his right hand.

"A beating's a terrible thing," said March from somewhere above. "But sometimes it's the only medicine. You understand, don't you, Viktor? I'll wager you've handed out a few yourself. What with you being such a badass and all." He was silent for a couple of ticks. "Polutin assures me you're a bright lad. And I'm inclined to agree ... though I'm not sure I'd go so far as saying you're a bloody genius. Which is Polutin's view of the matter. He's an absolute fan of your mental capacities. If mental capacity was rock and roll he'd be front row at all your concerts, blowing kisses and tossing up his room key wrapped in a pair of knickers." Another pause. "Am I getting through to you, Viktor?"

Chemayev nodded, a movement that set his cheekbone to throbbing more fiercely.

"That's good." March's legs came into view. "According to Polutin, your talents lie in your ability to organize facts. He tells me you can take a newspaper, the *Daily Slobova* or whatever rag it is you boys subscribe to, and from the facts you've gathered in a single read, you're able devise a money-making scheme no one's thought of before. Now that's impressive. I'm fucking impressed, and I don't impress easy. So here's what I'm asking, Viktor. I'm asking you to marshal that massive talent of yours and organize the facts I'm about to present. Can you handle that?"

"Yes," said Chemayev, not wanting to risk another nod. His elbow was feeling stronger and he wondered if the fall might not have jammed the bone back into its socket. He shifted his left arm, and though pain returned in force, he seemed to have mobility.

"All right," said March. "Here we go. First fact. Polutin loves you like a son. That may seem farfetched, considering the crap he rubs in your face. But it's what he tells me. And it's for certain fathers have treated sons a great deal worse than he treats you. Love's too strong a word, perhaps. But there's definitely paternal feelings involved. Why he'd want a son, now, I've no idea. The thought of fathering a child turns my stomach. The little bollocks start out pissing on your hand and wind up spitting in your face and stealing the rent money. But I had a troubled upbringing, so I'm not the best judge of these things."

He paced off to the side, moving beyond Chemayev's field of vision. "Second fact. Whatever game you've been playing, it's over. Terminated. Done. And by the way, I'll be wanting you to tell me exactly what it was. Every last detail. But that can wait till you've got the roses back in your cheeks. Third fact. You've made one mistake. You can't afford another. Are you following me, Viktor? You're on the brink of oblivion with ten toes over the edge. No more mistakes or you're going to fall a long, long way and hit the ground screaming." March's legs came back into view. "Fact number four. God is dead. The certain hope of the Resurrection is a pile of shite. You have my word on it. I've seen to the other side and I know."

Chemayev found he could make a fist with his left hand. To test his strength he tightened it, fingernails cutting into his palm. March's voice was stirring up a windy noise inside his head, like the rush of traffic on a highway.

"There you have it, Viktor. Four little facts. Organize away. Turn 'em over in your mind. See if you can come up with a scheme for living."

Chemayev wanted badly to satisfy March, to avoid further punishment; but the facts with which he had been presented offered little room for scheming. Instead they formed four walls, the walls of the lightless world in which he had been confined before meeting Larissa. It occurred to him that this was exactly what March wished him to conclude and that he could satisfy him by saying as much. But the thought of Larissa charged him with stubbornness. She was the fifth fact he could not ignore, the fact that had shattered those walls. Thanks to her there was a sixth fact, a seventh, an infinity of fact waiting to be explored.

"It's no brainbuster, Viktor. I'm not the least gifted when it comes to organization. Fuck, I can't even balance my checkbook. But even I can figure this one out."

As if his engine had begun to idle out Chemayev's energy lapsed. He grew cold and the cold slowed his thoughts, replaced them with a foggy desire to lie down and sleep. March put a hand on his shoulder, gave him a shake, and pain lanced along his cheekbone. The touch renewed his hatred, and braced by adrenaline, he let hate empower him.

"C'mon, lad." March said with a trace of what seemed actual concern in his voice. "Tell me what you know."

"I understand," said Chemayev shakily.

"Understand what?"

"I have a . . . a good situation. A future. I'd be a fool to jeopardize it."

"Four stars!" said March. "Top of the charts in the single leap! See what I told you, Viktor? A kick in the head can enlighten even the most backward amongst us. It's a fucking miracle cure." He kneeled beside Chemayev. "There's one more thing I need to tell you. Perhaps you've been wondering why, with all the rude boys about in Moscow, our Mister Polutin hired in a Mick to do his dirty work. Truth is, Russki muscle is just not suited to subtlety. Those boys get started on you, they won't stop till the meat's off the bone. I'm considered something of a specialist. A saver of souls, as it were. You're not my only project. Far from it! Your country has a great many sinners. But you're my top priority. I intend to be your conscience. Should temptation rear its ugly head, there I'll be, popping up over your shoulder. Cautioning you not to stray. Keep that well in mind, Viktor. Make it the marrow of your existence. For that's what it is, and don't you go thinking otherwise." March stood, reached down and took Chemayev's right arm. "Come on now," he said. "Let's get you up."

Standing, it looked to Chemayev that the stones beneath his feet were miles away, the surface of a lumpy planet seen from space. A shadowy floater cluttered his vision. The white leaves each had a doubled image and March's features, rising from the pale seamy ground of his skin, made no sense as a face—like landmarks on a map without referents.

"Can you walk?" March asked.

"I don't know."

March positioned himself facing Chemayev and examined him with a critical eye. "We better have you looked at. You might have a spot of concussion." He adjusted his grip on Chemayev's shoulders. "I'm going to carry you ... just so's you know I'm not taking liberties. I'll come back after and get your things."

He bent at the knees and waist, preparing to pick Chemayev up in a fireman's carry. Without the least forethought or inkling of intent, acting out of reflex or muscle memory, or perhaps goaded by the sour smell of March's sweat, Chemayev slipped his right forearm under March's throat, applying a headlock; then with all his strength he wrenched the Irishman up off his feet. March gurgled, flailed, kicked. And Chemayev, knowing that he only had to hang on a few seconds more, came full into his hatred. He heard himself yelling with effort, with the anticipation of victory, and he dug the grip deeper into March's throat. Then March kicked out with his legs so that for the merest fraction of a second he was horizontal to the true. When his legs swung down again the momentum carried Chemayev's upper body down as well, and March's feet struck the ground. Lithe as an eel, he pushed himself into a backflip, his legs flying over Chemayev's head, breaking the hold and sending them both sprawling onto the stones.

By the time Chemayev recovered March had gotten to his feet and was bent over at the edge of the circle, rubbing his throat. Stupefied, only dimly aware of the danger he faced, Chemayev managed to stand and set off stumbling toward the trees. But the Irishman hurried to cut him off, still holding his throat.

"Are you mad, Viktor?" he said hoarsely. "There's no other explanation. Fuck!" He massaged his throat more vigorously, stretched his neck. "That's as close as I've come. I'll give you that much."

Chemayev's legs wanted to bend in odd directions. It felt as if some organ in his head, a scrap of flesh he never knew existed, had been torn free and was flipping about like a minnow in a bait bucket.

Strands of hair were stuck to March's cheek; he brushed them back, adjusted the waist of his trousers. "It's the girl, isn't it? Liza . . . Louisa. Whatever her fucking name is. Back when I was of a mood for female companionship, there were more than a few knocked my brains loose. They'll make a man incorrigible. Immune to even the most sensible of teachings."

Chemayev glanced about, groggily certain that there must be an avenue of escape he had overlooked.

"I remember this one in particular," said March as he

approached. "Evvie was her name. Evvie Mahone. She wasn't the most gorgeous item on the shelf. But she was nice-looking, y'know. A country girl. Come to Dublin for the university. Wild and red-cheeked and full of spirit, with lovely great milky bosoms, and a frizzy mane of ginger hair hanging to her ass that she could never comb out straight. I was over the moon ten times round about her. When we were courting we'd sit together for hours outside her dormitory, watching the golden days turn to gray, touching and talking soft while crowds moved past us without noticing, like we were two people who'd fallen so hard for one another we'd turned to stone. Our hearts just too pure to withstand the decay and disappointment of the world." He stepped close to Chemayev, inches away—a wise white monkey with a creased, pouchy face and eyes as active as beetles. "After we became lovers we'd lie naked in the casement window of her room with a blanket around us, watching stars burn holes in the black flag flying over the Liffey. I swear to God I thought all the light was coming from her body, and there was music playing then that never existed . . . yet I still hear its strains. Is it like that for you, Viktor? That grand and all-consuming? I reckon it must be."

March clasped Chemayev's shoulder with his left hand, as if in camaraderie; he made a fist of his right. "Love," he said wistfully. "It's a wonderful thing."

* * *

Chemayev was not witness to much of the beating that then ensued; a punch he never saw coming broke his connection with painful reality and sent him whirling down into the black lights of unconsciousness. When he awoke he discovered to his surprise that he was no longer in pain—to his further surprise he found that he was unable to move, a circumstance that should have alarmed him more than it did. It was not that he felt at peace, but rather as if he'd been sedated, the intensity of his possessive attitude toward mortality tuned down several notches and his attention channeled into a stuporous appreciation of the blurred silver beam hanging in the darkness overhead . . . like a crossbeam in the belly of a great ark constructed of negative energy. He could hear water splashing, and a lesser sound he soon recognized to be the guttering of his breath. He thought of Larissa, then tried not to think of her. The memory of her face, all her bright particularity, disturbed the strange equilibrium that allowed him to float on the surface of this pain-free, boundless place. But after a while he became able to summon her without anxiety, without longing overmuch, content to contemplate her the way an Orthodox saint painted on an ikon might gaze at an apparition of the Virgin. Full of wonder and daft regard. Soon she came to be the only thing he wanted to think of, the eidolon and mistress of his passage.

Things were changing inside him. He pictured conveyor belts being turned off, systems cooling, microbes filing out of his factory stomach on the final day of operation, leaving their machines running and all the taps going drip drip drip. It was amusing, really. To have feared this. It was easier by far than anything that had preceded it. Though fear nibbled at the edges of his acceptance, he remained essentially secure beneath his black comforter and his silver light and his love. The thought of death, once terrifying, now seemed only unfortunate. And when he began to drift upward, slowly approaching the light, he speculated that it might not even be unfortunate, that March had been wrong about God and the hope of the Resurrection. Beneath him the garden and its pagan central element were receding, and lying with its arms out and legs spread not far from the ruined fountain, his bloody, wide-eyed body watched him go. He fixed on the silver light, expecting, hoping to see and hear the faces and voices of departed souls greeting him, the blissful creatures that patrolled the border between life and true eternity, and the white beast Jesus in all Its majesty, crouched and roaring the joyful noise that ushered in the newly risen to the sacred plane. But then he sensed an erosion, a turmoil taking place on some fundamental level that he had previously failed to apprehend. Fragments of unrelated memory flew at him in a hail, shattering his calm. Images that meant nothing. A wooden flute he'd played as a child. An old man's gassed, wheezing voice. Sparks corkscrewing up a chimney. Pieces of a winter day in the country.

Shards of broken mental crockery that shredded the temporary cloth of his faith, allowing terror to seep through the rents. Real terror, this. Not the fakes he'd experienced previously, the rich fears bred in blood and bone, but an empty, impersonal terror that was itself alive, a being larger than all being, the vacuous ground upon which our illusion breeds, that we never let ourselves truly believe is there, yet underlies every footstep ever taken . . . gulping him down into its cold and voiceless scream, while all he knew and loved and was went scattering.

T rembling and sweaty, Chemayev stared at the television set above the bar. A brown-haired teenage girl in a denim jacket and jeans was hitchhiking on a desert road, singing angrily—if you could judge by her expression—at the cars that passed her by. He watched numbly as she caught a ride in a dusty van. Then, astounded by the realization he was alive, that the girl was not part of the storm of memory that had assailed his dying self, he heaved up from the barstool and looked avidly about, not yet convinced of the authenticity of what he saw. About a dozen people sitting at various tables; the bartender talking to two male customers. The recessed door beside the fireplace opened and a woman in a black cocktail dress came into the lounge and stood searching the tables for someone. Still shaky, Chemayev sat back down.

All that had happened in the garden remained with him, but he could examine it now. Not that examination helped. Explanations occurred. He'd been given a drug in a glass of Yuri's special reserve—probably a hypnotic. Shown a film that triggered an illusion. But this fathered the need for other explanations. Was the object of the exercise to intimidate him? Were the things March had said to him about Polutin part of the exercise? Were they actual admonitions or the product of paranoia? Of course it had all been some sort of hallucination. Likely an orchestrated one. He could see that clearly. But despite the elements of fantasy—March's lyric fluency, the white trees, and so on—he couldn't devalue the notion that it had also had some quality of the real. The terror of those last moments, spurious though they had been, was still unclouded in his mind. He could touch it, taste it. The greedy blackness that had been about to suck him under . . . he knew to his soul *that* was real. The memory caused his thoughts to dart in a hundred different directions, like a school of fish menaced by a shadow. He concentrated on his breathing, trying to center himself. Real or unreal, what did it matter? The only question of any significance was; Who could have engineered this? It wasn't Polutin's style. Although March surely was. March was made to order for Polutin. The alternative explanations—magical vodka, mysterious Lebedevian machinations—didn't persuade him; but neither could he rule them out. . . . Suddenly electrified with fright, remembering his appointment, thinking he'd missed it, he peered at his watch. Only eleven minutes had passed since he'd drunk the vodka. It didn't seem possible, yet the clock behind the bar showed the same time. He had fifteen minutes left to wait. He patted his pocket, felt the airline tickets. Touched the money belt. Pay Yuri, he told himself. Sign the papers. There'd be time to think later. Or maybe none of it was worth thinking about. He studied himself in the mirror. Tried a smile, straightened his tie unnecessarily, wiped his mouth. And saw Niall March's reflection wending his way among the tables toward the bar. Toward him.

"I was hoping I'd run into you," March said, dropping onto the stool beside Chemayev. "Listen, mate. I want to apologize for giving you a hard time back there in the fucking ice palace. I wasn't meself. I've been driving around with that bastard Polutin all day. Listening to him jabber and having to kiss his fat ass has me ready to chew the tit off the Virgin. Can I buy you a drink?"

Totally at sea, Chemayev managed to say, no thanks, he'd had enough for one evening.

"When I can no longer hear that insipid voice, that's when I'll know I've had enough." March hailed the bartender. "Still and all, he's a fair sort, your boss. We held opposing positions on a business matter over in London a while back. He lost a couple of his boys, but apparently he's not a man to let personal feelings intrude on his good judgment. We've been working together ever since."

Chemayev had it in mind to disagree with the proposition that Polutin did not let personal feelings interfere with judgment—it was his feeling that the opposite held true; but March caught the bartender's eye and said, "You don't have any British beer, do you? Fuck! Then give me some clear piss in a glass." The bartender stared at him without comprehension. "Vodka," said March; then, to Chemayev: "What sorta scene do you got going on here? It's like some kind of fucking czarist disco. With gangsters instead of the Romanovs. I mean, is it like a brotherhood, y'know? Sons of the Revolution or some such?"

The bartender set down his vodka. March drained the glass. "No offense," he said. "But I hate this shit. It's like drinking shoe polish." He glanced sideways at Chemayev. "You're not the most talkative soul I've encountered. Sure you're not holding a grudge?"

"No," said Chemayev, reigning in the impulse to look directly at March, to try and pierce the man's affable veneer and determine the truth of what lay beneath. "I'm just . . . anxious. I have an important meeting."

"Oh, yeah? Who with?"

"Yuri Lebedev."

"The fucking Buddha himself, huh? Judging by what I've seen of his establishment, that should be a frolic." March called to the bartender, held up his empty glass. "Not only does this stuff taste like the sweat off a pig's balls, but I seem immune to it."

"If you keep drinking. . . ." Chemayev said, and lost his train of thought. He was having trouble equating this chatty, superficial March with either of the man's two previous incarnations—the sullen, reptilian assassin and the poetic martial arts wizard.

"What's that?" March grabbed the second vodka the instant the bartender finished pouring and flushed it down.

"Nothing," said Chemayev. He had no capacity for judgment left; the world had become proof against interpretation.

March turned on his stool to face the tables, resting his elbows on the bar. "Drink may not be your country's strong suit," he said, "but I'm forced to admit your women have it all over ours. I'm not saying Irish girls aren't pretty. God, no! When they're new pennies, ah . . . they're such a blessing. But over here it's like you've got the fucking franchise for long legs and cheekbones." He winked at Chemayev. "If Ireland ever gets an economy, we'll trade you straight-up booze for women—that way we'll both make out." He swiveled back to face the mirror, and looked into the eyes of Chemayev's reflection. "I suppose your girlfriend's a looker."

Chemayev nodded glumly. "Yes . . . yes, she is."

March studied him a moment more. "Well, don't let it get you down, okay?" He gave Chemayev a friendly punch on the arm and eased off the stool. "I've got to be going." He stuck out his hand. "Pals?" he said. With reluctance, Chemayev accepted the hand. March's grip was strong, but not excessively so. "Brothers in the service of the great ship Polutin," he said. "That's us."

He started off, then looked back pleadingly at Chemayev. "Y'know where the loo . . . the men's room is?"

"No," said Chemayev, too distracted to give directions. "I'm sorry. No."

"Christ Jesus!" March grimaced and grabbed his crotch. "It better not be far. My back teeth are floating."

The walls of the corridor that led to Yuri's office were enlivened by a mural similar to the mosaic that covered the bar in the lounge—a crowd of people gathered at a cocktail party, many of them figures from recent Russian history, the faces of even the anonymous ones rendered with such a specificity of detail, it suggested that the artist had used models for all of them. Every thirty feet or so the mural was interrupted by windows of one-way glass that offered views of small gaudy rooms, some empty, others occupied by men and women engaged in sex. However, none of this distracted Chemayev from his illusory memory of death. It dominated his mental landscape, rising above the moil of lesser considerations like a peak lifting from a sea of clouds. He couldn't escape the notion that it had been premonitory and that the possibility of death lay between him and a life of comfortable anonymity in America.

He rounded a bend and saw ahead an alcove furnished with a sofa, a coffee table, and a TV set—on the screen a husky bearded man was playing the accordion, belting out an old folk tune. Two women in white jumpsuits were embracing on the sofa, unmindful of Chemayev's approach. As he walked up the taller of the two, a pale Nordic blond with high cheekbones and eyes the color of aquamarines, unzipped her lover's jumpsuit to expose the swells of her breasts . . . and that action triggered Chemayev's memory. He'd seen this before. On the TV in the bar. Just prior to entering the garden where he had fought with March. The same women, the same sofa. Even the song was the same that had been playing then—the lament of a transplanted city dweller for the joys of country life. He must have cried out or made a noise of some sort, for the smaller woman—also a blond, younger and softer of feature—gave a start and closed her jumpsuit with a quick movement, making a tearing sound with the zipper that stated her mood as emphatically as her mean-spirited stare.

"You must be Viktor," the taller woman said cheerfully, getting to her feet. "Larissa's friend."

Chemayev admitted to the fact.

"I'm Nataliya." She extended a hand, gave his a vigorous shake. The sharpness of her features contrived a caricature of beauty, the hollows of her pale cheeks so pronounced they brought to mind the fracture planes of a freshly calved iceberg. "I am also friends with Larissa," she said. "Perhaps she has told you about me?"

"I don't know," Chemayev said. "Perhaps. I think so."

Before he could voice any of the questions that occurred to him she caught his arm and said, "Come. I'll take you to Yuri." Then turning to her lover, she said, "I'll be back as soon as I can." The smaller woman let out an angry sniff and pretended to be absorbed in watching the TV.

Nataliya led him along the corridor, chattering about Larissa. What a sweetheart she was, how kind she was to the other girls, even those who didn't deserve it. God knows, there were some impossible bitches working here. Take that cunt Nadezhda. This scrawny redhead from Pyatigorsk. Her father had stolen from Yuri and now his little darling was keeping him alive by faking orgasms with drunks and perverts. You should have seen her the day she arrived. A real mess! Weeping and shivering. But after a couple of weeks, after she realized she wasn't going to be raped or beaten, she started acting like Catherine the Great. Lots of girls went through a phase like that. It was only natural. Most came from awful situations and once they felt they had a little power, you expected them to get a swelled head. But Nadezhda had been here a year and every day she grew more intolerable. Putting on airs. Bragging about the rich men who wanted to set her up in an apartment or buy her a *dacha*. And now—Nataliya's laugh sounded as if she were clearing her throat to spit—now she claimed some mystery man was going to pay her debt to Yuri and marry her. Everyone tried to tell her these things never worked out. Hadn't lying beneath a different man every night taught her anything? In the first place, why would a man take a whore to wife when he could have what he wanted for a far less exacting price? Love? What a joke! Men didn't love women, they loved the way women made them feel about themselves. Most of them, that is. The ones who did fall in love with you, the ones who were fool enough to surrender their power to a woman. . . . because that's what love was in essence, wasn't it? A kind of absolute surrender. Well, you had to be suspicious of those types, didn't you? You had to believe some weakness of character was involved.

To this point Chemayev had been listening with half an ear, more concerned with the significance of having run into these women from his dream, trying fruitlessly to recall how the dream had proceeded after he had seen them, and thinking that he should turn back so as to avoid what might prove to be a real confrontation with March; but now he searched Nataliya's face for a sign that she might be commenting on his particular situation. She did not appear to notice his increased attentiveness and continued gossiping about the pitiful Nadezhda. She'd never liked the bitch, she said, but now she was about to get her comeuppance, you had to feel badly for her. Maybe she wasn't really a bitch, maybe she was just an idiot. And maybe that was why Larissa had befriended her. . . . Nataliya stopped as they came abreast of yet another window, touched Chemayev on the shoulder, and said, "There's Yuri now."

In the room beyond the glass, its walls and furniture done in shades of violet, a pasty round-shouldered man with a dolorous, jowly face and thin strands of graying hair combed over a mottled scalp stood at the foot of a large bed, seeming at loose ends. He had on slacks and an unbuttoned shirt from which his belly protruded like an uncooked dumpling, and he was rubbing his hips with broad, powerful-looking hands. Chemayev had seen Yuri on numerous occasions—or rather he had seen the man who officiated at the nightly auctions—but he had never been this close to any of the doubles, and despite the man's unprepossessing mien, or perhaps because of it, because his drab commonality echoed that of the old Soviet dinosaurs, the Kruschevs, the Andropovs, the Malenkovs, he felt a twinge of fear.

"Is that him?" he asked Nataliya.

She looked uncertain, then brightened. "You mean the one you're expecting to meet? He's upstairs. At the party."

"What are you talking about? What party?"

"At Yuri's place."

"His office?"

"His office . . . his apartment. It's all the same. He's got an entire floor. The party's been going on since Eternity opened. Eleven, twelve years now. It never shuts down. Don't worry. You'll do your business and meet some fascinating people."

Chemayev studied the double, who was shuffling about, touching things, pursing his lips as though in disapproval. He did not appear to be the magical adept of Polutin's description, but of course this was not the real Yuri—who could say what form he'd taken for himself?

"If you want to finish by the time Larissa gets off work," Nataliya said, "we'd better hurry."

"She's not working tonight," Chemayev said, still intrigued by the double.

"Sure she is. I saw her not half an hour ago. She was this young blond guy. A real pretty boy. Her last client of the night . . . or so she said."

She said this so off-handedly, Chemayev didn't believe she was lying. "She told me she didn't have to work tonight."

"What's she supposed to tell you? She's going to throw some asshole a fuck? You know what she does. She cares for you, so she lied. Big surprise!"

What Nataliya had told him seemed obvious, patently true; nonetheless Chemayev was left with a feeling of mild stupor, like the thickheadedness that comes with the onset of flu, before it manifests as fever and congestion. He leaned against the wall.

"The amazing thing is, you believed her," she said. "Who'd you think you were involved with? Lying's second nature to a whore."

"She's not a whore," he said, half under his breath.

Nataliya pushed her sharp face close to his. "No? What could she be then? A missionary? A nurse?"

"She didn't have a choice. She...."

"Sure! That explains it! Every other girl who becomes a whore has a choice, but not sweet Larissa." Nataliya made a dry sound in the back of her throat, like a cat hissing. "You're pathetic!"

Chemayev hung his head, giving in to the dead weight of his skull. To graphic images of Larissa in bed. It was unreasonable to feel betrayed under such circumstances, yet that was how he felt. He wanted to run, to put distance between himself and the corridor, but the violet room seemed to exert a tidal influence on his mood, pulling his sense of betrayal into a dangerous shape, and he had the urge to batter the window, to break through and tear Yuri's double apart.

"Want to watch? They're probably going at it in one of the rooms. I bet we can find them." Nataliya tugged at his jacket. "Come on! Treat yourself! I won't say a thing to Larissa."

Chemayev shoved her away, sending her reeling against the opposite wall. "Shut your fucking mouth!"

"Oo—oo—ooh!" Nataliya pretended to cower, holding her white hands like starfish in front of her face, peering through the gaps between her long fingers. "That was very good! Just like a real man!"

Chemayev's head throbbed. "You don't understand,"

he said. "I'm paying off her debt. We're planning to go away . . . to marry."

Nataliya was silent for a bit, then: "And now you're not? That's what you're saying? Now you've realized your whore is really a whore, you intend to abandon her?"

"No . . . that's not it."

"Then why waste time? Keep your appointment. Pay the money. You'll forget about this."

Chemayev thought this was good advice, but he couldn't muster the energy to follow it. His mental wattage had dimmed, as if he were experiencing a brownout.

Nataliya leaned against the wall beside him. "What I said about Nadezhda . . . about her telling us someone was going to pay her debt. I bet Larissa told her about you, and she took the story for her own. She does that sort of thing. Takes scraps of other people's lives and sews them into an autobiography." She looked off along the corridor. "I'm sorry for what I said. If I'd known it was you and Larissa. . . ." Her voice lost some value, some richness. "Maybe it'll be different for you two."

Her solicitude, which Chemayev suspected was only prelude to further abuse, snapped him out of his funk. "No need to apologize," he said. "I haven't taken anything you've said seriously." He headed off along the corridor.

"Oh . . . right! You have the surety of love to support

your convictions." Nataliya fell into step beside him. "I'm curious about love. Me, I've never experienced it. Mind telling me what it's like?"

Chemayev's headache grew worse; he increased his pace. They came round a sharp bend and he saw an elevator door ahead.

"All I want's a hint, you understand. Just tell me something you know about Larissa. Something only you with your lover's eye can see."

Enraged, Chemayev spun her about to face him. "Don't talk anymore! Just take me to Yuri!"

Half-smiling, she knocked his hands away and walked toward the elevator; then she glanced back, smiling broadly now. "Is this how you treat her? No wonder she lies to you."

Inside the cramped elevator, chest-to-chest with Nataliya, Chemayev fixed his eyes on a point above the silky curve of her scalp and studied the image of Stalin's KVD chief, Beria—the mural on the walls repeated the motif of those in the corridor and the bar, but here the figures were larger, giving the impression that they were passengers in the car. Contemplating this emblem of Soviet authority eased the throbbing in his head. Maybe, he thought, in the presence of such an evil ikon his own sins were diminished and thus became less capable of producing symptoms such as anxiety and headaches. The old thug looked dapper, dressed in a doublebreasted blue suit, sporting a red flower in his lapel instead of a hammer-and-sickle pin, quite different from the photographs Chemayev had seen in which he'd worn executioner's black. His quizzical expression and pince-nez gave him the air of a schoolteacher, stern yet caring, a man whom you'd detest when you studied under him, but whom you would respect years later when you realized the value of the lessons he'd taught. Not at all the sort of character to preside over purges and summary executions, watching from a distance, betraying no more emotion than would a beetle perched on a leaf.

Inching upward, the elevator creaked and groaned—the sounds of a torture chamber. The exhausted cries of victims, the straining of mechanical torments. Nothing like the noiseless efficiency of the one that had brought him to the theater. The car lurched, passing a floor, and Chemayev's thoughts, too, lurched. He reawakened to Nataliya's presence, felt her eyes on him. Bitch. He wanted to beam the word into her brain. What right did she have to ask him personal questions? *Tell me something you know about Larissa, something only you with your lover's eye can see.* What did she expect? That he'd bare his soul to her? Fat chance! There were lots of things he could have told her, though. A year-and-a-half's worth of things. Thousands of intimate observations. The problem was, his head hurt too much at the moment for him to think of any.

The elevator door rattled open and Chemayev

stepped out into a corridor with cement walls, smelling of urine and vomit, illuminated by the ghastly dim light from an overhead bulb. The floor was littered with empty bottles, crushed plastic containers, soggy news-papers, dead cigarette packs, used condoms. Partially unearthed from a mound of debris, a crumpled Pepsi can glittered like treasure. Heavy metal blasted from some-where close by. At the far end of the corridor a lumpish old man with stringy gray hair falling to his shoulders was wielding a mop, feebly pushing a mound of trash into the shadowy space beneath a stairwell. Along the walls stood buckets of sand—for use in case of fire. Che-mayev turned to Nataliya, who gestured for him to pro-ceed. As they passed, the old man peered at him through the gray snakes of his hair, his face twisted into a frown, and he smacked his lips as if trying to rid himself of a nasty taste.

If Chemayev had any doubt as to where he stood, it was dispelled by what he saw from the window at the foot of the stairs—he was gazing down onto the parking lot of Eternity, a view that could only be achieved from high up in one of the *krushovas*. This surprised him, but he was becoming accustomed to Yuri Lebedev's curious logic. As he started up the stairs, the music was switched off and he heard voices in the corridor above. At the top of the stairs, lounging against a wall, were two men in jeans and leather jackets, one with a shaved scalp, nurs-ing a Walkman to his breast, and the other with a mohawk that had been teased into a rooster's crest. They eyed Chemayev with contempt. The man with the Mohawk blew Nataliya a kiss. His face was narrow, scarcely any chin and a big nose, looking as if it had been squeezed in a vise. A pistol was stuck in his belt.

"Private party," he said, blocking Chemayev's path.

"I've got an appointment with Yuri," Chemayev told him.

The bald guy affected a doltish expression. "Yuri? Which Yuri is that?"

"Maybe Yuri Gagarin," said his pal. "Maybe this pussy wants to be an astronaut."

"Better let him pass," said Nataliya. "My friend's a real assassin. A faggot like you doesn't stand a chance with him."

The man with the pistol in his belt made a twitchy move and Chemayev grabbed his hand as it closed around the pistol grip; at the same time he spun the man about and encircled his neck from behind with his left arm, cutting off his wind. The man let go of the pistol and pried at the arm. Chemayev flicked the safety off, pushed the pistol deeper into the man's trousers.

The man's Adam's apple bobbed. "Go easy, okay!"

Chemayev wrenched the gun free and waved both men back against the wall. "Are you crazy?" he asked Nataliya. "Why did you antagonize him?"

She moved off along the corridor, heading for a doorway thronged with partygoers. "I have so few chances to watch you be masterful. Indulge me."

Chemayev shook his forefinger in warning at the two punks and followed her. The pistol—a nine-millimeter—didn't fit his holster; he wedged it in the waistband of his trousers at the small of his back.

The first thing he noticed about the party was that the instant he stepped through the door the stench of the hallway vanished, as if he had penetrated an invisible barrier impermeable to odors. The smells were now those you might expect of any Moscow gathering: perfume, marijuana and cigarette smoke, bad breath, the heat of people pressed together under the sickly lighting, crowded into an unguessable number of rooms. People of every description. Students in sweaters and jeans; old ragged folks with careworn faces, the sort you'd expect to find in the *krushovas*; beautiful women in couturier gowns; street prostitutes—some equally beautiful—in vinyl micro-minis and fake furs; men dressed like Chemayev himself, members of a *mafiya* or businessmen with more-or-less reputable interests; musicians with guitars and violins and horns; homosexuals in drag; uniformed soldiers; jugglers. In one corner several fit-looking men wearing jerseys tossed a soccer ball back and forth; in another two actors played a scene to an audience consisting of a blond middle-aged woman in a lab coat and thick spectacles, a thickset man in a wrinkled suit, the very image of a Party hack, and a pretty adolescent girl wearing leg warmers over her tights,

holding a pair of ballet slippers. On occasion, as Chemayev and Nataliya forged a path, being pinched and
fondled and grabbed in the process, incredible sights
materialized, as fleeting as flashes of lightning. A gei-
sha's painted face appeared between shoulders; she
flicked out a slender forked tongue at Chemayev, then
was gone. Soon thereafter he caught sight of a small
boy whirling as rapidly as a figure skater, transforming
himself into a column of dervish blue light. And not
long after that they squeezed past a group of men and
women attending a giant with a prognathian jaw and a
bulging forehead who, kneeling, was as tall as those
gathered around him; he reached out his enormous
hands and flickering auras manifested about the heads
of those he touched. To someone unfamiliar with Eternity these sights might have seemed miraculous; but to
Chemayev, who had witnessed similar curiosities on the
stage of the theater, they were evidence of Yuri's talent
for illusion. He accepted them in stride and kept pushing
ahead. Once he saw a brunette who might have been
Larissa laughing flirtatiously on the arm of a slender
blond man; he called to her, knocked people aside in his
determination to reach her, but she disappeared into the
crowd. There were so many people milling about it was
impossible to keep track of any single person, and they
were of such great variety it seemed a contemporary
Noah had scavenged the streets of the endangered city
for two of every kind and brought them to this place of

relative security, a cross between the Ark and the Tower of Babel. The hubbub, comprised of talking, singing, laughing—indeed, of every sort of human emission—was deafening, and the only impression Chemayev had of the general aspect of the place was derived from the objects that lined the walls. Overflowing bookcases; side-by-side refrigerators; an ornate China closet containing framed photographs; a massive secretary of golden oak; cupboards, reliquaries, travel posters, portraits, a calendar showing the wrong month and a picture of Siberian wheat fields. Items typical of a middle-class apartment. Smoke dimmed the lighting further, creating an amber haze, twisting with slow torsion into a menagerie of shapes that often appeared identifiable—ephemeral omega signs and kabalistic symbols and mutant Cyrillic characters—beneath which the closely packed heads of the partygoers bobbed and jerked. In various quarters couples were dancing and due to the heat, many—both men and women—had removed their shirts; but because of the overall exuberance and the general lack of attention paid to the topless women, the effect was not truly prurient and had the casual eroticism of a tribal celebration.

Eventually Nataliya and Chemayev forced their way into a large relatively under-populated room. No more than fifteen or sixteen people standing in clusters, some occupying the grouping of couches and easy chairs that dominated the far end. Nataliya drew Chemayev aside.

"This is ridiculous," she said. "For all I know we're following Yuri about. Sit down and I'll try to find him."

Oppressed, mentally fatigued, Chemayev was in no mood to argue. Once she had left, he collapsed into an easy chair, let his head fall back and closed his eyes. The workings of his mind were clouded, murky. It was as if the contents of his skull were the interior of a fishbowl that hadn't been cleaned for weeks, the water thickened to a brown emulsion in which a golden glint of movement was visible now and again. Though not altogether pleasant, it was an oddly restful state, and he became irritated when a man's voice intruded, telling a story about two young friends who'd come to Moscow from the north. He tried unsuccessfully to ignore the voice and finally opened his eyes to discover that the room had filled with decrepit, ill-clad men and women, typical denizens of the *krushovas*. The storyteller was hidden among them and his voice—a slurred yet authoritative baritone—was the only one audible.

"There was a special bond between them," the man was saying. "They were both misfits in the life they had chosen—or rather that had chosen them. They were romantics and their circumstance was the very antithesis of the romantic, suppressing the natural expressions of their hearts and souls. Nicolai—the livelier of the pair—he was more grievously affected. He fancied himself a poet. He aspired to be a new Mayakovsky, to give tongue to the millennial monsters taking shape from the funeral smoke of Communism. A talented, personable fellow. Blond, handsome. For all his bloody deeds, he had something inside him that remained untouched. A core of . . . not innocence exactly, but a kind of youthful arrogance that counterfeited innocence. That made innocence unnecessary. Who knows what he might have achieved in a more forgiving age?"

This reference to someone named Nicolai and the accompanying description charged Chemayev with new anxiety and caused him to shake off his malaise. He sat up and peered about, trying to locate the speaker. An old woman fixed him with a baleful stare, then turned away. Her faded print dress was hiked up in back, revealing a raddled, purple-veined thigh; one of her grimy stockings had sagged about her calf in folds, like a seven league boot.

"The morning in question," the man went on, "they got up well before dawn and drove to an open market north of the city. You know the sort of place. A muddy field where vendors set up stalls. Farmers selling vegetables and such. An old bus was parked at the edge of the field. It served as an office for Aleksander Fetisov, the small-time criminal they'd been sent to kill. Fetisov had grown dissatisfied with picking up the crumbs that fell from the table of the big shots. He had grand ambitions. But neither his strength nor his ingenuity had proved equal to those ambitions. When he stepped out of the bus with his bodyguards our heroes opened fire from behind the bushes where they had hidden themselves. The farmers ran away.

"Nicolai knelt beside Fetisov's body. He needed proof that they'd done the job. A watch, a ring. Some identifiable token. As his friend searched the dead man's clothing Viktor moved up behind him and aimed a pistol at his head. It would have been merciful if he had pulled the trigger right at that second, but he wasn't committed to the act. He was still trying to think of a way out ... even though he knew there was none. He couldn't understand why Polutin had ordered him to kill Nicolai. But for Viktor, lack of understanding was not sufficient cause to break ranks. In this he differed from Nicolai. And of course, though he couldn't see it at the time, this was the reason Polutin had ordered Nicolai's death—he had too much imagination to be a good soldier."

Bewildered and full of dread, Chemayev stood and began making his way toward the sound of the voice. He knew this story, he was familiar with every detail, but how anyone else could know it was beyond him. The elderly men and women shuffled out of his path clumsily, reluctantly—it seemed he was pushing through a sort of human vegetation, a clinging, malodorous thicket comprised of threadbare dresses, torn sweaters, and blotchy, wrinkled skin.

"Nicolai glanced up from the corpse to discover that his friend had become his executioner. For an instant, he was frozen. But after the initial shock dissipated he made no move to fight or to plead for his life. He just looked at Viktor, a look that seemed fully comprehending, as if he knew everything about the moment. The mechanisms that had created it. Its inevitability. And it was the composition of that look, the fact it contained no element of disappointment, as if what was about to occur was no more nor less than what Nicolai might have expected of his friend . . . that was the spark that prompted Viktor, at last, to fire. To give him due credit, he wept profusely over the body. At one point he put the gun to his head, intending to end his own life. But that, certainly, was an act to which he was not committed."

Standing near the door, his back to Chemayev, the center of the *krushova* dwellers' attention, was a squat black-haired man in a blue serge suit. Chemayev stepped in front of him and stared into the unblinking eyes of Lavrenty Pavlovich Beria, his clothing identical in every respect to that worn by the painted image in the elevator, complete down to the pince-nez perched on his nose and the red blossom in his lapel. Flabbergasted, Chemayev fell back a step.

"If it were up to me," Beria said, "I'd have you shot. Not because you betrayed your friend—in that you were only carrying out an order. But your penchant for self-recrimination interferes with the performance of your duty. That is reprehensible." He clicked his tongue against his teeth and regarded Chemayev dourly. "I suspect you'd like to know how I came to hear the story I've been telling my comrades. No doubt you're trying to rationalize my presence. Perhaps you've concluded that if Yuri could create doubles for himself, he might well have created a double for Beria. Perhaps you're thinking that when Lev Polutin sent you and Nicolai to kill Fetisov, he also sent a spy to make certain you did the job right, and that this spy is my source. That would be the logical explanation. At least according to the lights of your experience. But let me assure you, such is not the case."

Having recovered his poise somewhat, Chemayev seized on this explanation as if it were a rope that had been lowered from the heavens to lift him free of earthly confusion. "I'm sick of this shit!" he said, grabbing Beria by the lapels. "Tell me where the fuck Yuri is!"

An ominous muttering arose from the crowd, but Beria remained unruffled. "People have been trying to talk to you all evening," he said. "Trying to help you make sense of things. But you're not a good listener, are you? Very well." He patted Chemayev on the cheek, an avuncular gesture that caused Chemayev, as if in reflex, to release him. "Let's say for the sake of argument I'm not who I appear to be. That I'm merely the likeness of Lavrenty Pavlovich Beria. Not God's creation, but Yuri's. Given Yuri's playful nature, this is a distinct possibility. But how far, I wonder, does playfulness extend? Does he only create doubles of the famous, the notorious? Or might he also create doubles of individuals who're of no interest to anyone ... except, perhaps, to Viktor Chemayev?" A meager smile touched his lips. "That doesn't seem reasonable, does it?"

There was a rustling behind Chemayev, as of many people shifting about, and he turned toward the sound. An avenue had been created in the ranks of human wreckage from the *krushova* and sauntering toward him along it—the way he used to walk when he spotted you at a bar or on a street corner, and had it in mind to play a trick, his head tipped to the side, carrying his left hand by his waist, as if about to break into a dance step—was a blond, slender, blue-eyed man in a fawn leather jacket, gray silk shirt, and cream-colored slacks. His boyish smile was parenthetically displayed between two delicately incised lines that helped lend him a look of perpetual slyness. In fact, all the details of his features were so finely drawn they might have been created by a horde of artisan spiders armed with tiny lapidary instruments. It was the face of a sensitive, mischievous child come to a no less sensitive and mischievous maturity. He looked not a day older than he had on the last morning of his life three and a half years before.

"That's right!" Nicolai said, holding out his arms to Viktor. "In the flesh! Surprised?" He wheeled in a circle as if showing off a new suit. "Still the handsome twenty-two-year-old, eh? Still a fucking cloud in trousers."

Logic was no remedy for this apparition. If the floor

had opened beneath him to reveal a lake of fire, Chemayev would not have been more frightened. He retreated in a panic, fumbling for the pistol.

"Man! Don't be an asshole! I'm not going to give you any trouble." Nicolai showed Chemayev his empty palms. "We've been down this road once. You don't want to do it again."

Guilt and remorse took up prominent posts along Chemayev's mental perimeters. His breath came shallowly, and he had difficulty speaking. "Nicolai?" he said. "It . . . it's not you . . . ?"

"Sure it is. Want me to prove it? No problem." Nicolai folded his arms on his chest and appeared to be thinking; then he grinned. "What's that night club where all the whores dress like Nazis? Fuck! I'm no good with names. But you must remember the night we got drunk there? We screwed everything in sight. Remember?"

Chemayev nodded, though he barely registered the words.

"On the way home we had an argument," Nicolai said. "It was the only time we ever got into a fight. You pulled the car off onto the side of the Garden Ring and we beat the shit out of each other. Remember what we argued about?"

"Yes." Chemayev was beginning to believe that the man might actually be Nicolai. The thought gave him no comfort.

"We argued about whether the goddamn Rolling

Stones were better with Brian Jones or Mick Taylor."
Nicolai fingered a pack of Marlboros from his shirt
pocket, tapped one out. "Stupid bullshit. I couldn't chew
for a fucking week." He fired up his cigarette and ex-
haled a fan of smoke; he closed his right eye, squinted
at Chemayev as if assessing the impact of his words.
"Want more proof? No problem."

He dropped, loose-limbed, into a nearby chair and
began to reel off another anecdote, but no further proofs
were necessary. His unstrung collapse; his languid gestures; the way he manipulated the cigarette in his left
hand, passing it from one pair of fingers to another like
a magician practicing a coin trick—the entire catalogue
of his body language and speech were unmistakably Nicolai's. No actor alive, however skillful, could have
achieved such verisimilitude.

As Chemayev looked on, half-listening to Nicolai, a
consoling inner voice, a voice of fundamental soundness
and fine proletarian sensibilities that had been there all
the time but only became audible when essential to
mental stability, was offering assurances that beyond
the boundaries of his temporary derangement the world
was as ever, humdrum and explicable, and no such thing
as this could be happening—drugs, alcohol, and stress
were to blame—rambling on and on with increasingly
insane calmness and irrelevance, like the whispered lit-
any of a self-help guru suggesting seven simple methods
for maximizing spiritual potential issuing from a cas-

sette playing over a pair of headphones fallen from the head of gunshot victim who was bleeding out onto a kitchen floor. Yet simultaneously, in some cramped subbasement of his brain, urgent bulletins concerning zombie sightings and karmic retribution were being received, warnings that came too late to save the iniquitous murderer of a childhood friend. . . .

"Viktor!" Nicolai was staring at him with concern. "Are you all right? Sit down, man. I know this is fucked up, but we've got some things to talk about."

Unable to think of an acceptable alternative, Chemayev sagged into the chair opposite, but he did not lean back and he rested the pistol on his knee. Overwhelmed with guilt and regret, he had the urge to apologize, to beg forgiveness, but recognized the inadequacy of such gestures. His heart seemed to constrict into a dark nugget of self-loathing.

"You know it's me now, right?" Nicolai asked, "You don't have any doubts?"

Called upon to speak, Chemayev was unable to repress his urge for apology and emitted a sobbing, incoherent string of phrases that, reduced to their essence, translated into an admission of responsibility and a denial of the same on the grounds that he'd had no choice, if he hadn't followed Polutin's orders, Polutin would have killed him, his family. . . . The shame of the act never left him, but what else could he have done?

Nicolai shifted lower in his chair, reached down to

the floor and stubbed out his cigarette. He watched the embers fade. "I never expected to last long in Moscow," he said gloomily. "That's one of the differences between us. You always thought you were going to win the game. Me, I knew it was only a matter of time before I lost." He tapped out another cigarette. "I can't help how you feel. And believe me, I know. I saw your face when you pulled the trigger. I see your face now. You're not hard to read." He lit up again. "You'll never forgive yourself, no matter what I tell you. So why don't we put the subject aside for now. We've more important things to discuss."

Once again Chemayev could think of nothing to say other than to abase himself, to offer further apology. Tears streamed from his eyes, and though the tears were validation of a kind, evidence that his spirit, albeit tarnished, was still capable of normal reactions, they also infused him with shame. He struggled to control himself. "I don't understand," he said. "How is this possible? How can you be here?"

"With Yuri all things are possible," said Nicolai; then his glum mood lifted. "You know those American jokes? The ones with the punch lines that go, 'I've got good news, and I've got bad news'? It's like that. I've got good news, and I've got bad news. Which do you want first?"

This was the old Nicolai, always joking, trying to make light of things. Chemayev relaxed by a degree from his rigid posture.

"Come on!" Nicolai said. "Which do you want?"

"Good."

"Okay. The good news is there is an afterlife. The bad news"—Nicolai made a sweeping gesture that, for all Chemayev knew, might have been intended to include the apartment, Russia, the universe—"this is it!"

"What the fuck are you talking about?"

"This place." Nicolai gave a sardonic laugh. "This fucking night club. Eternity."

There must be, Chemayev thought, more to the joke.

"You still don't get it, huh? Christ!" Nicolai leaned forward and gave Chemayev a rap on the knee, like a teacher scolding—fondly—a favorite pupil. "For such a genius you're not too quick on the uptake."

"Eternity?" said Chemayev, incredulous, "Yuri Lebedev's Eternity . . . that's the afterlife? You're not serious?"

"Serious? What the fuck's that? Is Moscow serious? Starving people camped in the subways. Generals selling tanks on the black market. That old fart in the Kremlin swilling down a quart a day and promising us the capitalist paradise. It's no less serious than that." Nicolai wriggled in his chair like a kid with an itch. "Yuri, man . . . he's. . . ." He gave his head a shake, as if to signify awe. "You don't have to hang around the party long before you learn things about him."

"You mean that horseshit about he's a fucking wizard? A Master of the Mystic East?"

"They're things a guy like you might not be able to swallow. But for a guy like me, with what I've been through, I don't have any choice."

Chemayev looked down at his hands.

"Have you ever met anyone who knew Yuri?" Nicolai asked. "Any of his friends, his associates. Not just someone who used to work for him."

After giving this due consideration Chemayev said he had not.

"That's because they're dead. Grenkov, Zereva, Ashkenazy. All those guys. They're all dead and they're all at the party. Man, you wouldn't believe who's here! It's the goddamn Communist Hall of Fame. Yuri's a big fan of those power-mad old bastards. Lots of generals and shit. Not many poets, though. Yuri was never much of a reader."

"Oh. So it's the *party* that's the afterlife!" Chemayev gave a scornful laugh. "This is bullshit!"

Nicolai's face hardened. "Bullshit? Well, maybe you'll think this is bullshit too! When you shot me, I went out. One second I was staring at you. At your dumbass face! It looked like you were going to start whimpering. I had time to say to myself, 'Oh, fuck . . . yeah . . . of course. . . .' I figured things out, you understand. The way you were pouting—I knew it meant you'd scrambled over whatever pissy little moral hurdle the job had posed. And then"—he snapped his fingers—"I wasn't there anymore." He allowed Chemayev time to react and when no reaction was forthcoming he went on: "I don't remember much afterward. But at some point I began to hear a voice. I can't tell you what kind of voice. It was all around me . . . this enormous sound. As if I was inside the mouth that was speaking. Sometimes it seems I can almost repeat the words it was saying—they're on the tip of my tongue. But I can't spit them out." He made a frustrated noise. "The next thing I remember for certain, I'm walking down a dingy corridor toward a door. Toward the party. I'm wearing nice clothes. Cologne. It's like I just got out of the shower and I'm ready for a night on the town."

Nicolai took a hit of his cigarette and let smoke leak out between his lips, as if too enervated to exhale properly. "I suppose it does sound like bullshit. I can't explain it. Everybody says that while Yuri was building the club he was hanging out with some strange people. Experts on the Kabbala. Computer scientists. He even brought in a shaman from up near Archangel. They say he went through some drastic changes, and I believe it. Whatever he was like before, I'll bet it wasn't much like he is now."

"You've met him?"

Nicolai coughed, grimaced, butted his cigarette. "You don't meet Yuri. You experience him."

"You experience him." Chemayev gave a sarcastic laugh. "So you're saying he's like a sunset or something."

"A sunset. . . ." Nicolai looked as if he was mulling it over. "It's not a totally inappropriate analogy. But for sure he's not a guy you sit down and have a chat with. The fact is, I don't think he's a guy at all. Not anymore. The things he got into when he was building the club, it transformed him. The club, Yuri, the party . . . they're all the same somehow." Nicolai smiled crookedly. "That's pretty weak, isn't it? Maybe the best I can do is tell you what it's like being here all the time." He gestured at one of the walls. "Take a look around."

Chemayev had not paid much attention to the room when he had entered, but he was fairly certain the walls had not been covered, as they were now, with a faded earth-toned mural like those found on the walls of factories during the Communist era: determined-looking, square-jawed men and broad-shouldered women with motherly bosoms engaged in the noble state-approved pursuit of dump-truck-assembly, faces aglow with the joy of communal effort, their sinewy arms seemingly imbued with the same iron strength as the mighty girders and grimly functional machinery that framed them. Other than their two chairs, the room was empty of furniture. The *krushova* dwellers and Beria were gone, and the noise of the party had abated, replaced by a faint roaring, like the sound of blood heard when you put a seashell close to your ear. Chemayev thought he had become inured to apparitions, but a chill spiked in his chest.

"Shit changes all the time," said Nicolai. "Empty rooms fill up with people. You'll be having a talk with someone and it'll just end—like the rest of the scene was cut out of the movie. Snip! You're in another room, doing something else. You'll be sleeping in a bed, the next second you're dancing with somebody. There's no logic to it, it's all done on a whim. Yuri's whim. The physical laws of the place are his laws. Not God's, not nature's. It's like everyone here is inside him. Part of him. He's become a universe unto himself. One that contains the club and the party. . . . For all I know he's taken over the fucking world. But the difference between the places I'm familiar with—the club and the party—most people in the club are still alive." He started to take out another cigarette, then thought better of it. "We get visitors like you from the real world now and again. And various among us are privileged to visit the club. But. . . ." His mood veered toward exasperation, and Chemayev wondered, with only a touch of cynicism, if Yuri might not be editing his emotions as well as his scenes. "Don't you understand?" Nicolai asked. "Yuri's in control of everything that happens here. We're fucking figments of his imagination. Once you step inside Eternity you're subject to his whims the same as us. I don't know what kind of deal you're hoping to do with him, but take my word, it's not going to be what you expected. You should get the hell out. Right now." He chuckled. "Here I am trying to save your ass. Old habits. Of course"—he kept his face neutral—"I'm probably too late."

"If what you say is true," Chemayev said, "then logic would dictate that you're the subject of Yuri's whim at present. That's the reason for this . . . this confrontation. You must have something to tell me. The lecture on Yuri's power, I assume."

Nicolai jumped up and went to stand facing one of the muralled walls, as if compelled by the heroic figure of a muscular redheaded man holding up an ingot in a pair of tongs, staring at it with such unalloyed devotion, it might have been the sacred light of Mother Russia soon to become an axle joint. "That's what I've been waiting to hear," he said. "The voice of the heartless motherfucker who shot me. I knew it was in you somewhere." He wheeled about, his clever features cinched in fury. "You think this is a confrontation? My dear friend Viktor! My cherished boyhood companion! Don't you worry. You'll be back here one day . . . and maybe not just for a visit. Then we'll have a fucking confrontation!" He paced toward Chemayev and stood with his feet apart as if preparing to attack. "I do have something to tell you, but it's got nothing to do with what I said about Yuri. That was for old time's sake. For a while it was like we were friends again, you know. A couple of guys sitting around bullshitting. I can't figure why it happened, but that's how it felt."

Chemayev could relate to Nicolai's confusion. His own feelings, compounded of love, fear, guilt, and much more, were too complex to analyze, like a stew that had been simmering for three and a half years, new ingredients constantly being added, fragrant, rich, and savory, but ultimately indigestible. Nothing could be salvaged here, he realized. "What do you have to tell me?"

Nicolai plucked out his Marlboros, tapped the pack on the back of his hand. "Russian women. Ever think about how tough they are, Viktor? They get the crap beat out of them, they take the best abuse of drunks and addicts. Their fathers fuck them, their boyfriends pimp them. By the time they're sixteen they're world-class ballbusters. They're still sweet, still capable of love. But they've learned to do what's necessary. Most men don't see this. They don't understand that no matter what the woman feels for them, she's going to do what's in her own best interests. She's become just like a Russian man. Sentimental on the outside. Soft. But on the inside they're steel."

"Is this leading somewhere?" asked Chemayev.

"I fucked your woman tonight," Nicolai said. "Your beautiful Larissa. I did her twice. The second time I had her up the ass. She loved it, she went absolutely crazy. I've never considered myself a petty sort, but I must admit it gave me a great deal of satisfaction." He studied the pack of cigarettes, as if using it to focus his thoughts. "You know how it is with some women—when you make love to them their faces get twisted, distorted. Sex strips away their beauty, revealing the beast. But Larissa, man. . . . She's amazing. No matter how depraved the act, how degrading your intent, she just gets more beautiful. She had this entranced look. Radiant. Like a saint. Like the more I defiled her, the closer she grew to God." His soft laugh expressed a touch of incredulity. "But none of that's important, is it? She's a whore, after all. So she fucks a guy—even a dead guy—what's the big deal? She's doing her job. If she enjoys it a little, all that means is she's a professional." He came closer and perched on the arm of his chair. "After the first fuck we talked a while. She told me this was her last night, she was going away with the man she loved. She told me all about you. What a great guy you were. How much you loved her. All your virtues. I didn't try to illuminate her. I didn't have to. She realizes you're a calculating son-of-a-bitch at heart. She didn't say it, but it was implicit in what she said. She knows you. She loves you. How could she not? She's exactly the same as you. She'll do whatever she has to and there won't be a stain on her conscience." He repocketed the Marlboros without removing one. He stood, adjusted the hang of his jacket. "Okay. That's it. My duty's done."

He seemed to be waiting for a response.

In standing Chemayev was unsteady as an old man, he had to put a hand out to balance himself. He should be angry, he thought; but he only felt out of his depth. There was a gap between himself and his emotions too wide for any spark to cross. But because he believed he should react in some way, because not to react smacked of inadequacy, he pointed the pistol at Nicolai's chest.

"Give it a try," said Nicolai, he held both arms straight out from his sides, turning himself into a blond, expensively tailored Jesus on the Cross. "It worked the first time. I'm interested in what'll happen myself." He rested his head on his shoulder. "Wonder what Yuri will have to say?"

After pondering his options Chemayev decided it would be best to hurry past this part of things. "Where's Yuri now?"

As if in response the air between them began to ripple, a sluggish disturbance that spread throughout the room, infecting floor and ceiling and walls, and as it spread the dimensions of the room underwent a slow, undulant elongation, an evolution that seemed organic, like the stretching of a python's gullet when it prepares to swallow an exceptionally large object. Once the rippling ceased Chemayev found that he was standing at a remove of some forty feet from Nicolai.

"Haven't you heard a thing I've been telling you?" Nicolai's voice carried a slight echo. "In this place you can't get away from Yuri."

Before Chemayev could react, the rippling started up once again, accompanied by a dimming of the lights. Moved by an old reflex of mutual reliance he sprinted toward Nicolai, but the process of elongation was on this occasion so rapid, like the reduction in view achieved by narrowing the aperture of a telescopic lens, by the time he had gone only a couple of steps, Nicolai had dwindled to a tiny black figure at the far end of a long corridor. A foul-smelling corridor with stained, pitted concrete walls, littered with trash, ranged by warped wooden doors and buckets of sand. Hills of cans and bottles, stratified canyons of paper and plastic waste, dried-up riverbeds of urine and spilled vodka, altogether effecting a post-apocalyptic terrain laid out beneath a dirty white sky in which hung a jaundiced light bulb sun. It was the same corridor he and Nataliya had walked down earlier that evening.

The elevator door, battered, defaced by graffiti, stood about twenty feet away. Chemayev had the impulse to run to it, to seek shelter in the relative sanity of the night club. But he was fed up with being given the runaround; he'd entered into a straightforward business arrangement and he intended to see it through to a contract, no matter what games Yuri wanted to play. As for Larissa, if she'd lied . . . he could handle it. Their problems were every one associated with this psychotic country populated entirely by lunatics and their victims. By tomorrow night they'd be clear of all that.

He turned back, intending to frame a few last words that would convey to Nicolai both a more rational, more dignified portion of apology, and his acknowledgment of how things stood between them; but his former friend was nowhere to be seen. Looking at Chemayev from an arm's-length away was the swarthy old derelict who had been sweeping up the corridor. He had barely noticed him on first meeting, but now he marveled at the man's ugliness. With his stubby arms and legs, his swollen belly and narrow sloping shoulders, his smallish head, he might have been a toad that had undergone a transformation, only partially successful, into the human. He had about him a bitter reek reminiscent of the smell of the vegetation in the garden. The chest of his grimy T-shirt was mapped by a large, vaguely rectangular brown stain like the image of a spectacularly undistinguished continent whose most prominent features were bits of dried food stuck to the fabric along the south coast and central plain. His wool trousers were shapeless as those of a clown, supported by frayed suspenders. Filthy twists of gray hair hung from his mottled scalp, half-curtaining his eyes, and his face, sagging, pouchy, cheeks and nose sporting graffiti of broken capillaries, thick-lipped and dull. . . . It reminded Chemayev of dilapidated hovels in the villages of his childhood, habitations humbled by weather and hard times into something lumpish, barely distinguishable from a mound of earth, a played-out vegetable plot in the back, rusted garden tools leaning against bowed steps, its thatched roof molting, sided with unpainted boards worn to a shit brown, and something ancient, howlingly mad with age and failure, peering out through two dark windows with cracked panes.

It was fascinating in its lack of human vitality. More than fascinating. Compelling. It seemed to hold Chemayev's eyes, to exert a pull that intensified with every passing second, as if the mad absence within had the virtue of a collapsed star, a generating fire grown so cold and inert it had become fire's opposite, a negative engine wherein chaos became comprehensible and physical laws were reworked according to some implausible design. He could not look away from it, and when at last he did, not due to his own efforts, but because the old man moved, extending a hand to him, palm upward like a beggar, thus shattering the connection, he felt lightheaded and confused and frail, as if he had been winnowing away, unraveling in the depths of that bleak stare.

In his frail lightheaded confusion there were a few things Chemayev thought he understood. This liver-spotted troll, this mud man with a black hole inside him, was Yuri—he was fairly certain of that. He was also fairly certain that the old bastard had his hand out for money. For the gold certificates contained inside his, Chemayev's, money belt. What was he supposed to do? Just fork it all over? Fuck that! Where were the papers to sign? What guarantees did he have—*could* he have—with a creature like this. He wanted to establish some sort of security for himself and Larissa, but couldn't summon the words, and he realized with complete surety that fear had nothing to do with his inability to speak, words simply weren't part of Yuri's program—no more talk was needed, everything had been said, and now it was Chemayev's choice to give over the money and see what that bought him ... or to exercise caution for the time being.

That he accepted this proscription, that he believed Yuri had so much control over the situation, implied that he accepted Nicolai's assessment of the man. He would have liked to deny this, but it seemed undeniable. He should tell someone, he thought. Before leaving Moscow he should tip the media, get a TV truck out to Eternity, expose the fact that the great Yuri Lebedev was running more than a night club, the old geezer had become a minor fucking deity in charge of a franchise in the afterlife catering to murderers, hookers, and various relics of the Cold War. . . . This trickle of whimsy, edged with more than a little hysteria, dried up when Chemayev noticed that the walls and ceiling and floor of the corridor around and behind Yuri were billowing in and out with same rhythm as the rise and fall of his chest, as if the old man were the central image of a painting, a portrait of squalor floating on the surface of some gelatinous substance in a state of mild perturbation. He backed farther away, but the distance between himself and Yuri did not lengthen, and he saw that his body, too, was billowing, rippling, ruled by the tidal flux of Yuri's sluggish breath—it appeared they were both elements of the same semi-liquid medium. Horrified, he flailed and kicked, trying to swim away, but none of his exertions had the least effect ... unless they played a role in the steady expansion of Yuri's face. It was widening, distending, losing its cohesion like a shape made of colored oil, spreading to cover more and more of the fluid atop which it was suspended, resembling a face distorted by a funhouse mirror, and Chemayev felt that his own body was suffering a similar distortion, his legs elongating, his torso becoming bulbous, his head lopsided and pumpkin-sized, and that he and Yuri were flowing together.

Yuri's mouth stretched wider and wider, becoming a dark, gaping concavity that reduced his other features to tiny irrelevancies, like the glowing lures above the enormous mouth of an angler fish. It was curving to surround Chemayev, preparing less to swallow him than to incorporate him into its emptiness, and he thought briefly of the garden, the dark oval through which he had passed to reach it. If he could have screamed he would have made a cry that reached to heaven, but he was as voiceless as a strand of seaweed floating on an off-shore billow, going out on the tide toward the great hollow places of the sea, and as he passed into the darkness, Yuri's darkness, as it closed over him, his fear—like his voice—was subsumed by the myriad impressions that came to him from the place into which he was being absorbed.

He had a sense of the man Yuri had been, a quick

mental rumor that left flavors of crudity, brutality, lust-fulness, intelligence . . . an intellect that had aspired too high, that had sought a godlike invulnerability and created the means necessary to achieve it, but had lost everything of consequence in gaining it, for Yuri's character was merely a component of the thing, the place, he had become. Through a mingling of magic and science and will he had triggered a sort of spiritual fission, all the particulars of his flesh and mind exploding into an immense, radiant cloud that did not dissipate in the way of a mushroom cloud, but maintained its integrity at the moment of peak fury, sustained by a surface tension that might have been the residue of the spell he had caused to be pronounced. Not a god so much as an embryonic entity of unguessable nature, striving to reach its maturity, extending its influence through various human (and perhaps inhuman—who could say?) agencies, populating its vacancy with dead souls, partly just for company, to ease its aching emptiness, but also utilizing their knowledge to engineer plots designed to increase its power, always feeding, growing, becoming. . . . This was among the last thoughts Chemayev recalled before he was utterly subsumed, drowned in Yuri's black essence—that all Yuri's energies were being desperately directed toward the process of growth, of fulfilling whatever evolutionary destiny was now his—though perhaps he had no real destiny. That had come to be Yuri's torment, the one feeling of which he was capable:

the fear that he had trapped himself inside the prison of his own power, that he could only grow larger, that no matter how much power he gained, the dissolution and chaos of his new condition would never change, and he could impose no order, no equilibrium that would satisfy his original wish to be both man and god, he could merely unify his environment—whether this consisted of a night club, Moscow, Russia, or entire planet—under the disordered banner of Eternity. His circumstance posed an intriguing intellectual and philosophical puzzle. Through his machinations, his alliances with generals and politicians and the *mafiyas*, might not Yuri be responsible for the chaos overwhelming the old Soviet states, or were the two forces feeding into one another? And if Yuri came to dominate the world or a substantial portion thereof, if he could avoid being absorbed by a creature like himself, but vaster and more cruel, would anyone notice? Was not the current chaos of the world all-pervasive, were not genocides and serial killings and natural disasters and the unending disregard of one soul for another sufficient evidence of this? And that being so, could it be possible that this chaos had always been the product of sad invisible monsters such as Yuri, a ruling class gone unnoticed by everyone except for saints and madmen...? Chemayev was amused by the formulation of these questions. He thought if he could sustain his awareness a while longer he might learn the answers, and they in turn would lead to subtler questions, the ones Yuri himself had asked, and if he could learn *those* answers, benefiting from Yuri's experience, he might be able to avoid Yuri's mistakes. But at the moment it didn't seem worth the effort. Blind now, all his senses occluded, uncertain of his location, even as to which plane of existence he occupied, by all rights he should have been more afraid; but having practiced death once before, and having since witnessed a condition worse than death, he felt prepared for anything.

On regaining consciousness Chemayev realized he was back in the garden. Considering the cautionary flavor of his previous experience and the circular pattern governing the evening, he had little doubt that March would soon put in an appearance, but nevertheless he found the bitter smell of Yuri's vegetation and the sound of water spurting from the broken fountain and the silver bar of light floating overhead solid and comforting by contrast to the emptiness through which he had passed. Surprised to find that he was still holding the nine-millimeter pistol, he tucked it into his waist and headed for the fountain, pushing aside black branches clustered with white leaves bearing scatters of inky characters—he wondered now if these might not be fragments of the formula that had made Yuri's transformation possible.

Once he reached the edge of the cobblestone circle

he stationed himself behind some bushes, a position from which he had a clear view of the fountain. The abstracted calm that had eased his passage from the corridor to the garden remained strong in him, and waiting went easily at first. With its black serene sky, the silver bar in place of a sun, the ruined fountain and eccentric forest, the place had a Mexican *Twilight Zone* ambience—like an old B-movie set awaiting its Dramatis Personae—that appealed to him. But as the minutes wore on his anxiety resurfaced. He chastised himself for not having given Yuri the money. The moment had been brief, the circumstances problematic. But everything he'd worked for had been on the line. He should have been up to it. Of course paying the money might have been a fruitless gesture. God only knew what was going on. It was apparent that he was being manipulated. Equally apparent that Polutin had a hand in things— hadn't he implied that he'd done business with Yuri? Perhaps he'd managed to sour the deal Chemayev had negotiated. One way or another, he'd just have to find another way to get the money to Yuri.

He became so enmeshed in worry he nearly failed to notice March on the opposite side of the circle, half-hidden in the bushes. Not shirtless as before. Wearing his leather trenchcoat. Chemayev aimed his pistol at him, but let the barrel drop. Killing him seemed the safest course, but he had no clue what the repercussions might be. It might be wise to feel things out. Risky, perhaps. But the pistol boosted his confidence. He tucked it back into the waist of his trousers, concealing it beneath his jacket, and stepped out onto the cobblestones.

"March!" he called.

March's head snapped toward him. "Viktor! Christ, what're you doing here?"

"What am I doing here? Just taking a stroll. What are you doing here?" As he spoke Chemayev recognized that their dialogue was roughly the mirror image of what they had said to one another on his previous adventure in the garden. He didn't know whether to take this for a good or a bad omen.

"I'm not sure how to answer that." March edged forward. "Frankly, I've been having myself one hell of a time. A fucking asylum would feel like a rest home after this place."

It hadn't occurred to Chemayev that anyone else might have been having experiences similar to his own; but judging by March's behavior he thought now this might be the case. The Irishman kept casting furtive looks to the side, as if expecting some menace to emerge from the bushes.

"This Yuri character . . ." March's right hand fluttered up; he rubbed the back of his head fitfully. "Did you keep your appointment with him?"

"Not yet," said Chemayev.

"If I were you I might give it a pass."

"You've seen him, then?"

March shook his head in the affirmative, then said, "I don't know. Maybe." He moved another step toward Chemayev. "I was talking to this old geezer. The guy looked like he'd spent the night in the boneyard kissing corpses. Filthy bugger! About seventy years old going on terminal. He claimed to be Yuri."

"You talked with him?"

"Naw, we stared into one another's eyes! Of course we talked."

"What did you talk about?"

An angry tightness in his voice, March said, "Oh, this and that. The rugby final, the roots of British oppression. Chatty bits." He had another quick glance behind him. "Do you know of a way out of here?"

March's agitation lifted Chemayev's spirits. "How about the way you came in?"

"Are you fucking with me, Viktor?" March walked purposefully toward him, stopping close to the fountain, about twenty feet away. "I need an ally. If you're not an ally, I may have to take a bite out of you." He had regained some of his self-assurance, as if the show of menace had been restorative. "I've had a number of unsettling experiences. A premonition of violence as well. Perhaps it's all in my head. I'm not a'tall sure someone didn't put something in my drink. But no matter that, I'm sensing a hostile vibe between us. Why would that be?"

Chemayev considered showing March the pistol, but

decided against it. Confrontation had not served him well the last time. "Work it out for yourself. I've got my own problems." He started to walk away, but March said, "Hang on, Viktor." He was holding a chrome-plated automatic with a taped grip.

Chemayev gawked at it. "Where did you get the gun?"

"Picked it up during my travels. I was feeling a touch inadequate after checking my own weapon. But now"—he hefted the gun, as if appreciating its weight—"now I'm feeling twice the man I ever was."

He urged Chemayev toward the fountain, had him sit on carved fragments at its base. Chemayev arranged himself carefully, adjusting his left hip so the pistol came loose in his waistband. In his thoughts he remarked again on the role reversal taking place. During their previous encounter he had been the anxious one, the one to ask about Yuri, the one to decide for confrontation. Perhaps all this pointed to a happier conclusion. But did March suspect what he suspected? He'd mentioned a premonition of violence. Chemayev was forced to assume that this premonition had involved the two of them.

"Do you fancy Irish music, Viktor?" March asked out of the blue, he sat down cross-legged about fifteen feet away. "Bands, you know. Rock 'n'roll."

"U-2," said Chemayev absently. "I like U-2."

"Jesus! U-2!" March launched into a simpering parody of "In The Name of Love," and then made a flatulent sound with his lips. "Bono Vox, my ass! That ball-less little prat! I'm talking about real Irish music. Like Van Morrison. Van the Man! Not some gobshite got up in a gold jockstrap."

"He's okay," Chemayev said.

"What the fuck do you mean, 'okay'? That's soul music, man! Ahh!" He made a dismissive gesture with the automatic. "That's what I get for trying to talk rock 'n'roll with a Russian. Your idea of music is some fat asshole playing folk songs on the lute."

Chemayev leaned back against the base of the fountain. Out of the corner of his eye he could see the arc of water spurting from the broken pipe; overhead, a great crossbeam broadcast a benign silvery radiance. Black trees with leafy prayer flags stretched toward the light, and the round gray stones beneath him seemed to be eddying in their concentric circles. He allowed the fingers of his right hand to brush the pistol grip beneath his jacket. His chances were fifty-fifty, he figured. About the same as ever.

"You look almost happy," March said. "Did you have the good thought?"

"Happy's not the word for it," said Chemayev.

"What am I missing, Viktor? You seem so at ease. It's not like you. Do you know something I should know, or is it the drugs have just kicked in?"

"I don't know shit," said Chemayev. "I've been

having a bad night, too. Someone's been playing games with me."

"Games," said March. "Yeah, that's my feeling." He cracked the knuckles of his free hand by making a fist. "Do you recall me mentioning the dealings I had with your Mister Polutin over in London? A terrible business. Couple of his boys got taken out. Well, not long after I was passing the evening with this Rastafarian bunch in a squat in Chelsea. I won't go into the whys and wherefores—suffice it to say, it was part of a complex proceeding. At any rate, I was feeling comfortable with things when I made the mistake of smoking a joint one of those savages handed me. I'm not sure what was in it, but from the extreme paranoia that resulted, I'm guessing it was angel dust. The idea was, I gather, to fuck me up sufficient so the Rastas could carve me. I had the suspicion it was Polutin's idea . . . though considering the relationship we've had since, I may be mistaken. But the drug, whatever it was, didn't have the desired effect." The barrel of the automatic drooped toward his knee. "Not that I wasn't sick as a fish. Fucking hell! I was feverish. My thoughts buzzing like flies. Patches of color swimming around me. My bones ached. I thought my heart was going to burst out its bottom like a soggy sack full of red milk. But the paranoia . . . it organized me somehow. I became a calm at the center of the storm of my symptoms. I could see everything in the room with wonderful clarity.

"There was eight of 'em. All licorice-skinned and snake-headed. Eyes agleam. Lounging in the doorways, sitting on sprung sofas. Trying to orchestrate my paranoia with their whispered talk. Streetlight washed through the busted-out windows, painting a shine on their faces and exposing the shit spray-painted on the walls. Designs, mostly. A variety of strange devices that had to do with that mongrel religion of theirs, but which spoke to me in a way unintended by the artist. I could read the future in those mazes of squiggly lines."

A slackness came into March's face, as if he'd been brought hard against the memory of a transcendent moment. Chemayev inched his hand beneath the flap of his jacket, touched the pistol grip with his fingertips.

"Have you ever been close to death, Viktor?" asked March. "I don't mean nearly dead. I'm talking about the way you're close to a woman when you're lying with her in the act of love and there's not an inch of air between you that isn't humming with sweet vibration. That's how it was that night. I was in death's arms, fucking her slow and easy, and she was fusing her power with mine. I could actually see the bitch. She had a sleek silver face with a catlike Asian cast. The mask of a demoness. The silver moved as supplely as flesh to make her wicked smiles. Her hair was white, long and fine, and her breasts were corpse-pale, the nipples purplish. Like poison berries. When she opened her mouth I saw a silver word embossed on her black tongue. A character in the language I spoke before I was born, telling me it was time to act. That if I took action at that precise second, I'd come through the ordeal."

In his distraction March's pale face had an aspect of long-preserved youth, like that of a revivified mummy; the licks of black hair falling over his brow looked like absences in his flesh.

"When I drew my gun," he went on, "I was inside death. Hot and slick with her. Her legs locked about my waist, fingernails stabbing my back. Both of us screaming with release. I had six bullets, and every one went true. Six head shots. Their dreadlocks hissed and snapped, their eyes rolled up like horses' eyes. One of the survivors came at me with a machete, and I killed him with my hands. The last one fled." He ran the barrel of the automatic idly along his thigh. "That was strange enough, but what happened next was stranger yet. I was standing there, reviewing my work. Stoned as a fucking goose, I was. Reading the bloody sentences newly written on the walls. Obituaries of the recently deceased. Tributes to my marksmanship. When I turned my head, following the red script of those shattered lives, I found death was still with me. I'd assumed she was an ordinary hallucination, that she'd served her purpose and moved on. But there she stood, posed like Hell's calendar girl with hands on hips and one leg cocked, smiling at me. I'd only seen her close up before. Only been witness to half her beauty. The silvery stuff of her face flowed in sinuous curves to embellish her arms and legs. Silver flourishes coiled down her hips and framed her secret hair, which was trimmed to the shape of seven snakes standing on their tails. She beckoned to me, and I couldn't resist. I lay with her once again."

Chemayev had succeeded in securing a firm grasp on the pistol; but recalling March's quickness, he didn't trust the steadiness of his hand.

"It was a fool's act," March said, "to be coupling with what half my mind believed to be a product of madness. Especially with the dead lying around us, souls still tangled in their flesh. But I was in thrall. Her musk coated my tongue, her sweat formed a silvery sheen on my skin. My eyes went black with staring through the slits of her eyes into the thoughtless place beyond. She whispered to me. Not words of love, but a sibilant breath that entered through my ear and slithered into all my hollows, making an icy shape inside me. She stayed with me until the sky paled and flies began to gather like early fishermen at the edges of the spills of blood. But she never truly left me. I've seen her time and again since that night. Whenever trouble's near she comes to guide my arm." He gave Chemayev a sideways look. "I've seen her tonight."

"Maybe you're mistaken. It could have been one of Yuri's girls. They like to dress up." Chemayev thought if it weren't for the plash of water behind him, he would be able to hear the beating of his heart.

"I've seen her tonight," March repeated. "But I'm not so sure she's with me this time." He paused. "What do you think of my story, Viktor?"

"You mean apart from the obvious pathology?"

"Always ready to spit in the devil's eye." March lowered his head and chuckled. "You remind me of myself as a lad."

Chemayev's hand tightened on the pistol, but he failed to seize the opportunity.

"You probably think I'm having you on," said March, and was about to say more, when Chemayev, his patience for this game exhausted, broke in: "I don't know what you've got in mind, but I doubt you understand the implications of your story."

"And I suppose you're bursting to enlighten me?"

"Sure. Why not?" said Chemayev. "The idea that a man who's accustomed to violence, who thrives on it, has come to rely on a fictive alliance with death . . . with a comic book image of death . . ."

"All alliances are fictive," said March. "Haven't you figured that one out?"

Chemayev ignored the interruption. "The fact you've created an imaginary playmate to help enable your violence—even if just in a story—that implies slippage. Weakness."

March's face emptied. "Weakness is it?"

"What else? Maybe it's a touch of guilt. Some old flutter of religion. Something that demands you create a quasi-mystical justification for actions you previously considered utilitarian."

"Quasi-mystical." March blew air through his lips like a horse. "That cuts deep, Viktor, It's a brand I'm not sure I can bear. Especially coming from a featherless little chirper like yourself."

It seemed to Chemayev that March was fast approaching a moment of decision, a moment when he'd be preoccupied, all his attention focused on the possible consequences arising from the exercise of his anger, and as a result, for a fraction of a second he'd be slow to react.

"It may be a product of age," Chemayev said. "Your increasing awareness of mortality."

"Let it rest," said March. "Seriously."

"The brain could be in the early stages of decomposition. Logic decaying into fantasy, gasses collecting in the skull."

"Do you hear what I'm telling you, boy?"

"It must look like a fucking swamp in there." Chemayev tapped the side of his head. "Methane seeping from rotten stumps, gray scraps of tissue hanging down like moss. The brain a huge pale cheese wreathed in mist, rising from the black water. The creatures of your imagination peeping from its fissures. Most of them bullshit versions of yourself."

"You bloody little piss merchant! Shut the fuck up!"

"Bruce Lee March, Dylan Thomas March, Charlie

Manson March. Niall the Catholic Fishboy, old Father McConnell's favorite sweet. And let's not forget your masterpiece: Death. Based, I imagine, on some pimply little squinch who wouldn't let you have a bite of her muffin back in trade school. When the mists get really thick, they all pick up banjos and sing 'Toora Loora Loora.'"

"That's enough!" said March.

"You know, there's every chance you've developed a tumor. Brain cancer's known to cause delusions. Or maybe it's early Alzheimer's. You might want to get yourself checked out."

March's nearly colorless eyes appeared to lighten further, as if the black shadow of his soul had shrunk to a more compact shape, pulling back from his skin, and Chemayev, feeling certain the moment had arrived, slid the pistol from beneath his jacket and shot him twice in the chest.

The bullets twisted March, flipped him fishlike onto his side; the detonations blended with and seemed to enlarge his outcry. His feet kicked in sequence as if he were trying to walk away from the pain. He was still clutching the automatic; he fumbled with the trigger guard, the barrel wobbled down, the muzzle lodging between two cobblestones. He strained to lift it, his eyebrows arching with effort. The heightened pallor of his skin and the bright blood filming his lips gave him the look of an actor in a Kabuki drama. Chemayev finished him with a bullet to the temple.

He dropped the pistol onto the cobblestones. He had no remorse—March had intended to kill him, hadn't he?—but he was tired, desperately tired, and he felt an odd internal instability, as if the spiritual vacuum created by the death, the instantaneous decompression, had sheared off part of his soul and the remaining portion, now too small for the body it inhabited, was tipping this way and that like the air bubble in a carpenter's level. He sat down awkwardly, one leg sticking out, the other folded beneath him. Streams of March's blood fingered among the stones—Chemayev imagined them to be a cluster of gray environmental domes in a crimson flood, a mining colony amid the lava flows of Venus. The sound of the splashing water grew louder, troubling his head. He pressed his fingers to his brow, closed his eyes. Fuck. What next? Where did he stand with Larissa? With Yuri and Polutin? He had the suspicion none of it mattered anymore. The victor in this contrived war between himself and March would be trapped forever with an undecaying corpse on the stage set of a magical western, condemned to a limbo in which he would feed on deathly beetles and drink bitter water from a fountain whose splashing kept growing louder and louder. Becoming incredibly, irrationally loud. It was beginning to sound almost like applause. . . . He opened his eyes. Blinked rapidly due to the unaccustomed brightness. Then scrambled to his feet. The body was gone, the fountain was gone, the stones, the trees, it was all gone, and he was standing on the stage of Eternity's theater, tiers of white leather booths rising on every side into swirling fog, the elegantly attired men and women looking down at him, clapping and cheering. Stricken, overwhelmed by this latest transition, he turned in a circle, hoping to find a point of orientation, something that would explain, that would clarify. He caught sight of Polutin. The big man was standing in the aisle, his head tipped back, belly thrust out, applauding with such ponderous sincerity that Chemayev half-expected to see a ringmaster urging him on with a whip in one hand, a piece of raw fish in the other. On unsteady legs, giddy with the aftershocks of violence, stunned by all he saw, he made his way up from the stage and along the aisle and let Polutin guide him into the booth.

"Why did you take so long? What's wrong with you?" Polutin frowned at him, exasperated; but then he patted Chemayev's knee, the brisk gesture of someone ready to put the past behind them. "You did well," he said. "You may not think so now, but you'll see it eventually." In his sloppy; drink-reddened face was a bearish measure of self-satisfaction that seemed to answer all questions concerning his involvement in the evening's events; but Chemayev was unable to process the information. There was too much to think about. Just the idea that he and March had been part of the entertainment suggested a labyrinthine complexity of physical and metaphysical relationships sufficient on its own to confound him. And the odd certitude he had felt immediately prior to shooting March, the correspondences between that feeling and March's story about death—what could be made of that? For the life of him, he could not even recall how he had come to this moment. The road that led from a village along the Dvina was easy to follow up to the point he and Nicolai arrived in Moscow, but thereafter it was broken, gapped, and once it entered the darkness of Eternity, everything that had previously been easy to follow came, in retrospect, to seem unfathomable. Polutin began prattling on about a meeting scheduled for the next day with his Italian associates, and the talk of business calmed Chemayev. He tried to achieve a perspective, to reorder the universe according to Chemayevian principles, but the image of March intruded. Another ghost to join that of Nicolai. Not so much guilty baggage attached to this one. Though for a vicious killer, March hadn't been such a bad guy. A slant of wild hilarity broke through his mental overcast. Someday they'd say the same about him.

The background music changed—a saccharine swell of violins flowing into a romantic brocade of darker strings, French horns, trumpets. "Aha!" Polutin said. "The auction!" Disinterested, Chemayev glanced toward the stage. And sat bolt upright. Emerging from the center of the stage, borne upward on a circular platform, was Larissa. Naked. Carrying a silver tray on which lay a single long-stemmed rose. Their eyes met and she looked hurriedly away. Waiting for her on the stage, his thinning hair slicked down, natty in a white suit, holding a microphone, was one of Yuri's portly doubles. "LADIES AND GENTLEMEN!" he said, and with a florid gesture directed the general attention to Larissa. "THE ROSE!"

As Larissa walked up the aisle, serene in her nakedness, several men shouted bids, which were duly noted by Yuri's double, who plodded along behind her. When she reached Polutin's booth she stopped and trained her eyes on a point above Chemayev's head. Her expression was unreadable.

Chemayev said weakly, "Larissa?"

She betrayed no sign of having heard; he saw nothing but reflected dazzles in the darks of her eyes.

Polutin's arm dropped onto his shoulder. "So, Viktor. How much are you bidding?"

Uncomprehending, Chemayev looked at him, then at Larissa. The stoniness of her face in contrast with the soft vulnerability of her breasts and the gentle swell of her belly seemed to restate the conflict between what he hoped and what he feared. He had the impulse to take off his coat and cover her, but he didn't move a muscle. "I don't have any money," he said to Polutin. "Not for this. I have some, but . . . I . . . ." He looked again to Larissa. "Why aren't you at the bar?" He reached for her hand but she pulled away.

"Don't." Her chin trembled. "Don't touch me. Just do what you have to and let me go."

"What's happened? Larissa, please!" Chemayev made as though to slide out of the booth but Polutin caught his arm.

"Be very careful," he said. "I can't save you from this."

Chemayev shook him off, leaned across the table to Larissa. "For God's sake! I still have the money. All of it. What's wrong?"

Yuri's double moved between them, stared at him dispassionately, his thick lips pursed. "You refused to pay," he said. "You broke the contract. Now"—he shrugged—"you can either bid or you can remain here until your debt is paid."

"My debt? I don't owe you. . . ."

"The price of the woman," said the double. "You broke the contract, you forfeit her price."

A tiny nebula of platinum and emeralds glinted among the tangles of Larissa's dark hair. Someone must have given her new earrings. In the silvery light her nipples showed candy pink, her skin milky. A mole the size of a .22 caliber bullet hole on the small of her back above the high, horsey ride of her buttocks. Chemayev realized he was cataloguing these details, filing them away, as if he'd have to remember them for a long time.

"What can I do?" he asked her. "Isn't there anything . . . ?"

"Leave me alone," she said.

His desperation and confusion knitted into a third

emotion, something akin to anger but imbued with the sort of hopeless frustration an insect might feel when, after an enduring struggle, it has freed itself from a spiderweb only to fall into an empty jelly glass, where it is peered at by the incurious eyes of an enormous child. Chemayev's hand dropped to the money belt but he did not remove it.

"Make up your mind," said the double. "There are others who may wish to bid."

Chemayev had difficulty unbuttoning his shirt. His fingers felt thick and bloodless, and the inside of his head compacted, as if stuffed with gray rags. Stripping off the belt took an inordinately long time—it seemed to cling to his waist. Finally he managed it. The double grabbed the belt and gave it a shake. "There can't be much here," he said.

"Four million," said Chemayev emptily.

"Four million rubles?" The double scoffed at the figure. "The bid's already much higher than that."

"Dollars," Chemayev said. "It's in gold certificates."

Polutin was aghast. "Four million dollars? Where did you get such a sum?"

"I didn't steal from you. I played the German market. The Dax."

Polutin lifted his glass in salute. "And I thought I was familiar with all your talents."

"FOUR MILLION!" The double roared into his microphone. "VIKTOR CHEMAYEV BIDS FOUR MILLION DOLLARS!"

The assemblage began to cheer wildly, shouts of "Bravo!", fists pounding the tables, women shrieking. Chemayev put his elbows on the table, rested his head in his hands.

"Here," said Larissa, her voice like ashes. She thrust out the rose to him, the bloom nodding stupidly in his face, a knurl of convulsed crimson. He was unable to make sense of the thing. He tried to connect with her again, and when she looked away this time, his eyes ranged over her body like a metal detector over a snowy field, registering the fullness of her thighs, the razor-cut strip of pubic hair, the swollen underside of a breast. The least of her human details—she had withdrawn all else. She dropped the rose onto the block of ice. The bloom nestled against an empty bottle of Ketel One. Melting ice dripped onto the petals. Yuri's double took Larissa by the arm and escorted her toward the stage.

"It might be best for you to leave, Viktor," Polutin said. "Take the morning off. Come see me in my office around three. And be prepared for a difficult negotiation. These Italians will screw us good if they can."

Chemayev laboriously pushed himself up from the booth. People were continuing to cheer, to talk excitedly about the size of the bid. On stage Yuri sailed one of the gold certificates into the air where it burst into flames; the fire assumed the shape of a pair of flickering wings and then flew apart into a flurry of small orange birds. With gasps and delighted cries, the crowd marveled at what they assumed was a trick, but might well have been something more extraordinary. Yuri bowed, then sailed another of the certificates high—it floated above the heads of the crowd, expanding into a sunburst, becoming a stylized golden mask like the representation of the benign east wind on a medieval map. Golden coins sprayed from its mouth. One of the coins was plucked out of mid-air by a pale dark-haired man wearing a leather trenchcoat. Chemayev had only the briefest glimpse of him before he vanished in the swarm of people scrambling for the coins, but he could have sworn it was March. Niall your fucking Welcome Wagon March, the rage of Kilmorgan, the pale Gombeen Man. Chemayev could not sustain interest in the implications fostered by March's possible presence, but he wondered about the man. Who the hell had March been, anyway? What he said he was, who he variously seemed, or a surprise waiting behind the game show's mystery door?

"Come a little before three," said Polutin. "That way we'll be sure to have time to talk."

As Chemayev turned to leave he noticed the rose. Contact with the cold had darkened the edges of several petals, but it remained an alluring complexity, vividly alive against the backdrop of ice and white linen. After a moment's hesitation he picked it up. Chances were he would only throw it away, but considering the cost, he wanted no one else to claim it.

Outside, the snow was no longer falling. Long thin curves of windblown powder lay across the asphalt like the ghosts of immense talons; white crusts shrouded the windshields of the surrounding cars. Chemayev sat at the wheel of his Lada, the engine idling, wipers clearing a view of the bunkerlike entrance to Eternity. In the morning, he thought. In the morning when Larissa went to school he'd meet her at the door and ask why she had treated him so coldly. Was it simply because he'd failed her? Maybe they'd threatened her, lied to her. Whatever the reason, he'd be honest. Yes, he'd say, I fucked up. But it's this place that's mostly to blame, this broken down ex-country. Nothing good can happen here. I'm going to set things right and once we get away I'll be the man you believed in, the one who loves you. . . . Even as he rehearsed this speech he recognized its futility, but the plug of nothingness that had stoppered his emotions during the auction had worked itself loose, the speedball of failure and rejection had worn off, and all the usual passions and compulsions were sparking in him again.

A gaunt, gray-haired man in a tattered overcoat stumbled into his field of vision. One of the *krushova* dwellers, holding a nearly empty bottle of vodka. He lurched against the hood of a Jaguar parked in the row across from Chemayev, slumped onto the fender, then righted himself and took a pull from the bottle. He wiped his mouth, stared blearily at the Lada, and flung out his arm as if shooing away a dog or an annoying child. "Fuck off," said Chemayev, mostly to himself. The man repeated the gesture, and Chemayev thought that perhaps he had not been gesturing at him, perhaps he'd been summoning reinforcements. Dozens . . . no, hundreds of similarly disheveled figures were shambling toward him among the ranks of gleaming cars. Bulky women with moth-eaten sweaters buttoned wrong; men in duct-tape-patched hooded parkas, ruined faces peering grimly through portholes lined with synthetic fur; others in ill-fitting uniform jackets of various types; one in rubber boots and long johns. Shadowy drabs and drudges coming from every corner of the lot, as if they were phantoms conjured from the asphalt, as if the asphalt were the black meniscus of Yuri's brimful kingdom. Clinging to one another for support on the icy ground like the remnants of a routed army. Drunk on defeat. They stationed themselves along the row, all glaring at Chemayev, each with a charcoal mouth and ink drop eyes, faces with the ridged, barren asymmetry of terrain maps, the background figures in an apocalypse by Goya come to life, each beaming at him a black fraction of state-approved, party-sponsored enmity. Yuri's state. Yuri's party.

Less frightened than repelled, Chemayev drew a pistol from his shoulder holster, rolled down the window, and fired into the air. Instead of fleeing they edged forward, clumsy and tentative as zombies, confused by the brightness of life but full of stuporous menace. What did they intend to do? he wondered. Curse him? Puke on him? He poked his head out the window and aimed the pistol at the closest of them, a balding man whose seventy-inch-waist trousers appeared to support his upper half like a dessert cup filled with two scoops of yellowish cream pudding, the smaller topped by sparse hanks of white hair like shredded coconut, his sweatshirt proclaiming allegiance to the Central Soviet hockey team. He displayed no fear. And why should he? Who'd be fool enough to kill one of Yuri's people? Perhaps he was dead already. Chemayev ducked back into the car. Set the pistol on the dash. He had surrendered so much, he stubbornly refused to admit this last formal measure of defeat. But then the army of the *krushovas* came shuffling forward again and he understood that he had neither the confidence nor the force of arms to stand against them. He shifted the Lada into gear and pulled out along the row, going slowly to avoid hitting the shabby creatures who stood everywhere throughout the lot. They pressed close as he passed, like animals in a preserve, peeking in through the windows, and he had a surge of panic ... not true fright, but a less disabling emotion fueled by a shameful recognition of his relationship to these lusterless clots of anti-life, these exhibits in the existential sideshow. Sons and Daughters of the Soil. Old ragged male monsters with the hammer-and-sickle stamped on every cell of their bodies. Boring meat-eaters, ferocious farters, grunters, toilers, industrial oxen, blank-eyed suet-brained party trolls. Old lion-faced women with gray hair sprouting from every pore, ugly with the crap they'd eaten all their lives, their filth-encrusted nails as strong as silicon, breeding warmonger babies in their factory wombs, dead now like empty hangars, cobwebbed, with wheelmarks in the dust. . . . You couldn't hate them, that'd be the same as hating yourself, you could only say goodbye to all their grim Russian soul shit. You had to cut it out of yourself some-how, you had to sit down and pinch a roll of fat and slide a knife in, probe for that special Russian organ that made you such a bear for suffering, that prompted you to sit up with your mouth open when God came round with his funnel and his tube of black bile to forcefeed all the Russian as-yet-unborns he was fattening for some conflagration on the far side of infinity. You had to put some distance between yourself and this dirt with its own soul that reached up through the bottoms of your feet and moved you like a finger puppet. You had to find some way not to be like these relics, even if that meant killing the most vital part of your spirit. You had to run to America, you had to drown in its trivialities, bathe in its chrome wavelengths until all the scum of Mother Russia was washed off your skin, until your pores were so open the black oily essence of your birthright came seeping out like juice from a cracked bug. That's what you had to do. That was the only thing that could save you. But it was probably not possible.

Once clear of the *krushovas* Chemayev accelerated along the access road leading to the Garden Ring. Headlights penetrated the Lada, revealing patched brown plaid seat covers, a littered dash, bent ashtray stuffed with candy wrappers. The radio dial flickered, the heater whined and yielded up a smell of burning rubber. The crummy familiarity of the car consoled him, molding itself to him like a friendly old chair. He wanted a cigarette, but Larissa had made him quit. Shit. He rapped the top of the steering wheel with the heel of his hand. Not angrily. A call-to-order rap, a wake-up notice. He banished the feeling of unsoundness that had plagued him most of the night, took stock of his reserves. He pictured them straggled across a parade ground, the survivors of a force that had once numbered four million. He'd have to start over. He'd have to put tonight behind him. Approach tomorrow as if everything were normal. He'd permit himself to make no goals, not even where Larissa was concerned. He'd simply do his job and see what developed. He sped out onto the Garden Ring, merging with the stream of traffic headed for the city center. There was an ache in his chest that seemed part bruise, part constriction, and he knew it would worsen during the weeks ahead. Whenever he stopped for a solitary drink or tried to sleep it would send out fresh tendrils of pain, seeding despair and distraction; but he'd overcome those enemies before, and he could do it again, he would rise to the challenge. That was half of life, the way you dealt with challenges. Maybe more than half. It occurred to him, and not for the first time, that his obsession with Larissa was partially fueled by the challenge she presented, but as always he refused to diminish the purity he accorded the relationship by defining it as a logical consequence of his compulsiveness. He brushed the idea aside, concentrated on the road, and soon his mind began to tick along with its customary efficiency, plotting the day ahead. Call Larissa. See where things stood with her. Then business. What had Polutin said? The Italians. His office. Chemayev decided to set his alarm for eleven o'clock. That should give him plenty of time. No, he thought. Better play it safe. He'd set the alarm for ten. It would not do to be late.

WOLVES TILL THE WORLD GOES DOWN

GREG VAN EEKHOUT

MY BROTHER AND I flew recon over the gray Santa Monica beach, half-frozen rain striking our black feathers. Below, a skater swaddled in Gore-Tex swished around the curves of the bike path, while surfers in wetsuits bobbed in the dark waters.

It was the coldest winter on record in southern California. It was the coldest winter everywhere.

"Hey," said my brother. "Down there." Without waiting, he dove toward the sand where a dead Rottweiler rolled in the white foam. It had been a long flight and we were both ravenous. I angled in to follow, and soon we were absorbed in our feast.

A big gray gull challenged our salvage rights, screaming and beating us with his wings, but we tore him to shreds, ate him, then returned to the dog.

Later, my brother would be able to report every little

detail of the incident. He'd describe the precise markings on the gull's bill, the way he favored his left foot over his right, the iron and salt taste of his blood.

But he wouldn't be able to say *why* we'd killed him. He's expert at the *whats* and *whens* and *wheres*, but he leaves the *whys* to me.

His name is Munin, Memory. I'm Hugin, Thought.

Our hunger satisfied, we took to the skies again and continued south over the T-shirt shops and sunglass stands of Venice Boardwalk. When we reached the storm-shattered pier, we turned seaward, onward, away and beyond.

We heard a blue whale sing its last song before dying of old age. We watched an undiscovered species of fish go extinct. And we saw something enormous on the ocean floor, slithering on its belly and churning waves hundreds of fathoms above.

We flew and flew, carefully observing and cataloguing so that later we could give our boss, Odin, an accurate report. But first we had a special appointment to keep.

Well past the horizons of Midgard we came upon the shores of the dead. Hel is a dry place. It's a land of gray plains and twigs and dust. And in the center of this land there lived a pair of slain gods. We found them reclining atop the roof of a great timber hall, passing a cup back and forth.

The poets used to say that Baldr was so good and

pure he radiated white light, a sun compressed into human form. There used to be something about him, something that, when he walked by, made a man put down his drinking horn or stop hammering trolls for a second and just be glad he was alive to witness the moment. You knew that Baldr, somehow, was what the whole thing was about.

He was still beautiful, but not the same. Now he was cold and magisterial, a god of glaciers and dark stone mountains. He rose to his feet and announced our arrival to his brother.

Höd was a much humbler creature, thinner in the shoulder, longer in the face, his shriveled eyes lost in dark sockets. You really didn't want to look into those sockets. They went a long way down.

We landed on Baldr's outstretched forearms and dug our talons in a little to see if he'd flinch. He didn't, of course. Even exiled from the realms of the living, he was still a god. "Just when I was thinking you wouldn't come," he said. "I'm glad to see you. Let's go inside."

Getting welcomed to Hel isn't such an enormous thrill, but I politely thanked him anyway.

His hall was cold and dimly lit. Pale flames wavered in the hearth, their light barely pushing back the shadows. A long table bore a modest feast—a few loaves of bread, a pair of emaciated roast pigs.

Munin perched on the edge of the table and appraised the fare. "I guess it's a good thing we already ate."

Höd's jaw muscles clenched. "If you'd like to contribute to the meal, I can start plucking feathers right now."

Baldr laughed. "Brother," he said in his gentle voice, "we observe hospitality in my house."

I think Höd would have rolled his eyes had he been capable.

At the end of the table sat a plump old woman in a purple sweatshirt. The shopping cart beside her was filled with empty soup cans, magazines, rotting batteries, a sword hilt, a broken car antenna. Over her matted gray hair she wore a Minnesota Vikings cap. She clutched a long twig in her left hand.

"Sibyl," I said, nodding respectfully. I hadn't seen the witch-prophetess in a long time. Not since the world was younger and greener, when, in exchange for a meal, she'd told Odin how the world would end.

"There is an ash tree," she said now. "It's name is Yggdrasil. Lofty Yggdrasil, the Ash Tree, trembles, ancient wood groaning."

Not knowing if she was uttering an incantation or just making conversation, I indicated the twig with my wing. "Is that part of Yggdrasil?"

She shook the stick. "The world tree's an ash. Does this look like ash? Stupid bird."

Same old sibyl.

We sat around the table and picked at the skinny pigs for a while before Baldr asked us about affairs back in the land of men. Normally we report only to Odin, but how often do you get invited to Baldr's house? So Munin spoke of the weather on Midgard. Three winters, each colder and longer than the previous one, with little summer between. Floods, bad crops, people freezing in the streets, hoarding and price gouging and rioting and looting.

But Munin didn't say the *word*.

He didn't have to.

We all knew where this was heading; Ragnarök. The great monsters would do battle with the gods, and most of the gods would be slain. Heimdall. Hermod. Frey. Thor. Even Odin. A world without Odin. And the world itself would burn and crumble, and the ancient chaos that preceded us all would return. But from the ashes would rise the younger gods, and Baldr and Höd would end their exile in Hel to help them rebuild.

Munin went on and on, citing wind chill factors from CNN until Baldr put an end to his chatter. "Thank you, Munin," he said. "Most thorough. My father is lucky to have your counsel." He turned his gray eyes to me. "And you, Hugin, what will you tell Odin when next you see him?"

As if you didn't know, I almost said. But being Odin's agent has taught me to reflect before I speak. I'd play along for now. "I can tell you of two brothers," I said. "Like you and Höd, two sons of Odin." And there, in a vast dry hall situated at the center of Hel, with the sibyl worrying her twig, I told Baldr about an attempt to end the world.

Munin and I had watched the godling sons of Odin sail for many days and nights before they came to an island between worlds. As they neared the shore, Vidar threw the anchor over, jumped out and waded toward the beach. He was much like his father, lean and rangy with a voice that rarely rose above a dry whisper.

Vali was different. Forever a toddler, he scrambled over the gunwale and belly-flopped into the waves, thrashed about as he realized his feet couldn't touch the stony sea bottom, then gave a mighty kick that sent him flying through the air and onto the beach.

"Did you see?" he said, delighted. "I almost drowned!"

Vidar brushed sand off his half-brother's bottom. "I saw."

"I could have been killed!"

"Yes, you came perilously close to an untimely demise. Please follow, Vali. We have a task."

The beach sloped up sharply from the tide toward a towering wall of jagged basalt. The gods began to hike up the rise.

"Vidar, I'm hungry."

"Possibly because you didn't eat your supper?"

"Dried fish. I hate dried fish. I hate all fish."

"If I give you a piece of candy, will you be quiet?"

"No."

Vidar sighed-and gave him a piece of candy anyway. All the gods in Asgard knew it was easier if you didn't anger Vali.

They reached the rock wall and began to climb.

"Vidar, tell me a story."

"Now is not the best time."

Vali pouted. "You better tell me a story, or I'll rip open your tummy and pull all the tubes out, and then I'll choke you with the tubes, and then I'll make you eat the tubes, and then I'll—"

Vidar closed his eyes. "Once upon a time there was—"

"There was a god named Baldr," Vali cut in. "And Frigg, his momma, loved him, and everybody loved him, and he was always very nice. So Frigg got everything in the world to make a promise—all the animals and flowers and birds and *everything*—she asked everything to promise to never, ever, *ever* hurt Baldr."

A gust of wind picked up an unpleasant scent. Fur. Damp animal fur. Vidar continued the tale. "As you said, Vali, Mother Frigg exacted an oath from fire and water and metal and stones, and from earth and trees and beasts, from ailments and birds and poisons and serpents. She wrung a promise from every conceivable thing that it would do Baldr no harm. All except a young plant growing on the very skirts of Asgard, a small sprig of mistletoe. She felt it too small to be of any consequence."

Vali's grip slipped and he tumbled until a rock broke his fall. Vidar climbed down and retrieved him. "We don't have time for this," he said. "Climb on my back." They renewed the ascent, Vali riding piggyback.

"And so a game arose around Baldr's invulnerability," said Vidar. "He would stand at the highseat during assemblies, and the gods would hurl objects at him. Stones, spears, cauldrons of boiling water, wasp nests— all bounced off him and did no harm."

"But then Loki got all mad!" interrupted Vali. "And he put on ladies' clothes and tricked Frigg into telling him about the mistletoe. And there was Höd, and he was blind, and he couldn't play along, and Loki said, 'How come you're not playing?' And Höd said, 'I'm blind! They won't let me play.' And Loki said, 'That's not fair.' And he gave Höd the mistletoe, and said, 'Throw it! Throw it!' And Höd goes, 'I'm blind! I can't aim good.' But Loki helped him throw, and . . . and . . ."

"Catch your breath, brother. And try not to choke me."

"Your turn!"

Vidar crested the wall and peered over the summit. In the center of the island loomed a great, dark shape. The son of Odin swallowed and began his descent down the other side of the wall. Vali leaped off his back and scrambled after him.

"I said it's your turn, Vidar."

Vidar's mouth set in a grim line. "The mistletoe

pierced Baldr's breast," he said. "And it was . . . it was horrible. How can I tell you what it was like? You never saw him, brother. The skalds say he was beautiful, but it was more than that. You know how when you look at Thor, he's like a great dark thundercloud stepped down from the sky to assume human shape. And Njord, he's like the sea itself, tidal waves crashing in his eyes. Baldr was like that. Only he personified everything that was . . . I don't know, good? Worthwhile?" Vidar paused there, hanging off the side of the rock wall, his face haunted. Even Vali took notice and preserved the silence. Then, finally, Vidar said, "He died. Right there in front of all of us. You could almost see the world change color. Nobody knew what to say or what to do. And the next day, we put him in his ship and sent him off to Hel. That's the last any of us saw of him. And ever since we've been living out the sibyl's prophecy. We, the great and mighty Aesir. Puppets."

Something at the foot of the wall made a noise. A low growl, a clank of metal.

"Come on," said Vidar. "Let's cut some strings." They jumped the last twenty feet to the ground. Vidar drew his sword and led the way to a shadowy, massive form chained to a boulder. It turned its blue, liquid eyes to the brothers and watched them approach.

"But you didn't tell the good part of the story," Vali wailed. "The part when All-Father Odin got mad at Höd for killing Baldr, because he loved Baldr best of anybody, so he and my momma had me, and when I was just one day old I jumped on Höd's chest and I put my arms around his throat and squeezed and squeezed and squeezed, and then he was dead and he had to go to Hel, too. You didn't tell that part."

"You told it very well, Vali. Now let's finish our job."

"Was she pretty?"

"Was *who* pretty?"

"My momma. Was she pretty?"

"Vali, she was a giant."

Vali stopped walking, his lip curling into a snarl.

Vidar sighed. "All right. All right. Words are insufficient to describe her gigantic beauty. She was the most lovely giantess that ever was. Yes? Will that do?"

That satisfied Vali. The little god squared his shoulders, puffed out his chest, and took the lead toward the monster at the center of the island.

Viewed head-on, the wolf was merely the size of an adult grizzly bear. But if you squinted just so and looked at it through the corner of your eye, it was larger. Larger than the island that contained it, large enough to dwarf the mountains, to swallow the sun and the moon.

Vidar put a hand on his brother's shoulder, holding him firm. "This is Fenrir Lokisson, the wolf. He and I are destined to do battle at Ragnarök. And I will kill him. But not before he destroys the sky."

The wolf's jaws were propped open by a sword, and its legs were bound by a silk ribbon connected by a chain to a boulder.

Vidar raised his sword high in the air. The wolf stared at him placidly, his slow breaths sending clouds of steam into the gloom.

The ribbon binding him was made of six true things, from the roots of a mountain to the breath of a fish.

But Vidar's sword was made of seven.

He brought the sword down, parting the air with a thunderclap and sending up a shower of sparks as the blade cut through the ribbon. Then he gingerly removed the sword gag from the wolf's mouth. One day, Fenrir would devour Vidar's own father. And now he was free.

"Kill him!" screamed Vali. "Give me the sword!" The child god lunged at the wolf, but Vidar grabbed him by the arms, restraining him.

Fenrir bowed his great back, stretched his forelegs out and yawned. He shook dust from his tail, then turned to Vidar. His mouth formed something of a smile. "That was unexpected. Why set me loose?"

Vidar shrugged. "We're tired of sitting around waiting for Ragnarök to happen."

"Ah," said the wolf. "I think I get it. Why wait for the fulfillment of the prophecy when you can ignite it yourself? Hasten the destruction of several billion men, trolls, elves, giants, gods, horses, dogs, what have you. Usher in a sea of blood and fire and pain the likes of which not even Odin can fully imagine. Just so you and your brother and the other little godlings can step out of the wings and take charge of the remains now. A plot worthy of Loki."

"Actually," said Vidar, "I was just anxious to get to the part of the story where I kill you."

"I'll see you later, then," said Fenrir with a laugh. He leaped into the sky, momentarily eclipsing the moon, before vanishing into the dark.

The gods started back to the boat, and Munin and I circled overhead for a time, watching them.

"Well," I said to Munin. "What do you think about that?"

He flapped his wings twice to gain altitude. "Thinking's your department."

With the shadows deepening in Baldr's hall, Höd picked at the scant remains of the pig on his platter and shook his head. "It seems entirely unacceptable to me that a psychopathic little toddler is due to inherit the world after the Great Battle."

"Is that an objective opinion?" I asked. "That has nothing to do with the fact that Vali slew you?"

"It has *everything* to do with the fact that he slew me! If I wrung your feathered neck today, would you want to sit in council with me tomorrow? What kind of working relationship would that be?"

I turned to Baldr. "Maybe you could answer that question. What do you make of it when Aesir try to bring about the end of one world, just so they can hurry up and start ruling over the next?" I so badly wanted Baldr to say he found it reprehensible. I wanted him to

be angry with the young gods. I wanted him to tell me
he wasn't like them at all.

He regarded me with an almost cynical smile. On his
face, it was a sad thing to see. "Those gods are Odin's
progeny. The same as Thor or Höd or myself. They're
doing what we're all doing, what we've done for
thousands of years—playing their role in this hideous
prophecy. Only they realized it was possible to accelerate
the process. I admire their initiative. It's something we've
lacked for too long."

My feathers bristled. "They should be patient," I argued. "All they have to do is wait and they'll get what
they want. Let things happen in the way they were
meant to happen. The world ends, the gods and monsters
fight, and the young gods inherit a new earth. They
don't appreciate what a privilege that will be, to rule
over something new and fresh and green. They don't
appreciate what an honor that is." And now I looked
hard into Baldr's gray eyes. "It's wrong to interfere with
the prophecy."

The corners of Baldr's mouth curved up in a small
smile. Folding his ice white hands on the table before
him, he said, "What do you do, Hugin?"

I shifted my weight from one foot to the other and
cocked my head sideways. "What do you mean?"

"I mean what do you *do*? You fly around and watch
and analyze and calculate, and you whisper intelligence
in Odin's ear. But do you actually *do* anything?" The

hall had grown colder by many degrees as Baldr spoke. "Why do you judge those who have the courage to act, when you, Thought, have only the courage to think?"

Before I could devise a response, he turned his attention away from me and spoke to Munin. "Do you remember my funeral?"

"Of course. I'm Memory. I remember everything. Odin came with his Valkyries, and Frey came in a chariot drawn by a boar, and Freyja was there with her cats. Her dress was very pretty. And there were the trolls and elves, the mountain-giants and frost-giants. Everyone showed up. The Aesir wept. Thor kept blowing his nose, and it made a great *schnoork* sound that shook the leaves from the trees."

Leave it to Munin to remember the thunder of Thor clearing his nostrils. I remembered something else.

Odin the All-Father frightened me. In the dark hole left behind by his sacrificed eye, I saw his fear. He remembered the sibyl's prophecy from so long ago. She'd told him that Baldr would die, that his death would be the first step towards the doom of everything Odin had ever known. He'd always hoped that somehow the sibyl would be wrong. Sometimes witch babble is just witch babble. But now there was the shocking white corpse of Baldr, whom Odin loved not in the way a war god loves a warrior, but in the way a father loves a son.

That day, everything started to die.

I thought about some of the things Munin and I had

seen recently. The world-spanning serpent who churned the waters and brewed tidal waves and hurricanes. Thor's son, Modi, had loosed him a week ago. And there was the Ship of Dead Men's Nails, freed of its moorings by the young god Magni. I thought of the bloodbath Midgard was becoming, with people killing each other over a can of ravioli. All the portents were coming true.

Bent over her twig, the sibyl muttered softly to herself. "And the serpent rises, and children drown in its wake, and the blood-beaked eagle rends corpses, screaming. Ragnarök, doom of the gods, doom of all. Battle-axe and sword rule, and an age of wolves, till the world goes down."

She spat upon the twig, and now it wasn't a twig at all, but a spear with smoking runes burned down its side. I didn't recognize them. She put the spear in Höd's hands.

Baldr nodded. "Tell me what Odin did at my funeral, Munin." He wasn't looking at Munin. He was looking at me.

"He laid the gold ring Draupnir on your chest," Munin said. "And then he knelt at your side, brushed the hair off your forehead, just like he used to do when you were a boy. He whispered something in your ear."

"What did he whisper?"

Munin opened his beak, paused, shut it. He looked at me, and I shrugged. I didn't know either. On that awful day, Odin used his cunning and spoke in a voice not even I could hear.

The sibyl snorted. "I know what he said. I'm the one who gave him the words. And he had to say them, too. Didn't want to, but he had to. No choice. That was my price for giving him a heads-up about the future."

"Tell the ravens, please," said Baldr.

"This: The sibyl's magic can give you true death."

Baldr stood at the head of the table. "Now, Höd," he said.

"Wait," I squawked. "You're not really going to do this." Stupid, stupid bird. Baldr wasn't working with Vidar and Vali. He wasn't interested in freeing monsters. He wasn't trying to accelerate Ragnarök and end his days in Hel.

With a slight shudder, Höd rose to his feet. He fingered the mistletoe spear. "I don't want to do this," he said. "Not again. It's not fair. The prophecy says we get to live. That's what's supposed to happen. Not this."

Baldr's face darkened. "I thought we were agreed. Who are we to build a new world on the corpses of others?"

After a very long moment, Höd lifted the spear over his shoulder. He sighed. "I just . . . I just want to say thanks. For not ever being mad at me. Everybody else *hated* me for killing you. But you always treated me like a brother."

"It's all right," said Baldr. "You *are* my brother."

"This has all been for my benefit," I said to Baldr. "Mine and Munin's. That's why you sent for us. That's what this whole thing has been about."

Baldr nodded. "I wanted Odin to know what happened here tonight. I wanted him to know why I did it. I was always the first link in the chain. The most important link. Remove me, and the chain shatters. Send me to a true death. End my existence." Baldr closed his eyes. "Munin can tell Odin of my deed. But you, Hugin, you have to tell him . . . I don't know. You'll think of the right thing to tell him."

"I could tell him something right now," I said. "He'd never allow this. And if I don't stop to observe the world as I fly, I can be at his side before Höd lifts a finger."

"I know you can," said Baldr. "It would be very easy for you to do that."

I felt a tightness in my throat.

How often do you see a god defy the universe to save a world? How often do you realize that you can let it happen, or you can stop it? And how long do you have to think about it before you figure out the right thing to do?

Höd pulled the spear back a little farther and took a deep breath.

I took a deep breath, too.

"Your aim's too far right," I told him. "A little left. A little more. There."

Baldr smiled at me, this time with some of his old magic, and the hall seemed to warm, and I basked in him.

"Hey, wait!" said Munin. He was just now figuring it out. "Can they do this?"

I shushed him. "I think it'll be all right."

And Baldr stood there, his arms stretched out to his sides. And when the rune-burned mistletoe spear punched through his chest, he was laughing.

The world changed color again.

Munin and I left them there, Höd staring blindly at his hands, the sibyl reading her magazines. And Baldr, not just exiled from the living but truly and finally dead.

Later, after the long flight home, when we perched on Odin's shoulder and he asked us what we'd seen and heard, Munin told him everything in detail from his perfect memory. He told him of the break in the leaden clouds and the melting of the snow. He told him how we saw the great Fenrir wolf slink back to his rock, frightened for the first time of an unknown future.

And me, Hugin, Thought, I told him that he had better start making some plans.

Because Baldr had given us a whole new tomorrow.

And today, anything was possible.

THE LADY OF THE WINDS

POUL ANDERSON

SOUTHWARD THE MOUNTAINS LIFTED to make a wall across a heaven still hard and blue. Snow whitened their peaks and dappled the slopes below. Even this far under the pass, patches of it lay on sere grass, among strewn boulders—too early in the season, fatally too early. Dry motes blew off in glittery streaks, borne on a wind that whittered and whirled. Its chill searched deep. Westward, clouds were piling up higher than the heights they shrouded, full of darkness and further storm.

A snow devil spun toward Cappen Varra, thickening as it went. Never had he known of the like. Well, he had gone forth to find whatever Power was here. He clutched the little harp with numbed fingers as if it were his courage. The gyre stopped before him and congealed. It became the form of a woman taller than himself. She poised utterly beautiful, but hueless as the snow, save for faint blue shadows along the curves of her and eyes like upland lakes. The long, tossing hair and a thin vortex of ice dust half clothed her nakedness. Somehow she seemed to quiver, a wind that could not ever come altogether to rest.

"My lady!" broke from him in the tongue of his homeland.

He could have tried to stammer on with words heard in this country, but she answered him likewise, singing more than speaking, maybe whistling more than singing: "What fate do you seek, who dared so to call on me?"

"I—I don't know," he got out, truly enough. "That lies with my lady. Yet it seemed right to bring her what poor gift was mine to offer."

He could not tell whether he heard scorn or a slight, wicked mirth. "A free gift, with nothing to ask in return?"

Cappen drew breath. The keen air seemed to whip up his wits. He had dealt with the mighty often before now—none such as her, no, but whatever hope he had lay with supposing that power makes for a certain way of feeling, be it human or overhuman. He swept his headgear off, holding it against his breast while he bowed very deeply. "Who am I to petition my lady? I can merely join all other men in praising her largesse and mercy, exalting her name forever."

The faintest of smiles touched her lips. "Because of what you brought, I will hear you out." It ceased. Impatience edged her voice. The wind strengthened, the frosty tresses billowed more wildly. "I think I know your wish. I do not think I will grant it. However, speak."

He had meant to depart from Sanctuary, but not so hastily. After some three years in that famous, infamous city, he remembered how much more there was to the wide world. Besides, while he had made friends high in its life, as well as among the low and raffish—with whom he generally felt easier—he had also made enemies of either kind. Whether by arrest on some capital charge or, likelier, by a knife in some nighted alley, one of them might well eventually make an end of him. He had survived three attempts, but the need to stay ever alert grew wearisome when hardly anything remained here that was new to him.

For a time after an adventure into which he fell, rescuing a noble lady from captivity in another universe and, perhaps, this world from the sikkintairs, he indulged in pleasures he could now afford. Sanctuary provided them in rich variety. But his tastes did not run to every conceivable kind, and presently those he enjoyed took on a surprising sameness. "Could it be that the gods of vice, even the gods of luxury, have less imagination than the gods of virtue and wholesomeness?" he wondered. The thought appalled.

Yet it wakened a dream that surprised him when he recognized it for what it was. He had been supposing his inborn restlessness and curiosity would send him on toward fresh horizons. Instead, memories welled up, and longing sharpened until it felt like unrequited love. Westward his wish ran, across plains, over mountains, through great forests and tumultuous kingdoms, the whole way home to Caronne. He remembered not only gleaming walls, soaring spires, bustling marts and streets; not only broad estates, greensward and greenwood, flowerbeds ablaze, lively men and livelier women; he harked back to the common folk, his folk, their speech and songs and ways. A peasant girl or tavern wench could be as fair as any highborn maiden, and often more fun. He remembered seaports, odors of tar and fish and cargo bales, masts and spars raking the sky, and beyond them the water a-glitter beneath a Southern sun, vast and blue where it reached outward and became Ocean.

Enough remained of his share of Molin Torchholder's reward for the exploit. He need not return as a footloose, hand-to-mouth minstrel, showman, gambler, and whatever-else, the disinherited and rather disgraced younger son of a petty baron. No, if he could get shrewd advice about investments—he knew himself for a much better versifier than money manager—he would become a merchant prince in Croy or Seilles at the very least. Or so he trusted.

Summer was dying away into autumn. The last trader caravans of the year would soon be gone. One was bound as far as Arinberg. That was a goodly distance, well beyond the western border of this Empire, and the town said to be an enjoyable place to spend a winter. Cappen bought two horses, camp gear, and supplies from the master. The traders were still trading here, and did not plan to proceed for another week. Cappen had the interval idle on his hands.

And so it came about that he perforce left Sanctuary earlier than intended.

Candlelight glowed over velvet. Fragrances of incense, of Peridis's warmth and disheveled midnight locks, of lovemaking lately come to a pause, mingled with the sweet notes of a gold-and-diamond songbird crafted by some cunning artificer. No noise or chill or stench from the streets outside won through windows barred, glazed, and curtained. Nerigo, third priest of Ils, housed his newest leman well.

Perhaps if he visited her oftener she would not have heeded the blandishments of a young man who encountered her in the gaudy chaos of Midyear Fair and made occasions to pursue the acquaintance. At least, they might have lacked opportunity. But although Nerigo was not without vigor, much of it went in the pursuit of arcane knowledge, which included practices both spiritually and physically demanding. Today he had indicated to Peridis, as often before, that he would be engaged with dark and dangerous powers until dawn, and then must needs sleep in his own house; thereafter, duties at the temple would keep him busy for an indefinite span.

So she sent a note to Cappen Varra at the inn where he lodged. It went by public messenger. As she had made usual, her few servants retired to a dormitory shed behind the house when she had supped. If she needed any, she could ring a bell. Besides, like servants generally in Sanctuary, these cultivated a selective blindness and deafness.

After all, she must shortly bid her lover farewell. It would probably take a while to find another. She might never find another so satisfactory.

"You have asked about some things here," she murmured. "I never dared show you them. Not that you would have betrayed me, but what you didn't know couldn't be gotten out of you, were he to become suspicious. Now, though, when, alas, you are leaving for aye—" She sighed, fluttered her eyelashes, and cast him a wistful smile. "It will take my mind off that, while we rest before our next hour of delight."

"The wait will not be long, since it's you I'm waiting for," he purred.

"Ah, but, my dear, I am less accustomed than I . . . was . . . before that man persuaded me hither." With gold, Cappen knew, and the luxury everywhere around, and, he gathered, occasional tales and glimpses of marvels. "Let me rest an hour, to be the readier for you. Meanwhile, there are other, more rare entertainments."

A long silken shift rippled and shimmered as she undulated over to a cabinet of ebony inlaid with ivory in enigmatic patterns. Her single, curious modesty was not to be unclad unless in bath or bed. Having nothing else along, Cappen gratified it by resuming blouse and breeks, even his soft shoes. When she opened the cabinet, he saw shelves filled with objects. Most he couldn't at once identify, but books were among them, scrolls and codices. She paused, considering, then smiled again and took out a small, slim volume bound in paper, one of perhaps a dozen. "These amuse me," she said. "Let me in turn beguile you. Come, sit beside me."

He was somewhat smugly aware of how her gaze followed him as he joined her on the sofa. Speech and manner counted most with women, but good looks helped. He was of medium size, slim, lithe and muscular because hitherto he had seldom been able to lead the indolent life he would have preferred. Black hair, banged over the brow and above the shoulders, framed straight-cut features and vividly blue eyes. It also helped to have quite a musical voice.

She handed him the book. He beheld letters totally unfamiliar, laid it on his lap, and opened it. She reached to turn the pages, one by one.

Plain text mingled with lines that must be verse—

songs, because it seemed the opening parts were under staves of what he guessed was a musical notation equally strange. There were pictures too, showing people outlandishly clad, drawn with an antic humor that tickled his fancy. "What is this?" he wondered.

"The script for a rollicking comedic performance," she answered.

"When done? Where? How do you know?"

"Well, now, that is a story of its own," she said, savoring his attention. He knew she was not stupid, and wanted to be more to him than simply another female body. Indeed, that was among her attractions. "See you, Nerigo's wizardly questings go into different worlds from ours, alike in some ways, alien in more. Different universes, he says, coexistent with this one on many planes, as the leaves of this tome lie side by side. But I can't really understand his meaning there. Can you?"

Cappen frowned, abruptly uneasy. "Much too well," he muttered.

"What's wrong? I feel you go taut."

"Oh, nothing, really." Cappen made himself relax. He didn't care to speak of the business, if only because that would spoil the mood here. It was, after all, safely behind him, the gate destroyed, the sikkintairs confined to their own skies.

And yet, raced through his mind, that gate had been in the temple of Ils, where the high flamen made nefarious use of it. He had heard that, subsequently, the priests of the cult disavowed and severely discouraged such lore. They could have found themselves endangered. Yet search through the temple archives might well turn up further information. Yes, that would explain why Nerigo was secretive, and stored his gains in this house, where nobody would likely think to search.

"He only lusts for knowledge," Peridis reassured. Her tone implied she wished that were not his primary lust. "He does not venture into the Beyond. He simply opens windows for short whiles, observes, and, when he can, reaches through to snatch small things for later study. Is that so terrible? But the hierarchy would make trouble for him if they knew, and . . . it might strike at me as well."

She brightened. "He shares with me, a little. I have looked with him into his mirror that is not a mirror, at things of glamor or mirth. I have seen this very work performed on a stage far elsewhere, and a few more akin to it. True, the language was foreign to both of us, but he could discern that the story, for instance, concerns a love intrigue. It was partly at my wish that he hunted about until he found a shop where the books are sold, and cast spells to draw copies into his arcanum. Since then I've often taken them out when I'm alone, to call back memories of the pleasure. Now let me explain and share it with you as well as I'm able." Heavy-lidded, her glance smoldered on him. "It does tell of lovers who at last come together."

He thrust his qualms aside. The thing was in fact fascinating. They began to go through it page by page, her finger tracing out each illustration while she tried to convey what understanding she had of it. His free arm slid behind her.

A thud sounded from the vestibule. Hinges whined. A chill gust bore smells of the street in. Peridis screamed. Cappen knew stabbingly that the bolt on the main door had flung back at the command of its master. The book fell from their hands and they read no more that night.

A lean, grizzle-bearded, squinting man, clad in a silvery robe, entered. At his back hulked another, red-skinned, seven feet tall, so broad and thick as to seem squat, armed with steel cap, leather cuirass, and unfairly large scimitar. Cappen did not need Peridis's gasp to inform him that they were Nerigo and a Makali bodyguard.

The woman sprang to her feet. As the bard did, the little volume slid off his lap. Almost without thinking, he snatched it and tucked it down his half-open blouse. A bargaining counter—?

For an endless instant, silence held them all.

When Nerigo then spoke, it was quite softly, even impersonally. "I somewhat hoped I would prove mistaken. But you realize, Peridis, I cannot afford blind trust in anyone. A sortilege indicated you were receiving a visitor in my absences."

She stepped back, lifting her hands, helpless and imploring. Nerigo shook his head. Did ruefulness tinge his words? "Oh, fear not, my cuddly. From the beginning, I knew you for what you are. It's not rational to wax angry when a cat steals cream or a monkey disarrays documents. One simply makes provision against further untowardness. Why should I deny myself the pleasure that is you? No, you will merely be careful in future, very careful. If you are, then when I want novelty you shall go your way freely, unharmed, with only a minor spell on you to lock your lips against ever letting slip anything about me or my doings."

Cappen heard how she caught her breath and broke into sobs. At the back of his mind, he felt a burden drop off himself. He would have hated being the instrument of harm to her. Not that she had been much more to him than frolic; yet a man wishes well-being for his friends. Besides, killing beautiful young women was a terrible waste.

Hope flickered up amidst his dismay. He bowed low. "My lord, most reverend sir," he began, "your magnanimity surpasses belief. No, say rather that it demonstrates, in actual incarnation, the divine benevolence of those gods in whose service you so distinguish yourself. Unworthy though I be, my own humble but overwhelming gratitude—"

Nerigo cut him off. "You need not exercise that flattering tongue which has become notorious throughout Sanctuary," the sorcerer-priest said, now coldly impersonal. "You are no wayward pet of mine, you are a brazen intruder. I cannot possibly let you go unpunished; my demons would lose all respect for me. Furthermore, this is an opportunity first to extract from you everything you know. I think especially about the eminent Molin Torchholder and his temple of Savankala, but doubtless other bits of information can prove useful too. Take him, Yaman."

"No, no, I beg you!" Peridis shrieked, but scrambled aside as the giant advanced.

If he was hustled off to a crypt, Cappen knew, he would welcome death when at last it came. He retreated, drawing the knife at his belt. Yaman grinned. The scimitar hissed forth. "Take him alive," Nerigo called, "but I've ways to stanch wounds once he's disabled."

Cappen was no bravo or brawler. Wits were always his weapon of choice. However, sometimes he had not been granted the choice. Thus he went prepared. His knife was not just the article of clothing and minor tool commonly carried by men. It was razor-honed, as balanced as a hawk on the wing. When in his wanderings he earned some coins by a show of prestidigitation, it had often figured in the act.

He poised, took aim, and threw.

A hoarse, gurgling bellow broke from Yaman. He lurched, dropped his weapon, and went to his knees. Blood spurted. The blade had gone into his throat below the chin. If Nerigo wanted to keep his henchman, he'd be busy for a while. Mainly; Cappen's way out was clear. He blew Peridis a kiss and darted off.

A yell pursued him. "You'll not escape, Varra! I'll have you hounded to the ends of the Empire. If they're Imperial troopers who find you, they'll have orders to cut you down on sight. But first demons will be on your trail—"

By then he was in the vestibule, retrieving his rapier and cloak, whence he slipped forth into the street. Walls and roofs loomed black along its narrowness. A strip of stars between barely gave light to grope by. Oh, lovely gloom! He kept to one side, where the dark was thickest and there was less muck to step in, and fled as deftly as a thief.

What to do? tumbled through his head. The inconspicuous silver amulet hanging on his breast ought to baffle Nerigo's afreets or whatever they were. It protected him against any supernatural forces of less than divine status. At least, so the wizard who gave it to him years ago had said, and so it had seemed to work on two or three occasions since. Of course, that might have been happenstance and the wizard a liar, but he had plenty of worries without adding hypothetical ones.

Equally of course, if such a being did come upon him, it could seize him or tear him apart. Physical strength was a physical quality. Likewise for human hunters.

Yes, Nerigo would have those out after him, while

messengers sped north, south, east, and west bearing his description to castles, cantonments, garrisons, and watchposts. Once he had aroused the indignation of his colleagues, Nerigo would have ample influence to get such an order issued. Cappen's connections to Molin were too slight—how he wished now that he hadn't thought it best to play down his role in that rescue—for the high priest of Savankala to give him asylum and safeguard across the border. Relations between the temples were strained enough already.

The westbound caravan wouldn't leave for days. Well before then, Nerigo would learn that Cappen had engaged a place in it. There were several others, readying to go in their various directions. He could find temporary refuge and get information in one of the disreputable inns he knew. With luck, he could slink to the master of whichever was departing first, give him a false name and a plausible story, and be off with it—maybe even tomorrow.

That would cost, especially if a bit of a bribe proved advisable. Cappen had deposited his money with a reliable usurer, making withdrawals as desired. Suddenly it might as well be on the Moon. He was back to what lay in his pouch. It might barely stretch to getting him away.

He suppressed a groan and shrugged. If his most recent memories were dearly bought, still, they'd be something to enjoy on an otherwise dismal journey.

It was a long annual trek that Deghred im Dalagh and his followers made. Northward they fared from Temanhassa in Arechoum, laden with spices, aromatics, intoxicant herbs, pearls, rich fabrics, cunningly wrought metal things, and the like, the merchants and hucksters among them trading as they went. The route zigzagged through desert and sown, village and town, across dunes and rivers, by highroad and cairn-marked trail, over the Uryuk Ubur and thence the cultivated plains of the Empire, Sanctuary its terminus. That city produced little other than crime and politics, often indistinguishable, but goods of every kind flowed to its marts and profitable exchanges could be made. The return journey was faster, as direct as possible, to get beyond the mountains before their early winter closed the passes.

Well, Cappen consoled himself, this was not the destination he had had in mind, but needs must, he had never yet seen yonder exotic lands, and maybe he could improve his luck there.

It could stand improvement, his thoughts continued. Instead of the comforts he paid for and forfeited, he had a single scrawny mule, which he must frequently relieve by turning to shank's mare; a greasy third-hand bedroll; two similar changes of clothes and a towel; ill-fitting boots; a cheap knife, spoon, and tin bowl; and leave to eat with the choreboys, not the drovers.

However, he remained alive and at large. That was ample cause for cheerfulness, most of the time. Making friends came naturally to him. Before long his tales, japes, and songs generated a liveliness that drew the attention of the merchants. Not long after that, they invited him into their mess. Deghred gave him a decent kaftan to wear while they ate, drank, and talked; everybody concerned was fluent in the Ilsig language, as well as others. "I think you have possibilities, lad," the caravan master said. "I'll lodge you for a while after we come to Temanhassa and introduce you to certain people." He waved his hand. "No, no, not alms. A modest venture, which in the course of time may bring me a modest profit."

Cappen knew he had better not seem a daydreamer or a fool. "The tongue of Arechoum is foreign to me, sir. Your men can scarcely teach me along the way."

"You're quick to pick things up, I've seen. Until you do, belike I can help."

Cappen understood from the drawl and the bearded smile that Deghred meant also to profit from that help, perhaps considerably. Not that he was ever unnecessarily unkind or hostile. Cappen rather liked him. But business was business. At the moment, nothing better was in sight.

Beasts and men plodded on. The land rose in bleakening hills. Now and then, when by himself, Cappen took from his meager baggage the book he had borne from Peridis's house and paged through it, puzzling over the text and staves, smiling at the pictures, mainly recalling her and their nights. Thence he harked back to earlier recollections and forward to speculations about the future. It bore him away from the trek.

At a lonely fortress on a stony ridge, the commander routinely let them cross the frontier. Cappen drew a long breath. Yet, he realized, that frontier was ill-defined, and Nerigo's agents might still find him. He would not feel altogether safe until he was on the far side of the Uryuk Ubur.

Those mountains reared like a horse. Mile by mile the trails grew more toilsome, the land more cold and stark. Unseasonably so, Deghred said, and burned some incense to his little private gods. Nevertheless the winds lashed, yelled, and bit, clouds raced ragged, snow flurried.

Thus they came to the hamlet Khangaii and heard that if they went ahead, they would almost surely die.

A storm roared about the huts. Sleet hissed on the blast. Mosschinked stone walls and turf roof muffled the noise, a dung fire and crowded bodies kept the dwelling of headman Bulak odorously warm, but somehow that sharpened the feeling of being trapped.

"Aiala is angry," he said. "We have prayed, we have sacrificed a prime ewe—not in feast, but casting it into a crevasse of Numurga Glacier—yet she rages ever worse."

"Nor has she sent me a dream to tell why, though I ate well-nigh all the sacred *ulaku* left us and lay swooned through two sunrises." His elder wife, who was by way of being the tribal priestess, shuddered. "Instead, nightmares full of furious screams."

Flames flickered low on the hearth and guttered in clay lamps. Smoke dimmed what light they gave and blurred uneasy shadows. From the gloom beyond gleamed the frightened stares of Bulak's younger wife and children, huddled on the sheepskins that covered the sleeping dais. Three favored dogs gnawed mutton bones tossed them after the company had eaten. Several men and the senior woman sat cross-legged around the fire, drinking fermented milk from cow horns refilled out of a jug. They were as many as could well have been crowded in, Deghred and such of the merchants as he picked. The rest of the travelers were housed elsewhere. Even in this bad time, hospitality was sacred. Cappen had persuaded the caravan master that he, come from afar, might conceivably have some new insight to offer.

He was beginning to regret the mix of cockiness and curiosity that led him to do so. He had more or less gotten to ignoring the stench, but his eyes stung and he kept choking back the coughs that would have been impolite. Not that things were likely any better in any other hut. Well, maybe he could have slept. It was a strain trying to follow the talk. Bulak knew some Ilsig, and some of the guests had a smattering of his language.

Between stumbling pidgin and awkward translations, conversation did not exactly flow.

At least, though, the slowness and the pauses gave him a chance to infer what he could not directly follow, correcting his mistakes when context revealed them to him. It became almost as if he listened to ordinary speech. He wasn't sure whether or not the drink helped, if only by dulling his discomfort. Foul stuff, but by now his palate was as stunned as his nose and he readily accepted recharges.

"Have you not gods to appeal to other than this—this Aiala?" asked the merchant Haran im Zeyin.

Deghred frowned at the brashness and shook his head. The wife caught her breath and drew a sign which smoke-swirls traced. Bulak took it stolidly. "She rules the air over the Uryuk Ubur," he answered. Light wavered across the broad, seamed face, almond eyes, and thin beard. "What shall they of the Fire, the Earth, and the Water do?"

"It may be she is even at odds with them, somehow, and this is what keeps her wrathful," whispered the woman. "There is a song among the olden songs that tells of such a time, long ago, when most of the High Folk died before she grew mild again—but I must not sing any of those songs here."

"So it could worsen things to call on them," said Deghred with careful gravity. "Yet—may she and you bear with an ignorant outsider who wishes only to understand—why should she make you suffer? Surely you are blameless."

Bulak half shrugged. "How else shall she vent her anger than in tempest and chill?"

Irreverence grinned within Cappen. He remembered infuriated women who threw things. The grin died. Men were apt to do worse when beside themselves, and be harder to bring to reason. More to the point, he happened to be on the receiving end.

The headman's stoicism gave way for a moment. "I have had my day. Our tribe will live through the winter—enough of us—I think—and may hope that then she has calmed—"

"For she is not cruel," the priestess said as if chanting. "Her snows melt beneath her springtime breezes and fill the streams, while the pastures turn green and starry with tiny flowers and lambs frisk in the sunshine. She brings the fullness of summer, the garnered riches of autumn, and when her snows have returned we have been snug and gladsome."

Isn't that the sort of thing a goddess or god is supposed to do? thought Cappen.

"—but how many of our young will freeze or starve, how many of our littlest ones?" croaked Bulak. He stiffened his lips. "We must wait and see."

And, Cappen reflected, *few gods are noted for tender solicitude. In fact, they often have nasty tempers.*

If this is even a goddess, properly speaking. Maybe

she ranks only as a sylph or something, though with considerable local power. That could make matters even worse. Minor functionaries are notoriously touchy.

Supposing, of course, there is anything in what I've been hearing.

Deghred said it for him: "Again I pray pardon. No impertinence is meant. But is it not possible that what we have met is merely a freak, a flaw in the weather, nothing for the Lady Aiala to take heed of, and very soon, perhaps already tomorrow, it will go back to what it should be?"

Bulak shook his head. "Never in living memory have we suffered aught like this so early: as well you should know, who have passed through here, to and fro, for year after year. But there is the sacred song.... Push on if you will. The higher you go, the harder it will be. Unless we get respite within the next three or four days, I tell you that you will find the passes choked with snow and yourselves in a blizzard, unable even to go back. If afterward your bodies are found, we will make an offering for your souls." His smile held scant mirth. "Not that I'm at all sure 'we' means anyone here tonight."

"What, then, do you counsel we should do?"

"Why, retreat while still you are able. Tomorrow, I'd say. We cannot keep you through such a winter as is upon us. Barely will we be able to keep ourselves—some of ourselves. Go back north into the lowlands and wait. Could we High Folk do likewise, we might well, but if naught else, the Empire would seize on the chance to make us impoverished clients. We have had dealings with it erenow. Better that a remnant of us stay free. You, though, need but wait the evil out."

"At cutthroat cost," muttered Haran.

"Better to lose our gains than our lives," retorted Deghred. His tone gentled. "And yet, Bulak, we are old friends, you and I. A man should not turn his back on a friend. Might we, your guests, be able to do something? Maybe, even, as foreigners, give reverence and some unique sacrifice to the Lady, and thus please her—?" His voice trailed off.

"How shall we speak to her? In our broken Uryuk?" wondered another merchant. "Would that not be an insult?"

"She is of the winds," said Bulak. "She and her kind ken every tongue in the world, for the winds hear and carry the knowledge to each other." He turned to his elder wife. "Is that not so?" She nodded.

Deghred brightened. "Then she will understand us when we pray and make offerings."

The priestess pinched her lips together above the few teeth left her. "Why should she heed you, who are outlanders, lowlanders, have never before done her homage, and clearly are now appealing only to save—not even your lives, for you can still escape, but your mongers' profits?"

"Treasure? We have jewelry of gold, silver, and gemstones, we have garments fit for queens—"

"What are such things to Air?"

"To Earth, maybe," Bulak put in. "Aromatic woods might please Fire, spices and sweetmeats Water. Yet with them, too, I fear you would be unwise." Shrewdly: "For in no case will you offer your entire freight, when you can better withdraw and come back with most of it several months hence. It is . . . not well to try to bargain with the Powers."

That depended on which Powers, Cappen thought. He knew of some—But they were elsewhere, gods and tutelaries of lands less stark than this.

The drink was buzzing in his head. Dismay shocked through. *Why am I jesting? It's my life on the table tonight!*

Slowly, Deghred nodded. The one sensible thing for his caravan to do was retreat, wait out the winter, and cut its losses as much as might be. Wasn't it?

And absolute lunacy for Cappen Varra. Once he was back in the Empire, he himself would not bet a counterfeit lead bawbee on his chance of getting away again. The alert was out for him. If nobody else noticed first, one or another of his fellow travelers was bound soon to hear the description and betray him for the reward. Fleeing into the hinterlands or diving into some thieves' den would hardly buy enough time. Though his amulet might keep Nerigo's demons off his direct track, they could invisibly watch and listen to others, everywhere, and report everything suspicious to the sorcerer.

Stay here in Khangaii? Surely the villagers could feed one extra mouth. He'd pay them well, with arts and shows, entertainments such as they'd never enjoyed before, keeping heart in them through the grim time ahead.

Maybe they'd agree. Then maybe he'd starve or freeze to death along with so many of them. Or maybe Nerigo would get word of a vagabond who'd joined the men of Arechoum and stayed behind when they returned. He was not yet too far beyond the Imperial marches for a squad to come after him as soon as the ways became at all passable.

Deghred barked a harsh laugh. "Yes, most certainly not to dicker and quibble with a female already incensed," he said. "That would be to throw oil on a fire." He sighed. "Very well, we'll load up again tomorrow and betake ourselves hence. May we find it well with the High Folk when we come back."

The younger wife moaned softly in the shadows and clutched two of the children to her.

Let her live, Cappen thought wildly. *She's beautiful. Several of them that I've spied here are, in their way. Though I don't suppose I can beguile any—*

His heart leaped. His legs followed. The others stared as he sprang to his feet. "No, wait!" he cried. "Wait only a little span. A few days more at most. I've an idea to save us!"

"What, you?" demanded Deghred, while his traders

gaped and Bulak scowled. "Has a *yawanna* taken your wits? Or have you not understood what we were saying, how easily we can give the Lady offense and bring her fury straight against us?"

"I have, I have," Cappen answered frantically. "My thought is nothing like that. Any risk will be wholly my own, I swear. Only hearken to me."

Risk indeed. A notion born out of half-drunken desperation, maybe. But maybe, also, sired by experience.

He called up coolness, to be a wellspring for a spate of eager, cozening words such as a bard and showman had better always be able to produce.

D ay came bleak and bright. Washed clean, newly smooth-shaven, wearing the finest warm raiment to be found in the caravan's goods—plumed cap of purple satin, scarlet cloak, green tunic embroidered with gold and trimmed with sable, dark-blue hose, buskins of tooled leather—with a small harp in his hand from the same source, he left the village behind and made his way on up the path toward the heights. Wind whistled. Far overhead, a hawk rode it. The chill whipped his face. He hardly felt it, nor any weariness after sleepless hours. He was strung too taut.

But when he reached the cairn they had told him of, from which rose a pole and flew an often-renewed white banner, while a narrow trail wound off to the left, an abrupt sense of how alone he was hollowed him out. Though he seldom thought about it, his wish was to die, sometime in the distant future, with a comrade or two and a girl or three to appreciate his gallantry and his last quip.

He stiffened his sinews and summoned up his blood. He must not seem to be afraid, so best was to convince himself that he wasn't. Think rather of this as a unique challenge.

The trail went across the mountainside, near the edge of a cliff sheering down into dizzy depths. Elsewhere the land reached vast and tilted, here and there a meadow amidst the rock. A waterfall gleamed like a sword across the gorge. Its booming came faintly through the wind.

Before long he reached the altar where they prayed and sacrificed to Aiala, a great boulder squared off and graven with eroded symbols. Cappen saw few if any other traces of man. No sacred smoke, but thin gust-borne streamers of dry snow blew past. Here, though, if anywhere, she should quickly discern any worshipper.

He took stance before the block and turned his gaze aloft. Give her a short time to see, perhaps to wonder, perhaps even to admire.

The air shrilled.

Cappen tucked gloves into belt and positioned the harp. His fingers evoked the first chord. He began to sing.

It was a song he had used more than once over the

years, usually to good effect. Of course, it must be adapted to each occasion, even rendered into a different language, and he had lain awake working on it. However, if she really did know all human tongues, he could simplify the task by staying with the original Caronnais. If not, or if he was mistaken about her femaleness—He wouldn't weaken his delivery by fretting about that. He sang loud and clear:

"Be merciful, I pray, and hear my cry
Into the winds that you command. I know
That I am overbold, but even so
Adore the one whose queendom is the sky,
In awe of whom the moonlit night-clouds fly,
Who dances in the sunlight and the snow,
Who brings the springtime, when the freshets flow
And all the world goes green beneath her eye.
Yet worship is not that which makes me call
Upon you here, and offer up my heart.
Although I, mortal, surely cannot woo
As man to maiden, still, I have seen all—
No, just a little, but at least a part—
Of that alive enchantment which is you."

And she came to him.

"—However, speak," she said.

He suppressed a shiver. Now he must be as glib as ever in his life. "First, will my lady permit that I resume my cap and gloves and pull my cloak around me? It's mortal cold for a mortal."

Again something like amusement flickered briefly. She nodded. "Then say what is your name, your home, and your errand."

"May it please my lady, the caravaneers I travel with know me as Peor Sardan of Lorace." He was clearly from such parts. "But you of the high heavens surely recognize that this cannot be quite so." *Really? Well, anyhow, outright prevarication could be hazardous and should be unnecessary. She won't deign to give me away. If she chooses to destroy me, she'll do it herself. Battered to death by hailstones—?* "My motherland is farther west and south, the kingdom of Caronne, and I hight Cappen Varra, born to the noble house of Dordain. As for my errand, I have none fixed, being a wanderer—in spite of the birth I mentioned—who wishes to see something of the world and better his fortune before turning home. Rather, that was my only wish until this happy day."

"Yes, I've spied the pack train," said Aiala scornfully. "You hope I'll grant you better weather."

"Oh, my lady! Forgive me, but no. Who am I to petition you? Nor am I in their enterprise. I simply took what appeared to be an opportunity to visit their country, of which go many fabulous accounts. Now I see this for the velleity it was." He made his look upon her half shy, half aglow. "Here I find the fulfillment of my true and lifelong desire."

Was she taken a bit aback? At any rate, her manner grew less forbidding. "What do you mean?"

Cappen gestured from beneath his cloak. "Why, my lady, what else than the praise of Woman? She, the flower of earthly creation, in her thousandfold dear incarnations, no wine so sweet or heady as her presence, she is the meaning of my existence and my poor verses in her honor are its justification. Yes, I have found her and sung to her in many a land, from the soft vales of Caronne to the stern fjords of Norren, from a fisher but on Ocean shore to a palace in Sanctuary, and my thought was to seek her anew in yonder realm, perhaps some innocent maiden, perhaps some wise enchantress, how can I know before she has kindled my heart?"

"You are . . . a flighty one, then." She did not sound disapproving—what constancy has the wind?—but as though intrigued, even puzzled.

"Also, my very love drives me onward. For see you, my lady, it is Woman herself for whom I quest. While often wondrous, no one woman is more than mortal. She has, at most, a few aspects of perfection, and they changeable as sun-sparkles on the river that is time. Otherwise, the flaws of flesh, the infirmities of insight, the narrowness of dailiness belong to being human. And I, all too human, lack strength and patience to endure such thwarting of the dream for long. The yearning overtakes me and I must be off again in search of that prize which common sense tells me is unattainable but the spirit will not ever quite let me despair of."

Not bad, Cappen thought. By now he half believed it.

"I told you to speak in few words." Aiala didn't say that quite firmly.

"Ah, would that I could give you obedience in this as I shall in all else whatsoever," Cappen sighed into the wind. "Dismiss me, and of course I will depart, grieving and yet gladsome over what has been vouchsafed me. But until then I can no more curb my tongue than I can quell my heart. For I have glimpsed the gates of my goal, loftier and more precious than any knight before me can have beheld, and I jubilate."

"And never before have I—" escaped from her. She recalled her savage dignity. "Clarify this. I'll not stand here the whole day."

"Certainly not. The heights and the heavens await your coming. But since you command me, I can relate quite plainly that, hitherbound, I heard tell of my lady. Beyond, perhaps over and above her majesty and might-iness, the tales were of visions, dazzlements, seen by an incredibly fortunate few through the centuries, beauty well-nigh too great to bear—and, more than that, a spirit lordly and loving, terrible and tender, mysterious and merry, life-bearing and life-nourishing—in short, Woman."

"You...had not seen me...earlier," Aiala mur-mured.

"But I had, fleetingly, fragmentarily, in dreams and

longings. Here, I thought, must be Truth. For although there are doubtless other goddesses of whom something similar can be said, and I imply no least disrespect for any, still, Truth is One, is it not? Thus I strove to infer a little of the immortally living miracle I heard of. I wove these inferences into a humble tribute. I brought it to your halidom as my offering.

"To do worship is an end and a reward in itself. I dared hope for no more. Now—my lady, I have seen that, however inadequate, my verse was not altogether wide of the mark. What better can an artist win than such a knowledge, for an hour of his few years on Earth? My lady, I can die content, and I thank you."

"You—need not die. Not soon. Go back to the plains."

"So we had decided, the caravaneers and I, for never would we defy our lady's righteous wrath. Thence I will seek to regain my faraway birthland, that my country-men too may be enriched by a hint of your glory. If I fall by the wayside—" Cappen shrugged. "Well, as I said, today my life has had overflowing measure."

She raised her brows. "Your road is dangerous?"

"It is long, my lady, and at the outset—I left certain difficulties behind me in the Empire—trivial, but some people overreact. My plan had been to circumvent them by going roundabout through Arechoum. No matter. If the cosmic cycle requires that my lady decree an early winter throughout her mountains, I shall nevertheless praise her while blood beats within me."

"It's not that." Aiala bridled. The wind snarled. "No! I am not bound to a wheel! This is my will."

"Your wisdom."

"My anger!" she yelled. The storm in the west mounted swiftly higher. "I'll show them! They'll be sorry!"

"They?" asked Cappen low.

"Aye, they'll mourn for that they mocked me, when the waters of Vanis lie frozen past the turning of the springtime, and the earth of Orun remains barren, and the fires of Lua smolder out because no dwellers are left alive to tend them." Under his cloak, Cappen supressed a shudder. *Yes*, he thought, *human rulers don't take their subjects much into account either.* "Then they'll come to me begging my mercy, and I will grant it to them for a song."

I'm on the track. "But is it not my lady of the winds who sings to the world?" Cappen pursued, carefully, carefully.

"So they'll discover, when I laugh at their effort."

"I am bewildered. How could any being, divine or not, possibly quarrel with my lady?"

Aiala paced to and fro. The wind strengthened, the dark clouds drew closer. After a stark minute she halted, looked straight at him, and said, "The gods fall out with each other now and then." He forebore to mention that he well knew that. His need was for her to unburden herself. His notion that she was lonelier than she realized seemed the more likely when her tone calmed somewhat. "This—" She actually hesitated. "You may understand. You are a maker of songs."

"I am when inspired, my lady, as I was today." Or whenever called for, but that was beside the immediate point.

"You did well. Not that *they* could have appreciated it."

"A song was wanted among the gods?"

Locks streamed and tumbled the more wildly as she nodded. "For a wedding, a divine marriage. Your countrymen must perceive it otherwise, but in these uplands it is Khaiantai who wakens at the winter solstice from her sleep, a virgin, to welcome Hurultan the Lightbearer, her bridegroom; and great is the rejoicing in Heaven and on Earth."

On Earth in better years, Cappen thought. *Yes, the mythic event, forever new and forever recurrent.* A chill passed up his spine. He concealed it as best he was able. "But . . . the occasion is not always the same?"

"No. Is one day the same as the last? Time would come to a stop."

"So—the feast and—" his mind leaped—"gifts to the happy pair?"

"Just so. Of us Four, Orun may bring fruits or gold, Vanis a fountain or a rainbow, Lua an undying lamp or a victorious sword—such things as pertain to them—

while I have given an eagle or a fragrance or—We go there together; for we are the Four."

"But now lately—?"

Her reasonableness began to break. "I had in mind a hymeneal song, like none heard before in those halls but often to be again. They agreed this would be a splendid gift. I created it. And then—" Elemental rage screamed through an icy blast.

"And they did not comprehend it," Cappen proposed.

"They scoffed! They said it was so unworthy they would not come to the feast in my company if I brought it. They *dare!*"

Cappen waited out the ensuing whirlwind. When Aiala had quieted down a grim trifle, he ventured, "My lady, this is often the fate of artists. I have learned how eloquence is meaningless to the word-blind, music and meter to the tone-deaf, subtlety to the blunt-brained, and profundity to the unlearned."

"Good names for these, Cappen Varra."

"I refer to no gods or other high Powers, my lady," he made haste to reply. One never knew who or what might be listening. "No irreverence. Absolutely never! I speak merely of my small human experience and of people whom I actually pity more than despise—except, to be sure, when they set themselves up as critics. Yet even persons of unimpeachable taste and discernment can have differences of opinion. This is an unfortunate fact of life, to which I have become resigned."

"I will not be. Moreover, word has gotten about. If I come lamely in with something else than a song—No!" Aiala yowled. "They'll learn respect when I avenge my pride with disasters like none since Chaos rebelled in the beginning."

"Ah—may that perhaps conceivably be just a minim extreme, my lady? Not that I can judge. Indeed, I am baffled to grasp how your colleagues could reject your epithalamium. The music of the wind pervades the world, lulling breeze, sough in forests, laughterful rainsquall, trumpeting gale, oh, infinite is its variety, and its very hushes are a part of the composition," said Cappen with another sweeping gesture.

She nearly thawed. "You, though, you understand me—" she breathed. "For the first time ever, someone—"

He intended to go on in this vein until he had softened her mood enough for her to stop punishing the land. But she paused, then exclaimed, "Hear what I have made, and judge."

"Oh, my lady, I cannot!" gasped Cappen, aghast. "I'm totally unworthy, unfit, disqualified."

She smiled. "Be not afraid," she said quite gently. "Only tell me what you think. I won't take offense."

Too many others had insisted on declaiming their verses to him. "But, my lady, I don't know, I cannot know the language of the gods, and surely your work would lose much in translation."

"Actually," she said, "it's in classical Xandran, as we're wont to use when elegance is the aim."

He remembered white temples and exquisite sculptures in the South and West, too often ruinous, yet still an ideal for all successor peoples. Evidently the local deities felt that, while their worshippers might be barbarians, they themselves ought to display refinement. "But I also fear—I regret—my lady, I was not very dedicated to my schooling. My knowledge of Xandran was slight at best, and has largely rusted out of me." True enough.

Impulsive as her winds, she smiled afresh. "You shall have it back, and more."

"That would, er, take a while."

"No. Hear me. All tongues spoken by men anywhere are open to me."

Yes, so Bulak had said. How remote and unreal the Uryuk hut felt.

"For the sake of your courteous words, Cappen Varra, and your doubtless keen judgment, I will bestow this on you."

He gaped. "How—how—And how can this weak little head of mine hold so overwhelmingly much?"

"It need not. Whenever you hear or read a language, you will be able to use it like a native. Afterward and until next time, there will be only whatever you choose to keep and can, as with ordinary memories."

"My lady, I repeat, I'm wholly unworthy—"

"Hold still." Imperious, she trod over to him, laid hands on his cheeks, and kissed him.

He lurched, half stunned. A forefinger slid into either ear. He noted vaguely amidst the tempest that this was a caress worth trying in future, if he had a future.

She released him and stepped back. His daze faded and he could pay close heed to what he said. "I, I never dreamed that Woman herself would—For that instant I was like unto a god."

Her hand chopped the air, impatient. "Now you are ready to hear me."

He braced for it.

Gaze expectant upon him, she cleared her throat and launched into her song. Fantastically, the Xandran lyrics rang Caronnais-clear. He wished they didn't. As for the melody, she possessed a marvelous voice, but these notes took a drunkard's walk from key to key.

"The universe has looked forward with breath baited,
Not only Earth but the underworld and the starry
  sky,
For this day so well-known, even celebrated,
When all of us assembled see eye to eye
About the union of our shiny Hurultan, whose
  ability
It is the daylight forward to bring,
And dear Khaiantai, who will respond with agility,
So that between them they become parents of the
  spring—"

Cappen thanked the years that had taught him acting, in this case the role of a gravely attentive listener.

Aiala finished: " '—*And thus let us join together in chorusing my song.*' There! What do you think of that!"

"It is remarkable, my lady," Cappen achieved.

"I didn't just dash it off, you know. I weighed and shaped every word. For instance, that line '*Birds also will warble as soon as they hatch from the egg.*' That did not come easily."

"An unusual concept, yes. In fact, I've never heard anything like it."

"Be frank. Tell me truly, could I make a few little improvements? Perhaps—I've considered—instead of '*as ardent as a prize ball,*' what about '*as vigorous as a stud horse*'?"

"Either simile is striking, my lady. I would be hard put to suggest any possible significant changes."

Aiala flared anew. "Then *why* do Orun, Vanis, and Lua sneer? How can they?"

"Sneering comes easily to some persons, my lady. It is not uncommonly an expression of envy. But to repeat myself, I do not propose that that applies in the present case. Tastes do differ. Far be it from me to imagine how your distinguished kindred might perceive a piece like this. Appropriateness to an occasion need have nothing to do with the quality of a work. It may merely happen to not quite fit in—like, say, a stately funeral dirge in a series of short-haul chanties. Or vice versa. Professionals like me," said Cappen forbearingly, "must needs learn to supply what may be demanded, and reserve our true art for connoisseurs."

He failed to mollify her. Instead, she stiffened and glared. "So! I'm unskilled, am I? I suppose you can do better?"

Cappen lifted his palms with a defensiveness not entirely feigned. "Oh, absolutely not. I simply meant—"

"I know. You make excuses for them on behalf of your own feelings."

"My lady, you urged me to be forthright. I hint at nothing but a conceivable, quite possibly hypothetical reconsideration of intent, in view of the context."

Indignation relieved him by yielding to haughtiness. "I told you how I would lose honor did I by now give anything but a song. Rather will I stay home and make them sorry."

Cappen's mind leaped like a hungry cat at a mouse. "Ah, but perhaps there is a third and better way out of this deplorable situation. Could you bring a different paean? I know many that have enjoyed great success at nuptial gatherings."

"And the gods will know, or in time they'll discover, that it is not new in the world. Shall I bring used goods to the sacred wedding—*I*?"

"Well, no, my lady, of course not."

Aiala sniffed. "I daresay you can provide something original that will be good enough."

"Not to compare with my lady's. Much, much less exalted. Thereby, however, more readily blending into revelry, where the climate is really not conducive to concentrated attention. Grant me time, for indeed the standard to be met is heaven-high—"

She reached a decision. "Very well. A day and a night."

"Already tomorrow?" protested Cappen, appalled.

"*They* shall not think I waver weakly between creativity and vengeance. Tomorrow. In classical Xandran. Fresh and joyous. It had better be."

"But—but—"

"Then I will give you my opinion, freely and frankly."

"My lady, this is too sudden for imperfect flesh and feeble intelligence. I beg you—"

"Silence. It's more than I think I would grant anyone else, for the sake of your respectful words and song. I begin to have my suspicions about it, but will overlook them if you bring me one that is acceptable and that my winds can tell me has never been heard before on this earth or in its skies. Fail me, and your caravan will not get back to the plains, nor you to anywhere. Go!"

In a whirl of white, she vanished. The wind shrieked louder and colder, the storm clouds drew nearer.

Villagers and caravaneers spied him trudging back down the path and, except for those out forlornly herding the sheep, swarmed together to meet him. Their babble surfed around his ears. He gestured vainly for silence. Bulak roared for it. As it fell, mumble by mumble, he and Deghred trod forward. "What did you do yonder?" he asked, less impassively than became a headman.

Cappen had donned his sternest face. "These be mysteries not to be spoken of until their completion," he declared. "Tomorrow shall see my return to them."

He dared not spend hours relating and explaining, when he had so few. Nor did it seem wise to admit that thus far, in all likelihood, he had made matters worse, especially for the travelers.

Bulak stood foursquare. Deghred gave the bard a searching and skeptical look. The rest murmured, fingered prayer beads or josses, and otherwise registered an awe that was useful at the moment but, if disappointed, could well turn murderously vengeful.

Cappen went on headlong. "I must meditate, commune with high Powers, and work my special magianisms," he said. "For this I require to be alone, well sheltered, with writing materials and, uh, whatever else I may require."

Bulak stared. "Suddenly you speak as if born amidst us."

"Take that as a token of how deep and powerful the mysteries are." Cappen forgot to keep his voice slowly tolling. "But, but does anybody here know Xandran?"

Wind whistled, clouds swallowed the sun, three ravens flew by like forerunners of darkness.

"I have some command of the tongue," said Deghred, almost as if he suspected a trap.

"Classical Xandran?" cried Cappen.

"No. Who does but a few scholars? I mean what they use in those parts nowadays—that is, the traders and sailors I've had to do with. And, yes, once a crew of pirates; but I think that was a different dialect."

The foolish, fire-on-ice hope died. Still—"I may want to call on what knowledge you have. That will depend on what my divinations reveal to me. Hold yourself prepared. Meanwhile, what of my immediate needs?"

"We have a place," Bulak said. "Lowly, but all we can offer."

"The spirits take small account of Earthly grandeur," his elder wife assured them, for whatever that was worth.

Thus Cappen found himself and his few possessions in the village storehouse. It was a single room, mainly underground, with just enough walls beneath the sod roof to allow an entryway. After the door was closed, a lamp gave the only light. While the space was fairly large, very little was available, for it was crammed with roots, dried meat, sheepskins, and other odorous goods. The air hung thick and dank. However, it was out of the wind, and private.

Too private, maybe. Cappen had nothing to take his mind off his thoughts.

He settled in, a pair of skins between him and the floor, one over his shoulders. Besides the lamp, he had been given food, a crock of wine, a goblet, a crock for somewhat different purposes, and his tools—a bottle of ink, several quill pens, and a sheaf of paper, articles such as merchants used in their own work. Now he began wondering, more and more frantically, what to do with them.

Ordinarily he could have dashed something off. But a canticle in classical Xandran, suitable for a marriage made in heaven? Especially when the cost of its proving unsatisfactory would be widespread death, including his? He did not feel inspired.

The language requirement was obstacle enough. His wits twisted to and fro, hunting for a way, any way, around it. Through Deghred, he could now get a doubtless very limited acquaintance with the present-day speech. He recalled hearing that it descended directly from the antique, so much of it must be similar. How would pronunciation have changed, though, and grammar, and even vocabulary? In his days at home he had read certain famous poems five or six hundred years old. It had been difficult; only a lexicon made it possible at all; and the archaic idiom of the Rojan hillmen suggested how alien the verses would have sounded.

He glugged a mouthful of wine. It hit an empty stomach and thence sent a faint glow to his head. He did have a bit more to go on. When he concentrated, he could drag scraps of the proper classical up from the forgetfulness in which they had lain. Maybe his newly acquired facility helped with that. But they were just scraps. He had yawned through a year of this as part of the education that even a bastard son of a minor nobleman was supposed to receive, but declensions, conjugations, moods, tenses, and the dismal rest set his attention adrift in the direction of girls, flowery forests, rowdy friends, composing a song of his own that might seduce a girl, or almost anything else. What stayed with him had done so randomly, like snatches of his aunt's moralizings when he was a child and couldn't escape.

And then he had Aiala's lyrics. That wasn't by design. Every word clung to him, like the memory of every bit of a certain meal years ago that he had had to eat and praise because the cook was a formidable witch. He feared he would never get rid of either. Still, the thing gave him a partial but presumably trustworthy model, a basis for comparison and thus for a guesswork sort of reconstruction.

He drank again. His blood started to buzz faintly, agreeably. Of course; he'd need his reason unimpaired when—if—he got to that task. But "if" was the doomful word. First he needed the poesy, the winged fancy, concepts evoking words that in turn made the concepts live. Anxiety, to give it a euphemistic name, held his imagination in a swamp of glue. And wasn't that metaphor a repulsive symptom of his condition? Anything he might force out of himself would belong in yonder crock.

So he must lift his heart, free his spirit. Then he could hope his genius would soar. After which he could perhaps render the Caronnais into Xandran without mutilating it beyond recognition. The basic difficulty was that to create under these circumstances he must get drunk, no good condition for a translator. He suspected the necessary degree of drunkenness was such that when he awoke he wouldn't care whether he lived or died—until much too late. The lady of the winds did not expect to be kept waiting.

Besides—he spat a string of expletives—she demanded not only words but music. The two must go together as naturally as breath and heartbeat, or the song was a botch and a mockery. This meant they must grow side by side, intertwining, shaping one another, as he worked. Oh, usually he could find an existing melody that fitted a poem he had in process, or vice versa. Neither was admissible in this case; both must never have been heard before in the world. He could attempt a double originality; but that, he knew, would only be possible with the Caronnais native to him. To force the subsequent translation into that mold—well, give him a week or two and maybe he might, but since he had only until tomorrow—

He glugged again. He would doubtless be wise to

ballast the wine with food. It wasn't the worst imaginable food, caravaneers' rations, smoked meat and fish, butter, cheese, hardtack, rice cold but lately boiled with leeks and garlic, dried figs and apricots and—On the other hand, he lacked appetite. What use wisdom anyway? He glugged again.

If this was the end of his wanderings, he thought, it was not quite what he had visualized and certainly far too early. Not that he did well to pity himself. Think of his waymates, think of the poor innocent dwellers throughout these mountains. Surely he had enjoyed much more than them, much more colorful. It behooved a minstrel, a knight of the road, to hark back; as gladly as the wine enabled.

Most recently, yes, to Sanctuary. He had had his troubles there, but the same was true of every place, and the multifarious pleasures much outnumbered them. Ending with delicious Peridis—may she fare always well—and their last, so unfortunately interrupted moment—

He stirred on his sheepskins. By all the nymphs of joy, it happened he had brought away a souvenir of it! There he could for a while take refuge from his troubles, other than in drink. And perhaps, said practicality, this would liberate his genius.

Groping about, shivering in the chill, he found the book. Cross-legged, he opened it on his lap and peered through the dim, smoky, smelly lamplight.

The words leaped out at him. They were in no language he had ever heard of, nor was it anywhere named; but he read it as easily as he did his own, instantly understanding what everything he came upon referred to. Not that that brought full knowledge. The world he found was an abstraction, a bubble, floating cheerfully free in a space and a time beyond his ken. No matter. He guessed it was almost as airy there.

The musical notation stood equally clear to him, tunes lilting while he scanned them. Their scale was not too different from that common in the Westlands. He would need only a little practice before singing and strumming them in a way that everybody he met ought to like. What exoticism there was should lend piquancy. Yes, for his future career—

Future!

He sprang to his feet. His head banged against a rafter.

Hastily fetched through biting wind and gathering murk, Deghred im Dalagh hunkered down and peered at Cappen Varra. "Well, what do you crave of me?" he asked.

"In a minute, I pray you." Himself sitting tailor-fashion, the bard tried to arrange paper, inkpot, and open book for use. Bloody awkward. No help at all to the image of a knowing and confident rescuer.

"I've a feeling you're none too sure either," Deghred murmured.

"But I am! I simply need a bit of assistance. Who doesn't ever? The craftsman his apprentices, the priest his acolytes, and you a whole gang of underlings. I want no more than a brief . . . consultation."

"To what end?" Deghred paused. "They're growing dubious of you. What kind of Powers are you trying to deal with? What could come of it?"

"The good of everybody."

"Or the ruin?"

"I haven't time to argue." *If I did, I suspect you'd be utterly appalled and make me cease and desist. Then you'd offer an extravagant sacrifice to a being that no such thing will likely appease—for you haven't met her as I have.*

Deghred's voice harshened. "Be warned. If you don't do what you promised—"

"Well, I didn't exactly *promise*—"

"My men won't let you leave with us, and I suspect the villagers will cast you out. They fear you'll carry a curse."

Cappen was not much surprised. "Suppose, instead, I gain clemency, weather as it ought to be, and the passes open for you. Will they give me anything better than thanks? I'm taking a considerable personal risk, you know."

"Ah, should you succeed, that's different. Although

these dwellers be poor folk, I don't doubt they'd heap skins and pelts at your feet. I'll show you how to sell the stuff at good prices in Temanhassa."

"You and your fellow traders are not poor men," said Cappen pointedly.

"Naturally, you'd find us, ah, not ungenerous."

"Shall we say a tenth share of the profit from your expedition?"

"A tenth? How can you jest like that in an hour like this?"

"Retreating to winter in the Empire would cost more. As you must well know, who've had to cope year after year with its taxes, bribes, and extortionate suppliers." Getting snowed in here would be still worse, but Cappen thought it imprudent to explain that that had become a distinct possibility.

"We are not misers or ingrates. Nor are we unreasonable. Three percent is, indeed, lavish."

"Let us not lose precious time in haggling. Seven and a half."

"Five, and my friendship, protection, and recommendations to influential persons in Temanhassa."

"Done!" said Cappen. He sensed the trader's surprise and a certain instinctive disappointment. But the need to get on with the work was very real, and the bargain not a bad one.

Meanwhile he had arranged his things just barely well enough that he could begin. Dipping pen in ink, he said, "This is a strange work I must do, and potent forces are afoot. As yet I cannot tell of it, save to pledge that there is nothing of evil. As I write, I want you to talk to me in Xandran. Naught else."

Deghred gaped, remembered his dignity, and replied, "May I wonder why? You do not know that tongue, and I have only some smatterings."

"You may wonder if you choose. What you must do is talk."

"But what about?"

"Anything. Merely keep the words flowing."

Deghred groped for a minute. Such an order is not as simple as one might think. Almost desperately, he began: "I have these fine seasonings. They were shipped to me from distant lands at great expense. To you and you alone will I offer them at ridiculously low wholesale prices, because I hold you in such high esteem. Behold, for an ounce of pungent peppercorn, a mere ten zirgats. I look on this not as a loss to me, although it is, but a gift of goodwill."

Cappen scribbled. While he listened, the meanings came clear to him. He even mentally made up for the stumblings, hesitations, and thick accent. The language was his to the extent that it was the other man's; and he could have replied with fluency. What slowed him was the search in his mind for words that weren't spoken. "Knot" and "insoluble," for instance. How would one say them? . . . Ah, yes. Assuming that what he pseudo-remembered was correct. Maybe the connotations were strictly of a rope and of minerals that didn't melt in water. He jotted them down provisionally, but he wanted more context.

Deghred stopped. "Go on," Cappen urged.

"Well, uh—O barefaced brazen robber! Ten zirgats? If this withered and moldy lot went for two in the bazaar, I would be astounded. Yet, since I too am prepared to take a loss for the sake of our relationship, I will offer three—"

"Uh, could you give me something else?" Cappen interrupted. "Speech not so, m-m, commercial?"

"What can it be? My dealings with Xandrans are all commercial."

"Oh, surely not all. Doing business in itself involves sociability, the cultivation of friendly feelings, does it not? Tell me what might be said at a shared meal over a cup of wine."

Deghred pondered before he tried: "How did your sea voyage go? I hope you're not troubled by the heat. It is seldom so hot here at this time of year."

"Nothing more—more intimate? Don't men like these ever talk of their families? Of love and marriage?"

"Not much. I can't converse with them easily, you know. Women, yes."

"Say on."

"Well, I remember telling one fellow, when he asked, that the best whorehouse in the city is the Purple Lotus.

Especially if you can get Zerasa. By Kalat's cloven hoof, what a wench! Plump and sweet as a juicy plum, sizzling as a spitted rump roast, and the tricks she knows—" Deghred reminisced in considerable detail.

It wasn't quite what Cappen had meant. Still, association evoked words also amorous, but apparently decorous. His pen flew, scrawling, scratching out, spattering the paper and his tunic. When Degredh ended with a gusty sigh, Cappen had enough.

"Good," he said. "My thanks—albeit this is toward the end of saving your own well-being and prosperity too. You may go now. Five percent, remember."

The merchant rose and stretched himself as well as the roof allowed. "If naught else, that was a small respite from reality. Ah, well. You do have hopes? Are you coming along?"

"No," said Cappen. "My labors are just beginning."

Day broke still and cloudless but cruelly cold. Breath smoked white, feet crunched ice. When he emerged at mid-morning, Cappen found very few folk outdoors. Those stared at him out of their own frozen silence. The rest were huddled inside, keeping warm while they waited to learn their fate. It was as if the whole gigantic land held its breath.

He felt no weariness, he could not. He seemed almost detached from himself, his head light but sky-clear. His left arm cradled the harp. Tucked into his belt was a folded sheet of paper, but he didn't expect any need to refer to it. The words thereon were graven into him, together with their music. They certainly should be. The gods of minstrelsy knew—or would have known, if they weren't so remote from this wild highland—how he had toiled over the lyrics, searching about, throwing away effort after effort, inch by inch finding his way to a translation that fitted the notes and was not grossly false to the original, and at last, not satisfied but with time on his heels, had rehearsed over and over and over for his audience of turnips and sheepskins.

Now he must see how well it played for a more critical listener.

If it succeeded, if he survived, the first part of the reward he'd claim was to be let to sleep undisturbed until next sunrise. How remotely that bliss glimmered!

He trudged onward, scarcely thinking about anything, until he came to the altar. There he took stance, gazed across the abyss to peaks sword-sharp against heaven, and said, "My lady, here I am in obedience to your command."

It sounded unnaturally loud. No echo responded, no wings soared overhead, he stood alone in the middle of aloneness.

After a while, he said, "I repeat, begging my lady's pardon, that here I am with that which I promised you."

The least of breezes stirred. It went like liquid across his face and into his nostrils. In so vast a silence, he heard it whisper.

"I humbly hope my offering will please you and all the gods," he said.

And there she was, awesome and beautiful before him. A phantom wind tossed her hair and whirled snow-sparkles around her whiteness. "Well?" she snapped.

Could she too, even she, have been under strain? He doffed his cap and bowed low. "If my lady will deign to heed, I've created an epithalamium such as she desires, and have the incomparable honor of rendering it unto her, to be known forever after as her unique gift at the turning of the winter."

"That was quick, after you protested you could not."

"The thought of you inspired me as never erenow have I been inspired."

"To make it out of nothing?"

"Oh, no, my lady. Out of experience, and whatever talent is mine, and, above all else, as I confessed, the shining vision of my lady. I swear, and take for granted you can immediately verify, that neither melody nor lyrics were ever heard in this world, Heaven or Earth or the Elsewhere, before I prepared them for you."

He doubted that she could in fact scan space and time at once, so thoroughly. But no matter. He did not doubt that Nerigo kept his half-illicit arcanum and whatever came to it through his mirror that was not a mirror well sealed against observation human and non-human. Whatever gods had the scope and power to spy on him must also have much better things to do.

Aiala's glance lingered more than it pierced. "I do not really wish to destroy you, Cappen Varra," she told him slowly. "You have a rather charming way about you. But—should you disappoint me—you will understand that one does have one's position to maintain."

"Oh, absolutely. And how better could a man perish than in striving to serve such a lady? Yet I dare suggest that you will find my ditty acceptable."

The glorious eyes widened. The slight mercurial shivers almost ceased. "Sing, then," she said low.

"Allow me first to lay forth what the purpose is. Unless I am grievously mistaken, it is to provide an ode to nuptial joy. Now, my thought was that this is best expressed in the voice of the bride. The groom is inevitably impatient for nightfall. She, though, however happy, may at the same time be a little fearful, certain of loving kindness yet, in her purity, unsure what to await and what she can do toward making the union rapturous. Khaiantai is otherwise. She is a goddess, and here is an annual renewal. My song expresses her rapture in tones of unbounded gladness."

Aiala nodded. "That's not a bad theme," she said, perhaps a trifle wistfully.

"Therefore, my lady, pray bear with my conceit, in the poetic sense, that she sings with restrained abandon, in colloquial terms of revelry, not always classically correct. For we have nothing to go on about that save the writings of the learned, do we? There must have been more familiar speech among lesser folk, commoners, farmers, herders, artisans, lowly but still the majority, the backbone of the nation and the salt of the earth. To them too, to the Life Force that is in them, should the paean appeal."

"You may be right," said Aiala with a tinge of exasperation. "Let me hear."

While he talked, Cappen Varra, in the presence of one who fully knew the language, mentally made revisions. Translating, he had chosen phrasings that lent themselves to it.

The moment was upon him. He took off his gloves, gripped the harp, strummed it, and cleared his throat.

"We begin with a chorus," he said. Therewith he launched into song.

"Bridegroom and bride!
Knot that's insoluble,
Voices all voluble,
Hail it with pride.—"

She hearkened. Her bosom rose and fell.

"Now the bride herself sings.

"When a merry maiden marries,
Sorrow goes and pleasure tarries;
Every sound becomes a song,
All is right, and nothing's wrong!—"

He saw he had captured her, and continued to the bacchanalian end.

"Sullen night is laughing day—

All the year is merry May!"

The chords rang into stillness. Cappen waited. But he knew. A huge, warm easing rose in him like a tide.

"That is wonderful," Aiala breathed. "Nothing of the kind, ever before—"

"It is my lady's," he said with another bow, while he resumed his cap and gloves.

She straightened into majesty. "You have earned what you shall have. Henceforward until the proper winter, the weather shall smile, the dwellers shall prosper, and you and your comrades shall cross my mountains free of all hindrance."

"My lady overwhelms me," he thought it expedient to reply.

For a heartbeat, her grandeur gave way, ever so slightly. "I could almost wish that you—But no. Farewell, funny mortal."

She leaned over. Her lips brushed his. He felt as if struck by soft lightning. Then she was gone. It seemed to him that already the air grew more mild.

For a short while before starting back with his news he stood silent beneath the sky, suddenly dazed. His free hand strayed to the paper at his belt. Doubtless he would never know more about this than he now did. Yet he wished that someday, somehow, if only in another theatrical performance, he could see the gracefully gliding boats of the Venetian gondoliers.

AVE DE PASO

CATHERINE ASARO

MY COUSIN MANUEL WALKED alone in the twilight, out of sight, while I sat in the back of the pickup truck. We each needed privacy for our grief. The hillside under our truck hunched out of the desert like the shoulder of a giant. Perhaps that shoulder belonged to one of the Four-Corner Gods who carried the cube of the world on his back. When too many of the Zinacantec Maya existed, the gods grew tired and shifted the weight of their burden, stirring an earthquake.

I slipped my hand into my pocket, where I had hidden my offerings: white candles, pine needles, rum. They weren't enough. I had no copal incense to burn, no resin balls and wood chips to appease the ancestral gods for the improper manner of my mother's burial.

Manuel and I were far now from Zinacantn, our home in the highlands of Chiapas, Mexico. Years ago my mother had brought us here, to New Mexico. Later we had moved to Los Angeles, the city of fallen angels. But for this one night, Manuel and I had returned to New Mexico, a desert named after the country of our birth, yet not of that country.

An in-between place.

Dusk feathered across the land, brushing away a pepper-red sunset. Eventually I stirred myself enough to set out our sleeping bags in the bed of the truck. It wouldn't be as comfortable as if we slept on the ground, but we wouldn't wake up with bandolero scorpions or rattlesnakes in our bags either.

"Akushtina?" Manuel's voice drifted through the dry evening like a hawk.

I sat down against the wall of the pickup and pulled my denim jacket tight against the night's chill.

Manuel walked into view from around the front of the truck. "Tina, why didn't you answer?"

"It didn't feel right."

He climbed into the truck and dropped his Uzi at my feet. "You okay?"

I shuddered. "Take it away."

Sitting next to me, he folded his arms against the cold. "Take what away?"

I pushed the Uzi with my toe. "That."

"You see a rattler, you yell for me, what am I going to do? Spit at it?"

"You don't need a submachine gun to protect us from snakes."

He withdrew from me then, not with his body but with his spirit, into the shrouded places of his mind. I had hoped that coming here, away from the cold angles and broken lines of Los Angeles, would bring back the closeness we had shared as children. Though many people still considered us children.

"I don't want to fight," I said.

His look softened. "I know, *hija*."

"I miss her."

He put his arms around me and I leaned into him, this cousin of mine who at nineteen, three years older than me, was the only guardian I had now. Sliding my arms under his leather jacket, I laid my head against the rough cloth of his flannel shirt. And I cried, slight sounds that blended into the night. The crickets stopped chirping, filling the twilight with their silence.

Manuel murmured in Tzotzil Mayan, our first language, the only one he had ever felt was his, far more than the English we spoke now, or the Spanish we had learned as a second language. But he would never show his tears: not to me; not to the social workers in L.A. who had tried to reach him when he was younger and now feared they had failed; not to Los Halcones, the gang the Anglos called The Falcons, the barrio warriors Manuel considered the only family we had left.

Eventually I stopped crying. Crickets began to saw the night again, and an owl hooted, its call wavering like a ghost. Sounds came from the edge of the world:

a truck growling on the horizon, the whispering rumble of pronghorn antelope as they loped across the land, the howl of a coyote. No city groans muddied the night.

I pulled away from Manuel, wiping my cheek with my hand. Then I got up and went to stand at the cab of the truck, leaning with my arms folded on its roof. We had parked on the top of a flat hill. The desert rolled out in all directions, from here to the horizon, an endless plain darkening with shadows beneath a forever sky. This land belonged less to humans than to the giant furry tarantulas that crept across the parched soil; or to the tarantula hawks, those huge wasps that dived out of the air to grab their eight-legged prey; or to the javelinas, the wild, grunting pigs.

We had come here from the Chiapas village called Naben Chauk, the Lake of the Lightning. My mother had been outcast there, an unmarried woman with a child and almost no clan. After the death of Manuel's parents, my aunt and uncle, she had no one. So eight years ago she brought Manuel and me here, to New Mexico, where a friend had a job for her. But she dreamed of the City of Angels, convinced it could give us a better life. So later we had moved to Los Angeles, a sprawling giant that could swallow this hill like a snake swallowing a mouse.

"The city killed her," I said. "If we had stayed in Naben Chauk she would still be alive."

Manuel's jeans rustled when he stood up. His boots

thudded as he crossed the truck bed. He leaned on the cab next to me. "I wish it. You wish it. But Los Angeles didn't give her cancer. That sickness, it would have eaten her no matter where we went."

"The city sucked out pieces of her soul."

He drew me closer, until I was standing between him and the cab, my back against his front, his arms around me, his hands resting on the cab. "You got to let go, Tina. You got to say good-bye."

"I can't." It was like giving up, just like we had given up our home. I missed the limestone hills of the Chiapas highlands, where clouds hid the peaks and mist cloaked the sweet stands of pine. As a small girl, I had herded our sheep there, our only wealth, woolly animals we sheared with scissors bought in San Cristóbal de las Casas. Until an earthquake killed the flock.

As it had killed Manuel's parents.

I wished I could see my mother one last time, cooking over a fire at dawn, smoke rising around her, spiraling up and around until it escaped out the spaces where the roof met the walls. She would kneel in front of her *comal*, a round metal plate propped up on two pots and a rock, patting her maize dough back and forth, making tortillas.

"It's good we came here to tell her goody-bye," I said. "It was wrong the way she died, in that hospital. In L.A."

"We did the best we could." Manuel kissed the top of my head. "She couldn't have gotten medicine in Naben Chauk, not what she needed."

"Her spirit won't rest now."

"Tina, you got to stop all this, about spirits and things." Manuel let go of me. I turned around in time to see him pick up the Uzi. He held it like a staff. "This is how you 'protect your spirit.' By making sure no one takes what's yours."

"How can you come to mourn her and bring *this*." I jerked the gun out of his hand and threw it over the side of the truck. "She would hate it. *Hate* it."

"Goddamn it, Tina." Holding the side of the pickup, he vaulted over it to the ground. He picked up the Uzi, his anger hanging around him like smoke. Had I been anyone else, grabbing his gun that way could have gotten me shot.

I climbed out of the truck and jumped down next to him. He towered over me, tall by any standard, huge for a man of the Zinacantec Maya, over six feet. His hooknosed profile was silhouetted against the stars like an ancient Maya king, a warrior out of place and time, his face much like those carved into the *stellae*, the stones standing in the ruins of our ancestors. Proud. He was so proud. And in so much pain.

Faint music rippled out of the night, drifting on the air like a bird, strange and yet familiar, the sweet notes of a Chiapas guitar.

"Someone is here," I said.

Manuel lifted his gun as he scanned the area. "You see someone?"

"Hear someone." The music came closer now, stinging, bittersweet. "A guitar. On the other side of the hill."

He lowered the gun. "I don't hear squat."

"It's there." I hesitated. "Let's not stay here tonight If we went back into town, they would probably let us stay at the house—"

"No! We didn't come all this way to stay where she was a *maid*." Manuel motioned at the desert. "This is what she loved. The land."

I knew he was right. But the night made me uneasy "Something is wrong."

"Oh, hell, Tina." He took my arm. "I'll show you. No one is here."

I pulled away. "Don't go."

"Why not?" Manuel walked away, to the edge of the hilltop. He stood there, a tall figure in the ghosting moonlight. Then he disappeared, gone down the other side, vanished into the whispering night.

"Manuel, wait." I started after him.

The guitar kept playing, its notes wavering, receding, coming closer. Then it stopped, and the desert waited in silence. No music, no crickets, no coyotes.

Nothing.

"Manuel?" I called. "Did you find anyone?"

Gunshots cracked, splintering the night into pieces.

"No!" I broke into a run, sprinting to the edge where he had disappeared. Then I stopped. The slope fell away from my feet, mottled by mesquite and spidery ocotillo bushes, until it met the desert floor several hundred yards below.

"Manuel!" My shout winged over the desert.

No answer. I slid in a stumbling run down the hill, thorny mesquite grabbing at my jeans. About halfway down reason came back and I slowed down, moving with more caution.

I reached the bottom without seeing anyone. Yet a tendril of smoke wafted in the air. How? No fire burned anywhere.

Music started again, behind me. Turning, I faced the shadowed hill. My feet took me forward, toward the drifting notes, toward the hill, toward the music *in* the hill. Yet as long as I walked, as many steps as I took, I came no closer to that dusky slope. It stayed in front of me, humped in the moonlight.

With no warning, I was on the edge of a campfire. What I had thought was the hill, it was smoke, hanging in layers and curtains. I walked through the ashy mist, trying to reach the campfire that flickered red and orange, vague in the smoke-laden air.

Someone was sitting on the ground by the fire.

"Manuel?" I asked.

He didn't stir. I continued to walk, but came no closer to him.

It wasn't my cousin. The stranger gave no indication he knew I had come to his fire. He stared into the flames, a heavy man with rolls of flesh packed around his body.

The ground began to move under my feet, bringing him toward me, while I walked in place.

Guitar notes drifted in the smoke, joined now by drums, a Chamula violin, and a reed pipe. They keened for my mother. The melody hit discords, as if offended that it had to play for itself when I should have brought the music in her honor. But where in Los Angeles could I have found Zinacantec instruments or musicians to play them?

I had so little of what I needed to give my mother a proper burial. She lay in an unmarked grave in California. But I would do my best in this in-between place. Manuel should have been the one to perform the ceremony, as head of the family, but I knew what he would say if I asked him. He trusted his Uzi far more than the ways of our lost home.

The ground continued to bring the stranger to me. He stopped only a few paces away. With a slow, sure motion, he turned his head and smiled, a dark smile, a possessive smile.

"Akushtina." He pressed his hands together and lifted his arms. When he opened his hands, a whippoorwill lay in the cup of his palms.

"No!" I stepped forward. "Let her go!"

He clapped his hands and the bird screamed, turning into smoke when his palms smacked together. "She's gone."

I knew then that he had trapped my mother's spirit

when she died, catching it before she could return home to the mountains around the Lake of the Lightning. She hadn't been buried with the proper rituals, after a mourner's meal at dawn, her head toward the west. It had let this unnamed stranger steal her soul, just as he stole the spirit of the whippoorwill, her companion among the wild creatures that lived in the spirit world.

Wait.

The whippoorwill wasn't my mother's spirit companion. An ocelot walked with her. In her youth, she had met it in her dreams, as it prowled the dream corrals on the Senior Large Mountain. If the ancestral gods had been angry when she died, it was the ocelot they would have freed from its corral, leaving it to wander unprotected in the Chiapas highlands.

A whippoorwill made no sense. It came from this place, here, in the desert. During the year we lived in New Mexico, in the ranch house where my mother worked, she and I had often sat outside in the warm nights and listened to the eerie bird voices call though the dry air. So I thought of the whippoorwill when I thought of her. But if this stranger had truly captured her spirit companion, he would have shown me the ocelot.

Why a whippoorwill? I had no answer. All I could do was make the offerings I had brought. I pulled out the bag of pine needles and sprinkled them on the ground. The smoke around us smelled of copal incense, this stranger doing for himself what should have come from me. I fumbled in my pocket for the rum bottle. It wasn't true *posh*, a drink distilled from brown sugar and made in Chamula. This came from a store in L.A. But it was the best I could do.

The man snorted, giving his opinion of my offerings. He motioned at the rum. "You drink it."

Flushing, I tipped the bottle to my lips. The rum went down in a jolt and I coughed, spluttering drops everywhere. The rattle of the stranger's laugh made haze whirl around us, smoke curling and uncurling, hiding the desert, revealing it, hiding it again in veils of gray on gray.

Then I remembered the candles. Candles, tortillas for the gods. Taking them out of my pocket, I knelt down and set them in the dirt. They were ordinary, each made from white wax, with a white wick. When I lit them, they should have burned with a simple flame. Instead they sparked like tiny sky rockets straining to break free of the earth.

The man rose to his feet, ponderous and heavy. "This is all you have for me?"

I looked up, trying to understand what he wanted. A shape formed behind him, hazy in the smoke. It stepped closer and showed itself as a deer, a great stag with a king's rack of antlers. Two iguanas rode on its head, their bodies curving down to make blinders for its eyes, their tails curled tight around its antlers. They watched me with lizard gazes. The stranger had a whip in his hand now, not leather, but a living snake, its tongue flicking out from its mouth, its body supple and undulating, its tail stiffened into a handle.

I scrambled to my feet. "I know you," I rasped, my throat raw from the drifting smoke. "Yahval Balamil."

He stood before me and laughed, Yahval Balamil, the Earth Lord, the god of caves and water holes, he who could give riches or death, who could buy the pieces of your inner soul from a witch who took the shape of a goat, or trap your feet in iron sandals and make you work beneath the earth until the iron wore out.

Greed saturated his big-toothed smile. "You're mine now."

The smoke in the air curled thick around us. I tried to back away from him, but I was walking in place, my feet stepping and stepping, taking me nowhere.

"Mine," he said. "Both you and the boy."

"No! Leave us alone."

He cracked his whip, and it snapped around my body in coils, growing longer with each turn, pinning my arms. The head stopped inches from my face and the snake hissed, its tongue flicking out to touch my cheek. I tried to scream, but no sound came out.

"Mine," the Earth Lord whispered.

"Tina?" a voice asked behind me.

"Manuel!" I spun around. "Where have you been? Are you all right?"

"Yeah, I'm all right." He stood with the gun dangling at his side. "What's wrong?"

"Can't you *see* it?"

"See what?"

I glanced around. We were halfway up the hill, just the two of us. No snake, no spirits, no gods. The fire had vanished, and the smoke had solidified into the mountain.

Turning back to Manuel, I said, "He's gone."

"He?" My cousin scowled. "Why do you smell like liquor?"

"I drank some rum."

"When did you start messing with that shit?" He stepped closer. "I told you never to touch it. You know what happens when men see a pretty girl like you drunk? It makes them think to do what they shouldn't be doing."

"It was part of the ceremony."

"Ceremony?" He looked around, taking in the candle stubs and pine needles scattered on the ground. Then he sighed, the fist-tight knot of his anger easing. In a gentler voice he said, "There isn't no one here. I checked the whole area."

"Then why did you shoot?"

"It was a deer. I missed it."

I stared at him. "You shot at a deer with an Uzi?"

"It surprised me. I've never seen deer here before."

"What if it had been me who surprised you?"

He touched my cheek. "You know I would never hurt you."

"You didn't shoot at a deer. It was Yahval Balamil."

His smile flashed in the darkness. "Did I hit him?"

"Don't make fun of me."

"You're mine," the Earth Lord whispered.

With a cry, I jerked back and lost my balance. I fell to the ground and rolled down the hill like a log, with mesquite ripping at my clothes. When my head struck a rock, I jolted to a stop and my sight went black. A ringing note rose in the air like a bird taking flight, then faded into faint guitar music.

"Tina!" Manuel shouted, far away.

"Mine," the Earth Lord said. "Both of you." A snake hissed near my ear.

"Stop it!" I struck at the dark air.

"Oiga!" Now Manuel sounded as if he was right above me. "I won't hurt you."

My sight was coming back, enough so I could see my cousin's head silhouetted against the stars. He was kneeling over me, his legs on either side of my hips. "Are you okay?" he asked. "Why did you scream?"

"Mine," the Earth Lord murmured.

"No!" I said.

Manuel brushed a lock of hair off my face. "I didn't mean to scare you."

Smoke was forming behind him, tendrils coming together in the outline of a stag.

"Leave him alone!" I sat up, almost knocking Manuel over, and batted at the air, as if that could defeat the smoke and protect my cousin.

"What's wrong?" Manuel stayed where he was, his knees straddling my hips, his thighs pressing on mine. He grabbed my hands, pulling them against his chest. He held them in his large grip while he caught me around the waist with his other arm. "*Tu eres bueno, Tinita.* It's okay."

The smoke settled onto him, a dark cloud soaking into his body, smelling of incense. Curls of smoke brushed my hands where Manuel held them, my legs where his thighs pressed mine, my breasts where his chest touched mine. The invading darkness seeped into him.

Manuel jerked as if caught by the smoke. Then he pulled me hard against himself, his breath warm on my cheek, his body musky with the scent of his jacket, his shirt, his sweat. He murmured in Tzotzil, bending his head as if searching for something. I turned my face up— and he kissed me, pressing his lips hard against my mouth.

I twisted my head to the side. "No."

"Shhh . . . ," he murmured. "It's all right." He lay me back down on the ground, his body heavy on mine, like the weight of the dead.

"Manuel, stop!" I tried to roll away, but he kept me in place.

"Mine," the Earth Lord said. "Both of you."

"*No.* Go away!" A breeze wafted across my face, bringing the smell of sagebrush—?

And candles?

Manuel kissed me again and pulled open my jacket with his free hand. "Akushtina," he whispered. *"Te amo, bija."*

"Not like this." My voice shook as I struggled. "You don't mean it like this."

"Soon," the Earth Lord promised. The snake hissed again.

Panic fluttered across my thoughts. I still smelled candles. That scent, I knew it from when we had lived here. Luminarios. On Christmas Eve my mother had filled brown bags with dirt, enough in each to hold one candle. She lined the paths and walls of the front yard with the glowing beige lanterns. My mother's love in a paper bag, warming the darkness while distant whip-poorwills whistled in the night.

"We can go together." Manuel moved his hand over my breast. "Together."

"Manuel, listen." I was talking too fast, but I couldn't slow down. "Do you remember the luminarios?"

His searching hand stopped as it reached my hip. "Why?"

"Remember what we swore when we were watching them? About family? How we would protect each other?"

He lifted his head to look at me, his memory of that time etched on his face. The smoke that had funneled into his body seeped out again. It swirled around him, as if trying to go inside and finding its way blocked by the power of a memory. Finally it drifted away, into the night. Somewhere an owl hooted.

Manuel made a noise, a strangled gasp he sucked into his throat. He jumped to his feet and backed up one step, still watching me. Then he spun around and strode away. Within seconds the shadows of the hill had taken him.

I got up to my knees and bent over, my arms folded across my stomach, my whole body shaking. A wave of nausea surged over me, then receded. What if he had gone through with what he started? It would have destroyed us both.

What had he meant by *We can go together*? Go where?

Then I knew. Under the earth. Forever.

I scrambled to my feet and ran up the hill. It wasn't until I came over the top that I saw him, a dark shadow by the truck. My hiking boots crunched on the rocks as I walked. I stopped in front of him and looked up at his face.

Once I had seen a vaquero forced to shoot his horse after a truck hit it on Interstate 10. The dying animal had lain on its side, dismay in its gaze until the cowboy ended its pain. Manuel had that same look now.

He gave me the keys to the truck. "Go back to town."

"Not unless you come."

He shifted the Uzi in his hands. "I'm staying here."

I struggled to stay calm. "When people hurt, sometimes they do things they shouldn't. But you stopped. You *stopped*." I pushed at the Uzi. "Manuel, put it away."

"You're all I got left." His voice cracked. "And now I made that dirty, too."

I thought of his words: *Te amo*. "You said you loved me."

"You don't know nothing about how I meant it."

"I'm not stupid. I know." I shook my head. "It was *him*, making you act that way."

He stared at me, his stark face hooded by shadows. "It was me. It's always been there."

"But you didn't do it." I tried to find the words to reach him. "Everyone has darkness inside of him. You turned away from yours. That says how strong you are."

He snorted. "You got this seeing problem, Tina, like you look at me with mirror shades. They reflect away the truth about me, so you see what you want, this good that isn't there."

"It's there." For all that Manuel denied it, the good lived in him. The changes we had weathered in our lives had worn him down, eroding him like the wind and thunderstorms on the desert, in part because he was older, more set in his life, and had lost both his parents as well as my mother. But also because his height, strength, deep voice, and brooding anger frightened people. He looked like the warrior he would have been in another time, and in his frustration with a world that had no place for him, he had begun to live out that expectation.

"It's still there," I repeated, as if saying it enough would make him believe it.

He just shook his head.

"Mine," the Earth Lord whispered. "Both of you."

This time I gave no hint I heard. I kept watching my cousin.

"Take the truck," Manuel said. "Go back to town. Back to L.A."

"Why?" Everything that mattered to me was slipping away. I knew what he would do if he stayed alone here in the desert. "So you can take away the only family I have left?"

"You'll do better without me."

"No!"

A shadow moved on the cab of the truck, a small one, barely bigger than my hand. Whippoorwill. With a soft flapping of wings, it rose into the air and circled above us, then flew away over the hill, into the endless open spaces of the night.

"*Mine,*" the Earth Lord rasped. His voice had an edge now, no longer gloating, more like a protest.

Then, finally, I understood. My mother's spirit had never been the one in danger. It was the two of us here, Manuel and me. We couldn't accept what we had lost, our home, our lives, our parents. That was why we had come to this in-between place. Our grief had made us vulnerable.

"I was wrong," I said. "The bird that Yahval Balamil was holding, it wasn't Mama. It was me."

Manuel clenched his fist around the Uzi. "What the hell are you talking about?"

"The Earth Lord," I told him. "He's come for us. He knows we're hurting now. It makes us easy prey. He's come to take the pieces of our souls."

"Stop it." Manuel's voice cracked. "We're the only ones here. Not dead people or fat gods. Just *us*. No one else. *No-fucking-one else*." He flipped over the Uzi, holding it by the barrel, and swung it like a club, smashing it into the door of the truck, denting the weathered chrome. As I jumped back, he flipped the gun back over and aimed it at himself.

"Manuel, *no!*"

He didn't move, just stood like a statue, the Uzi pressed against his chest. I was afraid to breathe, to look away, even to blink.

Slowly, so slowly, he turned, and pointed the gun away from his heart, out over the desert—

And he fired.

Bullets punctured the night like rivets ramming metal. Shadow clouds of dirt flew into the air and rocks broke in explosions. He kept on firing, his long legs planted wide, his hands clenched on the gun, shattering the night, until I thought he would crack the land wide open and fall into the fissure.

After an eternity, the bullets stopped. Manuel sank

to his knees and bowed his head, holding the gun like a pole in front of him. He made no sound. After a span of heartbeats I realized he was crying for the first time in years, in silence, even now unable to give voice to the grief that had torn apart his life, as he lost almost everything and everyone that had ever mattered to him.

I went to him and murmured in Tzotzil, nonsense words meant for comfort. He drew in a choked breath. Standing up, he wiped his face with the sleeve of his jacket. We stood with space between us, a space that would always be there now.

I gave him the keys. "Will you drive?"

He stood watching my face. Then, finally, he said, "We can stay in town tonight. Leave for L.A. in the morning."

"Okay." My voice caught. "That sounds good."

I knew that our surviving this one night wouldn't solve the problems we faced in L.A. It wouldn't take away the inner demons Manuel wrestled or bring back my mother. We still had a long way to go.

But it was a start.

We had finally begun to ride the healing path.

So we drove away, through a land haunted with moonlight, leaving behind the bone-desert of our grief.

GRASS

LAWRENCE MILES

"Only in the context of a totality of the sciences do Jefferson's achievements make sense. This would for instance explain the apparent contradiction of how a man now famed for his contribution to the political sciences . . . [was also] purportedly the first westerner to fully reconstruct the remains of a prehistoric mammoth. It's more the failing of an over-enthusiastic age than of the man himself that Jefferson seriously believed such antediluvian beasts could have survived until the 1800s in the wilds of the unexplored midwest. . . ."

—D. P. Mann, *The Worlds of Thomas Jefferson (1958).*

IT STARTS WITH THE President of the United States of America, although we should be clear on exactly what kind of *gentleman* we're discussing here. Sitting behind the Presidential desk (rose-wood, as it happens, and very nice too) is a man whom later generations will call a polymath, a statesman-philosopher, a true product of the enlightenment. Oh yes, this particular President is a *creator*, with a portfolio that begins "We, the people" and works its way up to a big climax from there. He's also a man who distrusts priests of just about every denomination, which explains much of what's about to happen here: he's got a lot of time for the divine, this one, but mere mortal authority figures get his back up like nothing else on God's Earth. Now, we can't be sure that what we're about to see in this room is *bona fide* true, because the affairs of the President are traditionally left behind closed doors, and there are some rules even we're expected to follow. But we can put the scene together out of the pieces we know. Call it listening at keyholes. Call it history by degrees.

Mr. Jefferson—Mr. President—sits behind the aforementioned desk, in front of a vast window that looks out onto a garden of grass and cat's-ears, a garden quite specifically designed so as to in no way resemble the three million square miles of hostile territory beyond it. The light's flooding through the window onto the parquet-and-polish floor, while the President himself is leaning over the books with which he surrounds himself (this being a less literate time, however, "surrounds" makes the number of books involved sound greater than it really is), reaching for his little box of joy. The box is small and off-white, a gift from a visitor whose exact name and purpose Mr. Jefferson can't quite recall: he seems to recollect that it was a woman, probably French (he has no difficulty remembering this, as he's had a head for Frenchwomen ever since a certain remarkable incident in a brothel in Paris ... this is another story, and not the only "another story" which will be intercepting us today). History doesn't record what he keeps *inside* the box, though as we've imagined Mr. Jefferson as a free-thinking nineteenth century gentleman it could be anything from snuff to hashish. Let's give him the benefit of the doubt, and assume it's chewing tobacco. Undignified as it may seem.

"It has to be done—it *must* be done—it is our duty," he says, as he starts picking at the box's contents. He talks the way he writes, with far too many hyphens and pauses, and he's addressing the two men standing on the other side of his desk. "If we're to claim these lands for the good of our nation—if we're to prevent them being overrun by jackals and opportunists—if we're to have room in which to breathe, and not fall upon each other as they do in Europe...."

Now, it so happens that Mr. Jefferson's domain has recently grown, thanks to a certain land deal which is not only due to increase his running total of United States, but which will also give him vast tracts of what he believes to be lush and verdant farmland, possibly including that mythical easy route to the Pacific. And the two men who now stand in Mr. Jefferson's office, nodding in solemn agreement, will go down in history

as the first men to travel into the heart of this new terrain: or the first to take notes anyway, which is the way
history works. Their names are, from left to right, Mer-
iwether Lewis and William Clark. As expected.

(This is all quite ridiculous, of course. At least one of
these men already belongs to the President's inner circle.
If Jefferson wants to brief them on their mission, then
he's more likely to do it in a cozy drawing room with a
bottle of Cognac, swapping stories as Lewis lounges on
a chaise longue and Clark leans nonchalantly against
the fireplace. But how can we resist imagining it this
way? The two of them standing to attention before the
Presidential desk, being instructed to journey into the
dark heart of the Northwest and bring the land under
control. No doubt you're already imagining these two
great explorers, these two grizzled veterans of the wilderness, walking into the President's office dressed in
furs and racoon-skin hats. We need to believe they're
going to step out of the briefing and, without even pausing for breath, stride off into the jungles of uncharted
America. Such is history.)

Mr. Jefferson is telling the explorers that nobody can
say for sure what they'll find in the Northwestern ter-
ritories. The French who sold him the land have hardly
been forthcoming, and the Indians aren't likely to be
much help either. The President expects every form of
terrain imaginable, from the tropical to the simply peculiar. He's read the greatest naturalists of the age. He

has plans to meet with Alexander von Humboldt himself. He's even heard the theories of the Englishman Frere, who claims to have found human remains which blatantly defy the book of Genesis, something Mr. Jefferson greatly appreciates. Oh, yes indeed. As an enlightened gentleman, the President knows the *terra incognita* Lewis and Clark will find is no Biblical wasteland. It's to be an altogether more rational landscape, filled with all the wonders that biology and geology can produce. A new world, untouched by Church dogma, governed only by the laws of Nature and Nature's God.

This is the point when Mr. Jefferson tells. Lewis and Clark about the mammoths: Oddly—seeing as most of this patchwork conversation will be lost to posterity—the part about the mammoths is the one thing the history books *do* record.

It starts with the President, but in purely chronological terms the briefing in the office isn't the first thing to actually *happen*. Just look at this landscape, for example. Nothing behind-closed-doors here. The sky's a color which later generations will be unable to imagine as anything other than a kind of paint, a deep blue, a *dark* blue, that makes the green, green grass look as though it's glaring in the sunlight. The air's fresh, pre-industrial fresh, the kind of fresh you only get once it's been filtered through the lungs of several million herd animals and a couple of dozen Indian tribes (this is as fresh as nature gets, no doubt about it). The grass clings to the slopes, sticks close to the curves of the land, so the green's only broken up by the dirt-paths where animals have left their scents behind them like breadcrumb-trails. And mountains? Oh, there are mountains. Just waiting on the horizon, looking as if they'll *always* be just waiting on the horizon, wherever you stand on the surface of the Earth. Perfect idyll. Perfect Montana.

Timeless, we'd say. But from the President's point of view, we'd have to call it the past. Months before the briefing of Mr. Lewis and Mr. Clark, the white race has already set foot in the Land of the Shining Mountains.

Here she comes now.

Her name's Lucia Cailloux, and at this moment she's running barefoot through the grass, up the side of a slope which seems to have been put there just to warn travelers that the Rockies will be starting soon, and that they'd better get used to moving uphill. An observer would point out that Lucia—whose manner of dress is unusually masculine, but then, that's probably what you'd expect from someone who's spent so much time talking to damned heathen Indians—is technically wearing *boots*. But that's not how it feels to Lucia. No, she can feel the warm, warm earth between her naked toes, because in her head she's suddenly become an eight-year-old. As a twenty-year-old woman in the service of her government, this is hardly what she's being paid for, but right now her superiors are more than eight thousand miles away and Lucia can't help but feel she's going to get away with it.

You see, right now she believes she's *going* somewhere. When she was young, she once ran all the way up the Rue Viande, something of an achievement when you've got child-sized legs and no shoes, because the Rue Viande is a perfect slope and the sheer amount of dirt on it (in those days, anyway, before Napoleon started cleaning it all up) made the road feel like mud in the summer. On that day—running all the way to the tannery, right at the highest point of the street, where the skins were strung up like flags at the top of the world—the junior Lucia could feel the whole world cracking like glass behind her, with the wind ripping through her dirt-blonde hair and the sheer speed (all of, oh, two miles an hour) tearing at her little dress. And as she headed for the tip of that slope, she knew—*she knew*—she'd look down and see something big and wonderful on the other side, as her reward for running all the way. She knew she'd see the whole world, in all its truth and majesty. The face, if you will, of Nature's God.

She was right, as well. Young Lucia always *was* a perceptive little witch.

Now the older Lucia, barefoot and booted, knows the same thing. She can quite literally smell it on the wind. At the top of the slope, she stops, so this is the point when we finally see her face in closeup. Dirt-blonde hair ragged around her shoulders, pasty little freckles blistering in the sunlight, the pupils in her big, big eyes getting smaller as she brushes the last few drops of sweat and sunshine away from her forehead. It doesn't really matter whether we're looking at Lucia *now* or watching the eight-year-old flashback version, because as it turns out her hair's naturally dirt-blonde in color. Twelve years after the Rue Viande, even a clean Lucia looks that way.

Lucia can hear her co-traveler, the Indian, thumping his way up the slope behind her. He calls out to her: *"Quelque chose?"*

And Lucia calls back: *"Tout."* (But that's pretty much the last time we'll be hearing her words in their natural spoken tongue.)

So the world spins around us, vertigo-wise, until we can look down on the great grass-covered crater beyond the slope. The dimple in the world, where Nature's God herself has reached down and left a whacking great fingerprint on the landscape. A gentle pit, with slopes of green sunning themselves in the midday heat, letting troughs of rainwater simmer and merge on their skin.

And there at the bottom of it all, the mammoths.

Now Lucia finds herself running again, and for a moment she isn't sure whether it's *now* her running or *then* her, until she remembers that on the Rue Viande she never went down the other side of the slope. At the bottom of the basin, the mammoths are grazing. It'd be almost abstract, like seeing drawings of fluffy brown clouds on a painted backdrop, if it weren't for the smell.

(Of course, when the eight-year-old Lucia stood on the *other* slope, the view was quite different. What she saw was a cartload of corpses, blocking the street while the horseman stopped to flirt with one of the local girls, as if having a cartload of corpses was some kind of aphrodisiac. But then, that was the Revolution for you. *C'est la vie*, as they say everywhere except Paris.)

That smell's starting to bother Lucia now, because she's remembering the smell of dung on the Rue Viande. She's so busy separating the horse-smell from the mammoth-smell that she doesn't even realize how far inertia's taking her. Gravity drags her to the bottom of the crater, then keeps her going, so before she can think about it she's stumbling over the ridges where the beasts have chewed and trampled away the grass. Pity the poor woman. The second most momentous moment of her life so far, and all she perceives is a series of confusing, ragged-edged images. The red-brown blurs that she knows are impossible animals. The smears of green that mark the walls of the crater, plastered with spoor and crushed plants: and is that a baby there, a baby mammoth, a little smudge of hair trying to stick close to its bigger smudge of a mother . . . ?

This is when things get slightly out of hand. It's when Lucia turns, nearly falling arse over tit in the process, and finds herself staring at the absurdly huge shape which is even now bearing down on her. The bull-mammoth weighs just over seven tons, not that Lucia will ever know it, and when rising up on its hind legs (as it is now) it must be all of fifteen feet high. When it raises its trunk, and opens its mouth, and flexes its massive lungs, you know it's quite capable of destroying anything that threatens its own stomping ground.

Nonetheless, the first thing Lucia does when faced with this monstrosity is "protect" herself by putting her arms up in front of her face. And they call this the Age of Reason.

There was an Indian. You might have forgotten about him.

He's now standing on the crest of the slope, watching the great beast rear up over the woman who's nominally his employer, though as a product of a non-market culture the Indian considers this "employer" business to be a pile of deershit. The Indian's name (for our purposes, anyway) is Broken Nose, which is not, of course, a "real" Indian name. It was given to him by a group of Frenchmen with especially fat faces, and it was earned after a confrontation at a French trading post, during which—predictably—the Indian broke a French official's nose. The friends of the unfortunate fat-faced man, being typically European, found this amusing. Being *very* typically European, "Broken Nose" was their idea of irony.

It's apparently supposed to sound like an authentic Indian title, although Broken Nose himself considers it just a good excuse to punch future fat-faced men without them being surprised. Besides, his original Shoshoni name was even more embarrassing.

It has to be said, Broken Nose doesn't have a great interest in the aesthetic. Below him are creatures the American settlers would find unbelievable, which would probably trigger a religious spawn in the Catholics or the Jesuits whom Mr. Jefferson distrusts so much. However, Broken Nose simply finds the beasts stupid-looking, wearing thick wool all over their bodies despite the sunshine. Broken Nose is *slightly* concerned for his "employer," but he's well aware that she can look after herself.

On the first night of the expedition, when Broken Nose and Mademoiselle Cailloux made camp on the trail from Louisiana—where the Frenchwoman had arrived under the name of "Lucy Pebbles," and bartered for supplies in what sounded to the Indian like a perfect local accent—the two of them talked at length. Or as much as was possible, anyway, given that Broken Nose had been taught French by men who only needed to prime him for certain tasks. Without any due modesty, Broken Nose showed Mme. Cailloux the scar which had been ritually inflicted across his inner thigh (*not* by his own tribe, but that's another "another story"). And with less regard for her integrity than Broken Nose would have expected from a European woman, Mme. Cailloux bared her torso from her neck to her waist, revealing a scab left by a bullet which she claimed *should* have killed her, by all the known laws of Nature and science. This began a discussion about the great wars in Europe, about the little tribal elder called Napoleon and the weapons he could muster: guns like those Mme. Cailloux herself carried, but grown so large that they needed huge boats of their own. Broken Nose asked why the Europeans always insisted on fighting with each other, and that gave the Mademoiselle pause for thought.

"*Your* people fight, don't they?" she said.

Broken Nose told her that this was indeed the case.

"Then why do *you* do it?" the woman asked.

The obvious answer was "because you tell us to," naturally, but Broken Nose suspected this was missing the point. The reasons seemed to him to be to do with territory, with possessions, with differences in gods. . . .

"No," said Mme. Cailloux. "We fight to stop the other tribes becoming *whole*."

Broken Nose didn't understand that. He still doesn't, although Mme. Cailloux has assured him that he will, before their mission here is complete. That is, if she doesn't get herself killed by the bull-mammoth.

In all probability, it's impossible to describe how it feels to have a mammoth rearing up over you. Maybe it's like the feeling you get when you lie on your back and watch the stars, and for a moment—*just for a moment*—you suddenly realize the true size of what you're staring at, as your brain suddenly forgets to force your usual scale of perception onto things. Maybe. It might be interesting to ask Lucia, even though she has even less conception of the distances of stars than the rest of us (but she's probably wise enough to know that Uranus, the furthest-flung of the seven planets, is seventeen hundred million miles farther away than she'll ever travel).

For the record, the mammoth *isn't* going to trample her to death. But looking up at the beast now, seeing its great brown-black outline framed against the perfect blue, Lucia feels she's watching the very countenance of Nature's God. As with the cart of corpses on the Rue Viande, it's the little details that really bother her. The strands of crushed grass on the bottom of its big round feet. The curve of its maw, the upturned V-shape that she knows could swallow a man, if not whole, then certainly in no more than *two* mouthfuls. The chips in its tusks, tiny imperfections in arcs of ivory so long that no matter which way she turns her head, she knows she won't be able to see both tips at once. And then there's its breath. Its terrible and ancient mammoth-breath, washing over her as the animal bellows into her face (one of those things Lucia's never considered until now, and which she's sure the academics who study the bones of these beasts have never considered either).

Yes, these are the things Lucia has trouble coping

with. So many little creases and flaws, more than she could catalogue in half a lifetime, let alone in the raw seconds she believes she has left. The beast's stubby-but-oh-so-big front legs pedal the air in front of its body, and then it suddenly finds itself falling.

It doesn't push itself forward as it falls. It doesn't, as it were, *attack*. It drops to the ground in front of Lucia, not on top of her, and the impact would surely crack the Earth open if the ground here weren't so used to the abuse. This is the way a bull-mammoth warns off the opposition. Lucia's realizing that even as she peels her heart from the roof of her mouth and tries to stop herself falling over (noticing, as an incidental detail, that the smell of sweat which is starting to blot out the dung-scent is *hers* and not the fault of the herd).

The bull-mammoth is exhausted. It's not a creature built for rearing up on its hind legs, and the only con-clusion we—like Lucia—can reach is that it expects strangers to be so intimidated by its mass that it doesn't actually need to follow up the threat. Having made its point, having bellowed its great beef-heart out, it can't do anything more than stand still and get its breath back. Lungs the size of fat children inflate and deflate, inflate and deflate, under a heavy pelt that must be home to entire empires of insects. From four feet above her head, those huge black eyes are staring down at Lucia, as if the thing's daring her to try anything else.

Easy to call it the face of Nature's God. So big, so

blatant, that we can only assume it's been put there for a purpose. Which it has, as Lucia well knows. *All* animals are there for a purpose. Horses are for riding, pigs are for eating. As far as she's concerned, the mammoths are here as a kind of metaphor. These are *political* animals, hence Mr. Jefferson's interest.

(You must have been wondering, for example, where this herd originates: woolly skins and elephant-blubber hardly seem to fit in around here. The best explanation we can hope for is that a number of mammoths were once the property of Catherine of Russia, she who was known as "The Great" before some idiot in her court started spreading that God-awful story about the horse. Horse or no horse, Catherine had something of a reputation as a witch . . . a label applied to most efficient female rulers, it's true, but even before her death there were fabulous and revolting stories about the company she liked to keep, and the animal rites they used to perform. Horses for riding, pigs for eating, trained monkeys for ritual. It's not entirely clear what the link is between the Empress of Russia being a witch and the existence of live mammoths here in what will one day be the State of Montana, although Lucia has heard it said, with maddening vagueness, that one can easily lead to the other. History is full of these logical gaps. Certainly, it's rumored that one such hairy beast was given by Catherine as a gift to George III of England, but that George—half-crazed brute that he was—destroyed the thing in a fight with pit dogs without even realizing its value. Lucia is secretly of the opinion that if Russia had given such a gift to the French, they probably would have eaten it.)

But Lucia's mammoth just keeps gasping. It's vulnerable now. With its show of strength over, it's got nothing to protect it but its dignity. Gravity has *not* been kind to these creatures, which probably explains why they're ripping up the grass on the crater floor when there are so many nice fresh trees just a couple of hundred yards over the rim. So when Lucia takes a step forward, the mammoth doesn't even blink: it's impossible to imagine such a blink being anything but a major task, and taking anything less than an afternoon to complete. From the look on its face, we could almost believe it's *indignant.*

How can we help but try to read its expression? If the mammoths were put here as metaphors, then we can read them any way we like. It's hard not to find meaning in something that big.

There's a stillness now, Lucia regarding the mammoth, the mammoth regarding Lucia. It's only once Lucia has paid her respects to the silence that she raises her hand. The trunk is close enough to touch, and touch it she does. Her fingers run through the tiny brown hairs, across the leathery old skin, over the wrinkles and the patches of dirt. She almost expects the beast to flinch, or to purr like a cat.

It's vulnerable, anybody can see that. Now, and only

now, Lucia gets her one big chance to touch the impossible.

This is what passed between Mme. Cailloux and Broken Nose that morning, after they pulled themselves to their feet at dawn and began the final trek to the place of the mammoths:

Mme. Cailloux spoke of a man called Jefferson, the leader of the colonists who lived off in the eastern lands. Mme. Cailloux explained to Broken Nose that her own tribal leader, Napoleon Short-Arse, had agreed to *sell* a portion of the land to the aforementioned Jefferson (a notion which, like the "employer" idea, Broken Nose finds profoundly stupid).

"We're afraid," said the Mademoiselle. "All of us. Your people. My people."

Broken Nose told her that his people weren't afraid of anything, which was, in his experience, what the French expected to hear from a stupid Indian.

"There's a saying in Europe," Mme. Cailloux went on. " 'The other man's grass is always greener.' We fight for territory. We start wars to acquire the other man's land. Why?"

Broken Nose shrugged. "More room. For cattle."

"No," the Frenchwoman told him. "It's because we think . . . we secretly believe . . . that the other man's land is a paradise. We start to believe there are great secrets there. Secrets we have to know for ourselves. And when we take the land away from him, and we find there's no paradise there . . . then we tell ourselves it was the *other* man's kind of paradise. Not ours. You understand?"

"Your people are stupid," said Broken Nose. (Not entirely true: this is what he believes he said, *after the fact*, although his training in the French tongue doesn't cover the possibility of him insulting his "employers." In his head, *after the fact*, he hears the words in his own language.)

"Perhaps," he imagines that Mme. Cailloux said. "But it's a matter of warfare. In war, we attack the enemy's resources. If an enemy has supply lines, we cut them. If an enemy has a better kind of weapon, we rid him of it."

This sounded to Broken Nose like the first sensible thing she'd said.

She went on to explain many things which Broken Nose had either no understanding of or no interest in. She told him, for example, that in the possession of Napoleon Short-Arse there was a length of metal, which purportedly came from a weapon that had been used to cut the flesh of one of the white man's gods "while he hung on the cross," this metal having the power to induce divine visions (of the spirit-world, Broken Nose guessed) in anyone who was scratched by it.

"Imagine such a thing in the power of the Vatican,"

the Mademoiselle said, although Broken Nose had no idea what marked these Vatican out from any of the other European tribes. "The relic would prove them correct. It would show them to be justified in all their beliefs. Thus would their grass become greener, and their state grow stronger. They might even become *whole*."

"Whole?" queried Broken Nose.

"I saw the Revolution," replied Mme. Cailloux. "I know what happens when people get what they want. Or when they *believe* they do."

None of which told Broken Nose anything remotely useful, or even explained the woman's mission to find the mammoths before the land gets passed on to Mr. Jefferson. But now, in what we have to call the *present*, Broken Nose is trying not to trip over his skin-shod heels as he tumbles down the slope of the crater. Up ahead, he can see Mme. Cailloux, facing the largest of all the mammoths (or is it just the closest?). He can see the woman resting her hand on the monster's trunk, and he can see the beast keeping quite still, something which his fellow Shoshoni would probably take as proof of the foreign witch's powers over the animal kingdom. But Broken Nose has little time for the wonders of nature, and sees her only as being lucky.

He pulls himself to a halt as the ground levels out under his feet, stopping just a few yards from the bulk of the bull-mammoth. Its eyes are fixed on the woman, and it makes pained groaning noises when it breathes.

Slowly, and with some reluctance, Mme. Cailloux lowers her hand.

"*Tout,*" she says. (This is the original French, of course, but somehow it makes more sense that way.)

Broken Nose isn't really sure where he should look. It seems disrespectful, somehow, to disturb this union. There they stand, woman and monster, in a communion that would seem almost obscene if it weren't so unlikely. For some reason, Broken Nose remembers a folk tale from his childhood about a father who had an improper relationship with his daughter, and who was swallowed up by the Earth as a punishment. After a few moments more, he speaks.

"The cargo," he says, using a word he's more than familiar with even though it's not entirely the right one. "Our *tools.* . . ."

It's then that Mme. Cailloux regains her senses, preternatural or otherwise, and turns away from the beast. The mammoth never blinks, though, and never moves its head. The Mademoiselle looks up toward the top of the slope, presumably remembering the packs which she and Broken Nose have left over the rise, the equipment her own "employers" issued her before transporting her here to the Land of the Shining Mountains. (And just as we imagined Lewis and Clark standing to attention before Jefferson, so Broken Nose imagines Mme. Cailloux standing before Napoleon Short-Arse himself, although he's imagining Napoleon sitting in a position of honor around a roaring fire rather than sitting behind a desk: there is, of course, no Shoshoni word for "furniture.")

So it is that Mme. Cailloux draws away from the mammoth, to begin her slow climb back up the slope, with Broken Nose at her heels. Mme. Cailloux doesn't look back at the mammoth as she walks, something Broken Nose interprets as an almost incestuous shame. And the mammoth doesn't watch her go, simply continuing to stare at the spot where she once stood. So it's left to Broken Nose to glance over his shoulder on the way up the slope, to watch the woolly monster recover its strength after its four seconds' worth of rabid activity, while the rest of the herd-animals go on bellowing and sniffing at each other. He wonders if the bull-mammoth even understands the difference between its human visitors and the other beasts of the wilderness.

"These are Mr. Jefferson's animals," he hears Mme. Cailloux say, halfway up the rise. "They feed on Mr. Jefferson's grass."

He *still* doesn't know what she's talking about. Broken Nose is starting to feel that even the mammoths understand this mission better than he does, but then again, wouldn't you expect him to think that way? Being Shoshoni, when *he* uses the mammoths as a metaphor the results aren't particularly literary.

Which leads us back to the President of the United States of America himself, as he sits behind his rosewood desk in his rose-tinted office, picking snuff or hashish or chewing tobacco out of his little carved box. This is some months in what might be called Lucia's future, so Lewis and Clark have in the last few minutes dutifully marched out of the office in their unlikely racoonskin hats. No doubt a kayak is waiting for them outside.

But now Mr. Jefferson's alone with his thoughts, and we can make the usual array of guesses as to what those thoughts might be. The President is hoping that his explorers will bring him back news of a Northwest Passage, a trade route that could turn his republic into an empire almost overnight (not that he wants an empire, as such, but ... well, you know how it is). And then, of course, there's the prospect of mammoths. If such things are found, they're sure to be given a place of honor in the new American mythology. He briefly wonders if there's room for a mammoth on the national crest: possibly he can put one in place of the eagle. A beast which proves, by its very nature, that the Church is full of asses and the world runs to the will of the new sciences. Just for a second, for a stupid childish second, he imagines riding the back of such an animal in a parade along Pennsylvania Avenue, celebrating his second—oh, to hell with precedent, make it his third—term in office. Jefferson's monsters, that's what the Church would say. He imagines the mammoths' backs being draped in flags, decked out in the red-and-white stripes and the seventeen stars (although the flag which hangs above the window in this particular office only has sixteen, those artisans who handle such things being a little slower than the expansion of the new republic).

All this makes Mr. Jefferson consider the box again. He tries to remember the name of the woman who presented it to him, the well-spoken Mademoiselle who appeared in this very office just a few short months ago, her skins and furs making her look like an Indian coming home from a trek in the great forests. Naturally, it's ludicrous to think that a complete stranger, and such an ill-dressed one, should be allowed to stroll into the Presidential office without even officially presenting herself ... but the notion's as hard to resist as all the other things we've seen inside this virtual room. Whether or not the woman *did* introduce herself, the one thing Mr. Jefferson can remember is what she told him when she placed the little off-white box on his desk.

"Your new world, *Monsieur* President," she said. Well, maybe she didn't say "mister" in the French style, maybe Jefferson's just remembering it that way because he likes the accent, but the point remains that when he slid the box open he found inside it just a few blades of green, green grass. Mr. Jefferson fails to remember how he responded to this, or even whether he asked his visitor to explain herself: she may well have vanished from his office before he could so much as speak (after all, a mysterious entrance should always be complemented by a mysterious exit).

Here and now, the President believes the contents of the box to have been a kind of message, sent by some agency he has yet to identify. In fact, he's only half-right.

And this is Jefferson's future. More precisely, this is 1805, halfway through Lewis and Clark's two-year excursion into the wildlands, the point at which the two men (and all their followers, though right now they're gloriously irrelevant) finally stumble across a certain indentation in a certain grassland. A crater, if you will. It's here that the two explorers, being consummate outdoorsmen, find trampled ground and traces of spoor which suggest the trail of some grand animal herd. At first they conclude that the Indians have driven their cattle through the area, though this theory falters when they arrive at the bottom of the basin, where the graves have been dug. They *assume* there are graves here, anyway, given that the ground's been broken from one side of the crater to the other. Now, as not even the Shoshoni would do something as bizarre as grazing their animals on top of their dead—and as a quick search of the area uncovers European shell-casings in the grass—there's obviously some kind of mystery here.

Sadly, it's not one the explorers feel they have time to solve. Besides, even by this stage they're starting to learn that digging up native graves is a bad move, tactically speaking. There's some discussion about what might be called the "central" grave, the fifteen-foot-long tract of broken earth which, from its size, must surely indicate the last resting place of a great leader (proving to the leader-obsessed white men that the people who performed these burials must have been *partly* civilized, even though the Shoshoni contingent in the expedition claims not to recognize the style). Lewis and Clark steer well clear, deciding to give the mysterious fallen chief the respect he must surely deserve.

Later, in the oh-so-short years between the end of the expedition and Lewis's highly dubious suicide, the duo will theorize that the site was deliberately desecrated by rogue Frenchmen as some kind of political maneuver. A stampede must have taken place at some point, so the large animals, whatever they may have been, were probably used by the French as weapons of destruction.

Like Jefferson, these people excel at being only partly correct.

And however far into the future we go, Mr. Jefferson, President of the United States of America, fails to understand the significance of any of this. Well, what can we expect? Polymath and philosopher he may be, but he doesn't even understand the significance of the box. The little off-white box which remains in his possession for the rest of his term in office, a gift from one of the very few people who understood exactly what he wanted from his glorious new territory, and knew precisely why he couldn't be allowed to get it. A box Mr. Jefferson might have used for snuff, or hashish, or tobacco, which a Frenchwoman once claimed was all that remained of his virtual paradise, and which just happened to be made out of ivory.

SLIPSHOD, AT THE EDGE OF THE UNIVERSE

ROBERT THURSTON

O N SLIPSHOD, THE LARGEST of the asteroids at our edge of the universe, we set up a temporary camp. I guess "we" is inappropriate since I, as their prisoner, had nothing to do with the operation. With no atmosphere on Slipshod (the name given the asteroid by our exec officer, Elaine), we had to stay within the transparent dome. Actually, I did not have to stay within the dome. I could slip out and drift over the asteroid's surface. I had no need of atmosphere and was, by human definition, noncorporeal. Yet I could not waste energy reserves by going far. I had a substantial amount of reserve, but did not want to waste any in case a chance for a real escape came. And Slipshod was so plain and monotonous that scenic tours were out of the question.

Elaine traced her fingers along the surface of one of the screens in the computer where I was, by human definition, caged. As her fingers lingered on the screen, I sipped at her energy. At that moment I needed none of the human energy, but I could never resist absorbing some of it from this woman who was regarded as so beautiful among the others. In my own sense of beauty, she is beautiful for the energy I absorb from her, an energy that, as it dissipates through my system, gives me a feeling like no other, like no other species I have absorbed from. Humans had the best reserves of energy I had ever experienced, and the most flavorful as well. And Elaine's was the energy I most craved. Truly, it was superior to the energy received from any of my own kind whom I have loved or killed in the elongated span of my existence.

Days ago, according to their measure of time, Elaine and Casey, the ship commander, discussed the mission just after making love in her quarters. During their peculiar expressions of passion, the heel of Elaine's foot had pressed briefly, and hard, against the screen of her room's computer terminal and, as a result, I was riding on a surge of energy that sent me bouncing from circuit to diode to cable and back again. At the time I paid little attention to what the two were saying, although like everything else I ever heard I remembered it later.

"I have serious misgivings," Casey said, his words coming out of his mouth in odd groupings, nothing like the rhythm of speech he normally employed.

"About what?" Elaine asked, as she rubbed his chest. Casey was muscular, according to the impressions of others that I picked up when I absorbed from the humans aboard the ship. Muscularity, and for that matter, all corporeality drew my interest easily as a field of study.) The others regarded his face, however, as something less than beautiful, as they judged beauty. Elaine of course was the standard. She was beautiful, even with her face marred by its continual unhappiness, and Casey was not.

For a long while Casey lay with his eyes shut and steadied his breathing.

"Misgivings," Elaine prompted.

"Yes. About our goals. Our mission objective. The dark at the end of the tunnel."

"You're posing again."

"I have gotten through life this way. Don't stop me now. What I mean, Elaine, is that I always wanted my life to mean something."

"It does. You're a commander."

"Hollow triumph. I'm a commander who has never fought a major battle, never made an impact on political structures, never discovered anything significant during years of exploring the backwater regions of the universe."

I could understand Casey because of the rare absorptions I had drawn from him, but I tended to avoid his energy unless I was in a low-level state.

Elaine again accused him of posing and for a short while he became more direct.

"This mission is a punishment. No, not a punishment—that would imply someone out to get me. I am not that important. No one is out to get me. I am just someone in the command structure, and a lower-echelon commander at that, who can be given a futile mission because there is nothing important for him to do anyway. What are we doing, when you come right down to it? Someone a thousand light-years away has theorized the location of the edge of the universe and so, as outsiders and therefore expendable, we are sent to the nearest point that the theory says it might be. If there is no edge to the universe, then the universe is infinite, as we have always comfortably believed, and we can go on forever looking for it. Talk about being shunted aside."

Elaine stayed quiet. I could imagine her thoughts, though. She did not really like Casey, and she thought his skills at making love were just another part of his posing, but she needed the feelings, the sensations that the act provided, and he tended to provide these sensations most efficiently. So she let him pose, both in speech and manner because, for the time being, he suited her, and of course there was not much opportunity aboard a small ship, many of whose inhabitants had been surgically altered to deny normal human urges. The higher command officers were allowed to refuse the alterations.

"If there is no edge to the universe," she finally said, "then we will prove it, and that will be that, and in its way that'll be your contribution. In the meantime, while we wait for it, touch me there. Ah, I feel that all through me."

I agreed with Elaine. Whether or not there was an edge to the universe, a physical measurable border where it all ended, did not matter to me. What I am particularly irritated about, as I review that conversation, is Casey's statement that he had made no significant discoveries. They had, after all, come to my planet, mapped it, communicated with us, and then—in a peculiar and arrogant act of human assertion—had figured out a way to capture one of its beings—me—and store it in a computer to take it home for further study. By the time I had figured out how to bypass the netting of electrical impulses that had trapped me, their ship had carried me too far away from my planet to return. I do not know if I would have returned had there been an opportunity. This computer provides so many of the needs I had to struggle for at home that I find it quite relaxing. Besides, observing humans, or any other creatures, fascinates me. On our planet, we only had us.

The humans thought that snaring me was akin to imprisoning a ghost or pulling a being made of water out of an ocean, things that apparently human beings had accomplished in earlier expeditions in their history. History itself was a concept that I had struggled to understand. The whole idea of keeping a record of the past was anathema to me, and I suspected that, if my species had kept a history instead of an orally transmitted set of astonishing and ever-changing tales, our history would be longer than theirs but with less self-congratulation.

Now, according to every calculation and examination of physical data accomplished by the ship computer, we have reached the goal, the edge of the universe—surely, irretrievably, and all the other adverbs of certainty in the ingenious human lexicon. The absolute edge. On the other side of it was nothing. On this side of it were Slipshod and the last few asteroids on the way to the edge.

The concept of the edge of the universe meant little to me. I lived, for the time being, in the universe of this computer and it was a vast one. With its twistings and turnings, its loops and spirals, its way of curving back into itself, this was an infinite universe—as infinite as I needed, if that is not some sort of contradictory term. Humans worry about the convolutions and layered meanings of language, but I find them rich and abundant and representative of another kind of infinity, one which could occupy me forever. Humans call their good feelings happiness. That word is sufficient for me to describe the lack of resentment I feel at being separated from my own kind and imprisoned in this computer.

Sometimes I realized that I needed the humans for

the surges and bursts of erratic energy that kept me going. I am, like them, finite and, if they die without transmitting me to a place where there are more of them, I will die, too. Snap out of existence, and it won't matter. I can go on longer than they, since I have stored abundant reserves of their energy in the computer's dark places, enough energy to keep me going for a long period of their time, even after the computer itself fails. If I could absorb enough energy to leave them and go home across the void, I might try it. I have a good sense of where home is. It is mapped in their computer memory, and I can carry the information along with me—but I could only make it if I could count on encountering other beings, in other ships on their way to other places. The other way I could die is for the computer to be destroyed.

For now, though, we are on Slipshod, and with the humans I look out at the edge of the universe and try to see something more, some detail, some moving thing that would let us perceive what the other side of the universe was like.

"What are we looking for?" Casey said. "If we could see something out there, it would not be the edge of the universe. If the universe ends here, there can be nothing out there. Anything out there would just be an extension of our universe. I mean, even now, all we have are computer readings that indicate this is the edge along with an undeniably human fear to test it further."

The single foray the ship had made toward the edge had resulted in all the controls of the ship going haywire and forcing it to turn away and return to Slipshod.

"What about if this is not the absolute edge?" said Blackie, a crewman. Blackie was the physical opposite of Casey, small and unimpressive. "What about if this is the borderline with another universe? An edge, a border we can't cross, but another universe out there, existing separately?"

"If so, I hope it's better than this one," Elaine said, her voice strange, what the humans call distracted. "Another universe like this one would be a waste of time by whoever's building the universes."

"Multiverses," I said through the computer's audio system. Most of the crew were, as always, startled by one of my rare speaking intrusions. Either they forget me or do not, unlike Elaine, care to admit I am here, that I am, for good or ill, one of them, a crewmember, albeit undocketed. Apparently the reason they are uneasy with me is that I have no physical presence among them. "If where we are is a universe," I continued, "and there is another universe, then your God or Creator made multiverses."

"Is that so, what the spark-dog says, is that true, Casey?" Blackie asked. Blackie himself was never sure about anything and always asking others for verification.

"Semantics have never been my strong point," Casey

responded. "Thing is, now that we have pretty much verified this is the edge of the universe, what do we do now?"

Elaine, whose warm hands on the computer surface had been transmitting some complicated and thrilling energy, abruptly walked away from the computer, toward Casey, and said: "We are here to be sure, to check further. I'll go. Let me go."

"Go where?" Casey asked.

"To the edge. *Through* it."

She now stood in front of him, her posture defiant.

"It's too risky," Casey said. "You might—"

"I might die, I might be repelled as the ship was and smash to my death on an asteroid surface, or dissipate into the void, be snuffed out of existence, turned into a giant cosmic turnip? I'm aware of all that. I accept the risk."

I did not like what I felt then, as I saw the possibility of her actual death and, with it, my own loss of her peculiarly exhilarating energy, so I interrupted again: "What you say is of the highest probability. You will simply die, which will prove nothing."

She whirled around, walked angrily toward the computer, bent her head a bit as if to talk into one of the speakers, as if it were my mouth if I had a mouth: "And so what, you bundle of—of whatever you are? What do you really know of human life? We are here to discover, explore, whatever. If we just make notes, enter data, turn around, go slinking back to let the theorists have their field day, what is proven? If somebody doesn't take the risk of going too far, then what is life worth?"

"I am not certain about what you call the 'worth of life.' It is not much a part of my culture. We believe we live forever somewhere, in some state, in some—"

"God," Casey said, his eyebrows raising abruptly and with the kind of dramatic look that Elaine called a *pose*, "spare us the religious crap of a being who is no more than sparks and radioactive dust particles."

"I was not referring to religion, as you understand it," I replied, wishing I could place the emotional intonations and stresses into my speech the way Casey and Elaine did. "Religion is, for us, fact. We are not corporeal—therefore, we may speculate that we continue in some form. We cannot, we believe, be dissipated altogether."

I recalled their struggles to capture me and the further struggles to store me in this computer, efforts I never understood. The only reason I have discovered about why they needed to capture me is the expectation of profit from exhibiting me. Since I can only be detected and not seen, I am not sure how they planned to accomplish that.

Elaine stared at the computer for a long moment, then turned back toward Casey.

"Casey, give me the chance. I want to be footnoted in history for having tried, even if the note ends she was never seen or heard from again, okay? Okay?"

Casey glared at her, and the sense I received from him was genuine loneliness, the loss of her. But finally he nodded his head. "Sure, Elaine, go ahead with it. We'll load you down with recording equipment and bring that data home to the theorists, too. And, if you survive this, well, that'll shake them up good."

Elaine looked almost smug. I did not understand, could not understand.

"Foolish damn bravado, that's all it is," Blackie said angrily. "Suicide, you ask me. A wish to become nothing. I mean, if there's nothing on the other side, then that's what you'll be, nothing."

"Yes, but if it is indeed another universe, then . . . then we'll at least know."

We watched Elaine sail toward the edge of the universe. She propelled herself toward it with thrusters attached to her suit, using the thrusters to give her a direct and quick line to the edge. Blackie watched nervously, his mouth twisted into the most negative look he could imagine—for whose audience, I wondered. Casey was not looking at him at all. Maybe Blackie was not as godless as he pretended. His sour expression may have been intended to register with his god.

Casey's face was anxious, worried. He fidgeted while

he kept Elaine in a fixed focus on various scanner screens. As he touched a screen, I was there to draw out bursts of his energy. He glanced down at his hand as if aware of my absorptions.

Elaine slowed as she neared the area which the computer had calculated as the edge itself. There was no sudden rejection of her, no throwing back, as there had been with the ship. Spreading her arms as if diving into water she plunged right toward the edge.

For a moment she seemed to disappear. There was an instant of what might have been optical illusion as parts of her appeared chopped off before passing through the edge. Finally, she was gone.

It seemed momentarily darker where she had gone through. Casey made a strange, choking sound followed by a faint whisper. Blackie closed his eyes.

Suddenly Elaine was on the other side, looking back toward us. I wondered if the calculations had been wrong. If she could be seen, whole and unchanged, perhaps she had not really gone through the edge, gone through anything. Perhaps she was in between worlds, in some kind of airlock between universes.

According to the computer's tracking, she had vanished. The records showed a blip of nothingness during her pass-through and continued to go on registering nothing. Apparently, wherever she was, it was beyond the universe we were in, beyond the edge, in some other place.

Elaine was Elaine for only a short while, less than half a minute. Her physical change was rapid, but it progressed through perceivable stages. She split apart, at first into aspects of herself. Her face floated in front of her head; her arms and legs were visible as separate entities of skin, bone, muscle, veins, arteries. Her pressure suit intermingled with parts of her and broke up into bits of itself, before dissolving. At one point her torso and hips exchanged places. There was something about children's toys in the computer's memory banks, and the first stage of Elaine's transformation reminded me of it.

The next stage was a transmutation of Elaine's individual parts. They sent out thin, sparkling rays of light as they changed texture, color, then rejoined in no human order—she was no longer head, body, limbs—no longer even recognizably human. If anything she was a casual geometric construction with no logic to it but a great deal of knobby and gnarly surface. Even with no face she seemed to stare at us.

This new entity lasted only a short time. It shifted and there was a new splitting apart—now she was small bits, fragments, of swirling light.

I sensed that the energy of her had grown, and I knew what I could do. I collected my energy reserves and eased out of the computer, passed through the wall of the dome, and into the vacuum of space. Crossing to the edge of the universe used up nearly all of the reserves, more than I had anticipated, and I knew I could not return to Slipshod. For a moment it looked as if I might snap out of existence before I reached the edge. But, even with the diminishing reserves, I felt more alive than I had since I had been captured and shoved into the computer.

I barely noticed my passing through the edge. The other side was still, with a sense of no distance, no dimension, no existence. But I did exist, and I was there. And Elaine was right in front of me, as swirling iotas of energy. Sensing her welcome, I joined with her. I changed, too. She became my energy, the energy I now needed, and I became hers. I was Elaine and she was I, and she was no longer Elaine and I was no longer I. Neither one of us wanted to return to the others or go to any home planet or go anywhere. She believed that our union was not sexual, and I saw that it had nothing to do with the accumulation of energy I had craved. There was something more and we did not know what it was. We thought we might find out. Or might not. We were where we were, and that is where we are.

HELL IS THE ABSENCE
OF GOD

TED CHIANG

THIS IS THE STORY of a man named Neil Fisk, and
how he came to love God. The pivotal event in
Neil's life was an occurrence both terrible and ordinary: the death of his wife Sarah. Neil was consumed
with grief after she died, a grief that was excruciating
not only because of its intrinsic magnitude, but because
it also renewed and emphasized the previous pains of
his life. Her death forced him to reexamine his relationship with God, and in doing so he began a journey that
would change him forever.

Neil was born with a congenital abnormality that
caused his left thigh to be externally rotated and several
inches shorter than his right; the medical term for it was
proximal femoral focus deficiency. Most people he met
assumed God was responsible for this, but Neil's mother
hadn't witnessed any visitations while carrying him; his

condition was the result of improper limb development during the sixth week of gestation, nothing more. In fact, as far as Neil's mother was concerned, blame rested with his absent father, whose income might have made corrective surgery a possibility, although she never expressed this sentiment aloud.

As a child Neil had occasionally wondered if he were being punished by God, but most of the time he blamed his classmates in school for his unhappiness. Their nonchalant cruelty, their instinctive ability to locate the weaknesses in a victim's emotional armor, the way their own friendships were reinforced by their sadism: he recognized these as examples of human behavior, not divine. And although his classmates often used God's name in their taunts, Neil knew better than to blame Him for their actions.

But while Neil avoided the pitfall of blaming God, he never made the jump to loving Him; nothing in his upbringing or his personality led him to pray to God for strength or for relief. The assorted trials he faced growing up were accidental or human in origin, and he relied on strictly human resources to counter them. He became an adult who—like so many others—viewed God's actions in the abstract until they impinged upon his own life. Angelic visitations were events that befell other people, reaching him only via reports on the nightly news. His own life was entirely mundane; he worked as a superintendent for an upscale apartment building, collecting rent and performing repairs, and as far as he was concerned, circumstances were fully capable of unfolding, happily or not, without intervention from above.

This remained his experience until the death of his wife.

It was an unexceptional visitation, smaller in magnitude than most but no different in kind, bringing blessings to some and disaster to others. In this instance the angel was Nathanael, making an appearance in a downtown shopping district. Four miracle cures were effected: the elimination of carcinomas in two individuals, the regeneration of the spinal cord in a paraplegic, and the restoration of sight to a recently blinded person. There were also two miracles that were not cures: a delivery van, whose driver had fainted at the sight of the angel, was halted before it could overrun a busy sidewalk; another man was caught in a shaft of Heaven's light when the angel departed, erasing his eyes but ensuring his devotion.

Neil's wife Sarah Fisk had been one of the eight casualties. She was hit by flying glass when the angel's billowing curtain of flame shattered the storefront window of the café in which she was eating. She bled to death within minutes, and the other customers in the café—none of whom suffered even superficial injuries—could do nothing but listen to her cries of pain and fear, and eventually witness her soul's ascension toward Heaven.

Nathanael hadn't delivered any specific message; the angel's parting words, which had boomed out across the entire visitation site, were the typical *Behold the power of the Lord*. Of the eight casualties that day, three souls were accepted into Heaven and five were not, a closer ratio than the average for deaths by all causes. Sixty-two people received medical treatment for injuries ranging from slight concussions to ruptured eardrums to burns requiring skin grafts. Total property damage was estimated at 8.1 million dollars, all of it excluded by private insurance companies due to the cause. Scores of people became devout worshippers in the wake of the visitation, either out of gratitude or terror.

Alas, Neil Fisk was not one of them.

After a visitation, it's common for all the witnesses to meet as a group and discuss how their common experience had affected their lives. The witnesses of Nathanael's latest visitation arranged such group meetings, and family members of those who had died were welcome, so Neil began attending. The meetings were held once a month in a basement room of a large church downtown; there were metal folding chairs arranged in rows, and in the back of the room was a table holding coffee and donuts. Everyone wore adhesive name tags made out in felt-tip pen.

While waiting for the meetings to start, people would stand around, drinking coffee, talking casually. Most people Neil spoke to assumed his leg was a result of the visitation, and he had to explain that he wasn't a witness, but rather the husband of one of the casualties. This didn't bother him particularly; he was used to explaining about his leg. What did bother him was the tone of the meetings themselves, when participants spoke about their reaction to the visitation: most of them talked about their newfound devotion to God, and they tried to persuade the bereaved that they should feel the same.

Neil's reaction to such attempts at persuasion depended on who was making it. When it was an ordinary witness, he found it merely irritating. When someone who'd received a miracle cure told him to love God, he had to restraint an impulse to strangle the person. But what he found most disquieting of all was hearing the same suggestion from a man named Tony Crane; Tony's wife had died in the visitation too, and he now projected an air of groveling with his every movement. In hushed, tearful tones he explained how he had accepted his role as one of God's subjects, and he advised Neil to do likewise.

Neil didn't stop attending the meetings—he felt that he somehow owed it to Sarah to stick with them—but he found another group to go to as well, one more compatible with his own feelings: a support group devoted to those who'd lost a loved one during a visitation, and were angry at God because of it. They met every other week in a room at the local community center, and talked about the grief and rage that boiled inside of them.

All the attendees were generally sympathetic to one another, despite differences in their various attitudes toward God. Of those who'd been devout before their loss, some struggled with the task of remaining so, while others gave up their devotion without a second glance. Of those who'd never been devout, some felt their position had been validated, while others were faced with the near impossible task of becoming devout now. Neil found himself, to his consternation, in this last category.

Like every other non-devout person, Neil had never expended much energy on where his soul would end up; he'd always assumed his destination was Hell, and he accepted that. That was the way of things, and Hell, after all, was not physically worse than the mortal plane.

It meant permanent exile from God, no more and no less; the truth of this was plain for anyone to see on those occasions when Hell manifested itself. These happened on a regular basis; the ground seemed to become transparent, and you could see Hell as if you were looking through a hole in the floor. The lost souls looked no different than the living, their eternal bodies resembling mortal ones. You couldn't communicate with them—their exile from God meant that they couldn't apprehend the mortal plane where His actions were still felt—but as long as the manifestation lasted you could hear them talk, laugh, or cry, just as they had when they were alive.

People varied widely in their reactions to these manifestations. Most devout people were galvanized, not by the sight of anything frightening, but at being reminded that eternity outside paradise was a possibility. Neil, by contrast, was one of those who were unmoved; as far as he could tell, the lost souls as a group were no unhappier than he was, their existence no worse than his in the mortal plane, and in some ways better: his eternal body would be unhampered by congenital abnormalities.

Of course, everyone knew that Heaven was incomparably superior, but to Neil it had always seemed too remote to consider, like wealth or fame or glamour. For people like him, Hell was where you went when you died, and he saw no point in restructuring his life in hopes of avoiding that. And since God hadn't previously played a role in Neil's life, he wasn't afraid of being exiled from God. The prospect of living without interference, living in a world where windfalls and misfortunes were never by design, held no terror for him.

Now that Sarah was in Heaven, his situation had changed. Neil wanted more than anything to be reunited with her, and the only way to get to Heaven was to love God with all his heart.

This is Neil's story, but telling it properly requires telling the stories of two other individuals whose paths became entwined with his. The first of these is Janice Reilly.

What people assumed about Neil had in fact happened to Janice. When Janice's mother was eight months pregnant with her, she lost control of the car she was driving and collided with a telephone pole during a sudden hailstorm, fists of ice dropping out of a clear blue sky and littering the road like a spill of giant ball bearings. She was sitting in her car, shaken but unhurt, when she saw a knot of silver flames—later identified as the angel Bardiel—float across the sky. The sight petrified her, but not so much that she didn't notice the peculiar settling sensation in her womb. A subsequent ultrasound revealed that the unborn Janice Reilly no longer had legs; flipper-like feet grew directly from her hip sockets.

Janice's life might have gone the way of Neil's, if not for what happened two days after the ultrasound. Janice's parents were sitting at their kitchen table, crying and asking what they had done to deserve this, when they received a vision: the saved souls of four deceased relatives appeared before them, suffusing the kitchen with a golden glow. The saved never spoke, but their beatific smiles induced a feeling of serenity in whoever saw them. From that moment on, the Reillys were certain that their daughter's condition was not a punishment.

As a result, Janice grew up thinking of her legless condition as a gift; her parents explained that God had given her a special assignment because He considered her equal to the task, and she vowed that she would not let Him down. Without pride or defiance, she saw it as her responsibility to show others that her condition did not indicate weakness, but rather strength.

As a child, she was fully accepted by her school-mates; when you're as pretty, confident, and charismatic as she was, children don't even notice that you're in a wheelchair. It was when she was a teenager that she realized that the able-bodied people in her school were not the ones who most needed convincing. It was more important for her to set an example for other handi-capped individuals, whether they had been touched by God or not, no matter where they lived. Janice began speaking before audiences, telling those with disabilities that they had the strength God required of them.

Over time she developed a reputation, and a follow-ing. She made a living writing and speaking, and estab-lished a non-profit organization dedicated to promoting her message. People sent her letters thanking her for changing their lives, and receiving those gave her a sense of fulfillment of a sort that Neil had never expe-rienced.

This was Janice's life up until she herself witnessed a visitation by the angel Rashiel. She was letting herself into her house when the tremors began; at first she thought they were of natural origin, although she didn't live in a geologically active area, and waited in the doorway for them to subside. Several seconds later she caught a glimpse of silver in the sky and realized it was an angel, just before she lost consciousness.

Janice awoke to the biggest surprise of her life: the sight of her two new legs, long, muscular, and fully functional.

She was startled the first time she stood up: she was taller than she expected. Balancing at such a height without the use of her arms was unnerving, and simultaneously feeling the texture of the ground through the soles of her feet made it positively bizarre. Rescue workers, finding her wandering down the street dazedly, thought she was in shock until she—marveling at her ability to face them at eye level—explained to them what had happened.

When statistics were gathered for the visitation, the restoration of Janice's legs was recorded as a blessing, and she was humbly grateful for her good fortune. It was at the first of the support group meetings that a feeling of guilt began to creep in. There Janice met two individuals with cancer who'd witnessed Rashiel's visitation, thought their cure was at hand, and been bitterly disappointed when they realized they'd been passed over. Janice found herself wondering, why had she received a blessing when they had not?

Janice's family and friends considered the restoration of her legs a reward for excelling at the task God had set for her, but for Janice, this interpretation raised another question. Did He intend for her to stop? Surely not; evangelism provided the central direction to her life, and there was no limit to the number of people who needed to hear her message. Her continuing to preach was the best action she could take, both for herself and for others.

Her reservations grew during her first speaking engagement after the visitation, before an audience of people recently paralyzed and now wheelchair-bound. Janice delivered her usual words of inspiration, assuring them that they had the strength needed for the challenges ahead; it was during the Q&A that she was asked if the restoration of her legs meant she had passed her test. Janice didn't know what to say; she could hardly promise them that one day their marks would be erased. In fact, she realized, any implication that she'd been rewarded could be interpreted as criticism of others who remained afflicted, and she didn't want that. All she could tell them was that she didn't know why she'd been cured, but it was obvious they found that an unsatisfying answer.

Janice returned home disquieted. She still believed in her message, but as far as her audiences were concerned, she'd lost her greatest source of credibility. How could she inspire others who were touched by God to see their condition as a badge of strength, when she no longer shared their condition?

She considered whether this might be a challenge, a test of her ability to spread His word. Clearly God had made her task more difficult than it was before; perhaps the restoration of her legs was an obstacle for her to overcome, just as their earlier removal had been.

This interpretation failed her at her next scheduled engagement. The audience was a group of witnesses to a visitation by Nathanael; she was often invited to speak to such groups in the hopes that those who suffered might draw encouragement from her. Rather than side-step the issue, she began with an account of the visitation she herself had recently experienced. She explained that while it might appear she was a beneficiary, she was in fact facing her own challenge: like them, she was forced to draw on resources previously untapped.

She realized, too late, that she had said the wrong thing. A man in the audience with a misshapen leg stood up and challenged her: was she seriously suggesting that the restoration of her legs was comparable to the loss of his wife? Could she really be equating her trials with his own?

Janice immediately assured him that she wasn't, and that she couldn't imagine the pain he was experiencing. But, she said, it wasn't God's intention that everyone be subjected to the same kind of trial, but only that each person face his or her own trial, whatever it might be. The difficulty of any trial was subjective, and there was no way to compare two individuals' experiences. And just as those whose suffering seemed greater than his should have compassion for him, so should he have compassion for those whose suffering seemed less.

The man was having none of it. She had received what anyone else would have considered a fantastic blessing, and she was complaining about it. He stormed out of the meeting while Janice was still trying to explain.

That man, of course, was Neil Fisk. Neil had had Janice Reilly's name mentioned to him for much of his life, most often by people who were convinced his misshapen leg was a sign from God. These people cited her as an example he should follow, telling him that her attitude was the proper response to a physical handicap. Neil couldn't deny that her leglessness was a far worse condition that his distorted femur. Unfortunately, he found her attitude so foreign that, even in the best of times, he'd never been able to learn anything from her. Now, in the depths of his grief and mystified as to why she had received a gift she didn't need, Neil found her words offensive.

In the days that followed, Janice found herself more and more plagued by doubts, unable to decide what the restoration of her legs meant. Was she being ungrateful for a gift she'd received? Was it both a blessing and a test? Perhaps it was a punishment, an indication that she had not performed her duty well enough. There were many possibilities, and she didn't know which one to believe.

*   *   *

There was one other person who played an important role in Neil's story, even though he and Neil did not meet until Neil's journey was nearly over. That person's name is Ethan Mead.

Ethan had been raised in a family that was devout, but not profoundly so. His parents credited God with their above-average health and their comfortable economic status, although they hadn't witnessed any visitations or received any visions; they simply trusted that God was, directly or indirectly, responsible for their good fortune. Their devotion had never been put to any serious test, and might not have withstood one; their love for God was based in their satisfaction with the *status quo*.

Ethan was not like his parents, though. Ever since childhood he'd felt certain that God had a special role for him to play, and he waited for a sign telling him what that role was. He'd liked to have become a preacher, but felt he hadn't any compelling testimony to offer; his vague feelings of expectation weren't enough. He longed for an encounter with the divine to provide him with direction.

He could have gone to one of the holy sites, those places where—for reasons unknown—angelic visitations occurred on a regular basis, but he felt that such an action would be presumptuous of him. The holy sites were usually the last resort of the desperate, those people seeking either a miracle cure to repair their bodies or a glimpse of Heaven's light to repair their souls, and Ethan was not desperate. He decided that he'd been set along his own course, and in time the reason for it would become clear. While waiting for that day, he lived his life as best he could: he worked as a librarian, married a woman named Claire, raised two children. All the while, he remained watchful for signs of a greater destiny.

Ethan was certain his time had come when he became witness to a visitation of Rashiel, the same one that—miles away—restored Janice Reilly's legs. Ethan was alone when it happened, walking toward his car in the center of a parking lot, when the ground began to shudder. Instinctively he knew it was a visitation, and he assumed a kneeling position, feeling no fear, only exhilaration and awe at the prospect of learning his calling.

The ground became still after a minute, and Ethan looked around, but didn't otherwise move. Only after waiting for several more minutes did he rise to his feet. There was a large crack in the asphalt, beginning directly in front of him and following a meandering path down the street. The crack seemed to be pointing him in a specific direction, so he ran alongside it for several blocks until he encountered other survivors, a man and a woman climbing out of a modest fissure that had opened up directly beneath them. He waited with the two of them until rescuers arrived and brought them to a shelter.

Ethan attended the support group meetings that followed and met the other witnesses to Rashiel's visitation. Over the course of a few meetings, he became aware of certain patterns among the witnesses. Of course there were those who'd been injured and those who'd received miracle cures. But there were also those whose lives were changed in other ways: the man and woman he'd first met fell in love and were soon engaged; a woman who'd been pinned beneath a collapsed wall was inspired to become an EMT after being rescued. One business owner formed an alliance that averted her impending bankruptcy, while another whose business was destroyed saw it as a message that he change his ways. It seemed that everyone except Ethan had found a way to understand what had happened to them.

He hadn't been cursed or blessed in any obvious way, and he didn't know what message he was intended to receive. His wife Claire suggested that he consider the visitation a reminder that he appreciate what he had, but Ethan found that unsatisfying, reasoning that *every* visitation—no matter where it occurred—served that function, and the fact that he'd witnessed a visitation firsthand had to have greater significance. His mind was preyed upon by the idea that he'd missed an opportunity, that there was a fellow witness whom he was intended to meet but hadn't. This visitation had to be the sign he'd been waiting for; he couldn't just disregard it. But that didn't tell him what he was supposed to do.

Ethan eventually resorted to the process of elimination: he got hold of a list of all the witnesses, and crossed off those who had a clear interpretation of their experience, reasoning that one of those remaining must be the person whose fate was somehow intertwined with his. Among those who were confused or uncertain about the visitation's meaning would be the one he was intended to meet.

When he had finished crossing names off his list, there was only one left: "Janice Reilly."

In public Neil was able to mask his grief as adults are expected to, but in the privacy of his apartment, the floodgates of emotion burst open. The awareness of Sarah's absence would overwhelm him, and then he'd collapse on the floor and weep. He'd curl up into a ball, his body racked by hiccuping sobs, tears and mucus streaming down his face, the anguish coming in ever increasing waves until it was more than he could bear, more intense than he'd have believed possible. Minutes or hours later it would leave, and he would fall asleep, exhausted. And the next day he would wake up and face the prospect of another day without Sarah.

An elderly woman in Neil's apartment building tried to comfort him by telling him that the pain would lessen in time, and while he would never forget his wife, he would at least be able to move on. Then he would meet someone else one day and find happiness with her, and he would learn to love God and thus ascend to Heaven when his time came.

This woman's intentions were good, but Neil was in no position to find any comfort in her words. Sarah's absence felt like an open wound, and the prospect that someday he would no longer feel pain at her loss seemed not just remote, but a physical impossibility. If suicide would have ended his pain, he'd have done it without hesitation, but that would only ensure that his separation from Sarah was permanent.

The topic of suicide regularly came up at the support group meetings, and inevitably led to someone mentioning Robin Pearson, a woman who used to come to the meetings several months before Neil began attending. Robin's husband had been afflicted with stomach cancer during a visitation of the angel Makatiel. She stayed in his hospital room for days at a stretch, only for him to die unexpectedly when she was home doing laundry. A nurse who'd been present told Robin that his soul had ascended, and so Robin had begun attending the support group meetings.

Many months later, Robin came to the meeting shaking with rage. There'd been a manifestation of Hell near her house, and she'd seen her husband among the lost souls. She confronted the nurse, who admitted to lying in the hopes that Robin would learn to love God, so that at least she would be saved even if her husband hadn't been. Robin wasn't at the next meeting, and at the meeting after that the group learned she had committed suicide to rejoin her husband.

None of them knew the status of Robin's and her husband's relationship in the afterlife, but successes were known to happen; some couples had indeed been happily reunited through suicide. The support group had attendees whose spouses had descended to Hell, and they talked about being torn between wanting to remain alive and wanting to rejoin their spouses. Neil wasn't in their situation, but his first response when listening to them had been envy: if Sarah had gone to Hell, suicide would be the solution to all his problems.

This led to a shameful self-knowledge for Neil. He realized that if he had to choose between going to Hell while Sarah went to Heaven, or having both of them go to Hell together, he would choose the latter: he would rather she be exiled from God than separated from him. He knew it was selfish, but he couldn't change how he felt: he believed Sarah could be happy in either place, but he could only be happy with her.

Neil's previous experiences with women had never been good. All too often he'd begin flirting with a woman while sitting at a bar, only to have her remember an appointment elsewhere the moment he stood up and his shortened leg came into view. Once, a woman he'd been dating for several weeks broke off their relationship, explaining that while she herself didn't consider his leg a defect, whenever they were seen in public together other people assumed there must be something wrong with her for being with him, and surely he could understand how that was unfair to her?

Sarah had been the first woman Neil met whose demeanor hadn't changed one bit, whose expression hadn't flickered toward pity or horror or even surprise when she first saw his leg. For that reason alone it was predictable that Neil would become infatuated with her; by the time he saw all the sides of her personality, he'd completely fallen in love with her. And because his best qualities came out when he was with her, she fell in love with him too.

Neil had been surprised when Sarah told him she was devout. There weren't many signs of her devotion—she didn't go to church, sharing Neil's dislike for the attitudes of most people who attended—but in her own quiet way she was grateful to God for her life. She never tried to convert Neil, saying that devotion would come from within or not at all. They rarely had any cause to mention God, and most of the time it would've been easy for Neil to imagine that Sarah's views on God matched his own.

This is not to say that Sarah's devotion had no effect on Neil. On the contrary, Sarah was far and away the best argument for loving God that he had ever encountered. If love of God had contributed to making her the person she was, then perhaps it did make sense. During the years that the two of them were married, his outlook on life improved, and it probably would have reached the point where he was thankful to God, if he and Sarah had grown old together.

Sarah's death removed that particular possibility, but it needn't have closed the door on Neil's loving God. Neil could have taken it as a reminder that no one can count on having decades left. He could have been moved by the realization that, had he died with her, his soul would've been lost and the two of them separated for eternity. He could have seen Sarah's death as an wake-up call, telling him to love God while he still had the chance.

Instead Neil became actively resentful of God. Sarah had been the greatest blessing of his life, and God had taken her away. Now he was expected to love Him for it? For Neil, it was like having a kidnapper demand love as ransom for his wife's return. Obedience he might have managed, but sincere, heartfelt love? That was a ransom he couldn't pay.

This paradox confronted several people in the support group. One of the attendees, a man named Phil Soames, correctly pointed out that thinking of it as a condition to be met would guarantee failure. You couldn't love God as a means to an end, you had to love Him for Himself. If your ultimate goal in loving God was a re-union with your spouse, you weren't demonstrating true devotion at all.

A woman in the support group named Valerie Tommasino said they shouldn't even try. She'd been reading a book published by the humanist movement; its members considered it wrong to love a God who inflicted such pain, and advocated that people act according to their own moral sense instead of being guided by the carrot and the stick. These were people who, when they died, descended to Hell in proud defiance of God.

Neil himself had read a pamphlet of the humanist movement; what he most remembered was that it had quoted the fallen angels. Visitations of fallen angels were infrequent, and caused neither good fortune nor bad; they weren't acting under God's direction, but just passing through the mortal plane as they went about their unimaginable business. On the occasions they appeared, people would ask them questions: did they know God's intentions? Why had they rebelled? The fallen angels' reply was always the same: *Decide for yourselves. That is what we did. We advise you to do the same.*

Those in the humanist movement had decided, and if it weren't for Sarah, Neil would've made the identical choice. But he wanted her back, and the only way was to find a reason to love God.

Looking for any footing on which to build their devotion, some attendees of the support group took comfort in the fact that their loved ones hadn't suffered when God took them, but instead died instantly. Neil didn't even have that; Sarah had received horrific lacerations when the glass hit her. Of course, it could have been worse. One couple's teenage son been trapped in a fire ignited by an angel's visitation, and received full-thickness burns over eighty percent of his body before rescue workers could free him; his eventual death was a mercy. Sarah had been fortunate by comparison, but not enough to make Neil love God.

Neil could think of only one thing that would make him give thanks to God, and that was if He allowed Sarah to appear before him. It would give him immeasurable comfort just to see her smile again; he'd never been visited by a saved soul before, and a vision now would have meant more to him than at any other point in his life.

But visions don't appear just because a person needs one, and none ever came to Neil. He had to find his own way toward God.

The next time he attended the support group meeting for witnesses of Nathanael's visitation, Neil sought out Benny Vasquez, the man whose eyes had been erased by Heaven's light. Benny didn't always attend because he was now being invited to speak at other meetings; few visitations resulted in an eyeless person, since Heaven's light entered the mortal plane only in the brief moments that an angel emerged from or reentered Heaven, so the eyeless were minor celebrities, and in demand as speakers to church groups.

Benny was now as sightless as any burrowing worm: not only were his eyes and sockets missing, his skull lacked even the space for such features, the cheekbones now abutting the forehead. The light that had brought his soul as close to perfection as was possible in the mortal plane had also deformed his body; it was commonly held that this illustrated the superfluity of physical bodies in Heaven. With the limited expressive capacity his face retained, Benny always wore a blissful, rapturous smile.

Neil hoped Benny could say something to help him love God. Benny described Heaven's light as infinitely beautiful, a sight of such compelling majesty that it vanquished all doubts. It constituted incontrovertible proof that God should be loved, an explanation that made it as obvious as $1+1=2$. Unfortunately, while Benny could offer many analogies for the effect of Heaven's light, he couldn't duplicate that effect with his own words. Those who were already devout found Benny's descriptions thrilling, but to Neil, they seemed frustratingly vague. So he looked elsewhere for counsel.

Accept the mystery, said the minister of the local church. If you can love God even though your questions go unanswered, you'll be the better for it.

Admit that you need Him, said the popular book of spiritual advice he bought. When you realize that self-sufficiency is an illusion, you'll be ready.

Submit yourself completely and utterly, said the preacher on the television. Receiving torment is how you prove your love. Acceptance may not bring you relief in this life, but resistance will only worsen your punishment.

All of these strategies have proven successful for different individuals; any one of them, once internalized, can bring a person to devotion. But these are not always easy to adopt, and Neil was one who found them impossible.

Neil finally tried talking to Sarah's parents, which was an indication of how desperate he was: his relationship with them had always been tense. While they loved Sarah, they often chided her for not being demonstrative enough in her devotion, and they'd been shocked when she married a man who wasn't devout at all. For her part, Sarah had always considered her parents too judgmental, and their disapproval of Neil only reinforced her opinion. But now Neil felt he had something in common with them—after all, they were all mourning Sarah's loss—and so he visited them in their suburban colonial, hoping they could help him in his grief.

How wrong he was. Instead of sympathy, what Neil got from Sarah's parents was blame for her death. They'd come to this conclusion in the weeks after Sarah's funeral; they reasoned that she'd been taken to send him a message, and that they were forced to endure her loss solely because he hadn't been devout. They were now convinced that, his previous explanations notwithstanding, Neil's deformed leg was in fact God's doing, and if only he'd been properly chastened by it, Sarah might still be alive.

Their reaction shouldn't have come as a surprise: throughout Neil's life, people had attributed moral significance to his leg even though God wasn't responsible for it. Now that he'd suffered a misfortune for which God was unambiguously responsible, it was inevitable that someone would assume he deserved it. It was by pure chance that Neil heard this sentiment when he was at his most vulnerable, and it could have the greatest impact on him.

Neil didn't think his in-laws were right, but he began to wonder if he might not be better off if he did. Perhaps, he thought, it'd be better to live in a story where the righteous were rewarded and the sinners were punished, even if the criteria for righteousness and sinfulness eluded him, than to live in a reality where there was no justice at all. It would mean casting himself in the role of sinner, so it was hardly a comforting lie, but it offered one reward that his own ethics couldn't: believing it would reunite him with Sarah.

Sometimes even bad advice can point a man in the right direction. It was in this manner that his in-laws' accusations ultimately pushed Neil closer to God.

More than once when she was evangelizing, Janice had been asked if she ever wished she had legs, and she had always answered—honestly—no, she didn't. She was content as she was. Sometimes her questioner would point out that she couldn't miss what she'd never known, and she might feel differently if she'd been born with legs and lost them later on. Janice never denied that. But she could truthfully say that she felt no sense of being incomplete, no envy for people with legs; being legless was part of her identity. She'd never bothered with prosthetics, and had a surgical procedure been available to provide her with legs, she'd have turned it down. She had never considered the possibility that God might restore her legs.

One of the unexpected side-effects of having legs was the increased attention she received from men. In the past she'd mostly attracted men with amputee fetishes or sainthood complexes; now all sorts of men seemed drawn to her. So when she first noticed Ethan Mead's interest in her, she thought it was romantic in nature; this possibility was particularly distressing since he was obviously married.

Ethan had begun talking to Janice at the group support meetings, and then began attending her public speaking engagements. It was when he suggested they have lunch together that Janice asked him about his intentions, and he explained his theory. He didn't know *how* his fate was intertwined with hers; he knew only that it was. She was skeptical, but she didn't reject his theory outright. Ethan admitted that he didn't have answers for her own questions, but he was eager to do anything he could to help her find them. Janice cautiously agreed to help him in his search for meaning, and Ethan promised that he wouldn't be a burden. They met on a regular basis and talked about the significance of visitations.

Meanwhile Ethan's wife Claire grew worried. Ethan assured her that he had no romantic feelings toward Janice, but that didn't alleviate her concerns. She knew that extreme circumstances could create a bond between individuals, and she feared that Ethan's relationship with Janice—romantic or not—would threaten their marriage.

Ethan suggested to Janice that he, as a librarian, could help her do some research. Neither of them had ever heard of a previous instance where God had left His mark on a person in one visitation and removed it in another. Ethan looked for previous examples in hopes that they might shed some light on Janice's situation. There were a few instances of individuals receiving multiple miracle cures over their lifetimes, but their illnesses or disabilities had always been of natural origin, not given to them in a visitation. There was one anecdotal report of a man being struck blind for his sins, changing his ways, and later having his sight restored, but it was classified as an urban legend.

Even if that account had a basis in truth, it didn't provide a useful precedent for Janice's situation: her legs had been removed before her birth, and so couldn't have been a punishment for anything she'd done. Was it possible that Janice's condition had been a punishment for something her mother or father had done? Could her restoration mean they had finally earned her cure? She couldn't believe that.

If her deceased relatives were to appear in a vision, Janice would've been reassured about the restoration of her legs. The fact that they didn't made her suspect something was amiss, but she didn't believe that it was a punishment. Perhaps it had been a mistake, and she'd received a miracle meant for someone else; perhaps it was a test, to see how she would respond to being given too much. In either case, there seemed only one course of action: she would, with utmost gratitude and humility, offer to return her gift. To do so, she would go on a pilgrimage.

Pilgrims traveled great distances to visit the holy sites and wait for a visitation, hoping for a miracle cure. Whereas in most of the world one could wait an entire lifetime and never experience a visitation, at a holy site one might only wait months, sometimes weeks. Pilgrims knew that the odds of being cured were still poor; of those who stayed long enough to witness a visitation, the majority did not receive a cure. But they were often happy just to have seen an angel, and they returned home better able to face what awaited them, whether it be imminent death or life with a crippling disability. And of course, just living through a visitation made many people appreciate their situations; invariably, a small number of pilgrims were killed during each visitation.

Janice was willing to accept the outcome whatever it was. If God saw fit to take her, she was ready. If God removed her legs again, she would resume the work she'd always done. If God let her legs remain, she hoped she would receive the epiphany she needed to speak with conviction about her gift.

She hoped, however, that her miracle would be taken back and given to someone who truly needed it. She didn't suggest to anyone that they accompany her in hopes of receiving the miracle she was returning, feeling that that would've been presumptuous, but she privately considered her pilgrimage a request on behalf of those who were in need.

Her friends and family were confused at Janice's decision, seeing it as questioning God. As word spread, she received many letters from followers, variously expressing dismay, bafflement, or admiration for her willingness to make such a sacrifice.

As for Ethan, he was completely supportive of Janice's decision, and excited for himself. He now understood the significance of Rashiel's visitation for him: it indicated that the time for him to act had come. His wife Claire strenuously opposed his leaving, pointing out that he had no idea how long he might be away, and that she and their children needed him too. It grieved him to go without her support, but he had no choice. Ethan would go on a pilgrimage, and at the next visitation, he would learn what God intended for him.

Neil's visit to Sarah's parents caused him to give further thought to his conversation with Benny Vasquez. While he hadn't gotten a lot out of Benny's words, he'd been impressed by the absoluteness of Benny's devotion. No matter what misfortune befell him in the future, Benny's love of God would never waver, and he would ascend to Heaven when he died. That fact offered Neil a very slim opportunity, one that had seemed so unattractive he hadn't considered it before; but now, as he was growing more desperate, it was beginning to look expedient.

Every holy site had its pilgrims who, rather than looking for a miracle cure, deliberately sought out Heaven's light. Those who saw it were always accepted into Heaven when they died, no matter how selfish their motives had been; there were some who wished to have their ambivalence removed so they could be reunited with their loved ones, and others who'd always lived a sinful life and wanted to escape the consequences.

In the past there'd been some doubt as to whether Heaven's light could indeed overcome *all* the spiritual obstacles to becoming saved. The debate ended after the case of Barry Larsen, a serial rapist and murderer who, while disposing of the body of his latest victim, witnessed an angel's visitation and saw Heaven's light. At Larsen's execution, his soul was seen ascending to

Heaven, much to the outrage of his victims' families. Priests tried to console them, assuring them—on the basis of no evidence whatsoever—that Heaven's light must have subjected Larsen to many lifetimes worth of penance in a moment, but their words provided little comfort.

For Neil this offered a loophole, an answer to Phil Soames' objection; it was the one way that he could love Sarah more than he loved God, and still be reunited with her. It was how he could be selfish and still get into Heaven. Others had done it; perhaps he could too. It might not be just, but at least it was predictable.

At an instinctual level, Neil was averse to the idea: it sounded like undergoing brainwashing as a cure for depression. He couldn't help but think that it would change his personality so drastically that he'd cease to be himself. Then he remembered that everyone in Heaven had undergone a similar transformation; the saved were just like the eyeless except that they no longer had bodies. This gave Neil a clearer image of what he was working toward: no matter whether he became devout by seeing Heaven's light or by a lifetime of effort, any ultimate reunion with Sarah couldn't recreate what they'd shared in the mortal plane. In Heaven, they would both be different, and their love for each other would be mixed with the love that all the saved felt for everything.

This realization didn't diminish Neil's longing for a

reunion with Sarah. In fact it sharpened his desire, because it meant that the reward would be the same no matter what means he used to achieve it; the shortcut led to precisely the same destination as the conventional path.

On the other hand, seeking Heaven's light was far more difficult than an ordinary pilgrimage, and far more dangerous. Heaven's light leaked through only when an angel entered or left the mortal plane, and since there was no way to predict where an angel would first appear, light-seekers had to converge on the angel after its arrival and follow it until its departure. To maximize their chances of being in the narrow shaft of Heaven's light, they followed the angel as closely as possible during its visitation; depending on the angel involved, this might mean staying alongside the funnel of a tornado, the wavefront of a flash flood, or the expanding tip of a chasm as it split apart the landscape. Far more light-seekers were killed in the attempt than succeeded.

Statistics about the souls of failed light-seekers were difficult to compile, since there were few witnesses to such expeditions, but the numbers so far were not encouraging. In sharp contrast to ordinary pilgrims who died without receiving their sought-after cure, of which roughly half were admitted into Heaven, every single failed light-seeker had descended to Hell. Perhaps only people who were already lost ever considered seeking Heaven's light, or perhaps death in such circumstances was considered suicide. In any case, it was clear to Neil that he needed to be ready to accept the consequences of embarking on such an attempt.

The entire idea had an all-or-nothing quality to it that Neil found both frightening and attractive. He found the prospect of going on with his life, trying to love God, increasingly maddening. He might try for decades and not succeed. He might not even have that long; as he'd been reminded so often lately, visitations served as a warning to prepare one's soul, because death might come at any time. He could die tomorrow, and there was no chance of his becoming devout in the near future by conventional means.

It's perhaps ironic that, given his history of not following Janice Reilly's example, Neil took notice when she reversed her position. He was eating breakfast when he happened to see an item in the newspaper about her plans for a pilgrimage, and his immediate reaction was anger: how many blessings would it take to satisfy that woman? After considering it more, he decided that if she, having received a blessing, deemed it appropriate to seek God's assistance in coming to terms with it, then there was no reason he, having received such terrible misfortune, shouldn't do the same. And that was enough to tip him over the edge.

Holy sites were invariably in inhospitable places: one was an atoll in the middle of the ocean, while another was in the mountains at an elevation of 20,000 ft. The one that Neil traveled to was in a desert, an expanse of cracked mud reaching miles in every direction; it was desolate, but it was relatively accessible and thus popular among pilgrims. The appearance of the holy site was an object lesson in what happened when the celestial and terrestrial realms touched: the landscape was variously scarred by lava flows, gaping fissures, and impact craters. Vegetation was scarce and ephemeral, restricted to growing in the interval after soil was deposited by floodwaters or whirlwinds and before it was scoured away again.

Pilgrims took up residence all over the site, forming temporary villages with their tents and camper vans; they all made guesses as to what location would maximize their chances of seeing the angel while minimizing the risk of injury or death. Some protection was offered by curved banks of sandbags, left over from years past and rebuilt as needed. A site-specific paramedic and fire department ensured that paths were kept clear so rescue vehicles could go where they were needed. Pilgrims either brought their own food and water or purchased them from vendors charging exorbitant prices; everyone paid a fee to cover the cost of waste removal.

Light-seekers always had off-road vehicles to better cross rough terrain when it came time to follow the angel. Those who could afford it drove alone; those who couldn't formed groups of two or three or four. Neil didn't want to be a passenger reliant on another person, nor did he want the responsibility of driving anyone else. This might be his final act on earth, and he felt he should do it alone. The cost of Sarah's funeral had depleted their savings, so Neil sold all his possessions in order to purchase a suitable vehicle: a pickup truck equipped with aggressively knurled tires and heavy-duty shock absorbers.

As soon as he arrived, Neil started doing what all the other light-seekers did: criss-crossing the site in his vehicle, trying to familiarize himself with its topography. It was on one of his drives around the site's perimeter that he met Ethan; Ethan flagged him down after his own car had stalled on his return from the nearest grocery story, 80 miles away. Neil helped him get his car started again, and then, at Ethan's insistence, followed him back to his campsite for dinner. Janice wasn't there when they arrived, having gone to visit some pilgrims several tents over; Neil listened politely while Ethan— heating prepackaged meals over a bottle of propane— began describing the events that had brought him to the holy site.

When Ethan mentioned Janice Reilly's name, Neil couldn't mask his surprise. He had no desire to speak with her again, and immediately excused himself to leave. He was explaining to a puzzled Ethan that he'd forgotten a previous engagement when Janice arrived.

She was startled to see Neil there, but asked him to

stay. Ethan explained why he'd invited Neil to dinner, and Janice told him where she and Neil had met. Then she asked Neil what had brought him to the holy site. When he told them he was a light-seeker, Ethan and Janice immediately tried to persuade him to reconsider his plans. He might be committing suicide, said Ethan, and there were always better alternatives than suicide. Seeing Heaven's light was not the answer, said Janice; that wasn't what God wanted. Neil stiffly thanked them for their concern, and left.

During the weeks of waiting, Neil spent every day driving around the site; maps were available, and were updated after each visitation, but they were no substitute for driving the terrain yourself. On occasion he would see a light-seeker who was obviously experienced in off-road driving, and ask him—the vast majority of the light-seekers were men—for tips on negotiating a specific type of terrain. Some had been at the site for several visitations, having neither succeeded or failed at their previous attempts. They were glad to share tips on how best to pursue an angel, but never offered any personal information about themselves. Neil found the tone of their conversation peculiar, simultaneously hopeful and hopeless, and wondered if he sounded the same.

Ethan and Janice passed the time by getting to know some of the other pilgrims. Their reactions to Janice's situation were mixed: some thought her ungrateful, while others thought her generous. Most found Ethan's story interesting, since he was one of the very few pilgrims seeking something other than a miracle cure. For the most part, there was a feeling of camaraderie that sustained them during the long wait.

Neil was driving around in his truck when dark clouds began coalescing in the southeast, and the word came over the CB radio that a visitation had begun. He stopped the vehicle to insert earplugs into his ears and don his helmet; by the time he was finished, flashes of lightning were visible, and a light-seeker near the angel reported that it was Barakiel, and it appeared to be moving due north. Neil turned his truck east in anticipation and began driving at full speed.

There was no rain or wind, only dark clouds from which lightning emerged. Over the radio other light-seekers relayed estimates of the angel's direction and speed, and Neil headed northeast to get in front of it. At first he could gauge his distance from the storm by counting how long it took for the thunder to arrive, but soon the lightning bolts were striking so frequently that he couldn't match up the sounds with the individual strikes.

He saw the vehicles of two other light-seekers converging. They began driving in parallel, heading north, over a heavily cratered section of ground, bouncing over small ones and swerving to avoid the larger ones. Bolts of lightning were striking the ground everywhere, but they appeared to be radiating from a point south of

Neil's position; the angel was directly behind him, and closing.

Even through his earplugs, the roar was deafening. Neil could feel his hair rising from his skin as the electric charge built up around him. He kept glancing in his rear-view mirror, trying to ascertain where the angel was while wondering how close he ought to get.

His vision grew so crowded with afterimages that it became difficult to distinguish actual bolts of lightning among them. Squinting at the dazzle in his mirror, he realized he was looking at a continuous bolt of lightning, undulating but uninterrupted. He tilted the driver's-side mirror upward to get a better look, and saw the source of the lightning bolt, a seething, writhing mass of flames, silver against the dusky clouds: the angel Barakiel.

It was then, while Neil was transfixed and paralyzed by what he saw, that his pickup truck crested a sharp outcropping of rock and became airborne. The truck smashed into a boulder, the entire force of the impact concentrated on the vehicle's left front end, crumpling it like foil. The intrusion into the driver's compartment fractured both of Neil's legs and nicked his left femoral artery. Neil began, slowly but surely, bleeding to death.

He didn't try to move; he wasn't in physical pain at the moment, but he somehow knew that the slightest movement would be excruciating. It was obvious that he was pinned in the truck, and there was no way he could pursue Barakiel even if he weren't. Helplessly, he watched the lightning storm move further and further away.

As he watched it, Neil began crying. He was filled with a mixture of regret and self-contempt, cursing himself for ever thinking that such a scheme could succeed. He would have begged for the opportunity to do it over again, promised to spend the rest of his days learning to love God, if only he could live, but he knew that no bargaining was possible and he had only himself to blame. He apologized to Sarah for losing his chance at being reunited with her, for throwing his life away on a gamble instead of playing it safe. He prayed that she understood that he'd been motivated by his love for her, and that she would forgive him.

Through his tears he saw a woman running toward him, and recognized her as Janice Reilly. He realized his truck had crashed no more than a hundred yards from her and Ethan's campsite. There was nothing she could do, though; he could feel the blood draining out of him, and knew that he wouldn't live long enough for a rescue vehicle to arrive. He thought Janice was calling to him, but his ears were ringing too badly for him to hear anything. He could see Ethan Mead behind her, also starting to run towards him.

Then there was a flash of light and Janice was knocked off her feet as if she'd been struck by a sledgehammer. At first he thought she'd been hit by lightning, but then he realized that the lightning had already ceased. It was when she stood up again that he saw her face, steam rising from newly featureless skin, and he realized that Janice had been struck by Heaven's light.

Neil looked up, but all he saw were clouds; the shaft of light was gone. It seemed as if God was taunting him, not only by showing him the prize he'd lost his life trying to acquire while still holding it out of reach, but also by giving it to someone who didn't need it or even want it. God had already wasted a miracle on Janice, and now He was doing it again.

It was at that moment that another beam of Heaven's light penetrated the cloud cover and struck Neil, trapped in his vehicle.

Like a thousand hypodermic needles the light punctured his flesh and scraped across his bones. The light unmade his eyes, turning him into not a formerly sighted being, but a being never intended to possess vision. And in doing so the light revealed to Neil all the reasons he should love God.

He loved Him with an utterness beyond what humans can experience for one another. To say it was unconditional was inadequate, because even the word "unconditional" required the concept of a condition and such an idea was no longer comprehensible to him: every phenomenon in the universe was nothing less than an explicit reason to love Him. No circumstance could be an obstacle or even an irrelevancy, but only another reason to be grateful, a further inducement to love. Neil thought of the grief that had driven him to suicidal recklessness, and the pain and terror that Sarah had experienced before she died, and still he loved God, not in spite of their suffering, but because of it.

He renounced all his previous anger and ambivalence and desire for answers. He was grateful for all the pain he'd endured, contrite for not previously recognizing it as the gift it was, euphoric that he was now being granted this insight into his true purpose. He understood how life was an undeserved bounty, how even the most virtuous were not worthy of the glories of the mortal plane.

For him the mystery was solved, because he understood that everything in life is love, even pain, especially pain.

So minutes later, when Neil finally bled to death, he was truly worthy of salvation.

And God sent him to Hell anyway.

Ethan saw all of this. He saw Neil and Janice remade by Heaven's light, and he saw the pious love on their eyeless faces. He saw the skies become clear and the sunlight return. He was holding Neil's hand, waiting for the paramedics, when Neil died, and he saw Neil's soul leave his body and rise toward Heaven, only to descend into Hell.

Janice didn't see it, for by then her eyes were already

gone. Ethan was the sole witness, and he realized that this was God's purpose for him: to follow Janice Reilly to this point and to see what she could not.

When statistics were compiled for Barakiel's visitation, it turned out that there had been a total of ten casualties, six among light-seekers and four among ordinary pilgrims. Nine pilgrims received miracle cures; the only individuals to see Heaven's light were Janice and Neil. There were no statistics regarding how many pilgrims had felt their lives changed by the visitation, but Ethan counted himself among them.

Upon returning home, Janice resumed her evangelism, but the topic of her speeches has changed. She no longer speaks about how the physically handicapped have the resources to overcome their limitations; instead she, like the other eyeless, speaks about the unbearable beauty of God's creation. Many who used to draw inspiration from her are disappointed, feeling they've lost a spiritual leader. When Janice had spoken of the strength she had as an afflicted person, her message was rare, but now that she's eyeless, her message is commonplace. She doesn't worry about the reduction in her audience, though, because she has complete conviction in what she evangelizes.

Ethan quit his job and became a preacher so that he too could speak about his experiences. His wife Claire couldn't accept his new mission and ultimately left him, taking their children with her, but Ethan was willing to continue alone. He's developed a substantial following by telling people what happened to Neil Fisk. He tells people that they can no more expect justice in the afterlife than in the mortal plane, but he doesn't do this to dissuade them from worshipping God; on the contrary, he encourages them to do so. What he insists on is that they not love God under a misapprehension, that if they wish to love God, they be prepared to do so no matter what His intentions. God is not just, God is not kind, God is not merciful, and understanding that is essential to true devotion.

As for Neil, although he is unaware of any of Ethan's sermons, he would understand their message perfectly. His lost soul is the embodiment of Ethan's teachings.

For most of its inhabitants, Hell is not that different from Earth; its principal punishment is the regret of not having loved God enough when alive, and for many that's easily endured. For Neil, however, Hell bears no resemblance whatsoever to the mortal plane. His eternal body has well-formed legs, but he's scarcely aware of them; his eyes have been restored, but he can't bear to open them. Just as seeing Heaven's light gave him an awareness of God's presence in all things in the mortal plane, so it has made him aware of God's absence in all things in Hell. Everything Neil sees, hears, or touches causes him distress, and unlike in the mortal plane this pain is not a form of God's love, but a consequence of His absence. Neil is experiencing more anguish than was possible when he was alive, but his only response is to love God.

Neil still loves Sarah, and misses her as much as he ever did, and the knowledge that he came so close to rejoining her only makes it worse. He knows his being sent to Hell was not a result of anything he did; he knows there was no reason for it, no higher purpose being served. None of this diminishes his love for God. If there were a possibility that he could be admitted to Heaven and his suffering would end, he would not hope for it; such desires no longer occur to him.

Neil even knows that by being beyond God's awareness, he is not loved by God in return. This doesn't affect his feelings either, because unconditional love asks nothing, not even that it be returned.

And though it's been many years that he has been in Hell, beyond the awareness of God, he loves Him still. That is the nature of true devotion.

ABOUT THE AUTHORS

The term "visionary" is applicable to very few writers, but **Ursula K. Le Guin**'s intellectually provocative fiction has earned her the accolade in general literary circles as well as the fields of fantasy and science fiction. "Bones of the Earth," is set in the same world as her Earthsea saga, which includes *A Wizard of Earthsea*, *The Tombs of Atuan*, *The Farthest Shore*, *Tehanu: The Last Book of Earthsea*, and *Tales from Earthsea*. She has written other novels—including *The Lathe of Heaven*, *The Dispossessed*, *Malafrena*, and *Always Coming Home*—and her short fiction and many celebrated essays on the craft of fantasy and science fiction have been gathered in a number of collections.

Jack O'Connell is the author of the novels *Box Nine*, *Wireless*, *The Skin Palace*, *Word Made Flesh*, and the multi-volume epic *The Dreamlife*. He lives in a rust belt mill city in the northeast corridor of the American empire, where he is sustained, on a daily basis, by his wife and children.

Brian A. Hopkins is the author of "Something Haunts Us All," "Cold at Heart," "Wrinkles at Twilight," and "Salt Water Tears." He is the recipient of the Bram Stoker Award and has been a finalist for both the Nebula and the Theodore Sturgeon Memorial Award. Brian lives in Oklahoma with his wife and two children. You can learn more about him by visiting his webpage at http://bahwolf.com.

Rosemary Edghill is the author of over thirty novels and several dozen short stories in genres ranging from Regency romance to space opera, making all local stops in between. She has collaborated with authors such as the late Marion Zimmer Bradley and SF Grand Master Andre Norton. Her website can be found at: http://www.sff.net/people/eluki.

Lucius Shepard has won the John W. Campbell award, the Nebula award, and the World Fantasy Award for his fiction. Recent work has appeared in *The Magazine of Fantasy and Science Fiction* and *Isaac Asimov's Science Fiction Magazine*.

ABOUT THE AUTHORS

Greg Van Eekhout's short stories have appeared in *Starlight 3, Horrors! 365 Scary Stories*, and a scattering of other fiction venues. He has also written nonfiction for various magazines, scripts for CD-ROMs, and T-shirt slogans for fictitious liquor companies. A Los Angeles native, he now lives in Tempe, Arizona. He maintains a web site at www.sff.net/people/greg.

A multiple winner of the Hugo and Nebula Awards, **Poul Anderson** (1926–2000) has written more than 50 novels and hundreds of short stories since his science fiction debut in 1947. He has tackled many of science fiction's classic themes, including near-light speed travel, time travel, and accelerated evolution. Much of Anderson's fantasy is rich with undercurrents of mythology, notably his heroic fantasy *Three Hearts and Three Lions*. Anderson received the Tolkien Memorial Award in 1978. With his wife Karen he has written the King of Ys Celtic fantasy quartet, and with Gordon Dickson the amusing Hoka series. His short fiction has been collected in numerous volumes.

A challenger of rules since childhood, **Catherine Asaro** regards those which constrict literary genres with a why-not gleam in her eyes and a multi-talented hand. Her first novel, *Primary Inversion*, created a stir in the science fiction community, because she combined romance with hard science fiction. Among the many awards earned by the Columbia, MD, author of nine novels are the National Readers' Choice Award for *Best Futuristic Fiction* and the Homer Award for Best Novel for *The Veiled Web*; and Romantic Times magazine's Reviewers' Choice Award for Best Science Fiction Novel for *The Radiant Seas*.

Lawrence Miles lives and works in Britain, although as "Grass" was his first American-published work he's not sure he should tell anybody that. So far he's written seven novels, most of them TV tie-ins but quite good anyway, plus the audio series *The Faction Paradox Protocols* for BBV (www.factionparadox.co.uk).

Since 1970, **Robert Thurston** has published more than 40 short stories in various magazines and anthologies. His novels include *Alicia II*, *A Set of Wheels*, and *Q Colony*. An adminitrator and part-Humanities instructor at a university, he lives in New Jersey with his wife Rosemary and daughter Charlotte.

Ted Chiang burst onto the science fiction scene in 1990 with "Tower of Babylon," which won the Nebula Award for best novella. Since then, his work has appeared in several other venues, including *Isaac Asimov's Science Fiction Magazine* and *Full Spectrum 3*.